"*An Accident of Stars* stands head and fabulous shoulders above most fantasy books I've read, not just this year but in recent years."

Over the Effing Rainbow

"This book is such great fun you'll want to take a sick day to finish it in one sitting."

Pop Verse

"Sometimes I see books described as portal fantasy, and it just seems... insufficient. Not inaccurate, but in cases like this one, it's like trying to describe a beach by using adjectives that only apply to a couple of pebbles in the sand. *An Accident of Stars* is a lot more than a magic wardrobe."

I, Fat Robot

"This books is great. I loved it."

Properly Lex

"If you enjoy well-written, character driven fantasy with strong women featuring throughout, a cracking plot and beautifully constructed plot, then go looking for this book. I will be eagerly awaiting the sequel."

Brainfluff

"Words can't begin to properly express how awesome Meadows is at creating complex and realistic fantasy worlds and the cultures and people that dwell within."

Bibliotropic – Top Eleven Outstanding Books of 2016

"One of my favorite books I read in 2016. The book was super women and femme focused, and I loved that."

Odd Leopards, Strange Cats

BY THE SAME AUTHOR

THE MANIFOLD WORLDS
An Accident of Stars

Coral Bones (novella)
Solace & Grief
The Key to Starveldt

FOZ MEADOWS

A Tyranny of Queens

BOOK II OF THE MANIFOLD WORLDS

ANGRY
ROBOT

ANGRY ROBOT
An imprint of Watkins Me

20 Fletcher Gate,
Nottingham,
NG1 2FZ
UK

angryrobotbooks.com
twitter.com/angryrobotbooks
Worlds apart

An Angry Robot paperback original 2017
1

A catalogue record for this book is available from the British Library.

ISBN 978 0 85766 587 4
EBook ISBN 978 0 85766 589 8

Set in Meridien by Epub Services.
Printed and bound in the UK by 4edge Limited.

For everyone who's ever been
too brave to die, too scared to live;
for anyone
who tried on a death that didn't fit:
you are not broken.
I love you.
Stay.

"… the older I get, the more I see how women are described as having gone mad, when what they've actually become is knowledgeable and powerful and fucking furious."

Sophie Heawood

PART 1
Uncrossing the Rubicon

1
Boundaries

"It's all right," said Ruby, squeezing Saffron's hand. They stood at the threshold of Lawson High, the gates hanging open like jaws. "I'll protect you from asshats."

"I'm not sure you're meant to know that word," said Saffron. It was an old joke, as comforting to her as it was annoying to her sister, but it came out more faint than teasing. "Why do you know that word, huh?"

"I'm fourteen, Saff," said Ruby, bravely ignoring the slip. "I go to school. I have *the internets*." She squeezed her hand again, harder than before. "And you."

"Yeah," said Saffron, a lump in her throat. "You do." But for how long? That was the question.

As though she could hear the unspoken rider, Ruby sighed, releasing Saffron's hand. It was her right, five-fingered and untattooed. *Your good hand*, their mother had called it over dinner, natural as breathing – *pass the salt please, Saff – no, there, by your good hand* – and even though Saffron sometimes thought of it that way too, she'd burned to hear it so presumptively labelled by someone else. Her left hand twitched, three fleshy fingers and two phantom ones, but did not form a fist.

"Seriously," Ruby said, "I mean it. If anyone gives you shit–"

"You'll defend my honour?"

Ruby squared her slender shoulders. "Yes."

The posture was so reminiscent of Zech, her strength and pride as she'd stood before the Council of Queens, that Saffron almost stopped breathing. Zech had often reminded her a little of Ruby; the reverse, it seemed, was also true, and doubly painful for it. She gulped and nodded, unable to make a verbal response. Zech was only six days dead, but Saffron couldn't mourn her, because nobody here even knew she'd ever existed. As far as everyone on Earth was concerned, Saffron had spent the past few weeks in captivity, hurt and manipulated by an unknown assailant who'd eventually let her go. It was a lie, of course, and one whose vileness roiled her guts, but how else to explain the time she'd lost to another world, the injuries she'd sustained?

The last time she'd walked into Lawson High her blond hair had been shoulder-length, her skin unmarked by anything more than freckles and childhood scars. Now, in addition to her two missing fingers and new tattoo – a pair of intertwined snakes biting each other's tails, encircling her left wrist in vivid red-gold-black – she was missing a chunk of cartilage from her right ear. A trio of scars raked the right side of her face from just above her eye to the back of her skull, their raised lines clearly visible through the half-inch stubble of her hair. A similar triple-slash ran diagonally across her ribs on her left side, with assorted other, smaller scars on her outer thighs, arms, hips. Standing before her bedroom mirror, Saffron had touched each one in turn, an ache in her chest half loss, half dislocated pride.

Dragonmarks. Not that she could ever admit the provenance – even in Veksh and Kena, the Trial of Queens was shrouded in a secrecy she'd sworn to uphold – but she still knew the truth. *I fought with dragons and bled in the dark. I'm not afraid of school.*

"Come on, then," she said to Ruby. "Let's get this over with."

Together they crossed into Lawson High. It was utterly anticlimactic, but Saffron's pulse ticked up anyway. Everyone – her parents; her newly-appointed social worker, Ms Mays; even the headmaster, Mr Barton – everyone had said she could take more time before going back, had urged to the point of pleading with her to do so. *You've only been home for six days, Saff! We just want what's best for you.* But after weeks of autonomy in Kena, being treated as though she was made of glass was maddening, not least because her every attempt at self-assertion was either met with paternalistic worry (*You don't have to try and be strong for us!*) or was taken as proof of emotional instability. As though wanting fifteen consecutive minutes of privacy was somehow unreasonable!

As they passed the teachers' car park, Saffron kicked angrily at a discarded Coke can, watching as it clattered away towards the admin building. *God, I miss Gwen. I really miss Yena. I miss Zech.*

"You sure you don't want me to wait with you?" asked Ruby, as they reached the metal bench outside the music rooms where Saffron habitually sat of a morning. "You know, just until your friends show up?"

"I'll be fine," said Saffron. She made herself smile as she sat down. "Promise."

Ruby bit her lip. She was half a head shorter than Saffron, her proportions almost puppyish as her body raced to grow into itself. Her brown hair was tied back in a sloppy braid, escaping wisps framing her not-yet-fully-emergent cheekbones. Her eyes were greenish grey, but though they flashed with worry, in the end she nodded and said, "OK. I trust you." A ghost smile flickered on her face. "Sometimes, anyway."

I trust you. Three small words that meant the world, but which no adult had said to her since she'd come back. Saffron could have cried.

"Thanks, Ru," she managed, voice inexplicably hoarse. "I'll

see you later, OK?"

"Sure," said Ruby. She hesitated a moment longer, as though arguing with herself, then shouldered her bag and headed off to meet her own friends, braid swishing as she vanished around the edge of the building.

Saffron inhaled deeply, pulling her own bag onto her lap. It was, of necessity, new, her old one having been lost in Kena, and after a hurried weekend trip to the shops it was full of equally new possessions. Only her phone was unaltered – she'd left it charging by her bed the morning she'd first left Earth. When she hadn't come home that afternoon, she'd since been told, her parents had tried to call her, only to hear the answering ring from her bedroom. Later, when her friends had started texting, worried and urgent at her absence, they'd turned it off rather than listen to the constant chiming.

Saffron was yet to turn it on again.

Distractedly she fiddled with the hem of her skirt, trying and failing to quell her nervousness. Like the phone, her uniform was purchased pre-Kena – as though her life was now divided into two different eras, PK and AK, like an archaeological record – but after three weeks of continuous exercise, fatigue, injury, magical healing and simple (if often delicious) food, it no longer fit her properly. She'd been slim before, but now she was wiry-hard, her body so stripped of its meagre softness that her hipbones jutted like knifehilts. She'd had to pin the skirt's waistband so it didn't fall down, while the blouse was a half-size too big. Her shoes, though, were AK, shiny and new and still being broken in, her heels protected from blistering by a pair of Band-Aids. This last detail made her want to laugh out loud. Band-Aids! For her heels! After weeks spent barefoot in the wilderness! It just felt so... incongruous.

"Holy shit. *Saff*?"

She jerked her head up, mouth gone dry.

It was Lyssi.

Her friend looked stricken, an unfamiliar expression on a

familiar face, and for the second time in as many minutes Saffron could have cried. All the time she'd been in Kena, she'd barely thought of the people she'd left behind. At first, it had taken conscious effort, an active repression of loss and consequences, but at some point – she wasn't sure when; after the flight from the compound, maybe, or in the aftermath of the battle of the Envas road – the process had become automatic. *Compartmentalising*, that was the word: she'd put her Earthly life in a box and shut it tightly, focusing instead on that literal new reality, and even now that she'd come home she hadn't quite lifted the lid. Avoiding texts and social media both, she'd let her friends find out through the parental grapevine that she was back and, for a given value of the word, unscathed, and told herself it was pragmatism, not cowardice, to duck the responsibility of a more personal reassurance.

But now Lyssi was here, with her straight black hair and sparkly nail polish; Lyssi, who loved rabbits, hated seafood and was not-so-secretly addicted to Korean TV dramas; Lyssi, who'd been her best friend since their first day at Lawson High.

"Hi, Lyssi," Saffron whispered, and almost fell off the bench when her friend lunged forwards, wrapping her up in a hug. She stiffened at the contact, throat tight with a mix of panic and guilt and overwhelmed relief, and only belatedly remembered to hug back, her clenched hands resting lightly between Lyssi's shoulder blades.

"You're a... here!" gulped Lyssi, pulling back for long enough to claim the seat beside Saffron. Her light brown eyes were wide and worried, raking over the vivid lines of Saffron's scars. "Oh, oh *Jesus, Saff*–"

"Don't touch!" Saffron said quickly, grabbing Lyssi's outstretched hand. And then, more calmly, "Please."

Lyssi flushed, startled, but nodded compliance, and when Saffron released her she balled both hands tightly in her lap, as if warding against temptation.

"I'm sorry! I just, it's so... Jesus, I don't even know what to say, I thought you were just dead or lost and now you're *here*, you're... you're–"

"I'm me," said Saffron, who hadn't quite realised until that moment how badly she wanted someone else to affirm it. "I'm still me, Lyssi."

"Yeah, but–" Lyssi was tearing up, "–are you *OK*?"

And there it was: the question to which there was no simple answer, honesty being far too complex a prospect. What could she say, really? She had a sudden, manic urge to blurt out the impossible truth:

Well, Lyssi, I wasn't raped, if that's what you're asking – and I'm sure you are, everyone seems pretty obsessed with the possibility – but I wasn't exactly tortured, either. See, I actually followed a stranger through a magic portal and trapped myself in another world, in a country called Kena, where a nearly-queen cut off two of my fingers. I was rescued by a girl who turned out to be her daughter, only none of us knew that at the time, and after the ruling monarch set fire to our compound for harbouring his runaway consort, I ended up killing a woman (and a horse, too!) in an ambush on the road. I learned about how dream-magic links the worlds – which is how I'm meant to be checking in with my Kenan friends, by the way, only I'm terrible at remembering it all when I wake up, which is terrifying if I let myself think about it – and then we went to the neighbouring country, Veksh, to seek their aid.

And the girl who rescued me, Zech? She asked me to stand proxy for her in the Trial of Queens, so that we could speak to their Council, and I did. I ran a maze in darkness under an ancient city, and I fought as a dragon, with a dragon, which is where all these other scars came from – some sort of magical transference, and I still don't know if that's more or less strange than the fact that dragons exist at all – and because we survived it, Zech was made a queen. And then we went back to Kena, and her mother killed her anyway, and I ran home before I even knew that everyone else was safe, because I was scared and lost and my friend was dead, *so no, Lyssi, I'm not OK, but not for the reasons anyone thinks, and I didn't think lying about it would be easy, but I didn't know it would be this hard, either.*

What she actually said, after all this had flashed through her head, was, "I'm... about as good as I could be, really. I'm coping." And then, when Lyssi still looked distraught, "I'm OK, Lyss. Really."

Lyssi stared at her, not quite crying, a look of incipient protest on her face. Rather than let it come to fruition, Saffron leaned in and hugged her again, which was apparently the right decision: Lyssi made a heartfelt noise and gripped her back, the two of them swaying together.

I'm lying, Saffron thought wildly. *I'm lying my ass off to everyone.*

"I'm glad you're back," Lyssi whispered.

Saffron shut her eyes, the guilt like bile in her throat.

I'm not.

Yena knelt in supplication, watching her shorn curls fall to the floor. It was the sixth day of her mourning for Zech, and she could wallow no longer. Her family and friends in Kena were scrambling to secure their position, Kadeja still awaited trial, Safi was missing, and meanwhile the game of Vekshi politics continued unabated – a game from which Yena, by dint of her exegetical leanings and lack of legal status, was currently excluded. Yasha was no help on either front: with the Council yet to formally lift her exile and unlikely to do so until after Kadeja was dealt with, the matriarch was trapped in a cycle of rage and frustration, with Yena the only safe outlet for either emotion. Yena had little enough love for Yasha's vehemence at the best of times, which this wasn't, and she certainly had no sympathy for her pride. In Kena, in their now-burned compound, Yasha had been all-powerful, her word akin to Vekshi law, but in Yevekshasa her status was as nothing. For all her talk of politics and patience, Yasha lacked the humility to accept her demotion, even temporarily, preferring instead to exert control over her one remaining disciple.

But Yena had never been as loyal to Yasha as Yasha seemed to think; had only pretended, as Sashi had pretended, for the sake of peace in the family. But things had changed, and with Yasha refusing to bow her head and adapt it fell to Yena to make her own choices, not least because Yasha was maddeningly unconcerned with events in Kena. When Kikra, the Shavaktiin dreamseer, had told them about Leoden's flight, the anchored portal under the palace and – most disturbingly of all – the captive worldwalkers, Yasha had declared them irrelevant. Irrelevant, after years of Kenan scheming! Yena couldn't tell if her grandmother's sudden complacency was due to her change in circumstances, her reaction to Zech's death or some other factor: all she knew was that she couldn't share in it.

At present, they remained in Yevekshasa on sufferance, their movements curtailed, their legal rights negligible and their information limited. Something had to be done, and if Yasha wouldn't swallow her pride and do it, then Yena would.

Behind her, Mesthani a Vekte worked steadily, carefully, pausing only to dip her blade in a bowl of fragrant water.

"You've a good-shaped head," she murmured, swiping a gentle thumb across Yena's skull. "Shaved will suit you."

Suit my face, maybe. Yena bit back the acerbic qualification with some effort. Mesthani was a queen of Veksh; however uncertain Yena felt about her current transformation into a prodigal daughter, she couldn't voice such thoughts aloud and still be taken seriously.

The larger curls formed a soft black pattern on the stone, like some arcane script; her neck and shoulders itched beneath a dusting of finer strands. She wore a borrowed *nek*, a shapeless, sleeveless, undyed shift worn by Vekshi women as their hair was cut. Its plainness was part penitence, part practicality, which Yena thought a fair summation of much of Vekshi culture.

This observation, too, she kept to herself.

Instead of voicing heresies, she said, "My thanks for your help. I wasn't sure my message would reach you."

Mesthani chuckled. "Truthfully, it shouldn't have, but your Shavaktiin are surprisingly resourceful." In a slower, more careful tone, she added, "Surprising, that you didn't seek your grandmother's aid in this." And then, more carefully still, "Or perhaps it's no surprise at all."

"I honour Yasha a Yasara, of course, regardless of her status," said Yena, with equal delicacy. "But honour, as the Ryvke says, is not the same as obedience."

For the space of a heartbeat, Mesthani's hands stilled. The Ryvke was not quite a sacred text, but near enough to one: the collected writings and wisdom of the most revered queens and priestesses of Veksh, with new material added but rarely, posthumously, and only ever after fierce debate among the Archivists, whose relationship to the priestesshood of Ashasa could best be described as *complicated*. Mesthani had plainly not expected Yena to quote from it, which was either advantageous or a slight on her perception of Yena's competence. Yena, naturally, hoped for the former.

As though she hadn't hesitated, Mesthani said, "Yasha a Yasara's approach to the Ryvke, as I recall, was always somewhat selective, even when she sat the Council."

Now it was Yena's turn to freeze. Of course she had seen her grandmother's scars, a series of raking gouges on belly and thigh, and asked about their origins in childhood. Of course she had heard it whispered among the other expatriates and exiles at the now-burned compound in Karavos that Yasha had once sat the Council of Queens, along with a dozen other equally fanciful rumours. But the truth had always been taboo; not even her mother had ever confirmed it out loud. To hear it admitted so plainly now was dizzying.

Focus, she told herself sharply. Out loud, she said, as mildly as she could, "Is there a way to approach such a wealth of varied wisdom other than selectively? Or can one truly follow the precepts of both Cerei a Celah and Marui a Nhako without contradiction?"

Mesthani laughed – more delighted than shocked, Yena hoped. "If such a thing is possible, I'm yet to hear of it. Your learning does you credit." She dipped her blade in the water, resumed her shaving. "But this conversation is straying. As flattered as I was to be asked to perform the service, you want more of me, I think, than my skills with this particular blade."

"I did. I do." Yena took a steadying breath against her grief, pretending not to hear the slight emphasis Mesthani placed on the word *particular*. "I claim a sister's mourning rites for Zechalia a Kadeja."

This time, Mesthani did more than pause: she inhaled sharply, rocking back on her heels. "Ash of the hearth! Not by sire's blood, surely?"

"What? No!" Yena spun around, shocked. "By the sun, nothing so sordid. I meant by clan-claim. My mother, Trishka a Yasha, had her raising almost from infancy; though Yasha formally took her in, she was more her mentor than mother. But to my elder sister and I, she was always ours. And now–" she gulped, swallowing the loss that threatened to choke her, should she cede to it, "–now, I wish justice for her. Justice, and remembrance, and the right to see her honoured by those she loved."

Mesthani's expression was calm in a way that betokened great self-control. "Now *that*," she said, after a moment, "is a truly compelling point of law. I'm not entirely sure we have a precedent, and if you know as much Vekshi history as your recitation of the Ryvke suggests, you'll know how rare that is. Yasha a Yasara is still recorded as traitor and exile: she has the support of sufficient queens to plead her case to the Council–" this said in such a way that Yena couldn't tell if Mesthani was one such backer, "–but as yet, they've been too concerned with Motherless Kadeja to vote her through. Likewise, as Ruyun a Ketra pointed out when you first arrived here, not only has your mother never declared her own obedience to Veksh, but you – and please, forgive me the sin of acknowledging Ruyun's rudeness – you were giving the gift of soul-skin in the sight of false gods. Ordinarily, that would put you far enough outside the law to mitigate your kin-rights, whether claimed by blood or clan."

"But?" asked Yena, who'd reasoned this much herself.

"But Zechalia was a queen, and queens cannot be kinless; nor can they be motherless, unless they are mothers themselves, or have avowed heirs or sisters. We did not consider it at the time, because we had no expectation that so young a queen might die before declaring a clan, but... well. That she is a priestess's daughter by blood is beyond dispute, and yet the priestess in question is now declared traitor, exile, and twice the worst kind of murderer. Indeed, there's already a debate about whether her eventual punishment should reflect her status as one who killed a queen, or one who killed a childless daughter." Yena felt briefly sick at this, and was glad to see that Mesthani, too, looked disgusted by the question. "Ksa a Kaje acknowledged her before the Council, of course, but given Kadeja's status and the fact that they were strangers, their legal relationship is murky at best. Yasha is also exiled, and your own mother unconfirmed, which leaves... well, nobody. And yet you were surely raised with her – you, who are currently outside the law, and yet may mend that status, as I see is your intent. Which begs the question: can a queen have sisters, but no mother? I do not know, but if you persist, we'll certainly find out."

Throughout this speech, Mesthani had not touched Yena's hair, the cutting of which was still only half complete. Belatedly, they both recalled the chore and took refuge in its resumption, Yena once more facing away, head bowed, as Mesthani plied her knife.

"I do not require a Council vote to seek penance for consorting with false gods," said Yena, once they were back in rhythm. "Mesthani a Vekte, when my head is newly shaved, I ask that you escort me to the Great Temple, there to show contrition for seeking my soul-skin beyond Ashasa's sight, so that I might present a formal clan-claim as Zechalia a Kadeja's sister."

Mesthani didn't answer immediately, which was as Yena had expected. The request was hardly without consequence, and with everything she'd done on Zech and Safi's behalf since their arrival at Yevekshasa, Mesthani must have already expended a fair amount of her political capital in a short space of time. Yena's heartbeat quickened with every second of silence, tension coiling in her chest.

Her hair continued to fall.

It will grow back eventually, once I'm gone from here, she thought, trying to distract herself with vanity. *Not like Safi's fingers.*

Safi.

Warmth rushed through her with the name, half pang, half smile, all hope. She missed Safi dearly – worried for her daily, particularly in the absence of regular updates from Kikra and the Shavaktiin, even in the depths of grief – but savoured the sense of anticipation that yearning brought, the way she might press at a satisfying bruise. Safi, at least, she would see again.

Unlike Zech.

She shoved the loss down hard and fast and kept it there, a stone held underwater.

A last lock drifted to the floor, so featherlight it seemed to fight the very air for passage. The knifeblade scraped across her scalp, neatening what little hair remained. Mesthani sat back again, job done.

"Having supported Zechalia a Kadeja's bid to sit the Trial of Queens – and after I supported her plans in the Council – the least I can give her now is the grace of a sister's mourning," Mesthani said.

Yena's didn't turn, but kept her head bowed as the queen squeezed her shoulder. "Rise, Yena a Trishka. Bathe and dress, and prepare yourself for the Great Temple. I cannot guarantee your petition will be granted, nor can I guess what form your penitence might take, but I will stand for you."

Yena's heart was tight in her chest – with fear, with hope. A passing breeze brushed her now-bare neck. "Thank you, honoured Mesthani."

Aged eleven, Saffron had gone through a phase of yearning to be a celebrity. Together, she and Lyssi had plotted their future dominion of social media, gossip columns and magazine covers, though what they'd do to earn their fame had changed on a daily basis. They'd started with all the obvious things, like acting and modelling, until Lyssi, who loved science, had hit on the idea of being a rockstar chemist, prompting the development of a suite of increasingly specific – and eventually impossible – dream-careers. Saffron's favourite had been time-travelling adventuress, which, given her recent experiences, felt both deeply ironic and scarily prescient; Lyssi had settled on astronaut empress of Mars. It had bonded them, two awkward, socially peripheral girls on the cusp of adolescence dreaming of visibility, which was the only sort of power they felt confident in wanting.

Saffron did not feel powerful now.

Wherever she went, whispers followed. The horrified stares which raked her scars were as subtle as smashed glass, the rubbernecking induced by her presence so overt she could almost hear tendons snapping. She kept her head up and thought of Gwen, who'd been walking worlds for longer than Saffron had been alive, and of Viya and Zech, who'd fought for the right to be heard.

It hurt to think of Zech.

"It's OK," Lyssi, beside her, whispered – to herself, it seemed, as she didn't quite look at Saffron. They'd just come from homeroom, where Mrs Kirkland had gone ghost-pale at the sight of her prodigal student, and were headed for the ugly tedium of PDHPE. Or at least, Saffron was: Lyssi had Chemistry instead. "It's OK, it's OK, it's OK."

It wasn't OK. It could only be endured. Which meant it was high school as usual, just turned up to eleven.

It was a perversely reassuring thought. Saffron bit back a black-humoured laugh and forged her way past a gaggle of Year Seven girls, whose chattering conversation turned to slackjawed hush at the sight of her.

Her confidence faltered slightly when they reached Lyssi's turnoff for the science block, but somehow she managed to force a smile.

"I'll be fine," she said to Lyssi, cutting off whatever worried thing she'd been about to say. "Really, it's *health class*. What's the worst that can happen?"

Lyssi almost laughed. "True," she said, voice only a little watery. "I'll... I'll see you later, OK? Promise?"

"I promise," said Saffron, and watched her friend go with commingled guilt and relief.

Hefting her bag, she walked to her next class alone.

In hindsight, Saffron often had trouble understanding why she'd chosen PDHPE as one of her Year Eleven electives. True, the school's timetabling meant she'd *had* to pick something in that slot, and the other options hadn't exactly been stellar, but after the torture of last year's lessons with Mr Marinakis, it was a wonder she'd even considered it. Something about life skills, maybe? She imagined what Yasha might have to say about the Ottawa Charter for Health Promotion and snorted.

The brief flare of amusement died as she recalled explaining the concept of high school to Zech, who'd barely been old enough to attend; as young as Saffron and Lyssi had been, when they'd dreamed of being famous. Yet Zech really *was* famous, in her own world: through cunning and courage she'd made herself a queen of Veksh, one of the youngest ever to hold the title. Her life had been brief, but it would be remembered in the histories of two different nations.

It isn't fair. Saffron gripped her bag strap, fighting an irrational urge to smash her new possessions into the wall. What did remembrance matter to the dead? If Zech had lived, she would've grown up and made more history. *I'll be the Queen Who Returned*, she'd said, after bargaining her temporary absence from the Council in exchange for their aid in removing Vex'Mara Kadeja – her mother, her murderer – from Kena. And now she wouldn't ever return, and Saffron alone was left to carry the memory of that promise unfulfilled.

"Jesus," someone whispered, in a voice just loud enough to carry. Saffron jerked out of her reverie, belatedly noticing her classmates. They were clumped in a line outside the unopened door to their classroom, either staring openly or doing a pisspoor job of pretending otherwise. She swallowed, hating the blush that crept up her neck, and moved to the back of the line. She'd forgotten that the doors weren't always unlocked by the start of first period, especially on Mondays; that the teachers sometimes had to hunt for the key. She set her back to the sunwarmed bricks and stared at her new black shoes, as shiny and unscuffed as the rest of her wasn't. Maybe if she kicked around in the gravel through recess, they'd start to look halfway normal.

"So, is it true?"

The voice was familiar, loud and leering: Jared Blake, who showed up to this particular class so rarely that Saffron hadn't thought to anticipate his presence. She lifted her head slowly, cold dread in her stomach. Except for Jared, her classmates were quiet; she knew he was talking to her.

She looked at him, her face as blank as she could make it. Jared Blake was rangy and rawboned, his brown hair gelled into spikes. He was white-skinned in a way that left him permanently sunburned, pink circles flaking across the bridge of his nose, his sharp cheeks layered with freckles over acne scars, his neck scored with lines where he'd scratched at it with jagged, bitten fingernails. He wore a seemingly permanent smirk, and it was utterly unfair that a boy so full of malice should have the longest, thickest lashes she'd ever seen, fanning lazily over pale blue eyes.

"Is what true?" Saffron asked, boldly.

"Jared, dude," mumbled one of his friends, shifting uncomfortably beside him, "c'mon–"

"That some freak made you his bitch." He grinned sharply, running his fingers across his head in imitation of her triptych scars. "You fuck Edward Scissorhands, Saffy?"

Only one boy laughed, and then barely – a scared, gulping bark, like he'd tried to keep it in – while someone else whispered, "Oh, *shit*." Everyone else was deathly silent, eyes as wide as their tongues were bitten.

In that moment, Saffron was swept by a rage both colder and hotter than anything she'd ever felt in her life. To have survived the impossible and still be forced to contend with the mundane abuse of Jared Blake was beyond insulting; it was insupportable. She opened her mouth to say or scream she didn't know what, only that it needed to be said–

"Ah, good morning, everyone! Sorry to keep you all waiting – couldn't find the key, I swear it hides from me – there we go, in, in!"

The teacher, Mr Lane, had arrived, as brightly oblivious to the scene he'd interrupted as a toddler wandering into parliament. With the collective, sullen sluggishness of cats being shooed from a sunbeam, the students moved into the classroom, the stunned silence of moments earlier transmuting into a susurrus of gossiping whispers, all eyes flicking from Saffron to Jared and back again as they took their seats.

Inside, a horseshoe of desks and chairs bracketed an extra

two rows, forcing a brief traffic jam as students chose where to sit. Numb with unspent fury, Saffron beelined for a seat in the middle row, hands shaking as she pulled her books out of her bag. Up front, Mr Lane was rattling around in his desk drawers for a whiteboard marker, muttering a semi-happy narration as he did so. Mr Lane was something of an odd fish in Lawson High's PE department, in that he bore no obvious signs of ever having voluntarily gone outside. He was short, bearded and bookish, his side part a neat white line in his dark brown hair, and Saffron had a vague notion that he'd been shunted over from HSIE as a staffing stopgap without yet managing to be shunted back. Even so, he wasn't a bad teacher; just visually incongruous, and slightly more inclined than his departmental colleagues to look things up in the textbook.

Saffron flinched only slightly as the adjacent seats were taken: the room was too small for her to be given a wide berth, no matter her classmates' preferences. She risked a glance to either side, hackles lowering slightly at the people she saw there. Glitter James-Michaels, on her right, was more likely to spend the class covertly texting than giving grief, while Alfie Gowan, on her left, was a meticulous, silent note-taker. Saffron exhaled shakily, clicking open one of her brand new pens. *I can do this. Normal day.*

Something cold scraped the back of her neck. She whirled around, startled, and found herself staring at Jared Blake, a metal ruler lolling between his outstretched fingers.

"Scissorhands," he grinned, and twitched his knuckles, making the ruler jump. "Look familiar?"

"All right!" Mr Lane said, clapping for attention. Saffron didn't know whether to hate or thank him; she turned back, clicking the pen in impromptu stress relief, jaw clenched painfully tight. "Did everyone have a good weekend? Yes? No? Maybe? Excellent! Well, now that I've managed to find a marker, let's try to get off to a good start by reviewing–"

"Sir, Saffron's back!" yelled Jared.

"–the chapter on... What? Saffron –? Oh! *Oh.* Um. So she is, yes." Mr Lane blinked at her, mouth hanging open only a little. He shook his head, as if to clear it of unwanted cobwebs, and ventured a tentative, "Welcome back, Miss Coulter."

Saffron nodded, not trusting her voice.

Mr Lane returned the gesture, a brief smile on his lips, and launched back into his teaching spiel with a heartfelt, "Now, as I was saying..."

Saffron let the words wash over her, for once grateful for her total lack of interest in the subject. She focused on breathing, trying to calm her racing pulse, hands moving on autopilot as she turned to the relevant page in her textbook.

The ruler rasped across her neck, accompanied by a singsong whisper: "*Scissorhands.*"

Saffron had a sudden, visceral flashback to age nine, when her primary school teacher had taken to seating disruptive students beside her. Saffron's chief virtue, as Ms Carradine had seen it, was her non-responsiveness. The troublemaker – and it was always a boy, she realised now; not because the girls never misbehaved, but because this particular punishment was never used on them – would try to rile her up. Saffron would ignore him, and eventually, the boy would get bored and find some other, less vocal way to amuse himself. Saffron, meanwhile, had to concentrate twice as hard to get her normal work done, and was denied the pleasure of sitting with whatever friend the boy had displaced. Not that Ms Carradine ever seemed to realise that she was punishing both of them: so long as the overt disruption ended, the matter was considered closed.

But one day, Saffron had snapped. Having exhausted his verbal taunts, her neighbour, a boy called Alex, had defaulted instead to pinching her under the desk, starting just above her knee and moving steadily up her outer thigh. Unable to move out of range and with Ms Carradine preoccupied with helping someone else, Saffron had endured it for as long as she could before finally, in a fit of helpless anger, thumping him in the chest.

She didn't remember Alex's last name now, but she did recall, with shocking clarity, the delighted-wicked look on his face as he told her, *sotto voce*, "You're going to get in *trouble*." He'd started howling, clutching his chest and crying crocodile tears, his tale of woe supported by another boy to his right, who'd missed both the preceding pinches and subsequent vow of revenge while catching Saffron's blow. Ms Carradine hadn't asked for Saffron's side of things, but had sent her straight to the principal's office. It was the only time she'd ever incurred such a punishment, and by the time she'd walked to the admin building, she was crying, too.

Fortunately, if you could call it that, Alex had pinched her hard enough to bruise, the purpling marks all the proof necessary to see him summoned to penance in her place. She'd still been rebuked for hitting, of course – *You should've told the teacher*, the headmaster said, as though Ms Carradine's entire strategy wasn't contingent on Saffron's silence – but was spared detention. Alex, for his part, spent two consecutive lunchtimes copying lines inside, then took to sneering at Saffron from the other side of the playground, occasionally calling her names. When he changed schools the following year, Saffron had breathed a quiet sigh of relief and put him firmly out of mind.

Until now, when Jared Blake's taunting brought the memories back in technicolour. It was the same thing all over again: no matter how tightly Saffron tucked her chair to the desk, its wooden edge biting into her stomach, she couldn't get out of range of the ruler, which never seemed to land in the same place twice. Unlike the file he'd last tried to jam beneath her skirt in metalworking – an incident that felt years old, instead of just weeks – the ruler was sharp, and as the lesson dragged on Jared alternated tapping her shoulders with the flat, dragging the edge across her nape, or digging the corner-point into the side of her neck, and always with that accompanying whisper: "*Scissorhands!*"

Saffron gripped her pen so hard, the plastic creaked. *You're not nine any more. If you hit him, they won't care who started it. They'll call the social worker. They'll call your* parents. *Don't give them a reason to send you home.*

But another, angrier part of her thought, *If the school won't stop him, why shouldn't I? My being quiet doesn't make him go away; it makes him think he's winning.*

And not just Jared, she realised with a jolt: though Mr Lane remained oblivious, each tap and whisper timed to occur when the teacher's back was turned, her classmates were more perceptive. A low murmur now accompanied each new provocation, hisses and huffed laughter undercutting the ambient classroom noise. Though Alfie Gowan, blessings on his commitment to note-taking, hadn't looked up, Glitter James-Michaels had started casting her sympathetic looks, a minute shake of her head speaking volumes: *He's not worth it. Don't give him what he wants.*

But what about what I *want?* Saffron almost screamed. The ghost of that primary school headmaster appeared by her ear, enjoining her once more, in his grave, slow voice, to simply tell the teacher. Except that there was no way to explain why successive taps with a ruler and references to a decades-old Tim Burton movie were such felonious actions as to merit Jared's removal without repeating what he'd said outside, which Saffron emphatically didn't want to do, not least because there was no way to do so calmly – and she *had* to be calm, or Jared, who wanted to provoke an emotional reaction, would win anyway. She tried to imagine it: raising her hand, waiting for Mr Lane's permission, her voice unwavering as she explained... what? That Jared thought the idea of her escaping from a violent rapist was funny enough to goad her about it in public?

Which was, she realised abruptly, exactly what he was doing. For all he knew, she really *had* been abused that way, and he was trying to give her flashbacks – to set her off in the middle of class like a goddamn IED.

Epiphany hit like a slap to the face: if Jared was going to think he'd won no matter if she endured his crap or reacted to it, then the only sensible thing to do was whatever made *her* feel best. She stifled a furious smile and put her pen down, waiting for her chance.

This time, the whisper preceded the ruler: "*Scissorhands!*"

After the bloody ambush on the Envas road, Matu had helped alleviate Saffron's fear and helplessness by teaching her basic self-defence. Just a few moves, repeated over and over, until he felt sure she had the knack of them. It hadn't transformed her into a warrior like Pix or Yasha, but it had done wonders to improve her reflexes, especially when responding to threats that came from behind.

As the ruler tapped her shoulder, Saffron shot her hand back and grabbed hold. Then, in a single, whip-fast motion, she yanked it out of Jared's grasp and threw it forwards–

–where it struck Mr Lane in the back of the neck, the pointed edge digging in.

The teacher whirled with a startled yelp which, on any other occasion, would've earned a laugh at his expense. "Who –" he began, and then, his voice an uncustomary growl as he glanced up from the fallen ruler, "*Jared.*"

Because the ruler was, unquestionably, Jared's: Mr Lane couldn't possibly have missed him playing with it, even if he hadn't noticed the provocative tapping. Following his angry stare, half the class had swivelled in their seats, too, and were now arrested by the damning sight of Jared Blake leaning halfway across his desk, one arm outstretched in a futile bid to reclaim what was already lost.

"I didn't throw it!" Jared said, a note of genuine outrage in his voice. "Saffron did!"

"It's your ruler," Mr Lane countered, stooping to retrieve it. He smacked the flat of it into his palm, as though testing its heft. He raised a pointed eyebrow. "Isn't it?"

"Yeah," Jared retorted, "but *she threw it!*"

Mr Lane looked at Saffron. His expression was mild, but his eyes were furious. "Is that true, Miss Coulter?"

It was an axial moment: the world – or hers, at least – turned on it. Except for Alfie Gowan, who was staring at the tableau in clear bewilderment, the whole class knew she'd thrown the ruler. Just as equally, they knew why she'd done it; or at least, why she'd done *something*. So far, no one had chimed in to support Jared's story, but that might change if she lied outright. And if the whole class engaged in a lie of omission on her behalf, what would that prove except that Jared was an unlikeable dickhead and Mr Lane out of his depth? Both those things were already obvious. What Saffron wanted was less so, even to herself.

"He was scratching my neck with the edge," she said. She felt weirdly serene, as if detached from consequence. "I tried to pull it away from him. I guess I pulled too hard." Almost, she added a *sorry*, the habit of deference deeply ingrained, but stopped herself in time. It would've been a bigger lie, somehow, than claiming that the throw was unintentional.

Mr Lane's gaze narrowed. "Really."

"Really.'"

"Bullshit!" yelled Jared. "She did it on purpose!"

And then, in an utterly unexpected show of solidarity, Glitter James-Michaels said, "No, she didn't. It was an accident." She looked at Mr Lane, a perfectly contoured eyebrow raised in accusation. "He was hitting her with it for *ages*, sir. You should've noticed."

Someone did laugh at that, and Mr Lane flushed, the rebuke all the sharper for coming from such an academically non-partisan student.

"Right," said Mr Lane, after a moment. "Mr Blake, you

keep your hands and utensils to yourself in future, please."

"Whatever," said Jared, slouching in his seat. "Sure."

"And as for you, Miss Coulter," said Mr Lane, inhaling in a clear bid for calmness, "I would like an apology."

And Saffron, equally calm, said, "No."

2
Lost & Found

Trying to solve political problems, Gwen thought, was rather like backburning a forest: no matter how much space you cleared, the green shoots of new troubles soon sprang up to repopulate the landscape.

"What do you *mean*, proof of abdication?"

"Exactly what it sounds like," Pix said, wearily. They sat in a comfortable, private chamber adjacent to the Cuivexa's new rooms, a pot of tea abandoned on the low, ornate table between them. "According to the consensus of the House of the Mortal Firmament–" an elite parliament of prominent Kenan nobles, without whose support no monarch could be lawfully crowned, "–Iviyat and Amenet cannot be formally invested as Vexas until or unless there is legal proof that Leoden has abdicated the throne."

"And it took them *six days* to render that verdict?"

"More likely they'd reached a decision by the first afternoon," Pix said tartly. "The rest of it was finding the courage to tell me so."

A muscle twitched in Gwen's jaw. "I wonder they found such courage at all, when they know what the outcome must be. If Viya and Amenet cannot rule by such stipulation, then neither can anyone else."

"Except for Leoden," said Pix.

"Except for Leoden."

"To their credit," said Pix, after a moment, "they're not exactly thrilled with the prospect, either."

Gwen bared her teeth. "How very good of them."

"Quite."

In the wake of old Vex Ralan's death, Gwen and Pix had involved themselves in the succession debate in no small part because the House of the Mortal Firmament had been divided on the issue. Of those in the House who'd supported Amenet, a bare handful now remained, Leoden having killed the majority during his bloody coup. Those who'd cleaved to Tevet, Amenet's now-dead sister, had likewise seen their numbers thinned during her failed siege of Karavos, a bitterly ironic attempt to avenge a murder which, unbeknownst to all but a few, its subject had survived. And yet, Gwen suddenly realised, Leoden had never bothered to stack the House in his favour by replacing the dead with new, loyal appointees – a logical move for any new Vex or Vexa to make, let alone one ascending in such troubled circumstances. Gwen wondered that they hadn't noticed it before; but then, of course, they'd been busy fighting for their lives, not looking to borrow trouble.

She said as much to Pix, who blinked, startled.

"Perhaps he thought he had more time," she said, but frowned as she said it. "Either way, it's to our advantage now."

They shared a look at that: as intriguing as the question was, they had more pressing matters to deal with.

"As for proof of abdication," Pix said, after a moment, "do you have any bright ideas?"

Gwen sighed. "Not off the top of my head, no. Still, I've a conference later today with the Most Honoured of Ke's Kin that might prove useful – I've been trying to meet with her for days to discuss the anchored portal, but she's been too busy."

Pix raised an eyebrow. "Busy, or stalling?"

It was a fair question; Gwen thought carefully before answering. "Busy," she said at last. "From what her messengers have said, I suspect she's trying to figure out who in her order might have aided Leoden before she speaks to us, and if she was personally culpable, I doubt she'd have been so helpful with the jahudemet before the wards came back up."

"I take your point," Pix murmured.

It was thanks to this latter courtesy that Amenet, Matu and Jeiden had been brought ahead to the palace while the rest of their allies were still marching to Karavos. In asking Ke's Kin to restore the broken wards, Viya had taken advantage of the moment to request a portal be opened to Avekou before they came back up, as Trishka was too drained to do it herself. The Most Honoured had agreed, sending them a talented young acolyte for the purpose. With his help, it was the work of minutes to summon their closest allies, whose presence, once the initial stir of shock died down, did wonders to shore up Viya's position. The acolyte, Naruet, had impressed Gwen with the strength and precision of his magic; almost, she'd pulled him aside to examine the anchored portal. Only the knowledge that they weren't sure who in the hierarchy might be working for Leoden had stopped her – trusting too soon or too easily could be worse than not trusting at all. Still, she'd kept his name in mind for her meeting with the Most Honoured, should the head priestess decline to inspect the portal personally.

"What do you think–" Gwen began, but broke off at the sound of the chamber door opening. She looked up, smiling as Viya and Amenet entered. The monarchs-to-be had been cloistered with various petitioners, nobles and advisers practically since before dawn, and while Amenet looked typically unruffled, Viya had the distinct air of someone whose patience was worn thin.

"You're early!" said Pix, coming to her feet. "Did something happen?"

Viya snorted. "Talking," she said. "At *length*. And we still don't know where the godshitting Vekshi ambassador is." She cast a brief, longing glance at the couch, but didn't sit, sighing in resignation as Gwen, too, came to her feet. "My theory is that Kadeja vanished her, or killed her, or did something else untoward and violent to her person, assuming she wasn't a casualty during Tevet's campaign. There's no official record of her leaving the palace, her old staff are gone, and nobody can remember seeing her since before my marriage."

"What does Sashi say?" Gwen asked. "Are there any rumours in the Warren?"

"None that she's reported," said Amenet. "Though she did offer to spy for us there, if we felt it necessary."

Gwen blinked, surprised. With the compound burning, Sashi had taken the bulk of Yasha's Vekshi expatriates and fled to the Warren, a colourful, crowded section of Karavos known, among other things, for its heavy concentration of Uyun and Vekshi migrants. Sashi's safe return to the palace now had lifted a weight from Gwen's heart, not least because of what it meant to Trishka to have at least one of her daughters safe at hand. That Sashi would volunteer to go back in the field so quickly shouldn't have surprised her, and yet she felt oddly disquieted by the prospect.

"And will you take her up on that offer?" she asked, forcing herself to speak.

Amenet looked thoughtful. "Perhaps," she said, "but if Sene a Sati truly can't be found, then we'll need to appoint an interim Vekshi ambassador, and there are not so many Vekshi in the palace these days that we have a wide range to choose from. And..."

She broke off, the right side of her mouth twisting sadly, the better to match the already downturned left. She'd survived Leoden's poisoning, but not unscathed: her whole left side had been paralyzed as if by a stroke, and not even the most skilled healers of Teket's Kin could say if the damage was permanent, or to what extent.

"And," she continued softly, "as it's the ambassador's task to see Zechalia's body safely back to Veksh, I would rather entrust that duty to one who loved her than to a stranger."

Gwen's throat tightened; she looked away, as did they all, the death of the child-queen hanging between them like shadows.

"Trishka would thank you for that, I think," she said, humbly. "Even if it meant Sashi leaving again."

"And speaking of leaving," said Pix, false humour in her voice as she gestured at the door, "I believe we have another matter to attend to."

"Yes," said Viya, clearly grateful for the change in topic. From what Gwen had seen, the Cuivexa's relationship with Zech had been a complex, often antagonistic one, but only a fool would think Viya unhurt by her death. "The worldwalkers. We should... we should see them."

"After you," said Pix, bowing courteously.

By unspoken agreement, Amenet set the pace as they left the chamber. She walked now with two aids, one hidden, one visible. The former was a brace imbued with the *sevikmet*, supporting her bad leg; the latter was a gorgeous rhyawood cane, slightly tapered at the base and cunningly carved to resemble a trio of braided branches, topped with a sphere of amber that set off the glow of the lacquered russet wood. A beautiful adornment, but also a functional one: gripping something hard and round eased the muscles in Amenet's palsied left hand. It was just a bonus, she'd joked with Gwen, that it made the cane look like a lesser god's sceptre from a moon-tale.

To Gwen, who'd grown up with different stories, it resembled a wizard's staff, but in either case it gave Amenet an otherworldly air. Beside her, Viya looked... not young, although she was that, too, but somehow liminal, as though she were caught on so many cusps that she'd come to embody them. As both Cuivexa and Vexa-to-be, her power now was equal parts nebulous and concrete, a thing born solely of will. No aspect of her escaped the contradiction, least of all her appearance. Unlike Amenet, who wore her black hair in a neat betrothal braid, Viya's coiffure was, of necessity, more complex. Though Kadeja was returned to Veksh, and Leoden had vanished, under Kenan law, they were still her marriage-mates, which meant she ought to have worn an unambiguous triple-braid to acknowledge them. Instead, the two braids at her temples were barely three links each, a joint's length of bound hair tied off with white and black cords. In stark contrast, the rest of her locks were pulled loosely back until they formed a single, thicker plait at her nape – as close to a betrothal braid as she could come while still admitting her (existing, tenuous) marriage.

The four of them walked in silence, steadily traversing the levels of the palace – down, down, to where the once-captive worldwalkers were now held. As they reached the second of several flights of stairs, Gwen bit her tongue against the impulse to start an argument. After they'd been removed from the vault, she'd wanted to move the worldwalkers to the palace proper, to be housed and cared-for in one of the many guest wings, but to her chagrin, Amenet and Viya had overridden her.

"Their visibility would raise too many questions," Amenet had said, apologetically. "Never mind that they have no reason to trust us yet, and might well run if we don't keep them secured. We'll certainly make them comfortable, but for the moment, it's best they stay in the lower levels."

Which, after some in-depth consultation with the relevant castellan, had yielded their current location: a defunct barracks set beneath one of the many palace gardens, used for storage in the past decade, but hastily restored for their injured guests. The individual rooms were still too cell-like to Gwen's eye, but she'd seen they were as comfortably furnished as possible, and though she was yet to win her bid to have the rescuees given time outside, she hoped that their current excursion – Amenet, Pix and Viya's first to see the worldwalkers in situ, the practicalities having been delegated to Gwen and Louis – would change their minds. For what felt like the fiftieth time, she reminded herself that neither woman was unmoved by the abuse the captives had suffered, nor had they deliberately made themselves unavailable to see the worldwalkers before now. They'd all been run off their feet with the myriad urgent practicalities of regaining control of the palace, and while they might still have made time for it, Gwen wouldn't fault them for their choices.

And at any rate, she thought, back straightening as they alighted the final set of stairs, *they're still here now.*

As they approached the door to the former barracks, a muscular guard in what Gwen guessed was his late twenties or early thirties snapped to attention. He was rather good-looking, with a sharp-bladed nose, a neatly shaved jaw and eyes so pale a brown they were almost gold, contrasting nicely with the warmer brown of his skin. To her surprise, she recognised him as a man she'd seen the past few days in Louis's company, albeit in a more personal context; Rikan, that was his name.

"My ladies," said Rikan, bowing over his cupped hands to Gwen and Pix. He offered a deeper, more practiced bow to Viya and Amenet. "Your highnesses."

"Hello, Rikan," said Gwen. He startled slightly at being recognised; Gwen wondered if it was because he hadn't expected her to know his name, or because he was bedding her son. "Is this your first shift down here?"

"Second, lady," he said, somewhat bashfully. His accent and dialect both were lowborn, but he didn't hesitate to make eye contact with Viya and Amenet. "I'm honoured by your trust."

"Has anyone been by today?" Pix asked.

"Just two, lady – Halunet from Nihun's Kin and Aydi from Teket's, checking on them as needs it. Oh, and that lad who serves your betrothed," he added, turning to Viya and Amenet. "Jeiden, I think? He didn't come in, but he did ask if everyone was well, and I told him they were as hale as could be expected, under the circumstances."

Gwen felt a brief pang of guilt at the mention of Jeiden. As close as they'd been, Zech's death had hit him hard; that he still found time to worry about others spoke volumes about his character. With Matu serving as unofficial Vexa'Halat, it was Trishka who'd taken Jeiden under her wing, and while Gwen didn't doubt for a moment that the boy was being well cared for, she promised herself she'd look in on him later.

"Rikan," said Viya suddenly, eyes lit with belated recognition. "I know you! You're the guard who was on duty when Luy–" Gwen's lips quirked; as subtle as the distinction was, she alone called her son Louis "–smuggled me from the palace. You flirted with him and let us through."

Rikan blushed prettily. "I did, highness. Can't say I regret either part of it."

Gwen snorted, making a mental note to congratulate her son on his fine taste in men some other time. Out loud, she said, "Thank you, Rikan," lips quirking in a smile as he stepped aside and let them through the door to the common area.

At Gwen's instruction, each of the worldwalkers had been given an individual room, the doors to which could be closed, but not locked. She explained as much to the others as they looked about: the majority of doors were unsurprisingly closed, but the few that were open revealed a glimpse of worldwalkers either sleeping or resting.

"Do we know where they came from yet?" Viya asked, voice respectfully lowered. "Do any of them speak Kenan?"

"No," sighed Gwen, frustrated. "The priests and healers are doing what they can, but the ones who are lucid enough for the *zuymet* to work are terrified of magic. Most of their hurts are from long-term captivity, malnourishment, so we've been using mundane means to heal them instead of the sevikmet – providing food, letting them rest. I think they're starting to trust us, but the real problem is whatever Leoden did to them, or had done to them, with *ahunemet*: their minds were rifled, thoughts and selves and memories, and now… well. Halunet's tried to help a few, but that sort of restoration is hardly a peaceful process, and without being able to explain his intent it just looks to them like we're no better than Leoden was. We could do it by force, but I'd rather not. They've already been violated, and I see no reason to add to that."

"Indeed," said Amenet, quietly. "Whatever knowledge he sought from them, I'd rather remain in ignorance than duplicate his methods."

They reached the end of the common area, which branched off into separate rooms: one for bathing and ablutions, the other a dining hall. The four of them turned to retrace their steps, and Gwen felt a sudden, frustrated pang at the anticlimax of it all.

"Perhaps we could see about bringing them into the gardens each day," said Amenet. "Supervised, of course, and in small groups, but–"

She broke off sharply, stopping dead as she stared into one of the few open rooms. Her mouth hung open, knuckles pale where they gripped the amber head of her staff.

"Pix," she said, free hand grabbing blindly for the courtier's sleeve. "Look in there. *Look at her.*"

"What…?" said Pix, but when she looked her face went ashen. "Thorns and godshit," she whispered.

"What is it?" said Gwen, peering into the room in question. She'd assumed they were staring at one of the alien worldwalkers, but the single bed was occupied by a middle-aged human woman, fast asleep. She was pale-skinned, her hair a scraggle of mousy brown; Gwen had never paid her much attention before, and didn't understand why Amenet and Pix were suddenly both on edge. "What am I missing?"

Pix swallowed, ripping her gaze away from the sleeping woman. "Gwen," she said, "that's Sene a Sati. The missing Vekshi ambassador."

The hallway outside the counsellor's office was decorated in early funding cut. Faded motivational posters with slogans dating back to the late nineties stood as a sad archaeological testament to awkward adult attempts at teenage relatability. Saffron sat on a wonky chair, scuffing her still-new shoes on carpet older than she was, and tried to look like she wasn't actively eavesdropping. So far, neither the school's regular counsellors nor the Deputy Head had realised that conversations held in their respective offices could be overheard from the hallway even if their doors were closed, so long as the windows were open – which, given the general warmth of coastal Australian weather, they invariably were. As no counselee, miscreant or other lurking student had yet betrayed this strategic vulnerability, Saffron didn't want to be the one to let the side down, and so kept her expression carefully indifferent, staring at the opposite wall as she listened.

"I understand your concerns," the Deputy Head, Mr Laughton, said, "but this is a clear-cut disciplinary matter."

A dissenting noise from Mr Gryce, the counsellor. "Anthony, please. These are such extraordinary circumstances–"

"If they're so extraordinary that she can't conduct herself in class, then she shouldn't be here in the first place! Oh, don't look at me like that, I'm hardly unsympathetic – what she's been through scarcely bears thinking about – but you know damn well the school environment is hardly conducive to rehabilitation at the best of times."

"*This* school environment, anyway," Mr Gryce muttered.

Saffron fancied Mr Laughton's answering glare was audible.

"We're getting off topic," he said, in the tone of someone used to getting his way and irritable at being railroaded. "The point is that, regardless of the girl's motives and your opinion, under the terms of her return to Lawson, I'm obliged to inform both her parents and her social worker of any, quote unquote, *behavioural incidents*. That much is non-negotiable."

Saffron stilled, a sick feeling in her stomach. As calm as she'd felt in class, almost otherworldly in the face of Mr Lane's baffled anger, she was currently riding a pendulum between fury and fear. She hadn't known her parents had made such a deal with the school, and it choked her to think they'd discussed such a thing behind her back. Rationally, a small part of her understood – *if they think you're unstable, they're hardly going to ask you to weigh in on their protective measures* – but the rest of her was seething. Fists clenched, she forced herself to tune back in.

"…your opinion," Mr Laughton was saying. "We've got Tim's side of things, and we're about to hear hers, but once that's done I want your recommendation before I make any calls."

Saffron let out a breath. If they hadn't yet called her parents or Ms Mays, then there was still a chance, however slim, that she could talk them into dropping the matter. Not that Mr Laughton was exactly known for being either reasonable or sympathetic to the pleas of students, but if Mr Gryce was present – if Saffron could convince the counsellor – then maybe she had a chance.

Footsteps sounded from the office. Mr Gryce opened the door and poked his head into the corridor. He was rake-thin and balding, brows creased worriedly even as his mouth approximated a smile.

"Come in please, Saffron."

Saffron nodded and rose, her bag dangling loosely from one hand. Her pulse quickened, but as she passed the counsellor she was swept by the same, surreal calm that had claimed her in Mr Lane's class. *It doesn't matter what they say: I'm right. They can't change that.*

Mr Laughton stood beside Mr Gryce's desk, arms crossed.

"Please, sit down," he said, gesturing Saffron to a chair placed opposite Mr Gryce's own. She complied, lips twitching as the counsellor took his own seat behind the desk, as though he, too, were obeying.

"Now, Miss Coulter," Mr Laughton said, gravely. "I'm sure you don't need me to impress upon you the seriousness of your being here. We know about the incident in Mr Lane's class, and understand that you were, in part–" his gaze flicked to Mr Gryce, "–provoked by Jared Blake. What I don't understand is why, even when Mr Lane acknowledged this fact, you refused to apologise."

Saffron's hands were still as stone, her pulse as calm as water. "Because he didn't ask Jared to apologise to me."

Mr Laughton blinked, nonplussed. "Excuse me?"

"It was a double standard," Saffron said. "He only asked Jared to stop – as though Jared *ever* stops bothering *anyone* – but he wanted *me* to apologise."

Mr Gryce, at least, had the grace to wince. "And did you, ah, explain this to Mr Lane?"

"I did," said Saffron, levelly. "He said that, since he hadn't actually *seen* Jared harassing me, he didn't think it was fair to make him say sorry, but he *knew* I'd thrown the ruler."

"And what did you say to that?"

"I said he hadn't *seen* me throw the ruler, either: he only had my word for it, and if he was going to trust me on that, then why not trust I was telling the truth about Jared, too?"

"Miss Coulter," said Mr Laughton, exasperated, "the fact that you didn't think it was fair doesn't mean it wasn't also right to apologise. You were disrespectful to Mr Lane; you must understand why he had to send you here."

"What I *understand*," said Saffron, a flash of fury cracking her calm, "is that Jared made a joke about... about the idea that I was raped, and kept *on* making the joke while he tapped me with his ruler – *Scissorhands*, he was saying, because of the scars, right?" She pointed angrily to her face, and felt viciously satisfied when Mr Laughton flinched. "And Mr Lane didn't even *notice*, even though he's meant to be in charge. He believed me enough to ask Jared to stop, but not enough to make him apologise – but *I* should say sorry to *him*?"

"Miss Coulter–" he began, but Saffron was having none of it.

"You know *exactly* what Jared is, sir," she shot back. "I've tried to report him to you before, and you didn't do anything except tell me *boys will be boys*, because short of expelling him outright there isn't anything you think you *can* do that'll make him stop. So he bullies and gropes and harasses every girl in this school as often as he likes, and if a male teacher acted that way to his female colleagues, you'd have fired him after the first offence – hell, if a *teacher* did that stuff, they'd be *arrested*. But because he's our age we're just meant to put up with it, as though that's fair or right; as though it's *easy* to just get on with working afterwards. You know why I didn't say sorry to Mr Lane?" She looked Mr Laughton dead in the eye. "Because defending myself was not a worse crime than what I was defending myself *from*. So, no, I didn't say sorry, because I'm *not* sorry, and I'm sick of lying to people about how I feel because they're incapable of believing an honest answer!" She snapped her jaw shut, glaring.

A terrible silence fell.

"Saffron," Mr Gryce said gently, "it's a complicated issue. We can't just expel boys like Jared for misbehaving; he deserves an education, too, no matter how determined he is at times to throw it away."

"It's not just *misbehaving*!" Saffron choked out. "It's so much worse than that, and you know it! Is giving him an eighth chance to snap our bras and shove his hand up our skirts more important than *us* not having to deal with *him*? What about *our* education?"

Mr Gryce visibly floundered; Mr Laughton sighed.

"Is there anything else you'd like to add, before we call your parents?"

"Yes," snapped Saffron. "You're more protective of a proto-rapist than you are of the girls he hurts, and you should be *ashamed* of yourselves."

And with that, she stood and stormed out of the office, slamming the door behind her.

The head priestess of Ke's Kin was older than Gwen – and taller, too – yet younger than she'd been expecting. She looked to be in her early sixties, a willowy woman of six-foot-something who carried herself with all the grace and dignity of a retired prima ballerina. Her white robe was slim-fitted, showing the shallow curves of hip and breast, while her unbound hair, a sheet of iron and silver shot with gleaming white, hung straight to the backs of her knees. Her delicate skin was the purest shade of black that Gwen had ever seen on a living person; the beauty of it quite took her breath away. Within the sanctity of this, her temple, the priestess's feet were bare, and her face was calm. Yet her eyes – a shocking pale green, as striking as the rest of her – were worried, and when her hovering seneschal finally bowed and left the room, she gestured Gwen to sit with a motion that was more twitch than wave.

"Forgive me," Gwen said, as she took her chair, "but I don't think I know your name."

The head priestess laughed – a little weary, a little wry. "The peril and privilege of rank is that its titles soon supersede one's own. In the early days of my ascension, I counted that a blessing; now, it feels a loss." She folded her hands in her lap – her nails, Gwen saw, were lacquered in white – and said, with an air of pleasant occasion, "Properly, I ought to be addressed as Most Honoured; improperly – or personally, rather, which means the same more often than I'd like – my full name is Ktho'isa'n khoi'Sthe idi Ke." She smiled at Gwen, a hint of challenge in her face. "Few enough here can pronounce it; should you prove to be one of them, you may call me Ktho."

Something in the shape of the syllables tugged at Gwen, though it took her a moment to understand why. Then it clicked, and to Ktho's clear surprise and delight, she repeated her full name back to her without a hitch, capping the recitation with, "Forgive me any impertinence, but are your kin from the pearl-diving clans who live to the west of the Sea of Songs?"

Ktho's smile was wide and lovely, erasing the worry lines that creased her eyes. "I can count on one hand the number of dignitaries who've ever guessed as much, and one of those was a representative of the city where my *ntai* still trades." A very faint accent emerged as she spoke the foreign word: a gift of trust so unexpected, Gwen was moved to give back in kind.

"My wife, Jhesa, was raised in the river-city of Japhiin, in the west of Uyu. She is the storyteller of our mahu'kedet, and more than one of her tales has featured pearl-divers."

"Your mahu'kedet? Are you not a worldwalker, then?"

Gwen shrugged, a slight smile twitching her lips. "We have, I think, both travelled far from where we first called home."

They shared a look of understanding, and Gwen felt a sudden frustrated pang, that this wondrous woman had lived barely a stone's throw from her for all these years, and yet had never crossed her path before. Gwen flattered herself that Ktho was thinking along similar lines, for all at once the priestess laughed and said, in a lighter voice than she'd yet used, "Do you know, Gwen Vere, I believe our conversation has strayed from the path."

Gwen hesitated, then said, "Gwen Vere ore Jhesa'yu ki Solomon." More softly, she said, "You have gifted me with your true name. I feel I can do no less than to trust you with mine. Though mostly, I prefer just Gwen."

"Just Gwen, then," Ktho breathed, and straightened like a soldier. "Please, then: tell me what you must."

Gwen took a faltering breath. She had warmed to Ktho as she warmed to few people; it felt wrong, somehow, to jar the moment back to business. *And yet needs must, when the devil drives.*

"You know, of course, that when the Cuivexa and her allies returned to Karavos with Vekshi aid, the magic we employed effectively, if temporarily, stripped the palace of magical protection. This afforded one of your jahudemet-users the opportunity to open a portal and bring through Amenet ore Amenet ki Rahei from Avekou, with others of her entourage, before aiding in the restoral of the wards."

Ktho nodded. "I do recall."

"Just so," said Gwen. "Well. You will also know that, during these unusual events, Vex Leoden fled the palace."

"On that count, I have heard a number of competing theories. But yes: flight is certainly preeminent among them."

"As well it should be, as it's true. I witnessed it." Gwen bit her lip. "He... escaped, I think is the word... through an anchored portal situated in an ancient vault beneath the palace." She explained the facts of Leoden's capture and how they'd come to lose him: the shaking palace, his claim that a dangerous artefact under investigation by Sahu's Kin was responsible, their foolish decision to trust him. "However it was he activated the portal, I can't believe he felt so threatened by us as to have jumped the worlds blind. He must've had a plan, a destination; we just don't know what."

Ktho looked stunned. "Your missive spoke of an anchored portal, but I never imagined–" She cut herself off with visible effort, motioning for Gwen to continue.

Gwen sighed: now came the difficult part. "In the same vault as the portal, we also found twenty-three prisoners, all of whom, as best we can tell, are worldwalkers." She didn't mention Sene a Sati on the grounds that she didn't yet know if the woman's incarceration and torture had been meant as punishment for some other crime, or if she, too, was part of Leoden's wider plans. "All have been subject to torture, oftentimes physically, but always to some degree by a horrific abuse of the ahunemet and possibly the zuymet, too. It therefore seems reasonable to conclude that Vex Leoden – and, we assume, the Vex'Mara Kadeja – had been aware of the portal for some time; certainly, they knew enough to use it in pursuit of their own agenda, though what that is, or was, we don't yet know. In any case, the worldwalkers who remain in our care are traumatised, untrusting of our motives and terrified of the very magic we need to help restore them to themselves. It is… frustrating."

A gross understatement; Ktho, by the look of absolute horror on her face, clearly understood this.

"One other point of relevance – on this matter, at least. There is another, related issue I would raise with you shortly." Gwen forced herself to meet Ktho's gaze. "Though Vex Leoden lied about many things to trick us into taking him to the anchored portal, I don't think he lied when he said that the room in which it lay was originally a treasure vault belonging to Vexa Yavin."

Ktho hissed in angry recognition at the name. "But of course. Who else would make such a dangerous thing?"

"Who else indeed," Gwen murmured. For all she was a worldwalker, she'd spent enough time in Kena to have learned a great deal of its history – and where that history faltered or was absent entirely, surviving records all agreed, the fault was Vexa Yavin's. A ruler now four centuries dead, her reign was known as the Years of Shadow, both for her encouragement of twisted magic and for her destruction of what had once been Kena's greatest archives, both magical and historical. It didn't help that she'd also waged bloody war on neighbours and subjects alike, even going so far as to build a new capital in her own, grandiose image – Yavinae, a city abandoned since her reign's end, and whose ruins still stood south of the Bharajin Forest, an Ozymandian testament to her ambition.

"And so you wonder," Ktho said, voice heavy, "who but a devotee of Ke's Kin would have the knowledge necessary to enable such atrocity – to reactivate a jahudemet artefact of Vexa Yavin?"

"If it makes you feel any better," said Gwen, knowing full well it wouldn't, "we suspect he may have suborned some of Nihun's Kin, too."

"Suborned? My dear, he was – and is, though it pains us all – the rightful Vex. *Suborned* is not the word you want, for that assumes his accomplices were employed to subvert the law, instead of to uphold its arbiter's wishes."

"Which leads us," said Gwen, "to the other matter I wished to discuss."

As briefly as she could, she relayed the verdict of the House of the Mortal Firmament: that proof of Leoden's abdication was needed in order for Viya and Amenet to take the throne – proof which they manifestly did not have and could not obtain, unless some legal loophole existed to moot the issue.

Ktho absorbed this all with the composure of a saint, and Gwen wondered how and when a woman born so very far from the reach of Kena and its gods had come to find herself beholden to both. But of course, she realised belatedly, the answer – as in her own case – was portal-magic. By longstanding tradition, the head priests and priestesses of the temples of the nine gods of the first and second tier of the celestial hierarchy always possessed the magic associated with their sworn deity. The jahudemet was governed by Ke, the goddess of stars, and as rare and powerful as it was, its manifestation was invariably met either with greed, as in Trishka's case, or hostility, as was more common in Uyu and the various annexed territories that made up the ariphate. As little as she knew of the pearl-divers of the Sea of Songs, it wasn't hard for Gwen to imagine that Ktho's gift, whatever her family's reaction to it, had eventually forced her relocation.

"Suppose," said Ktho, and stopped, a hesitancy to her voice that hadn't been there before. She plucked at the sleeve of her robes, a motile gesture that clashed sharply with her stillness otherwise, and fixed her pale-jade gaze on Gwen. "Suppose, for an instant, that a foolish woman–" her lips quirked with sadness, anger, "–had for some time suspected that a student, a much-beloved and fixated student, had unofficially continued their pursuit of research from which they had been explicitly banned. Suppose such a student is far and away the most likely culprit behind the reactivation of your anchored portal, and is thus responsible, however indirectly, for the abuses visited upon those it was used to capture. Such a student, in violating so completely their oaths to Ke, would be legally subject to the authority of Ke's head priestess, who would have no choice but to order their death, or be herself caught in contemptuous violation of her most sacred oaths. A death to be enacted by her own hand, no less. By her very own magic. Understand, to even speak of reprieve in such an instance would be abominable, not least because she had in the past been accused, and not without merit, of favouritism towards this particular student, despite their many... enthusiastic transgressions."

"Such imaginings are vivid indeed," Gwen said, quietly.

Ktho swallowed hard. Her lacquered nails twitched again, pinching at the fabric of her robes. "In such a case, the formalities would have to be observed with absolute precision. It is customary, for instance, that when a temple head is obliged to enact a death penalty, the reigning Vex or Vexa has the right to declare such a criminal a traitor to the throne, and thus to claim the right to enact a... a different penalty, more fitting to the offence. Exile is the most common option, though in times of war and turmoil, conscription to military service at the direct discretion of the monarch has been, if not always a morally defensible option, then certainly a means of controlling certain skills that might otherwise have been lost along with their user."

"An option," said Gwen, voice suddenly hard, "that was favoured by Vexa Yavin."

"An option," Ktho said quietly, "that can only be enacted by a reigning monarch. Or monarchs, as the case may be."

Gwen stared at the head priestess. Unasked questions buzzed on her tongue like wasps, and were just as painfully swallowed. Had Ktho been manipulating her from the outset? Was all their camaraderie a lie – an emotional trap into which Gwen had naively fallen, betraying those deepest parts of herself without a second thought? The prospect was ice injected into her heart – *godfuckingdammit, Ktho, I liked you!* – and for a moment, rage rendered her blind and speechless both, though directed as much at herself as at the woman opposite. *The last time I trusted such seeming goodness, Leoden took the throne. Fool of a woman! Fool and twice fool! Have you truly learned so little of politics?*

But:

This is your mess, another voice whispered. *Who else should be charged with fixing it?*

Two wrongs don't make a right. Helping Ktho absolve a criminal doesn't mend what Leoden did.

But if it puts Viya and Amenet on the throne...

Be rational: whatever you do, they won't thank you for it. Which is just as well, because this isn't about thanks – it's about an entire country in need of leadership, and controlling the knowledge you need to recapture Leoden. At the very least, you need to know exactly what that portal is before you could ever destroy it, or use it, or rest easy at the prospect of it sitting beneath the palace like a mouth to some unknown hell.

And if Ktho kills whoever opened it, then only your living enemies will ever know what it does...

"In my native language," said Gwen, "we have a saying at times like this. Would you like to hear it?"

"I would," said Ktho, a little uncertainly.

In English, Gwen said, with feeling, "What an *utter clusterfuck.*"

"That's... very succinct," said Ktho, after a moment.

"It was very heartfelt," Gwen replied, deadpan.

Ktho's lips twitched, and though she tried to smother the expression, still that spark of humour shone through.

"Might I ask where this student is now?"

Ktho winced. "In seclusion," she said. "At my suggestion."

Gwen raised a pointed brow. "Will they stay there?"

"I believe so, yes," said Ktho. "For now."

Another silence descended, briefer and more tepid than the last, until Gwen, who'd already known what she was going to do, gave in and broke it.

"Suppose," she said, sighing at the pretence of it all. "Suppose I speak for the Cuivexa in this. Suppose we would require–" she waved a hand, trying to conjure up the mental image of exactly what, if anything, Ktho could provide as proof of abdication, "–the relevant, ah, *precedent* within the next three days, in order to present it to the House, before we could take custody of your student. Would such a thing be possible?"

"It would," said Ktho. "On my honour as idi Ke." More softly, she added, "And on my honour as khoi'Sthe, for what that means to you."

If that's manipulation, it's a hell of an act, Gwen thought bleakly.

In Kena, one did not shake hands to cement a deal. Instead, Gwen kissed two knuckles – the middle joints of the pointer and index fingers of her right hand – and touched them briefly to her forehead, a mercantile salute. Ktho copied the gesture, slow and sure.

Her lacquered nails gleamed like stars.

3

Blunted Blades

"We're not cross," said Saffron's father, his tone giving lie to his words. "Just a little frustrated."

"We did suggest waiting longer before going back, darling," her mother added. "But now that we know there's a problem—"

"But there's *not* a problem," Saffron said, struggling to keep her voice in check. She stared at her parents, willing them to understand, unable to reconcile the terrible hurt she felt with the tense, concerned smiles on their faces. "What they asked of me, it wasn't fair – it was Jared who should've apologised!"

"Oh, Saff." Her mother squeezed her knee, and her voice was kind, so fucking *kind*, that Saffron wanted to scream. "You know better than to react to teasing! Boys like that, you just have to ignore them until they go away."

The words hit like a suckerpunch. Saffron swallowed hard, hating how close to tears she was, how caged and helpless she felt. *I speak three languages now, but I'm using the only one you know. Why don't you understand?*

Ms Mays, the social worker, shifted uncomfortably in the armchair opposite. Though well into her twenties, she looked strangely young to Saffron's eyes. New to her job, without the sharp authority, calm worldweariness or simple, cheerful gallows humour Saffron associated with emergency services veterans, of which social work was surely a daughter discipline – in practice, if not in funding. Young and eager and, like everyone else on Earth, completely ignorant of what Saffron had been through. *Hearts age faster than bodies, I think. Does that make me older than you?*

"Actually, Mrs Coulter," Ms Mays said, a gentle correction, "there's considerable evidence that passive acceptance of bullying can simply encourage the initiator to try harder, or at the very least, to persist. Direct confrontation is more effective – but throwing rulers, I grant you, is usually not what we have in mind." She flashed a bright smile in Saffron's direction, a clear effort at playful camaraderie. Saffron ignored it; for all her mother flushed, rebuked, which was a victory of sorts, Ms Mays hadn't acknowledged her anger, either.

Do they even know *I'm angry?* The question brought her up short. To Saffron, her rage was obvious. She could hear the ugly shake in her voice; could see the skin pulled tight across her knuckles where she'd balled her hands in her lap; could feel the burning flush on her cheeks and throat. And she knew she wasn't unreadable, either: Gwen had seen her upset before, and Trishka, and Matu, and all three had known exactly what it meant. So why couldn't her parents see it? Why couldn't Ms Mays?

Carefully, not sure how the statement would be met, she said, "I'm angry. Right now, I'm very, very angry."

"Good!" praised Ms Mays. "That's very good communication, Saffron."

"And *that*," Saffron snapped, "is a wholly useless response to someone's anger. I've fucking *been* angry this whole damn time–"

"Language!" her father barked, shocked.

"–and if any of you were paying the *slightest* bit of attention," Saffron forged on, glaring at him, "I wouldn't have *had* to say it." She swung her gaze to Ms Mays. "I don't need you to tell me I'm communicating properly; I need the three of you to acknowledge what I'm saying – by *listening* to me and responding to *that*, and not just saying, *oh, good job on the words*."

"We are listening, Saffron," Ms Mays said, her voice suddenly serious. "Believe me, you're being heard. But what you need to understand is that listening to you doesn't mean agreement on all counts."

"It should when I'm telling you *facts*," said Saffron. "If I say that two plus two is four, it shouldn't be up for debate."

"And what do you think the facts are, then?"

"I think–" said Saffron, and stopped. Caught herself. Took a deep breath, pretended her parents' eyes weren't boring into her neck like drill bits. Channelled Gwen and Viya, Yena and Yasha, trying to borrow their strength, their eloquence. Started again. "I think there are three facts. One: I am angry. Two: I am *allowed* to be angry. Three: this shouldn't disqualify me from attending school. If you're going to pull me out because of one incident – because of something *someone else started* – then what you're saying is, you don't trust me to know myself, or to handle myself, or to improve at all. You're saying I either have to behave perfectly, or I have to stay home, and I'm sorry, but I was never perfect, not even when I had all my original body parts." She held up her maimed hand and waved it at Ms Mays, ignoring the way her mother paled. *See? Cheerful gallows humour! Easy as pie.* "Standing up to Jared Blake is non-negotiable. It was *always* non-negotiable." And then, more plaintively, "Don't you *get* that?"

"We understand why you threw the ruler," her father said, rubbing his forehead. "We can sympathise with it, even. The boy in question certainly sounds a menace. What we don't understand – the bone of contention, as it were – is why you didn't apologise to your teacher."

"We heard what you said," said Ms Mays quickly, as Saffron opened her mouth. "About double standards, that his approach was hypocritical. And we understand the moral point, we do. But Saffron, part of returning to school – part of life in everyday society – is learning how to compromise. What concerns me isn't your belief that your teacher acted unfairly; it's your refusal to see that your response was contextually inappropriate. Now, given what you've been through–" Saffron tensed; could feel her parents jerk to attention like marionettes, "–I understand your desire – no, your *need* – to assert your personal boundaries, both emotional and physical. And I want you to know, that's very good. A very healthy part of recovering from trauma. It's important you feel the confidence to assert yourself, and I don't want to diminish that in the slightest."

"But," said Saffron, bitterly.

Ms Mays inclined her head. "*But*," she allowed, "an equally important part of recovery is learning – or re-learning, as I've said – to compromise. To allow for imperfections or divergent opinions in others, and to react accordingly."

Saffron's voice was heavy with sarcasm. "To be convenient."

Her father sighed. "Saffron–"

"This just isn't *like* you!" her mother blurted, the words tight with anxiety. "You've always been so good, Saff, such a good, kind girl, and it hurts my heart to think that man, that *monster*, could steal that part of you away – could make you into someone hard, someone else–"

"You think I'm not good anymore? Not kind?" The words came out a rasp.

Ms Mays visibly winced. "I'm sure what your mother *meant* to say is–"

"No," said Saffron, shaking with hurt and crying now, god-fucking-*damn* it, hot tears slipping free of their own accord. She shot to her feet, staring down at her mother's dismayed, soft face, a snarl of grief in her chest. *They called me Safi a Ellen, do you know that? Daughters named for mothers, and I honoured you in Veksh, I honoured you, and you'll never know it, never understand it – you want me to be what I was before, but I'm not that girl, and I wonder now if I ever was–*

"I am angry," she choked out. "I am angry, *and* kind, *and* good. It's not a contradiction, but if goodness to you is the absence of anger, then I'm sorry, but I was never good; I only ever pretended. Before all this, I felt so awful all the time, so sad and hurt – I barely slept, do you know that? Every day, I went to school and felt like I was broken, I was so unhappy, but if all this has taught me anything, it's that I can *survive*, I don't have to put up with the same old crap that was killing me before, and now that I know that about myself, you want me to jump right back in that box and shut the lid? If you'd known I was always angry before, would you still have called me good? Am I not allowed to feel stronger now?" Her voice had risen to a shout, sharp salt on her tongue where the tears wormed past her lips. "I know *exactly* what compromise is, Ms Mays, and it doesn't mean pawning my heart! It *can't*, or it's not a compromise. It's surrender."

"But if you really hate school so much," her father said, strained, "why did you fight so hard to go back so soon?"

Because you both keep looking at me like I'm porcelain. Because you want so badly for me to be normal that I almost want it, too. Because it should be my choice, not yours. Because I need to do something, *and it's all you'll let me do.* But those were answers she couldn't give, their truth as unwelcome here as her anger was.

"Because even if I'd said I never wanted to go again," she said, voice shaking, "at some point, you'd still have made me. And because I can't stand to be stuck at home, inside, like a hermit crab. I wanted to try. I want..." She swiped a wrist across her eyes and laughed, a cracked, miserable sound. The tears had stopped, but their stinging scent remained. "Shit, I want to *keep* trying. But you're not going to let me, are you? Because I told the truth, and you didn't like it." And then, in reflex, in murmured Kenan, "*I've gone and put eyes on my neck.*"

Ms Mays looked up sharply at that; Saffron laughed again, gave an offhand wave of her undamaged hand. "Private joke," she said, with a gallows-grin.

"Saffron–"

"You know what? I think we're done here."

She turned and left the living room, a sob in her throat as she headed upstairs to her bedroom. Small comfort to think that Gwen would have understood; Gwen wasn't here, and would have no authority over her family even if she had been. *All she has is my respect, for what it matters. Which, I guess, it doesn't. Not to them. They don't even know what she is to me.*

Nobody called her back.

Fours, Yena knew, were sacred to Ashasa. The four key elements which formed the world (water, stone, darkness, fire, each of which had four permutations); the four primary authorities to which each woman owed her labour (her goddess, her queens, her motherline and mother); the four staff-fighting disciplines (mounted, single combat, formation, exhibition). It was therefore no surprise that, having offered herself in supplication to the Great Temple – having knelt in false contrition for consorting with Kenan gods and temples, as though there was any honest apology to be made for honouring her truest self – her penitence was to constitute four acts.

But that doesn't mean I have to like it, she thought, gazing at the white grass on which she knelt. It was evening now, the gleaming moons like coins in the sky. The Kenans called them Kei and Mei, the Greater and Lesser, but in Veksh, they were Ashasa's daughters, Katala and Vashti, sentinels in the dark of the Mother Sun's absence. *And what are they to me? Just moons? Just stories? Must I choose, or feel myself judged forever?*

This was Yena's second act of penitence: to kneel unmoving through the night in the Great Temple courtyard, as naked as the day she was born, the better to appreciate the grace of Ashasa's warming light – a grace evidently both metaphoric and literal, if her frozen nipples were anything to go by. *Stop that,* she told herself sternly, wishing with a sudden, fierce ache that Sashi was there to laugh with her; or *at* her, even, so long as she had company. *You're meant to be contemplating your gratitude to the goddess.*

Gratitude and icy areolas did not mix.

Her first act of penitence, some hours earlier, had involved letting an ancient, gnarled priestess dunk her in a freezing pool, to similar mystic purpose. Unpleasant as the experience had been, at least it had been over quickly: now, she had hours still to go, and a burning want of clothes.

You've only yourself to blame for this. And, if she was being uncharitable, Mesthani a Vekte, who hadn't thought to talk her out of it. Presenting Yena at the Great Temple, Mesthani had been every inch the queen, her gestures and language minutely calibrated to suggest no partisan motivations; merely the fulfilment of her duty to Ashasa. By prior agreement with Yena, she'd made no mention of Zech or sisterhood, either: "They might still suspect an ulterior purpose," she'd murmured, leading Yena up the broad stone steps to the temple doors, "but if you say nothing, they're less likely to weigh it against whatever they ask of you."

Advice that Yena was glad to have taken: she shuddered to think how long she might have been asked to kneel in the naked dark if she'd openly declared her desire to be a queen's sister.

The air was chill with altitude, her brown skin pebbled with goosebumps. The deep scar on the outer edge of her left hand, her legacy of the battle of the Envas road, ached with cold, the new skin shrunken-tight. Her teeth chitter-chattered like genteel Kenan courtiers in the palanquin of her jaw, their motion more felt than heard. Above all, she longed to hug herself for warmth, but such a stance, she'd been forewarned, did not befit a penitent. The point was to be cold; to yearn for dawn before thawing in the Mother Sun's – again, both literal and metaphoric – embrace. Her muscles were already painfully stiff, one calf twitching with imminent cramp: by sunrise, she'd be locked in shape like one of the salted Kamnei breads that came in artful knots. You could buy them at some bakeries in Karavos, though Yena had little taste for them; she didn't like how the outer texture clashed with the inner. Sashi loved them, though, when she could get them.

Zech had, too.

Yena shut her eyes, refusing to cry here, of all places. *This grief will last the rest of my life. No need to spend it all upfront, like a girl with her first blood's coin at a market-stall.*

Something scraped on the nearby stone, a drawn-out, grating sound. The hairs on Yena's nape stood up. Turning her head was unlikely to violate the terms of her penitence, and yet this felt enough like a test that she stilled even further, willing herself to breathe calmly.

"So this is a granddaughter of Yasha a Yasara," said a voice like cracking slate. "Am I to be impressed?"

It took Yena a moment to realise the question was not rhetorical. "I don't know," she said, head bowed, eyes trained on the ghostly grass. "Do you care to be impressed?"

A bark of laughter. "As the Ryvke says, 'those who care for little may be persuaded to much'."

"And you care for much?"

"I didn't say that."

Yena swallowed. If Yasha had taught her anything, it was subtlety, but it was hard to feel subtle with all your skin bare and an unknown woman staring at you. "To whom do I have the honour of speaking?"

"Kiri a Tavi. I am, as the parlance has it, a blunted blade. Tcha!" She made a disgusted sound, by which Yena gathered that Kiri now stood directly opposite her, perhaps on the edge of the flat stone path that ringed her bit of grass. It took all her willpower not to look up: even if she hadn't recognised the name – it was Kiri a Tavi who'd spoken for Zech at the

Council of Queens, a decisive voice to sway the tide – a former yshra, one of the feared Ashasa's Knives, was always to be respected. Even Yena, whose faith in Veksh was a hand-me-down thing, knew that much. "You do not, I think, have much of Yasha's look to you."

"Less than my mother does, certainly," said Yena.

"Your mother." Kiri's voice was bitter. "Yasha should never have been pushed to choose between Trishka's life and the will of the Knives. I was younger then, but not young enough to claim the excuse of folly. If I'd only seen...!" She clicked her teeth in self-reprimand. After a moment, she said, in more level tones, "Your sire was Kenan, I take it?"

"Kamnei," said Yena, startled into honesty. "A trader."

"Kamnei!" she cackled. "I stand corrected! That nation has borne one good thing besides its silks, at least. Or possibly more than one. Do you have any sisters?"

Yena's mouth was dry. "One living," she said, and raised her head to look at Kiri, taking in the bone-white hair, the sharp, lined face. "One newly dead, whose kinship I would claim in law."

Kiri a Tavi smiled like a skull. "I rather thought you might."

Naruet liked Ktho's desk. It had good, clean lines and was carved from rhyawood, which always felt to him like an Inside wood, not like whitegum at all, which was cheap and pale and had as such been grossly overrepresented among the furnishings in his novitiate quarters. But then, it was Ktho's desk, used for Ktho's official business, and was therefore like an extension of her body, which meant, firstly, that looking at the desk was almost like looking at Ktho herself, only easier, because the desk didn't move about so much; and secondly, that perhaps Naruet was predisposed to consider rhyawood an Inside wood because of this desk in particular, and not because it had some innate, amenable property. He frowned at that, trying to recall if he'd ever encountered rhyawood before Ktho: certainly, she'd told him what it was called, but otherwise–

"Naruet? Are you listening?"

"My ears were," said Naruet, shifting uncomfortably. It was hard to divide his attention, but harder still to neglect a line of thought before its conclusion. "My head needs a moment."

Ktho didn't sigh at him for this, like so many others did. Instead, she stayed silent, which meant he had permission to continue.

If Naruet were to list the reasons why Ktho was Inside, her not-sighing and her quiet would have ranked very highly. But no, no – he was getting distracted again. Lists were for later. *But if lists are for later, then desks can be, too.* It was a snap-thought, one whose sudden rightness tingled from head to toe. His body sang with the *yes* of it. Just like that, the rhyawood-thought folded up and tucked itself away in his chest like a paper flower. He gave a sharp nod, satisfied, and said, "The moment is done."

"Thank you," said Ktho. "Now: please tell me the last thing your head heard me say."

Naruet thought for a moment. "You said, *I have always done my best for you, but this is beyond my control. There are no alternatives left unless you run – and you are* not *to run, Naruet, because if you were found, I would still be forced to kill you, and that would kill the heart of me.*" He paused, considering the meaning of the words beyond their cadence. "And then my head stopped listening, because it was too hard to hear, but I'm listening again now."

"I understand," said Ktho, and Naruet didn't flinch even a little, because from Ktho it wasn't a lie. She took a breath, then said, in a tone that sawed and polished, "What I do *not* understand, Naruet, is why you continued your research at all, when I asked you so many times to stop – after all our conversations!"

Oh! Now, *that* was an easy question, enough so that Naruet lifted his gaze from the desk and looked at Ktho, who wasn't moving so much now, to answer it. He couldn't keep the joy from his voice, his smile broad enough to hurt.

"Because it was Vex Leoden who asked me to work – Vex Leoden himself! And you told me, Ktho, that the monarch comes before the temples, I *did* listen and remember, and you told me that if anyone knew you'd indulged me again, you'd get in trouble, and I didn't *want* you to get in trouble, and you said I should try to be unobtrusive, to do what was bid of me, and Vex Leoden bid me do my work, and how much more obtrusive would it have been to deny him? How could I have asked your advice without letting you know that I'd been called to my studies?"

Ktho looked first startled, then chagrined. "Yes," she murmured, tone unfathomable. "I did say that, didn't I. But, Naruet–" and here her voice turned pleading, "–I need you to understand, Vex Leoden used your research to do terrible things. He captured people, worldwalkers and innocents, with the portal you helped him open, and he *hurt* them, Naruet. He stole their secret memories with the ahunemet. He kept them chained in the dark."

Naruet froze, his throat gone suddenly dry. He looked at Ktho, really *looked* at her, and though he understood what she'd said, it didn't accord with what he knew of Vex Leoden.

"No," he said, firmly. "You're wrong. It didn't happen like that."

"How did it happen, Naruet?"

"I don't *know*," said Naruet, frustrated. "I *thought* I knew, because I was there, but I don't have all the right pieces. Vex Leoden was Inside, I was *right* to have him Inside – he was kind to me, and interested. But the people in the pit–"

"You *saw* them?" Ktho broke in, clearly horrified. "And did *nothing*?"

"He told me they were criminals!" Naruet said, voice rising

in distress. "He told me I'd be safe, that I needn't fear, that I had only to look away–"

"Oh, Naruet."

This time, Naruet looked away in shame, hot tears pricking his eyes. He tried to steady his breathing, shutting his eyes to help keep calm, and flicked his fingers in a slowdown rhythm, two-three-four against his thigh, rocking slightly, until his lungs felt full again.

"Regardless," Ktho said, some moments – or perhaps some minutes – later; she'd waited his panic out, as she always did. "Regardless, there is nothing else I can do. Within the next three days, you'll enter the custody of the Cuivexa Iviyat and the lady Rixevet ore Rixevet ki Tahun, in exchange for my provision of the precedent that lets them take the throne. They will, in all probability, request your assistance with the anchored portal–" Naruet jerked his head up at that, hardly daring to hope, "–and on this occasion, Naruet, I give you full sanction to help them, and to pursue your research inasmuch as it helps you to help them, until or unless they ask that you stop, or they send you back to me. But please, please – I beg that you be careful; that you try to recall my caution, even if you cannot embrace it fully, and that you keep to the temple until then. Will you do that for me, Naruet?"

Alight with the possibilities, Naruet beamed. "I will, Ktho. I promise."

"You swear to me?"

"I swear." And then, as though he were a novice still, "I will not risk the *metmirai*. I'll be a good student, a good son of Ke."

Ktho's face crumpled, a mix of relief and sadness. Stepping out from behind her desk, she held out her hands, silently asking permission to touch, which Naruet inclined his head to grant.

Palms lightly cupping his cheeks, Ktho dropped a kiss on his forehead. "My Naruet," she murmured. "You were born to go deeper in; perhaps, in this, your heart has always seen further than mine, and I am too slow to see it. I wish you Ke's guidance. Please, be safe."

"I will try, Ktho," said Naruet, awkwardly, staring at his feet.

Ktho sighed and stepped back, releasing him. "Go and pack your things now, in case you're wanted sooner rather than later. I'll come for you when it's time; until then, keep your head down."

"Yes, Most Honoured," Naruet said, his rare use of Ktho's proper title earning him an equally rare smile.

"Good lad," said Ktho, and then Naruet was turning away, departing for his quarters with a head full of thoughts and a heart full of plans. Of its own accord, his hand went to the spiral key he wore on a chain around his neck, hidden beneath his robes. It brushed against his binder, a tangible reminder of a promise sworn to a man he trusted. He didn't for a moment believe Leoden was guilty of harming innocents – harming *worldwalkers*, of all people – but he also knew that Ktho wouldn't lie to him about something so important. It unsettled him deeply to have two such trusted Insiders in conflict with one another, but the obvious contradiction also meant there was an equally obvious solution.

Neither Ktho nor Leoden would lie to him on purpose, which meant that, if they each believed themselves to be speaking the truth, then someone else – someone Outside – had lied to one or both of them.

And Naruet meant to find out who.

4
Unrest

"You're sure?" Gwen asked wearily, looking to the priest and priestess for confirmation.

Halunet, robed in the blue of Nihun's Kin, gave a short, decisive nod; Aydi, in Teket's purple, copied him a heartbeat later. Aloud, she said, "As sure as we can be. Her memories were rifled badly enough to scramble her sense of self, even her knowledge of language, but once she wakes–" she gestured to a nearby bed, where Sene a Sati lay sleeping, "– she ought to start remembering."

"I've restored her as best I can," said Halunet, "but there may still be gaps in her recollection, particularly relating to what was done to her." His lip curled with rage. "It's hard to tell, but it looks as though they first attempted to wipe their interrogations from her memory, and then, when the repeated trauma triggered its own, more visceral flashbacks, they attempted to wipe those, too. Such an abuse of the ahunemet – whoever was responsible for it must be made to answer to the temples!"

"I concur," said Aydi, with uncharacteristic venom. "Leoden's recruitment of kemeta was one thing, but *this*? I can scarcely conceive of it."

Gwen felt like she'd run a marathon. Aydi and Halunet had been working for hours, the former using the sevikmet to keep Sene in a healing sleep, the latter using the ahunemet to repair the damage Leoden had done. "My sincerest thanks to you both. How long will she rest, do you think?"

Halunet and Aydi exchanged a professional glance, as though conferring silently. Again, it was Aydi who answered first. "The longer she sleeps, the more she's likely to remember. But in such cases, consciousness is also important to help reorder the mind – too long in dreams, and she may yet substitute false thoughts for true. I would say, try to ensure she sleeps for at least a full day, but no longer than two, and if she can't be woken after that time, or exhibits any confusion, you should send for me immediately."

"It may also be worthwhile to send for an *ilumet*-user," Halunet added thoughtfully. "Not to impugn honoured Aydi's work, of course – her deftness is exemplary–" Aydi inclined her head in acknowledgement of the praise, "–but to ward Sene from entry to the dreamscape. Ordinarily, it's not something I'd advise–"

"–but this is not an ordinary situation," Gwen finished for him.

Halunet's handsome face was grim. "Just so."

Thanking the pair of them again, Gwen saw them as far as the outer door then swayed to a standstill, one hand clutching the wall. She was still in shock at having found the ambassador in such an appalling condition: from what Halunet said, she'd been subject to more and worse abuses of the ahunemet than any of the worldwalkers. Unless it was a plain act of cruelty, Gwen couldn't fathom the logic behind it: why, when Kadeja was a ready source of information about Veksh, would Leoden bother interrogating Sene? Why, when his interest was plainly in other worlds, would he care about someone from his own? It made no sense, and though it pained Gwen to admit it, if one of the guards had claimed to have identified Sene a Sati among the worldwalkers, her first instinct would've been to think them mistaken.

But Pix and Amenet, unlike Gwen, had both met the ambassador during Vex Ralan's reign; their identification of her was absolute. They didn't know how long she'd been imprisoned; only that enough time had passed for her hair to grow out. That Sene exhibited no awareness of this heretical lapse, even when they'd managed to rouse her to proper consciousness, was chilling. Gwen and Pix had been horrified, while Viya, somewhat more practically, had sent Rikan to fetch a Vekshi shaving knife from Sene's former quarters, adding that, if he couldn't find such a thing, he was to take one of Kadeja's old knives instead.

In his absence, the three of them had tried to question Sene about her experiences, but it was like talking to someone in their dotage: her sentences tailed off in the middle; she forgot questions only moments after being asked them; and when she did speak, it was in a fragmented mixture of Kenan and Vekshi, as though she'd forgotten the two were separate languages. After a fruitless and frustrating half-hour, they finally gave up; Amenet, Pix and Viya all had other business to attend to, though Pix was the one who'd taken time to summon back Halunet and Aydi.

In their absence, Gwen had sat briefly by Sene's bedside, trying to marshal her thoughts. She'd considered trying to shave the ambassador's head, but decided against it: not only had she no skill at the task, but thought that Sene, once recovered, might be ashamed to have needed help, preferring to do it herself. Instead, Gwen had badgered Rikan into finding a shaving mirror to go with the washbasin already in Sene's room, and then, once the guard was safely returned to his post, had hurried off to her meeting with Most Honoured Ktho.

I should've asked Aydi to put me in a healing sleep, too, Gwen thought, forcing her weary limbs to make the climb to her own apartments. The day had been inordinately long by any standard, and still she had the unpleasant sensation of time running out, though why, she couldn't have said. Leoden's absence gnawed at her; she half expected him to reappear at any moment, smiling as he ripped her world away. They'd posted guards at the anchored portal in case he had the power to open it from wherever he was now, but Trishka said she thought it was highly unlikely, a comfort to which Gwen clung like a child with a blanket.

By the time she reached her chambers, Gwen was exhausted. She thought of her marriage-mates Jhesa and Naku, safe at their home in Candle Bay; of Louis, enjoying an evening with Rikan; of Jeiden and Sashi, returned to Trishka's care. She thought of Saffron, worlds away but free from immediate danger; and of Yena and Yasha, penned with their allied Shavaktiin behind the high, strong walls of Yevekshasa.

Collapsing into bed, Gwen kicked off her boots and lapsed into a black sleep.

My worlds are safe from you, Leoden. You cannot steal them now.

Saffron couldn't sleep.

She'd been in bed for hours, looking at the constellations of glow-in-the-dark stars she'd stuck to the bedroom ceiling almost a decade ago. She hadn't gone down for dinner, her appetite non-existent after the confrontation with her parents and Ms Mays, and for once since her return they hadn't tried to coax her out. Even Ruby had kept her distance, though whether that was on her own initiative or at some parental behest, Saffron didn't know. It left her feeling anxious: thanks to her early collection from school and the subsequent bungled conference, she hadn't had a chance to fill her sister in on what had happened, though the Lawson High gossip mill had doubtless produced a few choice versions in her absence.

She rolled onto her side, her awful lethargy somehow failing to translate to actual sleep. In Kena, she'd had no insomnia, kept so busy during the days, both physically and otherwise, that she'd slept through sheer bodily exhaustion. Now, though, it was creeping back, and as she couldn't reach the dreamscape while awake, her inability to sleep at will left her on edge, cut off from her sole point of contact with the other world. Logically, she knew that the harder she tried to fall asleep, the more awake she'd feel, and yet she couldn't quite talk her panicky lizard-brain into relaxation.

The power light on her unused laptop blinked at her in blue reproach. She didn't need to go online to know that Lyssi had likely messaged her; that multiple conversational threads in varying digital forums would be discussing her actions and absence. There was probably even a newspaper article or two; there hadn't been a massive media blowup over her disappearance, thank god, but she knew at least one publication had asked her parents about a potential interview. A part of her was morbidly curious to see what was being printed, but a shred of self-preservation woke to speak that ancient digital adage: *don't read the comments.*

Instead, she turned on her reading light, reached into the drawer of her bedside table, and pulled out a spiral notebook. It was an expensive one, given as a birthday present two years ago, the pages so pristine and the hardbacked cover so gorgeous – a kind of fractal paisley pattern in lavish oil-colours, rich and strange – that she'd never dared to write in it before this week. Opening to her latest page, she propped herself on an elbow, took up her pen, and thought.

Back in Veksh, when Saffron and Gwen had worked out the lies she'd need to tell on returning, they'd discussed Gwen's use of the dreamscape as a means of keeping in touch with those in Kena. With decades of practice under her belt, it was comparatively easy for Gwen to reach Trishka, and vice versa; for Saffron, however, who barely knew what she was doing, the process was much harder. In Kena, she knew, she'd walked in the dreamscape with Luy and Zech – had planned with them, and learned with them, and any number of other things – but on waking, the knowledge had vanished like mist, returning only as unpredictable pangs of intuition or deja vu.

Like Gwen, but unlike Luy, Saffron had no inborn facility for dream-magic – oneiromancy in English, *ilumet* in Kenan – and so had to work at it. Based on what Gwen had said about developing her own talents, Saffron had been keeping a sort of dream-journal, writing down whatever she could remember at the moment of waking, patches and fragments whose vagueness was maddening, but whose consistency nonetheless suggested she'd been successfully meeting with Luy. She'd added some other entries, too, during her week at home, partly as an emotional valve for everything she couldn't say to her family, but mostly for the simple catharsis of having it written down. For security, she wrote in Kenan, though as the zuymet hadn't extended to teaching her either of the two forms of Kenan lettering, she made do with the English alphabet.

I miss the food. Which is strange, because it was never the kind of thing you're meant to drool for, pastries and cakes and elaborate dishes made in kitchens. It was just... good. There was fresh bread at the compound in Karavos, hot and yeasty, and on the road we ate dried fruit crystallised with honey and fresh greens and tubers that Jeiden would find for us, and fresh game, too, birds whose names I didn't know and running animals like hares, if hares had tiny fangs and spotted red-and-black fur. Everyone carried spices in their saddlebags, and everything was seasoned just so, with hard, blueish salt that came from a place called the Sea of Sighs, and something I think was kavish, *little brown nuts that baked in the coals with whatever you cooked and made it taste like peppersmoke and cumin.*

I don't mean to say that food here is bad, or that I'm ungrateful for it. Maybe I'm just being fussy. I never had a

problem before, even if I did always think that Lyssi's dad
was a better cook than mine. But when you see it all made
from scratch like that – when you see the pelt of the not-hare
set aside to line gloves and hoods, and the leather claimed
for tanning work, and the offal buried to help regrow the
edible plants you used on the traveller's trails, and the small
bones taken for whittling into needles and pins, and the meat
slowcooked in beer that somebody's aunt fermented with
grain she grew at home – the whole thing simmering all day
in a yaravadi, *a fireflask, which is a cookpot magicked to*
hold a temperature that travellers can hang from a pack or
a saddlehorn, so as never to be without a good hot meal at
the end of the day – when nothing is wasted, and you sit by
a campfire under the stars and eat it all with flatbread made
fresh in an earth oven, and nobody says you're too young to
have a sip of the spirits the adults pass around afterwards –
just a mouthful of something clear and sharp and strong, like
sticking my head in a waterfall, and Yena laughing because
I coughed, and Zech taking two big sips before Matu could
grab it away from her, and Jeiden scolding her like he hadn't
wanted to do exactly the same, and Gwen saying how none
of us had any taste, that nobody drank jixa *if they could help*
it –

I miss the food.

Hands trembling only slightly, Saffron returned both
notebook and pen to the bedside drawer, turned out her
light, and wiped the tears from her eyes. She missed Yena and
Zech and Jeiden with an ache so strong it doubled her over
like a stomach cramp. Before the road to Yevekshasa, she'd
barely ever shared a bed, and then only in childhood, during
sleepovers with friends or at family gatherings, when she'd
bunked with Ruby or one of their cousins. But curling up
with three other bodies had helped to keep her nightmares
at bay; had soothed her, despite the invariable kicking and

snoring and the occasional misplaced elbow. All alone in her narrow bed, she felt touch-hungry, longing for the comfort of contact that came without expectations.

Across the room, her door nudged open.

"Saff? Are you awake?"

It was Ruby, barefoot and rumpled, dressed in a faded Pokemon nightie that had once been Saffron's.

"Yes," Saffron whispered, gulping relief as Ruby came in and shut the door behind her.

For a moment her sister stood at the bedside, hovering in belated indecision. And then, in a rush, "Can I get in with you?"

Her timing was so perfect, Saffron almost laughed. "Sure," she said, and pulled back the covers, shifting over as Ruby slipped in. It was briefly awkward, until Saffron flinched away from Ruby's cold feet. "Your toes are *freezing!*"

"They'd warm up if you'd quit *hogging*," Ruby grumbled, grabbing for a larger share of the blanket.

"It's my bed!"

"And I'm your guest, which means *I* get the warm spot."

"You're a terrible guest," said Saffron.

"Am not," said Ruby.

Their eyes met in the low light of Saffron's digital clock. They grinned at each other, smothering laughter into the poorly-shared pillow.

"Sorry," said Ruby, after a moment. She sounded very small. "I just... I have trouble sleeping, sometimes. Wondering if you'll still be here when I wake up."

Saffron's throat tightened. "Ru–"

"I mean, I know you're not really going to vanish again or anything, that's just stupid. My brain's being stupid. Right?"

Saffron opened her mouth, but no sound came out. The lie was gross, impossible, and she'd already told too many. She swallowed it like Persephone had her pomegranate seeds, and braced for the consequences.

Beside her, Ruby stiffened. "Saffron? It's stupid, right?"

"I don't know." The words came out a whisper. She squeezed her eyes shut and gripped the hem of her pyjama top. "God, I don't know, I don't know anything anymore – I thought I could do this, Ru, but I can't, and it's so fucking *hard*, and everyone thinks I should've apologized to Mr Lane about Jared – you heard about that, right?"

"I did," said Ruby, suddenly fierce, "and everyone is an idiot. I told mum at dinner, I *told* her, if some dumb boy had done that to me and the teacher asked *me* to say sorry, *I* would've said no, too!"

"You did?"

"I did!"

"And what did mum say?"

"She said I was being silly, and that I shouldn't encourage you, because what happened today was an *exception to the rule*." Ruby made a frustrated noise. "But it's *not* an exception! It's a thing that *actually happened*, because Jared Blake is an asshat."

Overwhelmed, Saffron choked out, "Thank you."

Ruby just shrugged, like it was no big deal. And then she looked up, her expression once more vulnerable, and said, "So you don't have to run away, OK? I've got your back. You'll be all right."

"What if I'm not, though?" Saffron stared beseechingly at Ruby, willing her to understand. "I just… The things that happened to me – being gone like that – it's not, I mean… I'm not the same – it's not what everyone thinks."

"What is it, then?"

Do you believe in magic? A mawkish, ridiculous question, like something you'd hear in a B-grade fantasy movie. Slowly, carefully, not quite sure what she was doing but desperate to try, Saffron said, "Ru, have you ever had a secret? A real secret, I mean, not just something no one else knows. An important thing you have to keep safe, because it's too big or too real somehow, or doesn't wholly belong to you. Anything like that?"

Beside her, Ruby went very still. "Yes," she rasped, after a moment. "Just one."

"OK. You don't have to tell me what it is – that's not why I asked – but where I was, the reason I was gone: it's that kind of secret. And I'd tell you if I could, I really, *really* would–" she loaded sincerity into the words, praying Ruby believed her, "–but I can't, because I can't tell *anyone*, and it's not the thing that everyone thinks, that I was... that I was raped, or something like that–" Ruby let out a tightly-held breath, "–but it's still a secret, all right? And part of it means that maybe – probably–" *oh, god, please let this be the right thing to say, please please please please,* "–I'm going to go away again. Go somewhere else."

For a long moment, Ruby was silent. Then:

"I should tell mum and dad," she whispered fiercely. Saffron's heart forgot to beat. "I know I should – they'd want to know, they'd want to stop you–"

"*No,*" Saffron choked out, "Ruby, no, *please*–"

"–but I *won't,*" said Ruby, just loudly enough to cut her off, "if you promise me that, when you go – if you go – you'll let me know that you're OK, and that I can see you again." She reached over under the blankets, gripping Saffron's tattooed wrist. "You *promise* me, Saff!"

"I promise," Saffron croaked. "I swear to god – I swear to everything that matters – I swear by my name, Ru – I'll tell you if I'm going to go, and I swear that it won't be forever."

"Good," Ruby breathed, and after a final, rock-hard squeeze, she pulled her hand away. "Good."

The silence between them was blanket-thick, a thing of trust and tension. Saffron thought up a dozen different ways she might say *thank you,* and discarded them all as inadequate.

"Ruby?"

"Yeah?"

"How come you're OK with this?"

Ruby made a furious noise. "*OK?*" she hissed. "I am *so not*

OK, OK? I am the literal *farthest thing in the universe* from *OK*!"

"Then why–?"

"Because," she bit out, "I don't exactly have a choice! And *you*, at least – you told me to my face."

"What do you mean, at least *I* did?" Dread unfurled in her stomach. "Why don't you have a choice?"

"I couldn't sleep." Ruby's voice was barely a whisper. "My room is next to mum and dad's, and I usually sleep so quick and deep, they never keep their voices down, but I couldn't sleep and I heard them talk – I heard them through the walls." She gulped, eyes wide and scared in the darkness. "Saff, they want to send you away."

"They *what*?"

"To make you better again, they want to send you to some, some mental health place, for *recovery*, because dad said if you didn't want to stay at home and didn't want to go to school, then maybe they should try for an alternative, and mum said she just wanted you back, and *he* said maybe it was for the best, and *she* said wasn't it all too soon, and *he* said going back to school was too soon, too, and at least this time they'd know where you were, and *she* said *I suppose it's better too soon than too late*, and *he* said *exactly*, and *she* said *OK, but what will we tell Ruby*, and *he* said–" she hiccupped slightly, voice strained with pain and outrage, "*–easier to explain it to her once it's done, you know she's oversensitive.*"

The bottom dropped out of Saffron's world. She was caught in the netherspace between portals, here and not-here, a creature of atoms. Blindly, she reached for Ruby, and Ruby reached for her, the two of them hugging hard in the darkness.

"I don't want you to go, Saff." Ruby's voice was muffled against her collarbone. "But I'd rather you go because you want to, and not because you're being tricked."

Saffron sobbed, just once. "Love you, Ru."

"Love you, too, asshat."

They lay like that for a long, long time before either one fell asleep.

Luy scryed the dreamscape, bare feet firmly planted in the metaphorical earth of his crossroads, and waited for Saffron Coulter, just as he'd waited every night of the six days since her departure from Kena. He let his thoughts drift, clearing his mind of guilt and grief and every other unhelpful thing that currently plagued him in waking. In their place rose a Shavaktiin psalm, as soothing as it was simple:

Maker, moment, memory.
The Great Story moves, as hearts are moved.
Each moment, we make and remember.

"Luy?"

He looked up, blinking as his reverie broke. "Hello, Safi," he replied. As at their other recent meetings, she was barely present, her dreambody thin to the point of translucence, as though she were already on the brink of blinking out. "What do you have to tell me?"

"My parents want to send me away," she blurted, strongly enough that the crossroads beneath them shifted and blurred in response to her emotions. "I've been in trouble at school and my parents are trying, but my sister heard them talking and they want to send me *away*…" She rattled off the details, voice going choppy with anger. Luy felt a pang on her behalf, but didn't interrupt, nor did he remark upon the fact that her dreamself was dressed in a telling mix of Earthly and Vekshi styles, a tartan school skirt paired with a square-necked *dou*.

"I need a way out," she said, voice desperate. And then, with a gulp of belated need, "Is Yena well?"

Luy hesitated. He'd spoken with Kikra, the Shavaktiin dreamseer still in Yevekshasa, earlier that day, and knew of Yena's gambit to sit penance in a bid for Vekshi rights. Safi had a right to know, but he also saw no point in worrying her when she was clearly stressed already – not when she might wake and vanish before he could tell her everything, and certainly not when he didn't yet know the outcome.

"Yena is fine," said Luy, which wasn't technically a lie. Even so, he found himself telling her about Sene a Sati, partly to make up for the omission about Yena, but also because it was telling that her dreamself was partially clad in Vekshi clothes.

Saffron absorbed this information silently, as though mulling the implications, but even as she opened her mouth to speak her dreamself flickered in warning. "I'll speak to Gwen," Luy said quickly. "I'll tell her about your parents, about the deadline, and see what can be done. Come here as often as you can – I'll always try to be here, but write a message in the crossroads dirt if I'm not, and I should still find it."

"OK," gulped Saffron, flickering again. "OK, I'll –"

And then she was gone.

Luy sighed, suppressing the urge to chase her. Building a patch of consciously-maintained dreamscape took discipline, skill and time, all of which they manifestly lacked. Had they been more physically proximate, he might have entered Saffron's dreamscape and helped her to shape it, taught her how to meet him there instead of here, but at their current distance – both physical and magical – he would have access only to her unconscious self, untrained in the dreaming lucidity which his own patch of dreamscape facilitated, but which hers did not.

"Is that girl your pupil?"

The strange voice was so unexpected, Luy almost startled awake. Instead, he whirled to confront the speaker, a short, coltish – man? Boy? Youth, he decided after a moment: based on his current appearance, Luy judged him to be no older than twenty-two and no younger than eighteen, his foxish face completely bare of stubble. He'd spoken in Kenan, which accorded with his looks, a familiar cast to cheek and jaw and nose. His brown skin was darkened from the sun, his lank black hair worn unbound past his shoulders. His eyes were brown and clever-looking, but he didn't quite meet Luy's gaze, preferring to stare just past him. Most likely, he was an unconscious dreamer – someone whose sleeping mind had drawn him to an occupied patch of the dreamscape.

"Not exactly," Luy said. "Why do you ask?"

The youth blinked. "I'm not sure," he said. "But she seems important." He stared around the crossroads, long fingers flicking in quiet rhythm. "You've met her in waking?"

"I have." Luy's gaze sharpened; unconscious dreamer or not, the question was a probing one. "Why do you want to know?"

"I'm told it's polite to enquire of such things." Another blink, followed by near fifteen seconds of silence. At no particular signal, the dreamscape shifted around them, responding to the stranger's presence. Clumps of crystalline mushrooms shot up through the soil of the crossroads, puffing into swollen domes that exploded in bursts of dissolving shards, like quixotic fairy bombs. Faint music played at the edge of hearing, both like and unlike a mix of harps and water. Drifts of colour moved through the air, more reminiscent of gauzy, floating scarves than clouds. It was one of the most surreal and lovely alterations Luy had ever witnessed, making him feel more accepting of the stranger than he might otherwise have been, had his dreamscape proved more hostile. It wasn't precisely true that an ugly dreamscape meant a dangerous person, aesthetic taste and the dreamer's mood being both too fickle to count upon, and yet Luy couldn't help responding to what he liked. And so he waited patiently, more curious than wary, for the youth to speak again.

Which, eventually, he did. "I should ask your name. That, too, is polite, though I'll understand if you'd rather not tell me."

"I have no fear of names," said Luy, intrigued despite himself. "I'm Luy."

"You're Leoden's Shavaktiin," said the youth, surprised. His gaze snapped briefly into focus, an assessment all the more searing for being momentary. "I've seen you in waking. Veiled, but seen. I know your voice."

A shiver of premonition ran through Luy – an all-over warning, like a touch of electrical current. "Who are you? What do you want?"

"I'm Naruet. I'm a scholar of sorts, and as for your pupil, I wish her no harm. I only want to know how she fits in the pattern."

"Which pattern?"

"This. All of it." He waved a long-fingered hand at the air around them, as if indicating the entirety of the dreamscape. "The worlds, the puzzle they represent – the way they fit together. It's all part of my work."

"Your work? What work? Who do you serve?"

Naruet grinned, broad and genuine. "Kena," he said. "I serve Kena the way you serve stories. Or at least, I think I do." He frowned, the transition sudden as a shift in the wind. "Even with people Inside–" he gave the word a peculiar emphasis; Luy wondered why, "–it's always so hard to tell, and you're not Inside at all. You're a stranger to me, though I've seen you before. Do you realise you're missing pieces?"

"Inside?" Luy asked. And then, as a second question superseded the first, "I'm missing pieces? What does that mean?"

Naruet's head jerked up sharply, the crystalline mushrooms vanishing in a silent, unanimous puff. "It means I should go," he said, and promptly vanished, leaving Luy alone again and very much confused.

Who was Naruet, and why had he appeared at Luy's crossroads? He'd sounded like a Shavaktiin, which might account for why he claimed to know Luy in waking, and yet he'd delivered no threats or warnings about Luy's divergent interpretation of the Great Story, nor had he appeared to arrive by direct intention. He'd come across as equal parts curious and detached, and except for the odd remark about Luy missing pieces, he'd said nothing sinister at all. His name was vaguely familiar, but then it was hardly an uncommon one. But if he'd seen Luy around the palace–

Luy huffed, frustrated. It was exactly the sort of ambiguous encounter he ought to have reported to the Shavaktiin enclave, had he still been in contact with them; but as he wasn't, the question of what to do next was his alone. After all, Safi herself had first appeared to him as such a stray dreamer, too. The youth might not have meant to look for Luy, but that didn't mean he wasn't important, and as he'd claimed to have seen Luy in waking the least he could do was ask if anyone in the palace knew the name Naruet.

Thus decided, he let himself slip out of the dreamscape and, after a somewhat groggy transition, back into waking, his physical body warm and pleasantly sluggish.

Beside him, Rikan shifted in sleep, his breath tickling Luy's shoulder, arm twitching where it was flung across his stomach. Luy allowed himself a private smile, savouring the rightness of the arrangement. Rikan was an unexpected development, but a wholly pleasant one; he only wished Halaya was there to share in it with him.

Breathing deeply, Luy closed his eyes and let himself drift once more into sleep.

This time, he didn't dream.

5
Hide Me, Seek Me

Saffron woke with a yawning judder, one hand already reaching for the book and pen in her bedside drawer.

"Mmmph," mumbled Ruby, sleepily cross at being jostled. Saffron ignored her, clinging to the tattered scraps of her dream. Turning to a new page, she jotted down the date and wrote, in hasty shorthand:

Dreamed Luy crossroads meeting, asked advice re: parents sending me away. Luy to ask Gwen, report back. Something about an ambassador (?), Yena well last checked. Don't know if I mentioned Ruby or that I told her I'd leave again. Try again tomorrow.

She read it over carefully, trying to dredge up any further details, but none were forthcoming. As reassurances went, it was painfully inadequate, but it was all she had. Sighing, she shut the book and returned it to the drawer.

"You need a better hiding place for that."

Saffron froze. After a tense, silent moment, she rolled to her side and looked at Ruby. Her little sister squinted blearily, her expression somewhat reminiscent of Beastie the kitten's when his bowl of dry food was empty.

"Who says it needs hiding at all?" said Saffron – weakly,

given last night's conversation.

Ruby managed the impressive feat of rolling her eyes without actually opening them, then shoved her face back in the pillow.

"Whatever," she mumbled, and went back to sleep with enviable ease.

Sighing, Saffron swung herself out of bed and headed towards the bathroom. En route, she almost tripped over Beastie, who usually slept on Ruby's bed and was, Saffron presumed, disquieted by the change in his sleeping arrangements. He twined around her ankles in a friendly, menacing sort of way, swatted his needle-claws at her foot, then trotted off towards Saffron's bedroom, presumably in search of his slumbering mistress.

Smiling slightly, Saffron carried on.

Strange, how easily her morning routine came back to her, for all that performing it still felt surreal. After weeks without access to indoor plumbing, a hot shower felt like a miracle. But when she returned to her room to dress – her bed now devoid of sister, but with a black-and-white kitten curled in conspicuous insolence on the pillow – her uniform felt stiff and strange, for all it was still too loose.

Yesterday, after being sent to the office before the end of her first class and home before recess, she'd barely had a chance to reacclimatize to Lawson High. In the hours of lassitude following the argument with her parents and Ms Mays, she'd wondered how today would go: if she and Lyssi would pick up where they'd left off; if Jared would rear his head again; if she'd make it through a whole school day, or even just an hour, without incident. But now, knowing what her parents had planned for her – knowing that, regardless of returning to Kena, her old routines were gone beyond recall – she struggled to justify even leaving the house.

Where do I live, when all this is done?

The question brought her up short. Instead of stepping

through her bedroom door, as she'd been about to, she sat down against it, back to the wood. Her only model for what a worldwalker looked like was Gwen, and because Gwen clearly travelled between Earth and Kena, Saffron had let herself believe that she could do that, too. But Gwen had had over thirty years to establish her routines, to learn the perilous balance that meant reassuring her family in one world while adventuring in another. More importantly, she'd been nineteen when she started, which was almost three years older than Saffron was now – little enough difference in the long term, but she hadn't been a minor at the outset, granting a vital legal autonomy to her absences.

I could choose to stay on Earth. Accept it was a one-time thing, get back to my life. It was a dutiful thought, the implications as heavy within her as a lump of cold grease. She had a brief flash of envy for worldwalkers who'd found their portals in earlier decades and centuries – and surely they must have done; neither she nor Gwen could possibly be the first – before the current level of digital and bureaucratic scrutiny made vanishing for months or years a much trickier thing to navigate. Unless she finished Year Twelve and sat the HSC next year, she wouldn't have any high school qualifications – and how could she get through school, let alone university, if she was spending regular time in Kena? Gwen had managed to qualify as a teacher, but she'd still gone back, and in between she'd been old enough to live on her own.

Compared to the multiverse, Earth was like an abusive partner who didn't want her spending time with other friends. She could come and go from Kena without anyone there complaining, and if she ever travelled to other, wider worlds – her heartbeat quickened at the prospect – the same would presumably hold there, too, if only because she'd always be a traveller.

But what did she want to *do* in Kena, exactly? It wasn't as if she had any more career prospects there than here. That

Gwen seemed to make do worldwalking was no guarantee that Saffron either could or would want to copy her indefinitely, but she couldn't imagine walking away from the possibility now just because she might change her mind at some later date, either.

Whichever way she turned, she was off the map. But at least in Kena the people who wanted to help her – and she *did* need help; her nightmares were proof enough of that – at least knew what she'd been through. If her family sent her to some sort of rehab centre, who knew what might happen? Sooner or later, a therapist or social worker was bound to realise that she was lying about her experiences and draw the wrong conclusions as to why, not because they weren't good at their job, but because *accidental worldwalker struggling with bereavement and reverse culture shock* wasn't a diagnosis they'd ever think to consider. The thought of being medicated for something that wasn't an illness – of being forced to ward off ever more probing questions about her wellbeing and experiences, all while being restricted to smaller rooms and tidier routines – was enough to set off a choking panic.

I can't do it. Can't. Won't. She inhaled raggedly, struggling to get her breathing under control. If she only had a more reliable way of contacting Luy–!

"Saffron?" her mother called from the hall. "Are you all right in there, sweetheart? Do you need a hand with anything?"

"No, I'm fine! I'll be right out!"

A slight hesitation. "Well, breakfast is ready. We'll see you downstairs."

"OK!"

The sound of retreating footsteps. The sound of her heart in her ears.

Saffron wiped her sweaty palms on her tartan skirt and came shakily to her feet. She stood for a moment, staring at the brightly-inked tattoo encircling her left wrist. She remembered what Mesthani had told her after the Trial of Queens, the words engraved in her memory: *Your rights in Veksh are now effectively equal to that of a queen. You may call on any trueborn daughter of Veksh for aid, and expect it to be granted.*

Sighing, she dropped her hand and shouldered her bag, heading into the hallway. In the absence of any trueborn daughters, she'd just have to help herself.

"You're kidding," said Yena. She stared flatly at the priestess. "This is a joke, yes?"

The priestess sniffed, as if mortally offended by the suggestion that she'd ever told a joke in her life. She hadn't bothered to tell Yena her name, and Yena hadn't asked. "Does this mean you wish to withdraw from your penitence?"

"Withdraw, no. Survive, yes."

"Your life is Ashasa's, to do with as She pleases. If you would scruple to risk yourself in returning to Her light, you are not worthy of its warmth."

"And you want me to risk myself by *walking through fire*?"

"Yes."

"Right." She wondered, with no small degree of sympathy, if Safi had spent her entire time in Kena and Veksh feeling as angry, scared and baffled as Yena felt now, and how in the worlds she'd coped. "And is this, ah–" she tried for a diplomatic way of phrasing it, "–a common method of penitence?"

"In cases like yours?" The priestess raised an arch brow. "Yes."

Yena tried very hard not to bristle at what, exactly, *cases like yours* implied. She had no proof, of course, but couldn't escape the nagging fear that she was being judged for some aspect of her personhood beyond her control, though whether it was her Kenan upbringing, her skin colour – she'd seen a few darker Vekshi in evidence, but they were a clear minority – or her *alikrevaya* status, she didn't know. Possibly it was all three, though just as possibly, she was being paranoid. Or maybe it was something else altogether, her political affiliation with Zech and Yasha bleeding over into how the more conservative elements in the priesshood viewed her altogether.

This was, she conceded, the most likely option, and yet the nameless priestess looked at her with such visceral distaste it was hard not to wonder if her prejudice, at least, stemmed from some more personal objection. Either way, it didn't solve the problem before her: how could she possibly walk unscathed through fire? *Surely they wouldn't ask if it was impossible, or if I couldn't back out at the last. Mesthani would have warned me if I was in serious danger of being burned to death.*

Wouldn't she?

Out loud, Yena said, "Then I accept. I trust in the Mother Sun's judgement."

The priestess blinked, her sneer sliding into clear surprise. "You do?"

This time, it was Yena's turn to raise an eyebrow. "Is there some reason why I shouldn't?"

Blushing showed so clearly on such pale skin; Yena had always found it an endearing quality. The priestess bowed her head and said, somewhat stiffly, "I will inform the Second Voice of your decision."

Huh. That's interesting. Yena frowned as the priestess retreated, gaze fixed on the stone door to her borrowed cell. After surviving her night in the temple courtyard – and that tense, enlightening conversation with Kiri a Tavi – Yena had been ushered inside by the same, older priestess who'd formerly dunked her in water: a woman whose title was Third Voice, not Second. If oversight of Yena's penance had suddenly jumped a rung in the temple hierarchy, it wasn't an accident: either Mesthani was right, and someone had correctly anticipated her plans from the outset, or else Kiri's visit – or even her endurance of the vigil, if she'd been expected to fail – had caused new eyes to take notice.

At dawn, when the Third Voice had declared her second

penitence complete, more than one other priestess had borne witness. Had Yena been in any position to gauge their reactions to the pronouncement, she might now have a better idea of who her opponents were. But after the long night spent on her knees, she'd been in no position to do anything but let herself be helped to her feet. Aching and stiff with cold, she'd been put in the care of two midlevel priestesses, each one more than strong enough to bear her faltering weight. Grateful for the help, Yena had nonetheless been confused when they'd promised to warm her up with a series of increasingly hot baths, the first tepid and the last near scalding. Sharing an amused look, they'd taken her to a steamy chamber with a series of sunken baths carved into the sloped stone floor. Rather than needing to be filled by hand, as Yena was accustomed to, these had water piped in from somewhere underground, each one kept heated by magic. As promised, several of the baths were already filled, and Yena went happily boneless as she was lifted into the first.

It soon transpired that her aides were well-practiced in reviving the subjects of outdoor penance: though not always conducted naked, they explained, nightlong vigils in the courtyard were a common punishment for temple novitiates, as well as playing a part in the rituals undertaken when priestesses progressed in their devotions.

"It's worst in the rain, of course," one had said, shuddering as if in memory.

"Though at least it doubles as a water-trial," her companion quipped. The two of them had laughed at that, then helped Yena into the next-warmest bath.

Thus restored to some semblance of physical normalcy, Yena was towelled down, provided with a clean nek to wear and a simple meal to eat, and led to the novice's cell she currently occupied. With her belly full and her limbs warm, she'd quickly fallen asleep on the narrow cot, having dozed only fitfully the night before. At best guess, several hours had passed between now and then, and with the nameless priestess gone she was left alone to contemplate the impossible task before her.

Walk through fire. Of course. What else would the Mother Sun ask?

Rubbing her newly stubbled head, Yena considered her conversation with Kiri a Tavi. The old woman reminded her more than a little of Yasha, which ought to have been unnerving, and yet was an odd source of comfort. Yasha, at least, she understood, and after a lifetime of quietly – and, at times, not so quietly – subverting that formidable matriarch's control of her life, it was something of a relief to find the skill had practical utility. Like Yasha, Kiri spoke in bursts of stubborn frankness leavened with subtler cues and barbs as to her actual point; decoding such exchanges was practically Yena's fifth language.

(The third and fourth, after Kenan and Vekshi, were Maluyu, the main language spoken by the Uyun, and Lakik, the dominant tongue of Kamne. At Yasha's urging, Matu had used the zuymet to teach Maluyu to both Yena and Sashi years ago, the better to facilitate their eavesdropping in the Warren. Lakik she had taught herself the hard way, through struggle and repetition, by speaking to the Kamnei merchants who sold the bread her sisters loved. It was the language of her most secret self, imperfect and rarely used, yet treasured all the same: a thing about her that not even Sashi knew. Yena had never articulated aloud her reasons for learning it, but felt it keenly all the same: the curl in her hair that Sashi's lacked; the brown of her hand against Yasha's white; the memory of how she'd risen in her grandmother's esteem, the day she'd first admitted to being a girl. Of such fragments was her stubbornness forged and honed, like an arrowhead knapped from flint.)

Kiri a Tavi had spoken that same, doubled language with the fluency of a native. Without ever speaking these precise words, she had said: *Pass your penitence, and I will support you as Zechalia a Kadeja's sister. Fail your penitence, and you will fall so far beneath my notice as to envy a speck of dust.*

What did not need to be said, but was nonetheless equally clear, was this: *The position of Ashasa's Knives is perilous, but so too are their methods. You would do well to have a blade in hand.*

The novice's cell had a single window, little more than a slit. A rectangular shaft of sun fell through it, one bright corner cutting across the curve of Yena's knee. The light was so thick, so honey-gold, it seemed to stain the very linen of her nek, as though she were being illumed from the outside in. A fanciful thought, yet doubtless in keeping with one who played the penitent of Ashasa.

Lips quirked in a self-deprecating smile, Yena sat and contemplated the problem of walking through fire. The answer, she hoped, would come to her in time.

Naruet lay on the temple roof, arms pillowed beneath his head, a kitten asleep on his stomach. The stone had cooled overnight, leaching the heat from his limbs, and though the sun was on the rise the kitten remained his primary source of warmth. Ignoring the discomfort, he stared up at the dawnstreaked sky and looked for what lay beyond the light: the stars, the moons, the distant veldt of the firmament. There was something soothing about the sky, and after a night spent hunting the dreamscape for clues, it helped him anchor himself to Kena and its reality, the fact of his physical self.

He had a nagging urge to scry the worlds for Luy's mysterious pupil: the brief glimpse he'd caught of her had felt significant, somehow, in a way that talking to Luy had not. Searching for someone he'd never met across the vast web of worlds was always a difficult prospect, but he'd theorised years before that meditating on the idea of a person – and on any real knowledge he had of them – could help guide him to their location. It helped, too, that the ilumet and the jahudemet were ultimately two sides of the same coin: both gifts could allow a practitioner to scry across the infinite, and as you needed to know where to look for the jahudemet to work, the ilumet – or rather, the dreamscape – could be used as a map to its subject.

Not, of course, that Ke's Kin sanctioned such logic. By the rigid nature of the celestial hierarchy, and thus the magical purview of the temples themselves, all disciplines were meant to be kept separate. Ktho, when pressed, would sometimes hint at the existence of reasons for this beyond the arbitrary and historical, but never went into detail about them, leaving Naruet to conclude that they were either part of the deeper mysteries to which he was not privy, or else that she was aware of their flimsiness and didn't want to be questioned. This latter thought was, perhaps, unworthy of him, but Naruet had a curious heart, and was forever frustrated by any and all attempts to check his acquisition of knowledge.

He'd looked for the girl in the dreamscape, too, when his talk with Luy was done. He hadn't found her lucid again, but then, he hadn't expected to. What he had found was a resonance that felt like her, a suggestion of a girl moving between worlds, the barest wisps of crossroads dreams and the scent of burning flowers, all muddled up with grief and guilt and rage and the barest whisper of a name: *Safi*. And there was something else there, too, a hint of something sharp and scaled that burned like a swallowed comet; Naruet had no idea what it was, but he found it fascinating. He clung to those tenuous threads of the dreamscape, memorised their shape, and set the knowledge aside to be used as his starting point next time.

After that, he'd looked for Leoden.

Naruet knew no names for the worlds he scryed, though he'd begun to suspect that the temple might. In lieu of such titles, he thought of Leoden's current location as the Bazaar, a seething mass of strange sights and stranger people that was nonetheless recognisable as a species of market. The Vex moved through it with purpose, the uncommon shortness of his hair still startling to Naruet's eyes. It was a singleton's cut, a rejection of even the prospect of joining a mahu'kedet, and though Leoden, at their first ever meeting, had taken the time to answer Naruet's astonished curiosity on that point – *I didn't expect Vex Ralan to die so soon, nor to inherit the throne*, he'd said; *I loved Kadeja while he lived, but the Vekshi do not marry as we do, and I had no plans to wear marriage-braids* – still he found the visual incongruity of it shocking.

Not that the strangers Leoden dealt with found it so, doubtless judging his appearance against their own, more alien standards. Naruet, who'd often struggled to fit in, found it comforting to think that a world might exist where behaviour considered odd in Kena passed instead for local good manners; it meant he wasn't innately unsuited to socialising, just stuck in a place that didn't appreciate his defaults. Did the strangers at the Bazaar appreciate Leoden? The silent nature of his scrying made it hard to tell, but as the Vex appeared to successfully negotiate in conversations with various locals – aided and tailed by an unfamiliar figure who Naruet took for a native guide – he was at least moving with purpose.

But what purpose? That was the real question, and one that Naruet couldn't answer.

"I understand why he fled," Naruet said to the kitten, now. "The palace was sieged and he had to run. It was the obvious way out. But that doesn't explain why he hasn't asked me to bring him home." He shifted his weight, bringing one hand up to rub the kitten, a friendly calico, behind one white-and-orange ear. She purred in benign encouragement; Naruet, skritching gently, continued to think out loud. "Perhaps he didn't believe me? We discussed the theory more than once, in case he ever decided to worldwalk himself; he must know I can do it. But he hasn't signalled, which means he must have a plan. But what plan? And why didn't he tell me what it was?" He frowned, an anxious twist in his stomach as he recalled Ktho's talk of captured worldwalkers. "Did he worldwalk without me, then? Or did someone else bring them through? Did *she*?"

He shuddered at the prospect. *She* was as far Outside as anyone he'd ever met, for all he'd been forced to pay her deference; he hated to even think her name. And yet it made an awful sort of sense, to think that *she* was the liar he sought: he'd never understood why Leoden trusted her, but if *she* were the one who'd captured and chained the worldwalkers – if *she'd* been the one to tell Leoden they were criminals, and Leoden had believed her – then that would account for a great many things indeed. It was a tempting theory, but Naruet had learned the hard way that it was better to have more tangible proof for his conclusions than *it makes sense to me*; other people seldom believed his word alone, which was disheartening enough that he tried to avoid the experience.

The most frustrating thing was that he *knew* his judgement was often flawed; that most other people didn't use Inside/Outside to help them gauge who to trust, or to figure out what to say. But knowing his weaknesses meant he could try, in his own way, to account for them, which had to be worth *something*. If other people did likewise, he'd certainly never seen much evidence of it, and *they* were still allowed to make mistakes – but then, he supposed, it was exactly the kind of thing he often struggled to notice, so perhaps that meant he shouldn't judge after all.

"Life would be so much easier," Naruet told the kitten, "if nobody ever said anything they didn't really mean."

The kitten continued to purr, tilting her head to give his skritching fingers better access.

Naruet sighed. He could try to learn more of Safi later, assuming he wasn't summoned to the palace first. For now, he would do as Ktho had ordered: keep his head down and stay within the temple.

Naruet stretched on the warming stone, and skritched the cat, and watched as the sun came up.

6
Cut/Run

It wasn't that Saffron had planned on silence. Over breakfast she'd spoken to her parents and sister, trying her best to seem respectful without appearing sullen. She'd even spared a fond, exasperated word for Beastie, who'd stolen a toast crust off her plate with nary a trace of guilt. But once she stepped into Lawson High, the memory of yesterday's defiance a hot-cold lump in her throat, like food that was burned on one side and frozen on the other, her words just... fled. Ruby said goodbye to her as they passed the gates, and all she could do was smile and wave; a janitor called out a cheerful injunction not to step in some indistinct but sticky-looking muck on the stairs, and her attempt at polite acknowledgement choked out into a nod.

She didn't know how else to describe it. The will to speak was certainly there – her thoughts hadn't stopped, and she sure as hell had motivation, especially when Lyssi ran up and demanded to know what had really happened yesterday, and if she was feeling OK now, and whether she'd checked her messages yet – but when she opened her mouth to answer, nothing came out but air. It ought to have been frightening, and on some level it was, but it also felt like a beautifully perverse solution to her problem: if speaking her mind had landed her in trouble, then what better option was there than saying nothing at all?

Even so, to reach for words and find only stillness... It was jarring enough to show on her face, and Lyssi saw it, though it took her several further thwarted attempts at inquiry to correctly identify the cause.

"You... you're not talking?" she hazarded, brow scrunched in confusion. Saffron considered correcting her, explaining that it was less a voluntary thing than it was a go-with-it-until-it-goes-away thing, but couldn't trust that Lyssi wouldn't freak out. Thinking quickly, she managed a grin, rummaged around in her school bag, pulled out a pen and paper and wrote: *Silent protest for yesterday. I'm on a word strike.*

She'd hoped that Lyssi might laugh – shit, she thought it was at least a *little* funny – but all her friend did was stare wide-eyed, her obvious worry intensified. *Yena would've laughed,* Saffron thought, a little mutinously and a lot fondly. Ignoring the resultant pang, she tried to shrug in an offhand, reassuring way, like it was no big deal.

But Lyssi refused to be reassured. "Saff, this is serious. They sent you *home* for yesterday, and now you're going to just, what – go quiet until they apologise? What if a teacher asks you a question?"

They won't, Saffron wrote, with more confidence than she felt.

"You don't know that!"

If I don't, you don't either.

Lyssi glared at her, and Saffron grinned – it was such a Lyssi expression, and just for a moment the argument felt normal, the sort of back-and-forth banter that had once characterised their friendship. But rather than grinning back, Lyssi's face crumpled.

"I don't *understand* you!" she shouted, two high spots of colour on her cheeks. "You don't check your messages, you don't text or call or come online, and now you're not even *talking*? Jesus, Saff – I know you've been through hell, and I know this isn't easy, but did it ever occur to you that *I* might need my friend back, too?" Her eyes brimmed with tears, and Saffron felt abruptly sick to her stomach. "You *vanished*, OK? And then we find out you're alive, you're here, and I'm sitting at home like a dumbass for *six days* waiting for you to call or talk to me or just, I don't know, just fucking *acknowledge* the fact that you vanishing screwed me up a bit, or a lot, and all I want to do is talk to you about it, and I know it was so much worse for you, I know I'm being selfish as hell, but it's like you don't even care who I am anymore, like you didn't even *miss* me, and I just – I don't know what to *do* with that, OK?"

I'm sorry. I'm so, so sorry. The words were on her tongue, and she didn't understand why she couldn't just *say* them – or say anything else, for that matter – because she'd figured the silence was something she was really doing on purpose, even if she didn't quite know how or why, and that if it truly mattered, she'd be able to talk again. But though she pushed and pushed and *pushed*, she couldn't do more than open her mouth, her throat staying stubbornly still.

Lyssi waited for an answer, hope and anger finally turning to hurt resignation when she realised Saffron wasn't going to talk. Belatedly, Saffron remembered that she could still write, but before she'd managed to scribble more than *I'm* in her notebook, Lyssi grabbed her wrist and yanked the pen from the page.

"*No*," she fumed. "You want to talk to me, you do it using actual human words, OK? I'm not some asshole teacher or some even-more-asshole boy or… or whoever else it is you're angry at. And if you're really not ready to be my friend again, I can wait until you are. I *can*." She said it with a stubborn jut to her chin, like the time she'd eaten an entire large pizza because Saffron had teased that she never managed to finish even a medium one. "But I can't… I can't just hang around on the outside of whatever you're feeling and wait to matter to you again, if all it's going to do is hurt. And it *does* hurt, and I hate it, and no matter what you went through, I don't deserve to have to feel like this. So I'm... I'm just going to walk away for now, OK? You find me when you're ready."

No. Saffron grabbed for her, silently pleading, but though Lyssi's expression wavered, she still dodged the contact, retreating backwards across the asphalt.

"Bye, Saff," Lyssi whispered, and then she turned and ran, her brightly hued school bag banging against her back.

Saffron started after her, then froze in place, a wrenching pain in her chest. Worse even than her inability to speak was the terrible knowledge that Lyssi was right: Saffron *had* barely thought of her during those weeks in Kena, and Lyssi – funny, clever, loyal Lyssi – deserved so much better than that. She hung her head, tears welling up as she stared at the ground. She'd promised Ruby she'd say goodbye before running off again, but what would her absence do to everyone else? She'd told Ms Mays that compromise didn't mean pawning her heart, but trampling on other people's was hardly an improvement, either. *No matter what I do, I'm hurting someone.*

If the only choice you could reasonably make was between selfishness and martyrdom, was it really a choice at all? Being forced to choose between her own happiness and the happiness of those around her was starting to feel like Jared Blake all over again: if she was going to get screwed no matter what, then the only sensible thing was to do what she wanted. *Assuming I figure out what that is, and whether it's even possible.*

"Hey. Hey, are you alright? That looked pretty brutal."

Blinking tears away, Saffron lifted her head and found herself staring into the surprisingly concerned face of Glitter James-Michaels. Once again, words failed her, which was almost a relief – it would've been mortifying to be able to talk to Glitter when her silence had just driven Lyssi away. She shrugged, shook her head, but couldn't find a way to play it off: even without a mirror handy, she knew her eyes were red, her cheeks puffy and tear-streaked.

Glitter paused, considering. She was lean-limbed and pretty in a conventional, white-girl-on-a-magazine-cover way that Saffron had never found particularly appealing, and so had an unfair tendency to dismiss. Her hair, though naturally a darkish blonde akin to Saffron's own, was dyed a lighter, more Scandinavian shade, pulled back in an immaculate long ponytail. She wore light makeup – or Saffron guessed it was light; she'd never been that great at the subtleties of contouring – and her eyes were the blue of coloured contacts; Saffron had a vague idea that her irises were hazel underneath, but couldn't have said for sure.

"Are you really not talking to anyone?" Glitter asked. And then, with an odd, soft shrewdness, "Or can you just not talk?"

Saffron swallowed, throat painfully tight. Nodded.

An unreadable expression flicked across Glitter's face – Glitter James-Michaels, the golden girl with garrulous friends and a godawful name, who'd barely said more than ten words to Saffron since the start of the year, and yet who'd somehow understood her better than Lyssi did.

"OK," said Glitter. "OK. I'm, ah. Guessing this is a new thing?"

Another nod.

"Right. Shit." She laughed and glanced around, smoothing a palm across her perfect hair. "And I'm guessing you can't ditch to try and deal with it, or your 'rents and the teachers and everyone'll freak out because of all your other crap, right?"

A fervent nod, this time.

"Shit." Glitter bit her lip. "You've got Kirkland for homeroom, right? You happy to cut, so long as you don't get in trouble?"

A sharp nod: *god, yes, please and thank you.*

"All right. You come with me and just, ah... you know. Try to look trustworthy."

Trustworthy. Right. Because that makes sense. But after a moment, she thought that maybe it kind of did, if Glitter was planning what Saffron thought she was planning, and when the other girl looped her arm through Saffron's she was happy just to follow. The bell rang as they set off: all around them, students streamed towards their classes, laughing and shouting and groaning in solidarity at the unavoidable bullshit of it all. Except that Saffron *was* avoiding it, at least temporarily, walking against the salmon-spawn flow of bodies as Glitter towed her towards the sickbay.

Though technically attached to the admin building, the sickbay had its own entrance; Glitter opened the glass-fronted door, kicked it shut once Saffron was in, and called, "Ms Wickie? It's Lita. Are you here?"

Lita? Saffron thought, looking anew at Glitter. As if sensing the question, Glitter – Lita – glanced and shrugged, a faint blush on her cheeks. Quietly, she muttered, "I hate my stupid name, OK? But so far, she's the only one calls me Lita. Everyone else just thinks it's a joke."

She, presumably, was Ms Wickie, the school nurse, a cheerfully freckled woman who emerged from the sickbay's second room a heartbeat later. She smiled at Glitter – *Lita*, Saffron forcefully corrected herself; under the circumstances, the least she could do was try to call the other girl by a name she actually liked, even if only in her head – but her gaze turned businesslike when she looked at Saffron, taking in the scars, the missing fingers and chunk of ear, the tattoo. With a sinking heart, Saffron realised that the nurse must already know who she was; would probably be obliged to call her parents, just like Mr Gryce and Mr Laughton had been.

"How can I help you girls?" said Ms Wickie. Her accent was country-broad, with just the faintest nasal twang to betray a New Zealand upbringing.

"This is Saffron," Lita said, finally releasing her captured arm. "She choked on her drink, and I'm sure she's fine, but she just wants to sit in the quiet a bit before she goes to class. Rest her throat, you know. But you'll need to send Mrs Kirkland a note to say where she is, or they'll panic."

Ms Wickie studied them both with the practised scrutiny of a woman used to being lied to – but somehow, it was Lita, not Saffron, at whom she looked most closely. "Tell me," she said, "would I be right in thinking that you'd like to stay with your friend, to make sure she's OK?"

"If I could," said Lita, humbly.

It was such an outrageous bid, Saffron half expected Ms Wickie to burst out laughing. Instead, she sighed – not at the request, but at some more intangible worry – and said, "As it happens, I need to speak to Mrs Kirkland this morning anyway. I'll explain the situation to her, and ask her to pass the message on to Saffron's first period teacher. Will that suit?"

"Thank you, miss," said Lita, ducking her head.

"Well, then." She cocked a thumb at the smaller room she'd previously exited: the sickbay proper. "In you go. I'll be back in fifteen or so. If anyone else drops by, you tell them to wait." And with that, she swept out of the building in presumable search for Mrs Kirkland.

Wordlessly, Lita led Saffron through to the sickbay, shutting the secondary door behind them. Three small cots lined the walls; Lita sat down on the nearest one, and after a moment's hesitation, Saffron sat down beside her.

Why did that work? What just happened? The question nudged at Saffron's lips: unable to speak, she could only express it by looking at Lita with what she hoped was grateful curiosity. Lita glanced away, shoulders hunching. She always seemed so put-together, but in that moment she looked as achingly human as Saffron felt, and when she spoke it was softly, her eyes on the floor.

"Ms Wickie... knows. Um. About some stuff that's happened to me that, that I couldn't... I didn't have anyone else to ask for help, but she was good about it, made sure I got what I needed, and when – it was months ago now, but I get... I get these moments, sometimes, where I need to lie down, or I need to be still, and there's nobody else who understands, and so she lets me come here with a friend, if I've brought one, or on my own if I haven't – and if I bring someone, she knows they won't know why I'm really here, so she never asks them any questions, she just... lets me have the company, no matter what stupid story I tell to get them in, and after yesterday, I figured, I just–" she looked at Saffron, pleading and proud and raw, "–if there was anyone else in this whole stupid school who might understand, it's you. Even if it didn't, you know, if it wasn't exactly the same – even if he didn't, with you, *to* you..."

She broke off, clearly struggling to put it all into words, but Saffron didn't need to hear any more, stomach twisting with awful understanding. Moving slowly, she put an arm around Lita's shoulders, squeezing gently, heartsick for the both of them. Lita exhaled hard and leaned into the contact, resting her head on Saffron's shoulder. After a moment, her own arm curled around Saffron's waist, her fingers gently gripping her shirt in lieu of holding her hip.

They sat like that for at least ten minutes, quietly breathing together. And then – Saffron didn't know if it was the quiet, the physical contact, Lita's confession or the simple passage of time; perhaps it was a combination of all those things, or something else entirely – her words came back. There was no fanfare, no telltale click in her jaw or mouth: she just suddenly *knew*, and wondered that she'd ever thought her sudden muteness voluntary.

"Thanks, Lita," she whispered.

Still pressed against her, Lita laughed, raspy and sad. "Yeah, well. At least my being a fuckup's good for something, right?"

"You're not a fuckup."

"You're not a freak."

Two heartbeats; three.

"I wasn't raped," said Saffron, softly. "Everyone thinks I was, but I wasn't."

"I was," Lita said. The admission came out small and flat. "But everyone I tried to tell said I wasn't. Everyone except Ms Wickie."

Saffron nudged Lita's knee with hers. "I have it on reliable authority that everyone's an idiot."

Lita choked out a laugh. "Yeah?"

"Yeah. My little sister said so and everything."

"Smart chick, that one."

"Yeah."

They sat together until Ms Wickie came back; until the second period bell forced them to go their separate ways to separate classes. Saffron watched Lita disappear, and felt the quiet solidarity of the sickbay spooling out between them like string in some mythological labyrinth – invisible, but uncut.

"And Saffron didn't tell you any more than that?" Gwen asked, when Louis had finished speaking. For the sake of both comfort and privacy, they were using English.

Her son shook his head, shrugging slightly. Freed from its former cornrow braids, his hair was pulled back in a tight, puffy tail, the pensive expression on his face a near-perfect echo of his father's, minus only Naku's crowsfeet. Ever since the incident with Kadeja, her son had foregone his Shavaktiin veils around the palace, saying that, as he'd begun to play a personal role in the story, there was little point in hiding from it. Gwen had been too happy at seeing his face to ask – as she would never ask Halaya or Kikra, with a mother's tart mistrust of a child's abnegation – exactly what role he'd been playing before then, if not a personal one. Louis had likely sensed the unspoken remark, but he'd let her conspicuous lack of comment pass without comment in turn, and thus did they preserve their equilibrium.

"There was nothing more to tell," he said. "Even assuming her sister's information was correct, that's no guarantee her parents have already found a place to send her, nor does it mean they want her to go immediately."

"And yet."

"And yet."

Gwen drummed her fingers on the tabletop, forcing herself to be mercenary. She'd always known that Saffron had risked exactly this sort of complication by returning home; that bringing her back to Kena might be tricky at best and impossible at worst. "Did she tell you what she wanted? Does she truly want to, to…" *become a worldwalker* felt too presumptuous, "… return to us, or is she simply struggling to adapt?"

"I don't know." Louis opened and closed his palm, a frustrated gesture. "It doesn't help that she's so new to the dreamscape – it was one thing to speak to her when we were sharing a world, but at such a remove and untrained as she is, she struggles to stay present for very long. She feels… yearning, I think, is the best word for it. She yearns, though I cannot rightly say for what. But if we're going to give her the choice, she might be on a shorter clock than we realised."

Gwen made a pained noise of assent, filed the information away, and moved on to the next urgent topic. "And what about Yena? Have you had more news from Yevekshasa?"

Louis snorted. "Whatever she means by seeking Ashasa's penance, she hasn't exactly confided in either Yasha or the Shavaktiin. Kikra's doing the best he can to find out more, but the Great Temple is warded against the ilumet, which means that neither of us can ask her directly."

"Luck save me from adventuresome children," Gwen muttered.

"But bloodmother," Louis said, impish in his translation of the Kenan term, "your dotage would be fearful dull, if not for the likes of us!"

"Dotage!" Gwen feigned a swipe at his head; Louis play-

dodged easily. "I'll be lucky to reach it, the way you run me ragged."

"Am I interrupting something?"

It was Matu, sauntering into the chamber as unconcernedly as if he owned it – which, once Viya and Amenet were crowned and Matu named their Vexa'Halat, he would, as this particular room was part of the (currently unoccupied) Halat consorts' wing. He looked as beautiful as ever, dressed in a sumptuous *enha* – an open, sleeveless surcoat that fell to his ankles – heavy with gold embroidery over black *nashi*: low-slung, hip-hugging trousers with voluminous, skirtlike legs. His muscular chest was bare, except for where a long rope necklace of black pearls and unworked gold nuggets brushed his pectorals, with matching pearl-and-gold drops hanging from both ears. Like Amenet's, his inky waterfall of hair was pulled back in a single betrothal braid; unlike Amenet's, his was tied off with green and lilac strings, respectively the colours of Lomo and Hime, who embodied the essence of *halat* – vitality – in the mahu'kedet of the gods.

He looked, in other words, exactly like a betrothed Halat consort should, and Gwen took a moment to appreciate the full effect before replying, in Kenan, with, "Nothing that can't stand to wait on beauty."

Louis snorted in amusement. In the same language, he said, "Mother. *Please*."

"Oh, as if you don't have eyes! I've seen your Rikan, you'll recall – he blushes quite prettily."

"*Mother.*"

"Rikan? He of the lovely honey-eyes?" said Matu, in a tone of professional interest.

"The very same," said Gwen.

Matu whistled, looking on Louis with new approval. "Oh, *nicely* done."

"Luck save me from adventuresome mothers," Louis muttered.

"Don't spurn your heritage, dear," said Gwen. "Or do I need to tell you again about how I met your firstmother?"

"Gods, no," groaned Louis. Feigning put-uponness, he appealed to Matu, "You see now why I became a Shavaktiin – how else was I to survive the onslaught of such narratives?"

Appealing to Matu in such matters, Gwen thought smugly, was always a tactical error: like any good halat-in-waiting, he merely smiled and said, "I can think of worse fates. And your bloodmother, if I may say it, is a *very* striking woman."

To her dying day, Gwen would deny blushing. Nonetheless, Louis glanced between her and Matu, used his astute Shavaktiin powers of observation to draw something approximate to the correct conclusion, and made a noise that was half laughter, half exasperation. "The Great Story fancies itself a comedy, it seems."

Grinning with an air of self-satisfied victory, Matu draped himself in a handy chair. "I should hope so," he said. "It would hardly be worth telling, otherwise."

Louis looked rather taken by the notion. "Do you know, there's a school of thought within the Shavaktiin enclave that suggests–" he caught himself, blinked, coughed, and converted this into, "–something I ought not, in all devotional responsibility, disclose to outsiders."

Gwen gave him a mock-reproving look. "I am your *mother*."

"I believe we've rather established that," said Louis, dry as good vermouth. "Yes."

"Right. Well," said Matu, examining his nails. "If we're all done being clever, I had actually come to say that I've spoken to certain trusted friends and former colleagues at the temple of Sahu, and none of them have any reason to believe that Leoden was researching Vexa Yavin, anchored portals, worldwalkers or even so much as a recipe for festival cake." At Gwen's alarmed look, he shot her a very Pixish look and said, "Please, credit me with some subtlety. No, I did not ask any of that outright, and yes, I do trust the discretion of those

I questioned, or I wouldn't have gone to them in the first place."

Gwen raised a brow, impressed. "And here we've all been acting on the assumption that you're constitutionally unsuited to court politics."

Matu gave a genteel shudder. "Unsuited, no. Unwilling, yes. Well. Mostly unwilling. I can always be persuaded by a just cause." He winked slyly at Louis. "Or a good story."

"As a point of academic interest," Louis asked mildly, "do you have any shame to speak of?"

"On an average day? No. But when the occasion calls for it, I can self-flagellate with the best of them."

"I feel almost reassured."

"I'm very reassuring."

Gwen rolled her eyes at the pair of them. "And here I thought we were done being clever."

"You might be," said Matu, "but in Yasha's absence, I'm feeling rather indulgent. On which note," he added, flowing abruptly to his feet, "I have an elsewhere to be. Do let me know if I can be of any further assistance. In *whatever* capacity." He smirked at Louis, who looked equal parts flattered and offended, smiled sincerely at Gwen, and sauntered towards the door with the same air of feline entitlement with which he'd entered.

"Do you know," said Louis, aiming to be overheard, "your Matuhasa is almost more terrifying than Leoden, at times."

"He's not *my* Matuhasa," said Gwen, the fondness in her tone perhaps belying the sentiment. "But I take your point."

"Changing the subject," said Louis, "do you know anyone in the palace called Na–"

"My lady! Gwen!"

The gasping, panicked voice from the doorway cut over Louis's question: it was Rikan, wild-eyed and out of breath. Matu, having sprung aside to make way for him, now hovered in his wake, curious as to the furore. Both Gwen

and Louis shot to their feet, Louis to place a steadying hand
on his lover's arm and Gwen to demand, "What is it? What's
happened?"

"It's the ambassador, lady. Sene a Sati." He gulped, his
brown skin ashen with shock. "She woke up from the healing
sleep, started ranting in Vekshi, crying and wailing like her
heart was broke. I tried to calm her down, get her talking
sense, and I thought she'd quieted – I swear by every god,
lady, I barely left the room, and only to ask Sathika to send
for a healer – I figured she was in shock, like, on account of
having woken too early – but then I went back in, and it was
already too late even if I'd had the sevikmet, she'd cut so
deep–"

Gwen went cold all over. *"Cut? What–"*

"She's dead, lady. Suicide." Trembling, Rikan leaned into
Louis's touch, his lovely eyes full of guilt. "Put a blade right
through the vein in her neck. Bled out before she hit the
ground, I'd guess, by the... by the way it sprayed."

But she had no knife! Gwen wanted to yell – the worldwalkers
weren't even given table knives, it should have been
impossible–

And then she remembered the Vekshi blade that Viya had
ordered brought to Sene's cell, and which Gwen herself had
left there: a show of good faith, so that Sene might shave her
outgrown hair in privacy.

"Thorns and godshit," she whispered, shaken to her core.
What in the worlds did Leoden do to you?

"We just think it would be for the best," said Saffron's mother,
hands fidgeting in her lap. "Just... until you've found your
feet again."

"We love you more than anything, Saff," her father added,
"and if you'd rather not be stuck at home or stuck at school,
we don't see why you shouldn't..."

Be stuck somewhere else? Saffron thought viciously, forcing herself to wait for her father to find a more tactful phrase.

"...benefit from an alternative," he said, with an air of benevolent finality.

"Now, there are a few different options to consider," Ms Mays said, smoothing the brochures she'd laid on the tabletop. "All private facilities, obviously – the public system is woefully overloaded – but these are the ones your parents and I think would be the best fit." She hesitated, then said, with a sidelong glance, "I should mention, however, that this facility, Gracewood–" she nudged a brochure forward of its fellows, like a magician asking *is this your card?* "–as well as being the closest to home, has an opening from this Friday."

"You hear that, Saff?" said her mother. "This Friday!" Ms Mays winced, and Saffron didn't blame her. In fact, she was beginning to feel rather sorry for the social worker, who was after all only trying to do her job and being stymied in it, not just by Saffron's resistance, but through the tactless, overbearing affection of her parents. Even at her coldest, most objective remove, it twisted her heart to see them stumbling so doggedly in pursuit of an aim their efforts were actively hindering, like a blindfolded child swinging for a piñata already crushed underfoot.

"Sure," said Saffron, voice leaden. "Friday. That works."

Her father frowned. "You really should try to make an informed decision–"

"Informed? You mean, like the way you're keeping *Ruby* informed by telling her to hide upstairs until Ms Mays is gone?" It was easy to let the borrowed anger bleed into her voice; easier than grabbing the brochures and ripping them into bits. "Are you actually going to tell her about any of this, or did you just figure you'd wait until I'd vanished again and see if she noticed?"

It was a low blow, given her inside knowledge, but justly aimed for the same reason: her mother paled, her father winced, and Ms Mays, seeing both reactions, looked horrified.

"Ellen, Daniel, I have to stress in the *strongest possible terms* the inadvisability of denying Ruby input into this decision, even at the planning stages. Asking her to deal with the sudden absence of her sister after an equally sudden loss – it could prove devastating."

"I understand your concerns," her father said, in the tone that usually meant a hard no was forthcoming. "Believe me, I do, but this isn't something Ruby should be able to veto just because she's too young to fully understand why Saffron has to go."

Her stomach clenched. "*Has* to go? What happened to giving me a choice?"

Her father flushed, but Ms Mays got in first. "You have lots of choices, Saffron, but that's not the same as having infinite options. Now, I know you had a better day at school today, and if you really want to keep trying I'll support you in that, but none of us were in favour of you returning so soon in the first place, and if you miss the Gracewood window and *then* decide school isn't the right choice, you could have a long wait ahead of you. Remember, sometimes it's necessary to compromise."

"Compromise. OK." Saffron seized on the word, heart pounding as her thoughts flew. "Here's my compromise: I'll say yes to Gracewood – I'll look at the other brochures if you really want, but like you say, there's a time limit here – if *you–*" she looked squarely at both her parents, "–call Ruby down here, now, and explain this to her. I get why none of you think I'm acting rationally, but that doesn't mean she should have to suffer for it, too."

Her father blustered. Her mother wavered. But in the end, Ruby was summoned, because the Coulter family was many things, but willing to have a full-blown emotional argument in front of an outside witness was not one of them.

"Yeah?" said Ruby, sauntering into the lounge room in a pair of paisley boxers and a singlet top, her hair still wet from the shower. "What do you... oh!" She blinked, clearly surprised to see Ms Mays still present: their mother had called up the stairs to her, but hadn't explained why. "Um. Hello, Ms Mays."

"Hello, Ruby." The social worker smiled, patting the space beside her on the couch. "Your parents and I talked it over, and we thought it was best you be present for this part of the conversation. Is that all right with you?"

"Sure, I guess." Ruby slunk to the indicated spot, for all the world a disinterested teen. She didn't look nervous, but Ruby had an excellent poker face, right up until she didn't. Settling herself, she inhaled to ask a question – and froze, catching sight of the brochures on the table. Gulping, she hovered a hand over the splayed papers, not quite touching them. She jerked it back, her gaze snapping urgently to Saffron's.

"You're going away?"

"Yes," said Saffron, meeting her stare for stare. "I'm, that is… I'll be leaving soon. This week, maybe." She hesitated, fumbling for a phrase that would work as a double statement, some callback to their earlier conversation, and finally settled on, "It won't be forever. I promise."

Ruby inhaled sharply: message received. When she spoke again, she sounded unbearably small. "Can I… Will I be able to visit, sometime? You know, once it's, once you're all settled?"

"I don't know," said Saffron, voice raw. "It's not really up to me. But I hope so, Ru. I'd really like that." And as she said it, she realised it was true.

"Oh, Gracewood encourages visitors!" Ms Mays said, warming to her theme, and launched into a spiel extolling the virtues of its recovery program, rooms, grounds, methods.

Saffron didn't hear a word of it, too busy watching Ruby who looked as though she'd never listened so hard to anything in her life. Her heart began to pound, desperate for Ruby to turn and acknowledge her, to share in the absurdity of the moment, but her sister stared fixedly at Ms Mays, her neck and shoulders rigid.

"It… sounds like a really nice place," said Ruby, when Ms Mays finally fell silent. She shook her head and blinked, a minute ripple of returning awareness, and only then did she look at Saffron, grey eyes soft and pleading. "Doesn't it sound nice, Saff? Nicer than–" she gulped, cheeks flushing, "–than lots of other things?"

An icy hand gripped Saffron's heart and squeezed. *No,* she thought, distantly numb. *Please, no.*

"It sounds OK," she said, striving for an ambivalence she was nowhere close to feeling.

"I just… This sounds like it could be really good. Or not so bad, at least."

"I guess–"

"So you'll try it, right? You'll give it a go?"

Saffron could feel the moment when the adults realised there was a subtext to this exchange that jarred with their understanding of things. The shift in attention was palpable, like a tightening in the air. It panicked her: she'd told Ruby a fragment of the truth precisely because she didn't want to lie to her, but with her parents and Ms Mays present, there was no way to be honest without betraying herself.

"Right," she said, lurching to her feet. "Right. OK. So, that's settled – I'm going, I'm gonna just… So I'll go, now – to my room, I mean, I'm going and–"

"Saffron?" asked her mother, concerned. "Are you alright?"

"I don't think we're quite done here," Ms Mays added. "I think we need to discuss this further–"

"Fine!" Saffron blurted. "No, I mean, I'm fine, it's fine, it's just–" She knew she was babbling, knew she was giving herself away, but couldn't make herself stop; she was backing away as she spoke, edging out of the room like a nervous crab, "–you know, we've decided, so I think… I just need to process it all, I need some time to, to–"

"Don't run away!" Ruby shrieked.

Saffron froze.

"I don't think–" their father began, just as Ms Mays said, "Why would you assume–"

"Don't you get it?" Ruby cut them both off, her face splotchy red. "She's going to run away, she told me, and it's all my fault – I overheard you saying you didn't want to tell me about Gracewood, and I was so angry, I told Saff, and *she* said she wanted to *leave*–"

"Ruby, stop!" Saffron begged. She felt feverish, her skin both cold and overheated, an ugly panic clawing at her throat. "That's not–"

"She wasn't kidnapped!" Ruby was crying now, thin tears streaking her cheeks. "She went somewhere else, somewhere secret, and she wants to go back because none of you ever *listen*–"

"What do you mean, she wasn't kidnapped?" Ms Mays's voice was high and sharp, cutting the rest of the conversation dead.

Ruby clapped a belated hand to her mouth, eyes wide and appalled. She looked helplessly at Saffron who felt as though she'd turned to lead. Time went syrupy, viscous against the sudden weight of her body. She viewed the scene as though it was fixed in amber: Ruby's terrified contrition, Ms Mays's dawning comprehension, her mother's shock, her father's incipient outrage. A fragment of something Luy had once told her in the dreamscape came back to her in a jagged flash – *there is only one moment in all of existence, and that moment is always now* – and just like that, her heart was set, her choice as singular and immutable as the north star.

Saffron looked at Ruby. "It's all right, Ru," she said, swallowing thickly. "I don't blame you. This isn't your fault, OK? I love you. I'll always love you, and that's why I forgive you." Her throat burned, tight and hot, as she glanced at her parents. "All of you."

"Saffron, what–?"

She ran.

7
Open Doors, Like Open Wounds

Sene a Sati lay in a cooling pool of her own fluids, a raggedy gash in the side of her neck. As though it had been painted on, an arcing streak of scarlet dripped across her mirror and wall at just the height she would've been standing: true to Rikan's morbid assessment, she'd likely been dead as she hit the ground. The speed and precision of her self-inflicted strike was all the more impressive when you saw how deep she'd had to drive the blade before wrenching it out again, a final spasm of furious, annihilating will.

Arterial spray is one of nature's absurdities, Gwen thought, suppressing a manic and highly inappropriate urge to say so out loud. *So garish! All that red just spurting out like tickertape – one good stab, and your neck's a bloody Jack-in-the-box by way of Jackson Pollock.*

Instead, she reached down and closed Sene's eyes, flinching only slightly from the stench of new death. The knife lay where the ambassador's twitching fingers had dropped it, coated now in a layer of congealing blood.

"I oughtn't have left her," Rikan whispered. He hovered in the doorway, ashy with shame and nausea. "Not as she was, not even for a second–"

"This isn't your fault," Gwen said sharply. She straightened, resisting a reflexive urge to wipe her fingers on her thigh, and met the guard's stricken gaze. "Ambassador or not, she was Vekshi-trained with a blade and clearly determined. If you'd tried to intercede, she might have struck you, too, or at least made a valiant effort to that effect."

Rikan looked like he wanted to find this comforting, but couldn't quite manage it. "I'm a guard, lady. It's what I do. I'm meant to stand between harm and others, even if it's from themselves, and doubly so if they're in my charge."

"You'll forgive me if I neglect to see your survival as a failure of duty," Louis murmured. He stood slightly back and to the side, offering as much support as Rikan would accept, and caught his mother's eye over Rikan's shoulder.

"Go and rest," said Gwen, gently commanding. "Look after yourself. Until or unless I say otherwise, that's the only order you need follow. Though of course," she added, mercy tempered by necessity, "I'll have to send one of Nihun's Kin to take a record of your memories. Sooner rather than later, if I can manage it." Halunet, she thought, recalling the priest who'd tended to Sene in the first place – she'd liked his calm manner and easy voice. Or was her trust in him, too, misplaced? Could he have been responsible for Sene's death, implanting her suicidal impulse with the ahunemet? The very idea made her head hurt, and not because it was in any way an implausible theory. *I can't keep suspecting every priest in the hierarchy of collusion with my enemies, or I'll wind up as twisted as Vexa Yavin.* Out loud, she said, "Do I make myself clear?"

Rikan slumped, voice watery with gratitude. "Yes, lady."

Thank you, Louis mouthed, and with a final, troubled glance at Sene's body, he led his lover away, leaving Gwen alone with the body and far too many thoughts.

The sight of Matu dressed as a proper halat consort was still new and startling enough that, even in the midst of crisis, Viya was hard-pressed not to take notice. She'd just initiated a discussion of Gwen's intemperate (but admittedly pragmatic) bargain with the high priestess of Ke's Kin with Pix and Amenet – who hadn't taken the news well – when he'd rushed in to tell them of Sene a Sati's suicide. It was such a strange, incongruous thing that Viya hadn't initially understood it, heart pounding in the misplaced terror that something ugly and violent was about to happen to *her*. She was halfway out the door before the truth truly registered, and nearly to the scene itself before her pulse had returned to anything near its normal rhythm.

They found Gwen standing just outside a bloodied cell, a hand held over her mouth to guard against the smell.

"It's truly suicide?" Pix asked, and Viya flashed her a grateful look for asking the question to which she most wanted an answer.

"As best I can tell," said Gwen, voice grim. "See for yourself."

And so they did, though one at a time: even without a dead body taking up the floor, the cell was too small to have comfortably housed the five of them at once. Viya glanced numbly at what remained of Sene a Sati, gaze skating over the ghastly image: she hadn't wanted to look at all, and yet she felt some obscure sense of duty – to Zech? to Trishka? to Veksh itself? – to bear witness to the ambassador. Matu hissed sharply through his teeth; Amenet stared, grey-faced, before jerking away again. Pix looked the longest, her face a mask of cold anger, before suggesting – once more to Viya's relief – that they all remove to the common area.

It was a sensible suggestion for more reasons than one. In addition to two increasingly stressed honoured swords – a burly man, unfamiliar to Viya, and a woman called Sathika – the hall outside the cell was starting to fill with worldwalkers, alarmed enough by the commotion to come seeking its source.

"We have to tell them," Gwen hissed. "They trust us little enough already – if they think we killed Sene, or drove her to die, we'll never get them home!"

"They haven't seen anything yet," Pix countered, albeit worriedly. "If we just send them back to their rooms–"

"What, and ask them not to notice that one of them has gone missing?"

"Sene wasn't one of them!"

"Do they know that?"

Pix opened her mouth to reply, hesitated, then borrowed one of Yasha's favourite bits of Vekshi invective. "*Arsegullet!*"

"If they won't believe us either way," said Viya, gaze flicking to Amenet, "then surely we should tell them whatever's most likely to keep them calm."

Amenet gripped the amber head of her cane and closed her eyes, considering Viya's proposal. Matu watched her with a sort of soft, focused reverence, waiting for her to render her half of their joint verdict. It ought to have been infuriating, and yet Viya, who'd grown up a spectator to secondmother Sava casting such looks at Hawy, found the habit oddly endearing. That was the way of the mahu'kedet: though all worked together, some hearts were always bound more closely together than others, and however freely Matu flirted, his devotion to Amenet was beyond question.

His timing was exquisite, courtier-perfect. The instant Amenet's eyes came open, lips parted on the brink of speech, Matu dropped gracefully to one knee, head bowed: a halat consort's public intercession with his monarch.

"My lights," he murmured, tactfully including Viya with the plural, though he spoke only to Amenet, "you know I have the zuymet. May I attempt to explain things to our guests? In their eyes, perhaps I am not so threatening as an honoured sword, nor so damnably familiar as a priest."

Seeing Matu dress like a consort was one thing; witnessing his active fulfilment of the role was quite another. Viya experienced a jarring moment of dislocation, trying to reconcile this version of Matu with the wry explorer-teacher she'd met at the compound, who smoked and swore and fought and flirted with all the raucous abandon of a tomcat. It wasn't just that he was embracing the role of Vexa'Halat, supporting his beloved Amenet's authority even as he used its weight to enhance his own; he was, she realised, enjoying himself immensely. Not the situation with Sene and the worldwalkers, of course – Matu was not so callous as that – but the theatre it entailed, the performative submission of his deference.

Amenet, looking on Matu, did not smile with her mouth, though her eyes shone. She touched him lightly on the forehead, releasing him from his posture, and said, "What do you think, Iviyat?"

"I think," said Viya shrewdly, "that our Vexa'Halat is clever enough in his role to be Vexa'Sehet, should he wish it. But yes," she said, forestalling reply to the former comment by waving a magnanimous hand between Matu and the worldwalkers. "By all means, Matuhasa. Make your attempt."

"As my lights command," said Matu, inclining his head. "If you would all step back from the doorway, please?"

Another theatrical request, but one that made sense, given that his next move was to hail the honoured swords – being Matu, he knew them both by name – and ask them, too, to stand down. They obeyed without question and with a great deal of relief, to the clear surprise of the several hovering worldwalkers.

As Matu approached, their collective anger morphed into uncertainty: one man fled to his cell, but another six remained, including one who was demonstrably non-human. This last was a short, hairless being whose flesh was covered in soft, lattice-fine scales more piscine than reptilian, their pale blue base patterned with black and gold false-eyes at throat and flank, with green stripes banding thir legs and forearms. Thei wore no clothes and had no genitals that Viya could recognise as such, though thei did have two small nipples. A faint webbed crest lay flattened against thir skull, rising slightly as Matu halted before the group.

Strangely – or not, depending on his priorities – it was the non-human he looked at first, head tilted in consideration: as tall as he was, Matu loomed over all the worldwalkers, but the alien especially. He appeared to realise this in the same instant Viya did – and then, just as he'd done for Amenet, he knelt to them, albeit on both knees this time, and waited to see what happened.

Beside her, Amenet tensed, her knuckles pale where she gripped her cane. "If they hurt him–"

"They won't," Viya said quickly. "The guards are still here."

"Even so–"

"Careful," Pix breathed, and when Viya looked back to the tableau, she understood why: Matu was stretching out a hand, palm-up, towards the scaled being.

Time slowed. The worldwalker blinked thir sideways-lidded eyes, extending a sharp-nailed, four-fingered hand with tentative precision. Butterfly-light, thei touched Matu's palm, and in that moment, the leap of the zuymet was almost audible, a whipcrack connection between them. Matu jolted in place, his spine going rigid beneath his enha – and then he spoke, a string of words in a sibilant, hissing, clicking language.

The non-human recoiled, snatching thir hand away, crest flattening hard again. One of the other worldwalkers shouted; another started towards Matu, only to be restrained by a third, while the remaining humans froze in place, watching as the non-human, recovering from thir shock, slowly lowered thir trembling hand. Faint pulses of colour rippled outwards through thir blue scales, yellow-green-white, thir skull-crest slowly lifting. Hesitantly, thei opened a mouth full of needle-sharp teeth and replied in kind. A whistling inflection coloured thir speech, as though to signify a question – or a challenge, Viya thought, heart leaping in sudden fear.

Matu hesitated, and for a horrible moment it looked as though the gambit had failed. But then – in response to what question, Viya didn't know – Matu ducked his head and pulled off his necklace of gold and pearls, proffering it to the alien.

The effect this had on the group was electric: all the humans began to talk at once – in a shared language, Viya realised in shock; as varied as their appearances were, she hadn't considered that some might share a heritage – while the non-human's crest came all the way alert, thir liquid eyes wide as thei looped the necklace over thir head. Thei spoke again, the clicks and hisses sounding somehow friendlier than before, and when Matu again extended a hand, the alien took it eagerly. This time, they clasped palms as equals, the protracted touch lasting almost a minute. It ended when the alien, with surprising strength, hauled Matu to his feet. Matu swayed a little, clicking something in reply, but didn't protest when one of the humans suddenly darted forwards and grabbed his hand in a copycat gesture, speaking eagerly all the while.

Matu laughed, the sound loud in the space, his free hand motioning in a *wait, wait* gesture. One of the human women made a disparaging sound, causing her companion to cuff her on the shoulder; meanwhile, the man holding Matu's hand went silent as the zuymet passed between them. *He translates worlds,* Viya thought with a pang of awe and envy. *Is any gift more powerful than that?*

When Matu finally let go, his fatigue was visible: he staggered a little, shoulders drooping, but managed to stand without support, voice rasping faintly as he addressed the group in that same, shared tongue. A brief back and forth followed: Viya didn't know what was being said, but it was very clear when Sene a Sati's death was finally mentioned. The worldwalkers recoiled in collective shock – even the non-human startled, suggesting thei understood that other language, too – their collective expressions running a gamut of fear, disbelief, anger.

Wearily, Matu continued talking, gesturing at Sene's room, until the alien stepped forward – a volunteer, or had thei been deputised? – and went to peek in through the door. Viya stared at thim in fascination: thir spine was slightly ridged, and when thei finally saw Sene's body, thir scales pulsed frantic colours again, a pattern of red-orange-red that seemed to connote distress. But when thei turned to look back to their fellows, crest dipping and raising again in some less obvious gesture, the other worldwalkers looked... relieved? It was hard to tell, but after another quick exchange with Matu – and with a few parting, suspicious glances towards the guards, Viya and the others – all six returned to their cells, leaving Matu, triumphant and exhausted, to report on his findings.

"I may need to sit down," he said, grinning wearily. He waved off Pix's hovering concern with fraternal aplomb, but was unable to do likewise with Amenet, who cupped his cheek in her palm and asked, thumb stroking tenderly, "Can you manage the stairs?"

"I think so," said Matu, "so long as we do it now."

With her wonderment satisfied, Viya's characteristic impatience returned in a sudden rush. Gritting her teeth against a demand for immediate answers, she set about issuing orders to the guards: which priests of which kin to summon, who was to clean the bloodied cell, the removal of the body. Both honoured swords bowed low to her over their cupped hands and set about obeying, Sathika staying to guard the hall while her burly companion dashed upstairs ahead of them, hurrying to fetch the requested help.

The rest of their party ascended more slowly, confined to Matu's faltering speed. Halfway up, Amenet shot Gwen an imploring look; without hesitation, Gwen slipped an arm around Matu's waist and took some of his weight, earning herself a grunt of grateful surprise.

"Thanks," he murmured, slightly sheepish. "I hadn't quite anticipated how tiring that would be. Teaching at speed, without a common language already in place – without a cultural frame of reference, or even a shared biology, for that matter – is… draining."

"And you did it twice," Gwen replied, "and are now wasting breath explaining to me instead of focusing on climbing stairs."

Matu huffed a laugh. "I never said I was smart. Vexa'Halat, not Vexa'Sehet, remember? Or I will be, once–"

"Just shut up and walk," Viya said, getting in ahead of Gwen, and Matu, with a panting grin of acknowledgement, complied.

Yena had expected to be made to wait, if only for the proper effect, but she hadn't thought it would take *this* long. Four possibilities for the delay occurred to her: there was some uniquely Ashasan reason for performing a firewalking penance at sunset or whatever distant, propitious hour was writ in law; the ritual itself required a lengthy set-up; the Second Voice wanted to keep her anxious, fearful and off-balance for as long as possible; or something important had happened – or was happening – that took precedence. Instinctively, she favoured the latter. Exactly what this occurrence might be, she didn't know, but in the long hours of her isolation in the novice's cell, she'd had plenty of time to dwell on each of the myriad alternatives. What if Kadeja's trial had started? What if there was news from Gwen or Safi? What if–

She shoved the thoughts aside, reminding herself that until she'd figured out how to walk through fire the delay was all to the good. *Boredom is not a good reason to wish to burn.*

Apart from the obvious, physical difficulties entailed by such a challenge, the problem was that beyond the wisdom contained in the Ryvke, the bulk of Vekshi customs and history were oral records, not written ones. Though Yena had grown up in a compound full of first-hand sources, the very fact of their removal from their homeland had tended to render them biased, unapproachable or both, with Yasha being a prickly case in point. Yena had studied the Ryvke for the same, inarticulate reasons that she'd learned to speak Lakik, and likewise in secret, borrowing Yasha's hidden copy and poring over the contents only at times when the matriarch's absence and the business of others ensured her privacy. For all that Yasha had held the compound accountable to Ashasa's law, her reckoning of what that meant had been at sufficient variance to the prevailing opinion as to earn her exile – what other such customs had she never deigned to mention? And beyond all that, the temple manifestly had its own traditions: even had Yasha been voluble on the subject, there was no guarantee that Yena would've learned everything.

And yet she felt maddeningly sure that firewalking *was* mentioned in the Ryvke, if only in passing. Something about Ashasa's scions, whatever that meant, but the relevant passage remained stubbornly beyond recall. The harder Yena chased the memory, the faster it retreated: all she could do was leave it be and hope that it surfaced in time to be of use. Sighing, she lay back down on the cot and tried for inner calm.

Something sailed through the window and struck her square in the forehead.

Yelping in shock and indignation – and pain, too; she'd be lucky not to have a bruise – Yena scrambled to her feet and cast around for the mystery object. She eventually found it under the cot: a fist-sized pot of some clear unguent, which, when the lid was removed, smelled faintly of copper. Inside the lid was a scrap of paper, stuck in place with a dab of the jar's contents. Frowning, Yena gently plucked it free and read the message, written in the spiky Vekshi script:

Cover yourself and hide the jar. Hurry.

Shredding the note, Yena stared at the jar's contents, considering the logical alternatives. Theory one: the unguent would protect her against fire and was meant to help her. Theory two: the unguent was flammable or poisonous, and would kill her either quickly or slowly, depending on intent. Theory three: the whole thing was a test of her faith in Ashasa, and by using the unguent, she'd fail.

"Arsegullet," Yena whispered. Not for the first time, she thought of Safi – specifically in this case, of the horrible scarring she'd incurred while sitting the Trial of Queens. (Zech had suffered likewise, but she couldn't think about Zech, or she'd be lost.) Violence and the sufferance of it were built into the bones of Vekshi law: what basis did she have to imagine that her penance wouldn't ask for blood? Fury built in her at the thought – did the Second Voice imagine the child she'd been had possessed the option of returning to Veksh to sit the rites that bestowed her soul-skin, when neither mother nor grandmother could have accompanied her or spoken on her behalf? Ought she to have stayed in a body outgrown from birth, the better to suit some future idea of obedience?

No. Be calm. You're overthinking, getting distracted. Yena inhaled and forced herself to consider the jar and its implications in a different light. *As I am, I cannot walk through fire. But possibly, with help, I might.* These were the only facts she could verify, and thus the lynchpins of her choice.

She stripped off her nek and started to apply the unguent, rubbing it into her skin. After a moment of lathering her forearms, as she might do with Pix's skin-softening cream, she forced herself to think more practically: the jar was small, and some body parts were more vital – and more vulnerable – than others. Swallowing, she sat down on the cot and applied a liberal coating to the soles of her feet, the palms of her hands, the sensitive skin of her breasts, inner thighs and between her legs – the thought of being burned *there* was terrifying – and, finally, to her face and throat, taking care not to neglect her ears and eyelids.

Only then did she deal with the rest of her body, though this latter coating was increasingly thin. She'd scraped the jar bare by the time she finished, and there were still patches of skin on her back and flanks that felt uncomfortably exposed. Just as worryingly, instead of remaining as a visible, tangible barrier, the unguent was quickly being absorbed, until only a faint gleam betrayed its usage. Gulping around a lump in her throat, Yena pulled her nek back on, sat down, remembered the injunction to remove the jar and, seeing no other alternative in the barren cell, lobbed it back out through the window.

Just in time: she'd scarcely reassured herself that the jar hadn't shattered or struck anyone when the door rattled open, revealing the same, disapproving priestess as before.

"Come," she said, voice unreadable as Yena rose to her feet. "It's time to face the fire."

"I shouldn't have left her," Rikan said, the words no less heartfelt for the repetition.

"Shh," said Luy, kissing the nape of his neck. "It wasn't your fault." With just a touch of humour, he added, "Even my bloodmother said so, and she's a very wise woman. Trust her word, if not mine."

It was a low trick, appealing to Rikan's obvious sense of duty, but one that seemed to work. Rikan sighed, rolling so that they were face to face, the two of them curled in the guard's narrow bed. Rikan dipped his head, the slight withdrawal belied by the calloused palm he slid up Luy's bare chest. It was sensual, not sexual, but welcome in either case: they'd removed shoes and tunics – and, in Rikan's case, armour – on lying down, but in deference to the awaited arrival of whichever representative of Nihun's Kin would be tasked with taking Rikan's statement, they'd kept their trousers on. Luy set his own hand to Rikan's hip, thumb brushing the bone above his waistband, and waited for him to speak.

"I've seen death before," he said, finally. "And ever since Vex Ralan's passing... well. I hardly need say what the city's been like. But this, the ambassador... it strikes hard, that she'd choose such an end with the danger gone."

"Because she was safe?"

"Not that," said Rikan, softly. "Because maybe she was right to fear she wasn't." He looked up again, gaze troubled. Luy sucked in breath. "What Leoden did to her – what he did to all those worldwalkers – he did that on our watch, Shavaktiin. Yours and mine. We were both here, in the palace, and we saw nothing, knew nothing, and likely couldn't have fixed it if we had. And I don't know about you, but that shames me."

A lump formed in Luy's throat. "It shames me, too."

Rikan slid his hand to Luy's ribs, the touch oddly hesitant. "I haven't asked it of you, as I know you saved Cuivexa Iviyat, and if none of them who rule in this has doubted you, it's not my place to start. Always figured asking questions was trouble for a man like me. But maybe... maybe there's times when not asking is worse."

"You want to know if I knew," said Luy, softly. "If I stood at Leoden's side and let him just –"

"No," said Rikan quickly. "Not that. If I figured you for complicity, I'd never have bedded you." He flashed a quick smile, almost shy, and not for the first time Luy found himself wondering how such a man was yet without a mahu'kedet. "I want to know why you came here in the first place. I'd thought at first it had to do with your lady mother, but she's not a Shavaktiin, and whatever her reasons they're plainly not yours. So. Why work for Leoden?"

"Now *that*," breathed Luy, "is a very difficult question."

"If it helps," said Rikan, "I can go first."

Luy blinked. "I'm sorry?"

"About why I'm here. Or rather–" he sighed, looking down again, "–about why I stayed. Not as there's much to the story, but still. I served here under Vex Ralan, though not with any distinction, and when Leoden was first touted as successor I paid it little mind. But what he did to the lady Amenet... it was wrong, Luy. I knew it then as sure as I know it now; as sure as I saw his arakoi fill our ranks and take the places of those who died or left when they had the chance."

"But you stayed?"

"But I stayed." Rikan squeezed his flank, a brief, rough pressure against his ribs. "The guards who left on principle were good folk, but most who replaced them weren't. And I thought, if Leoden got his way in that, that'd be another type of wrong all over, because there'd be no one left to check such evils as happen when backs are turned. Not saying I always succeeded, mind, and there wasn't a damn thing I could do about him keeping Cuivexa Iviyat penned in her rooms, but... other things. Smaller, maybe, to them as deal with nations, but I caught more than one arakoi bullying the servants, or worse than bullying, and I did what I could to check it."

"You're a good man," said Luy, and leaned in to kiss him, shallow and sweet. Halaya would like Rikan, and the thought of her approval – of their meeting, even – was a complex ache in his chest. Shavaktiin were not formally forbidden to marry, and yet it was preferred that they did not, the better to keep service to the Great Story as the primary narrative in their own lives. Informal relationships with other Shavaktiin were viewed in a more favourable light, and while those with grown or distant children were admitted to the order, the birth of a new child meant resigning an active role for all parents, becoming sworn lorekeepers instead of participants.

Once, Luy had thought it all a sensible division; increasingly, though, he chafed at it. Neither his bloodmother's wanderlust nor her involvement in distant politics had ever diminished her familial relationships, nor had her role in their mahu'kedet restricted her elsewhere. It was one of the reasons why, despite his faith in the Great Story, he'd felt confident enough in his divining of it to strike out on his own, against the instruction of his elders. Now, though... now, he wondered.

With a parting brush to Rikan's lips, he pulled back, trying to parse his thoughts into some semblance of order.

"The Shavaktiin believe that stories are the foundation of worlds, and that one story above and encompassing all others, the Great Story, is our map to the best possible ending. To that end, we look for signs, for ways to keep the Story on its intended path, but there are... there can be disagreements as to interpretation, where to go, what to do, how to do it. And when Leoden was crowned as Vex – when my bloodmother and her allies realised the extent of his deception and were forced to regroup – I went deeper into the dreamscape than I'd ever been before. And what I saw... I knew someone needed to come here, to help, to intervene. But the elders of the Shavaktiin enclave disagreed. They refused to sanction my actions, and so I was forced to come alone. And for that, I am... not outcast, exactly – I still belong to the Shavaktiin – but marked as a renegade."

"You have some supporters, though?" asked Rikan. "That is, I had thought... I've heard of allied Shavaktiin in Yevekshasa, them as aided Cuivexa Iviyat in her escape. Are they not your fellows?"

"They are," Luy admitted, "but to their detriment. Their support of me has likewise set them at odds with the enclave." He hesitated, and then said, with a certain fond exasperation, "My Halaya, of whom I've spoken, is among them."

Rikan smiled. "And does she follow your example through faith alone, or did you sway her with–" he grinned, hand sliding to squeeze playfully at Luy's ass, "–more creative methods?"

It was a teasing question, lightly asked, and so the accompanying sting of self-recrimination Luy felt at his disgrace having touched Halaya was lighter than usual; light enough that he answered honestly.

"I don't rightly know," he said, and Rikan, sensing the serious undercurrent, converted his grope to a caress, moving infinitesimally closer. "I would not wish to insult her judgement or her intelligence by suggesting affection for me could lead her to disregard both, did she truly think my interpretation flawed; and yet I can't help wondering if it cast the deciding vote."

"A friend can be as biased as a lover," Rikan pointed out. "More so, even, depending on the cause. As well to wish you'd swayed an enemy instead, the better to see their defection as proof of your rightness."

Luy felt a rush of affection for the man, laughing as he leaned in to place a kiss at the corner of Rikan's mouth. "What business is it of yours, to be so sensible? How am I meant to wallow in charismatic self-doubt if you cut me straight off with a reasoned argument?"

"Well," said Rikan, cheek dimpling as he pretended to give the matter serious consideration, "you could always tell me, in detail, about that deep dreamscape vision as led you here. Really rake through the particulars for signs of flawed reconnaissance, bad reasoning, that sort of thing."

"I co–" Luy began, then pulled up cold. A terrible chill washed through him, crown to soles.

Rikan's lips twitched as though in anticipation of a joke, but as the seconds ticked by and Luy remained silent, his expression turned worried.

"Luy?"

"It's gone." The words were faint with disbelief and no small degree of fear. "I can't… Rikan, I don't understand, it's *gone*–"

"What's gone?"

"The memory!" Luy sat bolt upright in bed, heart pounding. He looked at Rikan with desperation, struggling to articulate the sick, cold void that lay where the vision should be. "I can talk around it, I know that there's a vision to miss, but when I try – when I reach for it, for the details, there's just this, this *emptiness*, and I can't – I don't–"

"Luy. Breathe." Rikan sat up beside him, one hand on his shoulder, the other gently tilting his chin so that Luy looked at him. "Look at me. Can you breathe?"

Luy sucked in air, nodding on a ragged inhalation. Rikan breathed with him, clear and slow, until Luy could manage again. But still that terrible feeling remained, unmissable once noticed. It was like discovering he'd lost a tooth, the compulsion to probe the socket more powerful even than the need to feel whole. Luy stared at Rikan, stupid with the shock of it – and then the logic snapped into place, and he shuddered all over.

"Oh, gods. He took it." He gripped the sheets, knuckles aching. "Leoden, with the ahunemet – whatever he did to the worldwalkers, to Sene a Sati, he did it to me, too. Don't you see?" And then, in English, with a vehemence he seldom felt, "He *stole* my fucking *memory*!"

8
The Sun's Mouth

Fire filled the room, blossoming from raw stone like some impossible flower, red and gold and white. The room was easily twenty-five paces from door to door, though the flames were thick enough that Yena had to squint to see her intended point of egress. Heat rolled out in waves, like standing before Ashasa's own forge, its shimmer distorting the air. It would have been terrifying even without the expectation that she cross unscathed, a task that looked less like penance and more like suicide. What if the unguent didn't work, or was sweated away before she could cross the room, or caused her to burn even faster? Yena had imaged a bonfire, perhaps, or a floor of hot coals, but nothing on this scale.

"Pass through the sun's mouth, Yena a Trishka," the Second Voice said. They stood side by side on the threshold of fire, but not alone: both the chamber in which they stood and its twin beyond the fire were filled with attending priestesses, just as had happened after her frozen vigil. "Pass, and show your penitence."

It was a special type of madness that Yena even considered it – Vekshi madness, Sashi would call it – and yet she didn't know what else to do. There wasn't a soul in Veksh who could stop her from privately mourning Zech as a sister, penitence or not, but if she failed, she lost her chance to continue what

Zech had started, which was a far more fitting memorial than lonely grief or abstract justice could ever be. She looked at the Second Voice, searching for some hint as to what was expected of her, the right choice to make, but the priestess's expression was sternly blank, like a door closed to conversation.

Yena looked at the burning room. The fire was magically sustained, burning solidly on floor, walls, ceiling, the base carpet of flames erupting in violent, white-hot jets at irregular intervals. She gulped, thinking distantly that it was a waste of space to dedicate an entire room to fire, assuming it had no dual purpose the rest of the time–

The sun's mouth.

She blinked, thoughts racing in belated recognition of the phrase. Where had she heard it before? Though she was sweating fiercely from the radiant heat, her blood chilled when it finally came to her – a snippet of lore gleaned, not from the Ryvke, but from eavesdropping as her mother and grandmother speculated about the source of Kadeja's expulsion from Veksh and the temple.

"Well?" asked the Second Voice, a touch of impatience colouring her voice. "Will you cross? Or do you refuse the burden of penitence?"

"I do not refuse my penitence," Yena said, pitching her voice to carry. "But the sun's mouth is a trial and punishment reserved for proven heretics, which I am not."

An angry murmur from the assembled priestesses; Yena could only hope it was in her favour. Ignoring the pinched set of the Second Voice's mouth, she added quickly, "I am, of course, willing to accept a fire penance – I wouldn't be here if I wasn't. But I am not a heretic, and this is not a trial."

"It should be!" hissed the Second Voice. Her sudden vehemence took Yena aback. The priestess was in her fifties, rake-thin and hatchet-faced; compared to the Third Voice, whom she outranked, her youth spoke volumes about her ambitious ascent through Ashasa's hierarchy. She jabbed a bony finger into Yena's chest, hard enough that Yena, who hadn't been expecting it, stumbled closer to the door. "Look at you! Child of an exile's exile, hair uncut and flesh remade by heretic gods, and daring to claim kinship with a queen who ought never have won the name?" Her pale eyes glinted in the firelight, needle-sharp and scalding. "I am the Second Voice of Ashasa Herself, and *I* say you are a heretic!"

Lightning-fast, she gripped Yena hard by the scruff of her neck and hauled her bodily forwards. Yena yelped, struggling to free herself, but the priestess's hold was inexorable. Other women were shouting now, but all Yena heard was the roar of fire, that brilliant inferno blooming ahead like bright-hot death.

"Sun's mouth take you!" the Second Voice cried, and flung Yena into the fire.

Yena twisted as she fell, eyes wide with shock and terror as the door slammed shut. In the split second before the heat truly hit, she clamped down hard on the urge to scream – *there's no air in here, you can't scream, you'll suffocate, just move, move!* – and flailed for balance, barely managing to keep upright.

And then there was nothing but fire, bright and hot and raw and searing, lashing flame-tongues edged like knives that ate her skin and cut her eyes and licked the stubble from her scalp as she stumbled forwards, burning aching shrieking red and her soles were scorched and her arms and face – her nek burned up like a tallow-candle, wreathing her in oilburn-pain, and somehow she was still moving, lurching desperately towards the exit. She shut her eyes and shut her mouth and slip-slid-shuddered through an agony that felt both motionless and infinite, throat aching with the need to scream and needles in her lips and thighs and every scrap of skin a blister, burning down to bloodboiled nothing–

She burst into air, and fell, and sobbed, and fainted.

•••

There was no particular reason why, after leaving the worldwalker barracks, they'd ended up in Viya's rooms, and yet she felt strangely flustered by the choice of venue. As they waited for Gwen to return with Trishka – the former having suggested, not unreasonably, that it was wise to include the latter in their confidence – Viya busied herself with making tea. Matu certainly looked in need of a restorative, and so she made it a point to pour him the first cup, even though they were in her rooms and that honour, by custom, was more properly hers.

"Oh!" said Matu, startled by the courtesy. His long fingers wrapped around the dainty ceramic, flexing slightly against the warmth. "Thank you, Iviyat."

"Drink up," said Viya, trying and failing to cover her flush as both Matu and Amenet smiled at her. Her future marriage-mates were both very beautiful, and Viya, who yet considered herself too young for carnal speculation, was not so far removed from its spectre as to be wholly unmoved by the fact.

Mercifully, she was saved from further embarrassment by the arrival of Gwen and Trishka, who said their hellos and took their seats at the table. Viya poured the next cup of tea for herself, as was proper, and then went around the table until everyone was served. Matu sipped and swallowed, colour slowly returning to his face, his body angled subtly towards Amenet. Everyone waited patiently, and after a moment, he began to speak.

"The worldwalkers are traders," he said. "Or at least, the ones I spoke to are, and possibly more – ever since we unchained them, they've been trying to find out about the others, but they're encountering the same trust issues we are. After what Leoden did, nobody down there is eager to talk to strangers, and I can't say I blame them. They only accepted my overture because I demonstrated a willingness to trade with them – it's why I gave them the necklace."

Gwen blinked, taken aback. "You mean they're all from the same world?"

Matu shook his head. "Yes and no. They're from a place... I don't think it's accurate to call it a world. The closest Kenan translation for the name they gave it is *ko'asthasi*." An archaic term, one it took Viya a moment to place, before she remembered her moon-tales: asthasi were the hidden roads between the mortal world and the home of the gods, while ko was a genitive form of an old word for *place*. Matu paused, considering this linguistic puzzle, then added, "In English, I suppose, you might call it... a *crossroads*? Or a *nexus*, perhaps?"

"*Nexus* suits," said Gwen. "Although–"

"Nexus, then," said Viya, indicating with a short, irritable wave of her hand that she didn't care what alien language the place was named in, so long as they could move on to discussing it. "In what sense is it not a world?"

"It's hard to explain – hard for me, anyway," he added, shooting Gwen an appraising look. "The way the zuymet works, you acquire flashes of concepts along with new words, and when I looked for their name for home – I was trying to steer my acquisition, keep it to relevant terms – the images that came through were... peculiar."

"Whose images, though?" asked Amenet. "Is this from the humans, or the, ah... scaled person?"

Matu frowned. "Both," he said, after a moment. Then, forestalling Pix's disbelief, "No, no – let me try to explain, I'm not being deliberately obtuse." He took another sip of tea, his now-bare throat working gently. "The scaled person, as you have it, is a member of a race called the Qashqa. Thir true name is–" a fluted series of noises, inexpertly rendered, "–but goes by Rill among humans, who thei call, ah... well, it's an affectionate-derogatory term, of sorts, and I suspect the meaning is more obvious in their own language, but it came through as something like *mute-skins*. And I mention this," he said, again catching Pix's impatience, "because Rill speaks two languages – thir own, the Qashqa tongue, and the shared human trade-tongue, as thei belong to a Qashqa enclave within the Nexus, which is... close, somehow, to their world of origin, though I wasn't sure if that meant geographically or as measured by some other criteria."

Viya felt the hairs on her neck stand up.

"A difficult concept to discuss in Kenan," Gwen murmured, almost to herself. "Your terms are so much more magical than the scientific."

"And that matters why?" asked Viya, striving to sound more curious than irked.

"Without the right language," Gwen said, wryly, "linguistic problems are somewhat hard to explain."

Viya opened her mouth to protest that she'd only reiterated the problem rather than answering the question, then closed it again when she caught Gwen's meaning. The worldwalker flashed her a small, quick smile, then said, in a tone that suggested she was choosing her words very carefully, "This Nexus, Matu. Was it a natural place, do you think? Or more of a... a domed metal realm in the firmament?"

Across the table, Matu jolted. "You're thinking it might be a, a ..." he fumbled for words, then said – completely nonsensically, to Viya's mind, "...an upper-sky waystation?" And then he winced, chuckling sharply. "Yes, I quite see what you mean about the scientific."

"An *upper-sky waystation*?" Amenet said, completely bemused. "Yemaya's breath, what does that mean?"

"It's a very poor translation of an English term," Gwen said, quickly. "A thing we call a *space station*. It means, ah... a sort of moving city in the firmament, beyond the curve of the world."

"Like the realm of Ke and Na?" Viya asked.

"Not quite," said Gwen, shifting uncomfortably in her seat. "I mean something made by people."

"By people!" Viya exclaimed. "But that's–" she wanted

to say *sacrilegious*, or maybe just *impossible*, but remembered in time that Gwen was speaking of other worlds, and who was she to judge on either count? "–extraordinary," she said instead, and earned herself another pleased expression in return.

Pix, by contrast, looked almost offended; Amenet merely appalled. Trishka remained unflappable, listening with characteristic calm.

"Worldwalkers," Pix muttered, rolling her eyes.

"I don't think so," Matu said at last, in answer to Gwen's original question. "These worldwalkers have a word–"

"What, another one?" Pix quipped wryly.

Matu shot her an unusually venomous glare. "Please, dear sister – by all means, denigrate the labour of a magic you neither possess nor understand! I'm sure the zuymet looks simple enough when you've never learned another tongue, but no language ever maps perfectly to another. Words are tools altered to fit the needs of their speakers, and what one people requires, another disdains, or is yet to invent, or cannot comprehend. These traders think of *borders*, and their commonest word for it doesn't mean the same as ours – to them, it's a sort of looping edge, a static place where reality blurs, where the bravest merchants and explorers go to chart a map that is never fixed, yet ever-necessary. If you can offer a clean translation of *that*, dear Pixeva, then by all means enlighten us – but if you cannot, then I'll thank you to keep your burrs from my bedroll and *listen*."

It was, Viya thought, the sharpest rebuke she'd ever heard Matu give his sister, and judging by Pix's current angry flush, she knew it. Shoulders taut, the courtier opened her mouth to respond – but Trishka, in a sudden breathless burst, got in ahead of her.

"These borders," she said urgently, gaze fixed on Matu. "Would you call them *metmirai*?"

The word she'd used was, if possible, even more archaic

than ko'asthasi, and while she vaguely recognised it, Viya was startled realise that she didn't know the meaning. Too proud to ask aloud, she cast a hopeful look at Amenet, but for once her betrothed was as puzzled as she; as was Pix, for that matter.

This time, it was Trishka who rescued them, Matu having been stunned into uncharacteristic silence. "It means... magic-ragged, I think, is the most modern approximation, though that still misses a great deal of the subtlety. It's a word we really only use now in myths and moon-tales, referring to something – most often a place, but very rarely an item or person – destroyed or reduced by magic, though destroyed in what way, we don't really know."

Matu looked thunderstruck. "Gods damn me, but I just might," he said, staring at Trishka with a sort of startled awe. "How in the worlds did you make that leap?"

"Something I once heard from a daughter of Ke's Kin," said Trishka. "It was years ago, now – I won't bore you with the details of how I met her, but we fell to discussing the jahudemet, and in the course of our conversation, she told me that, had I been trained in the temple, I likely would've been taken 'deeper in'. I'd never heard the phrase before, and the priestess said that, within the temple, those with the strongest gifts are bound most tightly to the order's secrets, tapped for mentorship early on and trained along different lines. Being of lesser ability herself, she was almost as much an outsider to those mysteries as I was; all she knew was what her fellows called them. When I told her I could make portals she said that I should be careful of making too many, lest I leave my home metmirai. I'd never heard of that, either, and she laughed said it was a temple saying, something they told the younger acolytes when they first started to use their magic – not a serious warning, she said, but a joke to instil caution, the same way you might tell a child not to break their neck during play. I let it pass at the time, but later I wondered if there was more than habit to the usage; if it was really meant as a hint to those who go deeper in."

Trishka spread her hands. "Whenever I open portals for Gwen, I have to be careful not to overuse a particular location, lest that patch of world rip open. That's easier here, where magic works smoothly, but on Earth, it's harder. Fewer places are suitable to begin with, and they tend to thin more swiftly. We lost so much knowledge in the Years of Shadow, and metmirai as a concept is, I think, at least that old. And so I wonder – what if it originally referred to the jahudemet, to the consequences of its overuse? Our moon-tales mention portals and worldwalkers, but though we here–" she gestured around the table, "–know better than most how real they are, most Kenans hold such concepts to be the province of tales alone. We only think my gifts are rare because we see no portal-magic otherwise, but among Ke's Kin, their strongest jahudemet-users are taken deeper in, initiated into mysteries and secrets known to few others.

"Perhaps I'm not so unique, after all; or at the very least, perhaps I wasn't always. That anchored portal, the one Leoden found – it's not just built with the jahudemet. I've been trying to figure it since the Cuivexa took me down there–" she shot Viya a grateful look, which Viya returned with a controlled nod, heart racing at Trishka's words, "–and I think the other element is the *maramet*. And I don't just mean as an interwoven magic," she added, over Pix's startled hiss at such a reference to blood magic. "I mean that the portal was mortared with blood, the blood of those with the jahudemet. That's why it's so strong, so stable – it's like the Vekshi effect, the way they use multiple magic-users to create a single oversized portal, but done in death. A permanent gestalt." She hesitated, then said, voice low, "It would have cost a great number of lives to make, I think. To have lasted this long, to have such a reach, the maramet binding magic to blood to stone – many tens of deaths, at least. Perhaps a hundred. Perhaps even more than that."

An eerie silence fell across the room.

"Thorns and godshit," Amenet whispered. "Vexa Yavin was truly monstrous."

"So," said Gwen, after a moment had passed. "The worldwalkers Leoden found all come from the same world, this Nexus, which isn't so much a world entire as a bordered place, whose edges are metmirai. We don't know why he wanted them, except that he robbed their memories for information, and did the same – again, inexplicably – to Sene a Sati, the former Vekshi ambassador."

"They weren't the only ones," said a new voice, heavily.

Viya turned, as did the others: the speaker was Luy, entering from the antechamber with Rikan and a son of Nihun's Kin in tow, having been admitted by the guard. Luy looked grey-faced, almost ill, and Gwen was on her feet in an instant, concern in her eyes as she looked him over.

"What do you mean, they weren't the only ones?" Gwen asked. There was a general shuffling as room was made at the table; the priest declined to sit, preferring to stand nearby, but chairs were swiftly found for Rikan and Luy, the pair of them sitting hip to hip between Gwen and Trishka.

"I mean," said Luy, "that my memory of why I came here – the vision I had in the dreamscape that set me at odds with the Shavaktiin enclave – has been taken from me, and more besides. Honoured Halunet has confirmed it." He waved a hand at the priest, whose expression was caught somewhere between anger and apology.

"Tell me," Gwen said, voice threaded with steel.

Halunet bowed over his cupped palms, acknowledging the room as a whole. "Cuivexa, my ladies, lords, I have two reports to make, if you will allow it. The first, as you've heard, concerns the unlawful use of the ahunemet on Luy ore Jhesa'yu of the Shavaktiin; the second concerns the final words of the Vekshi ambassador, Sene a Sati, as witnessed by the guard Rikan ki Anaket." He paused, and Viya waved for him to continue. "Per your request for a member of Nihun's Kin to assess Rikan's memory, I arrived at the guard's quarters where I found both gentlemen in a state of some distress. At Luy's request, I assessed his memories for interference, just as I did the ambassador, and I regret to say that I found some evidence of it, though effected with far more surgical precision. Whatever memories were taken – and I can say that there was more than one, though thankfully still few – were removed with such care and delicacy as to make the loss almost undetectable to the subject. Which is to say, unless Luy attempts to think directly about whatever was taken from him, he will not – indeed, cannot – feel the absence."

"I tried to tell Rikan what brought me here," Luy said, voice tight. "And I knew that there was something to remember, but when I reached for the details, it was just… gone."

Matu and Pix both swore; Gwen took her son's hand and gripped it, hard. Amenet and Trishka both looked horrified, but Viya felt a surge of fear so profound, she almost choked.

"Honoured Halunet," she said, voice shaking, "would you… that is, would you mind assessing me, too, to see… to see if I have suffered similar interference? If it can't be readily detected, I… I would fear – I lived with Leoden, too, and–"

"Of course, Cuivexa," said Halunet, saving her from her stammering. Moving around the table, he came to stand at her shoulder, one hand hovering lightly beside her temple. "With your permission?"

"Please," Viya breathed, and shut her eyes at the gentle brush of his magic. Around her, it felt as though the whole room was holding its breath, and when Halunet finally withdrew the ahunemet, she felt her lungs seize.

"You are intact, Cuivexa."

Viya's noise of relief was perilously close to a whimper. She opened her eyes again, forcing herself to meet Luy's gaze. "I'm sorry," she whispered. "I don't mean to detract from you. But I had to know."

"Don't apologise for that," Luy said, and his voice, too, was raw. "Gods, I'm just happy he drew the line somewhere."

"And the ambassador?" Amenet asked, recalling them to the moment. "What of her last words?"

"I reviewed Rikan's memories of the event, and transcribed them as best I could – bearing in mind, of course, that I speak no Vekshi." Reaching into his robes, Halunet withdrew a sheet of neatly folded parchment. Following the line of Amenet's gaze, he stepped away from Viya and handed it to Matu, who took it with murmured thanks. Gently, he unfolded the document, brow furrowing as he read. His lips quirked, though not disapprovingly.

"For someone with no knowledge of the language, Honoured Halunet, you've done a fair job at deciphering the cadence – very little run-on, good word separation."

Halunet looked surprised, but pleased. "Thank you, my lord."

Matu waved a hand, not looking up from the parchment. As he read, his expression altered, sliding into shock. He glanced up sharply when he was done, studying Halunet, but didn't insult the priest by asking if he was sure of his accuracy.

"Well?" Pix demanded, getting in ahead of Viya. "What does it say?"

"Or rather, what did Sene a Sati say," Matu murmured. He resumed his seat, looking oddly pale. "She was distressed on waking, as Rikan reported – crying, shouting in Vekshi. According to this, she was begging Ashasa's forgiveness for her transgressions." He began to read aloud, an uncommon shake to his voice. "*Mother Sun, forgive me, but I told them everything. All my research, all my secrets, every truth I vowed to keep – they know it, and they'll use it, and I can't – I should never have looked for Vikasa, never questioned – the Archive was right to demand my silence, I am a fool, a fool – I've killed us, don't you see? I've doomed Veksh and Kena both, and shamed Ashasa with my pride, my weakness. I cannot bear it!"* He put down the parchment, expression grim.

Silence filled the room like fluid flooding a cyst.

"Shit," said Pix. She looked around, bewildered. "What does any of it mean?"

"And what – or who – is Vikasa?" said Amenet.

"I don't know," said Gwen. She looked at Louis, at Matu and Viya, and shivered. "But I'd wager it's nothing good."

Saffron ran, the world a liminal blur.

It was early evening, parts of the sky still gleaming umber-blue within the dominant black, the moon a Cheshire grin. It was maybe twenty minutes since she'd left the house, and in that time, she'd barely stopped running, terrified of what would happen if she were caught. Her initial departure had been sudden and shocking enough that neither her family nor Ms Mays had immediately realised she was fleeing more than just the room: their belated outcry had only come with the telltale opening creak of the front door. With her father's shouts drifting on the still air, she'd turned sharply down a pedestrian track between two rows of houses, then cut across someone's garden to access the bush, not wanting to stay where a car could easily catch her.

The bushland was national park, thin strips of greenery both paralleling and merging with the residential areas like the interlaced fingers of two mismatched hands. Not so long ago, Saffron would have flinched from running through it barefoot, as she did now – she hadn't had time to grab her sneakers, let alone don them – but after weeks of shoeless travel in the wilds of Kena, her soles were leather-tough. Which was just as well: as dark as it was, and as fast as she was moving, she was in no position to pick a dainty path through the scrub. Broken glass was the real danger, but so far, she hadn't encountered any: just sticks, stones, gumnuts and other such native detritus.

Through the trees, she glimpsed the occasional flash of suburban streetlights, pools of molten white like profane halos. There was little traffic sound, but above the ragged rasp of her breathing, she caught occasional birdnoise: the *brp-brp-brp* of a startled brush turkey, the rushing flap of nameless wings, and from far overhead the mournful cries of gang-gangs, presaging rain.

Beyond the occasional heartfelt wish for luck, Saffron had never prayed before, but in the silent clamour of her thoughts, she did so now – though not to anything so tenuously capricious as a deity.

Trishka, can you see me? Luy, can you hear me? Please, please, help – I need a portal, I need a way out – I need to come back to you all, to come home–

A sob burst on her lips like a soap bubble. *Home.* She didn't know if she meant Kena itself, the people who lived there or the possibilities they represented; only that it now lay ahead of her, not behind.

She stumbled over a dropped branch, wincing as a sharp stick scraped a red line up the side of her foot, but forced herself to keep going. If she could just get to the train station ahead of her parents and Ms Mays – if they hadn't thought ahead to where she might run, or drafted others in the search – then she could put enough distance between herself and them to... what? Fall safely asleep, then beg Luy in the dreamscape for a portal? It was a horrible, fragile plan, and the fact that she didn't have an alternative was hardly reassuring. She barked with laughter, dodging around the silvery bole of a greygum as her chosen path suddenly ended, with the typical abruptness of the suburban bush, on the edge of a cul-de-sac. A loose semicircle of houses sat opposite, and there, beside them, the thin, snaking footpath that led to the station.

Saffron slowed to a fast walk, wincing slightly as her smarting feet encountered the loose gravel of the road: it wasn't unbearable, and she wasn't taking damage, but that didn't mean it was comfortable. The flat cement of the pavement felt like a balm by contrast, and as she jogged lightly towards the station, she considered anew the problem of her own conspicuousness. Barefoot, scarred, tattooed, shaven-headed – *my kingdom for a hoodie!* – and clearly lacking a bag or wallet, she made a memorable sight. The sole positive was her lack of a school uniform, which would've been doubly damning given the hour: instead, she was wearing black drawstring pants and an oversized grey T-shirt, clothes chosen for their softness and comfort value prior to Ms Mays' arrival.

As she started up the ramp that led into the station proper, she slowed to a walk, fighting the urge to duck her head. It was a small stop, which meant that she could access the platform without having to pass through a ticket barrier. A train was just pulling out on one side, and Saffron felt a lurch of relief that its departure had emptied the place, but when she glanced at the electronic boards, she flinched to see that the next arrival wasn't for seven more minutes. She swallowed, clenching her hands to stop their trembling. *It's not that long,* she told herself, walking up to the far end of the platform. *They won't be here yet. I can manage seven whole minutes without–*

"Saffron?"

She stopped dead, rigid with fear. The voice – familiar, feminine – had come from behind her, and with the end of the platform just meters away there was nowhere to run. Heart pounding, she forced herself to turn.

It was Glitter James-Michaels, still in her school uniform, a worried look on her face. Saffron wanted to cry.

"Hi, Lita," she croaked.

They stared at each other, silent seconds ticking by. Lita cocked her head, a look of sudden understanding washing across her face.

"You're running," she said.

It wasn't a question. Saffron nodded, not trusting her voice.

"I did that, once," Lita said. Her voice was meditative, though her eyes were sharp. "In the holidays, just after… well, after. You know. They found me, though. Brought me back. Obviously." She shrugged, lips twisting. "Didn't really know where I was going, anyway. Just that it was *away*."

Saffron gulped. "I know. Where I'm going." *I think. I hope.*

"Really?"

"Yes."

Lita considered this. "They're chasing you right now? I mean, you don't have any shoes or whatever, so I'm guessing–"

"Yeah."

"Shit." Lita laughed, crooked and wry. And then, as they both caught the squeal of tyres from the station carpark, followed swiftly by a car door slam and the sound of running feet, "Oh, *shit*."

"Please." Saffron barely stopped herself from grabbing Lita's wrist. They were the only two people in sight, the platform empty of any other travellers. She glanced around for a hiding place, gaze lighting on the platform's toilet kiosk. "*Please*, Lita."

Lita hesitated, and for a horrible moment Saffron thought she was done for. Then:

"Yeah," breathed Lita. "Yeah, OK." She gave Saffron a shove towards the kiosk. "Go on, get in, quick!"

Saffron made a noise that wasn't quite *thank you* and complied, hurrying into the tiny, vacant stall and holding the door shut from the inside. She didn't dare lock it, in case the red OCCUPIED somehow gave her away, but clung to the handle and crouched down, heart rabbiting as she waited.

There was a vent on the lower half of the door, a series of angled metal slats. You couldn't see in through them from the outside, but if you put your face to them from the inside, as Saffron did now, you could just see out, a thin glimpse of the platform's edge and Lita's shoes and legs.

And then a second person appeared, tan slacks and brown loafers. *Dad*, Saffron thought, and bit her lip, straining to hear him through the door.

"...seen her? We need – she needs to come home, we have to talk–"

"Yeah," said Lita, "I've seen her."

Saffron stopped breathing, tasting betrayal in her mouth like blood, like spinal fluid shaken loose by some indescribable blow. It was Ruby all over again, and how had she been so *stupid*? She clung to the door handle, fingers slippery with sweat, and thought wildly that if she reached over and locked herself in, at least they'd have to fight to get her out–

"You just missed her, though," said Lita, calmly apologetic. "She caught the Sydney train, the one that left a few minutes ago? She ran on just as the doors were closing – almost got her foot stuck. They've probably passed the next station by now, but if you hurry–"

She didn't catch her father's reply, assuming he made one; just watched as he turned and fled the station, footsteps echoing loud as slaps as he bolted back up the stairs. She stayed where she was, dizzy with relief, for a count of sixty, then stood up, wiping her hands on her shirt.

She'd barely opened the door when Lita turned, caught her gaze and mouthed, *No, wait*, her fingers flicking in urgent negation. Saffron froze in place and jerked the door almost closed again, peeping out through the crack between wood and frame.

The rattlerush of an incoming train filled the station, and for a moment Lita was a fixed point, silhouetted against its silver bulk. And then she smiled – a fey, triumphant thing – and raised a hand in mock salute, two fingertips brushing her temple. The gesture squeezed deep in Saffron's chest, but there was no way to return it, no space in which to call out any last words – like *thank you*, or *tell Lyssi I'm sorry* – before the train doors opened and Lita stepped aboard. She was briefly obscured by a scatter of exiting commuters, then reappeared as the train doors shut, still smiling through the glass.

Saffron watched the train pull out of the station, whisking Lita away. Slowly, the platform emptied again; she stepped out of hiding, breathing deeply. The night air was cool on her skin, and she was alone.

A warm, sharp sensation burned down her throat and into her stomach, as though she'd swallowed a hot coal. She felt a brief tug behind her navel, a jolt of longing and something else, a feeling she couldn't name. The hairs on her arms and neck stood up; she was wreathed in silence, atoms, space.

Colour sparked in the grey-lit air at the end of the platform – a burst of light, like a tiny firework. Saffron walked towards it, joy coiling in her heart as the light steadied and grew, irising outwards into a portal. Its heart was black, and the world around and behind it was all in shadow: only a faint ring of rainbow-edged magic delineated the edges. It was perfectly circular, a CGI lens flare come to life, such a beautiful, timely rescue that Saffron was halfway through before she realised, with a sickening jolt, that it bore no resemblance to Trishka's magic. She faltered on the threshold of worlds, then made her choice and stumbled through, the station vanishing from sight as the portal snapped shut behind her.

Saffron blinked and looked around – and stilled.

"Oh, *shit*," she whispered, awed and more than a little terrified.

"Huh," said Leoden, cocking his head. "You're not what I expected."

PART 2
Whose Margin Fades

9

Through & Into Fire

Yena woke to a bright slash of pain across her arm and the sounds of a heated argument. The combination was so disorienting and her head so muzzy that she didn't think to cry out. Instead, she bucked against the – bed? Floor? Table? Whatever it was she was lying on – and struggled to blink the gunk from her eyes. *Context. I need context. What happened?*

"–there!" said one of the arguers, in a tone half relief, half triumph. "How's *that* for your precious stone trial, Kashkati?"

"It is witnessed," came the cold reply. "Her penance is done. We admit her within the welcoming circle of the Mother Sun's arms. But–"

"But nothing!" snapped a third speaker. "Avani broke her covenant and you know it. And don't try to claim the girl accepted the charge of heresy, either – half the hierarchy heard her denunciation!"

"That doesn't mean we should grant her clan-claim out of guilt!"

The first voice spoke again, dryly: "And the legal basis for refusing it now would be…?"

"You'd ask me to prove a negative, Mesthani? There *is* no basis, because there is no *precedent*, as well you know! There's no need–"

"She's awake," said the third voice, suddenly. "Jesit, your healing, please?"

Yena made a low noise of frustration. Her vision was blurry, but she could still make out a figure moving towards her from the background. Cool fingers closed around her throbbing arm, probing gently with magic. A healing tingle hummed through the flesh, like stars sparking under her skin. Memory and clarity both returned in a rush, the faces above resolving into familiarity. Or three of them, anyway: the first speaker was Mesthani a Vekte, the second the priestess who'd initially overseen her penance, the Third Voice of Ashasa, whose name was evidently Kashkati. The healer, Jesit, was the same priestess who'd so grudgingly told Yena she was to walk through fire, her sneering expression replaced now by cool focus. Yena might well have imagined the quick flash of apology in Jesit's gaze as she pulled away; she was certainly dazed enough to be misreading people.

She sat up – she was on a narrow cot, not a proper bed – and rubbed warily at her newly-healed arm. A faint scar marked where she'd been cut with the same stone blade now sitting innocuously on a nearby table – *stone trial, hah!* – but as to whether she'd been burned...

She squeezed her eyes shut, taking a moment to flex her limbs and digits, testing for damage.

The memory of crossing the sun's mouth hit her like a gutpunch, visceral heat and snapping flames and the faint scent of burning skin and hair.

Yena hunched over, trembling violently, both arms wrapping her knees.

"You're all right," Mesthani murmured, low and soft. "Your burns were only superficial, and Jesit healed them cleanly. You've some light scarring on your legs and back, but otherwise you're undamaged."

Yena made a choking noise, rage and pained relief all twisted together. She didn't trust herself to look up, but hugged her knees tighter – she was wearing another nek, she realised belatedly – and focused on breathing evenly, making herself take deep, slow breaths until her pulse had settled. Strange how the mind could hold two contradictory positions at once: she'd never for a second believed that Safi's scarring diminished her or made her anything other than whole, and yet she was overwhelmed with relief at not being likewise marked. She struggled to reconcile the dissonance, then huffed a laugh when a line from the Ryvke popped into her head.

"*It is easier to forgive from a distance than from within,*" she murmured, lifting her head. It was an oddly steadying thought, for all that part of her still wanted to burst into hysterical laughter. She looked at Kashkati; the old woman snorted, rising unsteadily to her feet.

"In your own blood burn the consequences," she muttered, her sharp tone contrasting with the gentle hand she clapped to Mesthani's shoulder in parting. "Ashasa forgive us all."

Yena watched her go, a strange thrum in her chest. She looked questioningly at Mesthani, who sighed.

"Kashkati is a species of mild traditionalist," she said. "Very fond of precedents, so long as she's not the one setting them. She'll recover." And then, to Jesit, "My thanks for your labours. You may rejoin your senior."

Jesit flushed, eyes lowering. Rather than answer, she stepped back from Yena's bedside, inclined her head to the three of them and hurried off after Kashkati, though whether in search of the Third Voice or some other priestess, Yena didn't know.

Exhaling, she let her gaze drift from Mesthani to the room's other occupant, the still-unknown woman who'd spoken in her favour. Her brown hair, streaked with grey, was bound back in a long braid, marking her as a senior priestess more clearly than even the blood red of her robes. There was something familiar in the lines of her face, though her missing left eye distracted Yena from giving it too much consideration. The socket was scarred and lidless, an arresting asymmetry against her high, even cheekbones.

"Forgive my ignorance," Yena asked, "but who are you?"

The priestess smiled, sharp and sad. "I am Ksa a Kaje," she said. "Your kinswoman in mourning, it seems." And then, at Yena's blank incomprehension, "Motherless Kadeja was once my child."

Yena swallowed. "Oh. Ah. You're not, ah..."

"What you were expecting?" Ksa raised the eyebrow over her empty socket. The effect was so disconcerting, it passed right through eerie and came out the other side. Once you got over the shock, it was almost charming.

"Actually," said Yena, "I was going to say, you didn't think it a presumption?" She faltered slightly at the startled looks both Ksa and Mesthani shot her, but ploughed on with, "That my clan-claim was granted, that is. Or has it been granted? You were talking before, and I thought–"

"It has been granted," Mesthani said. "When Avani – the Second Voice – threw you into the sun's mouth, the Council called an emergency quorum of senior queens and priestesses to decide her punishment. I raised the issue then, and pending your completion of the stone trial–" she nodded to the fresh scar on Yena's forearm, "–it was allowed. Not least because Kiri a Tavi spoke for you." She shot Yena a sharp look, as though in search of an explanation; Yena kept her expression studiedly blank, though her stomach lurched in gratitude.

"Congratulations," Ksa said, not without irony. "You are the sole inheritor of a queen's clan, which I may now claim as an offshoot of my own line, should you ever bear daughters. And no, I don't think you presumptuous." Her single eye shone like wet slate. "I'm only grieved at what we both have lost."

For a moment, Yena didn't know what to say. She didn't dare think too deeply about Zech, for fear of losing herself in grief; even so, her throat constricted around a sudden lump. Then she looked at Ksa – really looked – and said, without quite thinking, "She had your eyes, I think."

Ksa laughed raggedly. "My thanks," she said. She inhaled, running a trembling hand across her face. She let it fall slowly, gathering herself before speaking again. "One day, when some time has passed, would you tell me about my granddaughter?"

"I will," Yena whispered. The promise clenched her heart; she took a moment to steady herself, then turned to Mesthani and asked, in a more normal voice, "Does Yasha know?"

"She does," said Mesthani, "though whether she's more proud or angry is anyone's guess. Either way, you've clearly surprised her."

"No small accomplishment, that," Ksa murmured.

Yena nodded, absorbing this. "Has she asked to see me?" She waved a hand as Mesthani opened her mouth, answering her own ridiculous question. "Of course she has, of course. But they won't let her in without my permission, will they?"

"They can't," said Mesthani, simply. "Even if your mother were acknowledged under Vekshi law, Yasha is still technically an exile. But if you wanted to see her –"

"I don't." Yena gulped the admission. "Not yet, at least." *Not until I have something to show her for what I've done.* "But my penitence was accepted? I have Vekshi rights, and the rights of a queen's sister?"

Ksa inclined her head. "You do."

"Then I want to know: why hasn't Kadeja been dealt with?"

"Because..." Mesthani began, then hesitated.

"Because we do not have Zechalia's body," Ksa said, heavily. "And without a body, there can be no proof of death, and thus no trial."

"Oh," said Yena, oddly faint. Her stomach churned.

"The problems in this case are legion," said Mesthani. She

sounded irritated, but not as much as Ksa or Yena. "It's been more than a century since a queen last died on foreign soil, and that was during a military campaign where retrieval by her forces was comparatively easy. If Zechalia had been a popular queen, or one installed in her office for any length of time, then it would be considered a matter of principle to demand her swift return, even to offer reprisals in the event of delay. Instead, she was new, young, inaugurated under extraordinary circumstances, in pursuit of a goal whose realisation further complicated our relationship with Kena – the nation in which she was raised, I might add, for all she was Vekshi-born. And of course, she was one on whom the sun smiled and frowned–" *shasuyakesani*, the Vekshi term for Zech's mottled skin evoking a judder of remembrance, "–which… well." She glanced apologetically at Ksa. "It doesn't help."

Ksa winced. "Quite."

"The point being," Mesthani said, after a moment, "that the Council is both dithering and divided. Though Ruyun a Ketra was imprisoned for her public attack on Zechalia, her faction still has some sympathisers, to say nothing of those conservatives and moderates who, like Third Voice Kashkati, dislike the number of unprecedented questions these events have raised. As Kadeja stands accused of killing a queen, she is imprisoned, but until a body is produced she cannot be interviewed – not even by the queens themselves – by the law of Ashasa's Knives. She is completely alone, and while I doubt it pleases her to be thus isolated, it doesn't advance our cause. And so we wait on Kena's pleasure, and hesitate to judge the woman we risked ourselves to reclaim."

Carefully, Yena said, "The Shavaktiin here are in contact with our friends in Karavos. If I were to ask the dreamseer to inquire about the return of my sister's body, with what weight would any reply he gave me be considered?"

"That would depend," said Mesthani, equally careful, "on whether you chose to divulge the source of your information.

Were you, for instance, to say simply that you'd had word from your allies – not your family, note; the distinction there is already fraught enough – and leave it at that, then as Zechalia's kin, your word ought to be held as bond."

"Ought," said Yena, not missing the inference.

Mesthani grimaced. "Just so. And yet such a declaration would still, I think, be better than nothing."

"At the very least," Ksa said dryly, "it would be a new nothing for them to debate."

Yena nodded, making a mental note to track down Halaya and Kikra at the earliest opportunity. She realised with a jolt that she had no concept of how much time she'd lost recovering from her so-called penance – long enough for the queens and priestesses to meet, certainly, but longer than a day? Multiple days?

"How long have I been here?" she blurted, unable to keep the question in.

Mesthani laughed. "Only a few hours. Your healing was near immediate, thanks to Jesit, and swiftly accomplished. If you hadn't worn the firebalm, however…"

"Firebalm?" Yena asked. "Oh! You mean that unguent?"

"Just so."

So it had helped, after all. "I didn't know what it was," she admitted. "I didn't know if it was meant to protect me or make me burn faster, so I almost didn't use it."

Ksa paled. "You didn't know?"

"Should I have?"

"I suppose not. My apologies." She smiled, her one eye crinkling at the corner. "I've been so long a priestess, it didn't occur to me that one raised outside the hierarchy, let alone Veksh itself, would require an explanation."

Yena blinked, startled. "*You* sent it to me?"

"Of course!" said Ksa, shocked. "I wasn't about to let you burn." At Yena's continuing incomprehension, she clicked her tongue, chiding herself. "Fire trials are set for many reasons within the hierarchy, not just for penitence. It's an open secret that, if your cause is approved by a senior priestess, you'll be given firebalm to ameliorate the damage – the better to show Ashasa's benevolence to those she approves, of course, the Mother Sun having instructed Her devotees in the best course of action. But for those considered too radical, unrepentant or simply in disfavour, no such mortal aid is forthcoming. Your penitence was rigged against you the moment Second Voice Avani got involved; I merely restored the balance that should always have existed. Acting on the Mother Sun's inspiration, of course."

"Of course," said Yena, faintly. And what of the trial-set priestess who knew the secret of firebalm, but waited in vain for a prophylactic that never came? She shuddered at the cruelty of it, biting down on her sarcasm. *For now, you are a loyal daughter of Veksh. Don't jeopardise what you've won.*

For the first time since beginning her penitence, she let herself think of the other reason she'd sought her new status: to help solve the mystery of the anchored portal. Kena's historical record had been largely destroyed by Vexa Yavin, but the Archives in Yevekshasa were old and deep. It was a slim hope, perhaps, but Yena was curious enough to want to view them for her own sake, and if she was forced to wait on the arrival of Zech's body before Kadeja could be dealt with, then she'd much prefer to have something to occupy her.

"And what if I wanted to search the Archives?" she said, addressing the question to both Ksa and Mesthani. "To, ah…" she paused, hunting for a plausible excuse that didn't sound like a betrayal of Veksh, "…look for any helpful precedents?"

Ksa's face lit up, a sly smile spreading across her face. "Now *that*," she said, "I can certainly arrange."

For five full seconds, Saffron didn't breathe. Her whole body was frozen, staring at Vex Leoden – the man who'd poisoned Amenet, burned Yasha's compound, hunted them on the

Envas road and murdered Viya's mother – with a mix of horror and confusion, heart rabbiting with fear. But Leoden didn't make any move to hurt or restrain her: just stayed where he was, several paces away, and watched her. Saffron gulped a belated lungful of air, and only then did she fully register their surroundings, which were startling enough in their own right that she almost seized up all over again.

Wherever they were, it wasn't on Earth, and it certainly wasn't Kena.

For one thing, the sky was green.

Heedless of this geographical quirk, Leoden raised a curious eyebrow, favouring Saffron with an expression of faint curiosity. In Vekshi, he said, "I don't suppose you understand me, do you?"

His choice of language was so surprising, it was another moment before the thunderbolt realisation hit: *he doesn't know who I am.* She almost laughed out loud, giddy with the strange relief of it. Saffron knew Leoden, of course: his face was one of the few true recollections she'd retained from her time in the dreamscape with Zech, the knowledge further cemented by that final, frightening glimpse of him she'd caught when fleeing the palace. But Leoden had never seen *her* – and judging by his current reaction, he didn't suspect her of being involved with his enemies.

Which begged the question: who, then, did he think she was, and what did he want with her? *You're not what I'd expected,* he'd said – also in Vekshi, now that she had the wits to consider it – and if not for his second question she might logically have assumed he was waiting for Vekshi aid, some old ally of Kadeja's or enemy of the Council of Queens who'd braved the Many to meet him.

Except that neither her silence nor her seeming incomprehension were a surprise to him.

She studied Leoden, trying to gauge his thoughts, and failing. He had a good face, with dark, clever eyes, an expressive mouth, a high forehead and a nose somewhere between Greek and aquiline. His short black hair was shot with silver, devoid of marriage-braids – a singleton's cut, Matu had once explained – and yet it still struck her as faintly incongruous, though she couldn't have said why. His clothes were equally strange: Saffron didn't remember exactly what he'd worn the last time she'd seen him, but she felt certain it bore no resemblance to his current garb, which likely came from whatever world this was. To her eye, he looked more like a steampunk biker than a king: tall boots, dark leather trousers, and a long brown leather coat (her fingers twitched covetously) over a creamy shirt and tan suede vest. There was even a pair of chunky, dark-lensed goggles hanging around his neck, as though he'd just come from piloting an airship.

Protective gear. The phrase leapt into her head of its own volition, and for the first time she let herself take in their bizarre surroundings. The ground beneath her feet was bare earth, reddish gravel and silver-black dust interspersed with clumps of weird, thin grass – or something that looked like grass, at least – which was ultimately less green than silver, the sheen on it faintly metallic. A chill wind whipped by, redolent with the sharp tang of ozone and something like bleach fumes burning at her nostrils. The sky overhead was an angry malachite shade, as though perpetually caught in the throes of an invisible thunderstorm. Or perhaps not quite so invisible, after all: a crack like lightning juddered sideways across the sky – *across*, not down – and bloomed into white-light spiderweb patterns that lingered like afterimages.

Behind Leoden, the silvery soil ran in twining paths through what looked like an alien scrapyard, piles of junk metal and unnamed detritus stretching out in all directions. Or at least, Saffron assumed it was rubbish – how else to explain the miscellany of strange objects that protruded from the towering piles? Broken statues, decaying organics, mammoth struts and juts of white that might have been bones and might have been branches, rusting iron and glowing metals and colourful hunks of she didn't know what, all jumbled together with smaller items that looked domestic only in comparison to their larger counterparts. It made the hairs on her neck stand up, though she couldn't articulate why.

Unsettled, she glanced over her shoulder – she knew her arrival portal was likely long gone, but felt a vague compulsion to make sure – and froze, awed and riveted by what she saw. Barely metres away, the world turned into an Escher drawing, hanging columns and sheets of mist that looked like veils in the air, static rain flowing sideways broken by ghostly silhouettes that winked in and out of existence. *Does it stand, hang or stretch?* Her brain cramped even trying to take in the impossible vista: the longer Saffron stared at it, the less sense it made. It was like the blurred map-edges of an old video game, graphics glitching as some hazy avatar brushed the bounds of their pixelated reality, except that it *was* real, impossibly so, and almost painful to look at.

In Kenan, Leoden said, "Do you speak this tongue, either?"

Saffron jumped, spinning to face him, but managed to keep herself from answering. If he thought she couldn't understand him, perhaps he'd speak freely around her, let slip some hint of where they were and what it meant for Kena. He watched her, gauging her non-responsiveness, then tried again in some third, unknown language – or at least, she assumed that's what it was. When this, too, elicited no reaction, he snorted, the sound more amused than impatient.

"I don't know why I'm surprised," he murmured, switching back to Kenan. "Nothing here makes sense."

And where is here, exactly? Saffron thought. And then, when she realised he wouldn't understand her, she repeated the words aloud, in English.

Leoden blinked, nonplussed. "So you do speak," he said, reverting to Kenan. "Just not any useful tongue. Oh, that's *very* good."

Keeping up the pretence of linguistic confusion, Saffron gestured to the surreal landscape behind her, figuring tone might convey what the words themselves didn't. "I don't know where the hell we are, but this doesn't seem safe. Should we go somewhere else?"

The absurdity of the question almost made her laugh out loud. Leoden himself was anything *but* safe; by rights, she ought to have run away the moment she stepped through the portal. And yet there was a terrible thrill to being incognito: to standing before this man who'd hurt so many people she cared about and passing without recognition. But more than that, her portal was gone: until or unless she could reach Luy through the dreamscape, she had no access to either Earth or Kena, and whatever else it was, this world was clearly dangerous. If Leoden didn't see her as a threat – if, as his questioning suggested, he thought she was here to help him, regardless of why or to what end – then it made more sense to stick with him, if only for the short term. And if she took the opportunity to learn more about his motives while she was at it, then so much the better.

"We should go," said Leoden, though whether he meant the words for Saffron or himself, she couldn't tell. He tipped his head, motioning to a path that wove between two of the nearest, towering junkheaps, then took a step in that direction, beckoning with his hand.

Saffron didn't have to feign her moment of indecision. She ought to have been terrified, or heartsick at the very least, but something in Lita's letting her go had felt like absolution. *I'm a worldwalker,* she told herself, swallowing around the burn of bleach and ozone air. *And this is a world. So, walk!* And yet her feet stayed rooted to the ground.

"Come on," said Leoden, a touch of impatience colouring his tone, and underneath that, the faintest thread of fear. Saffron might have wondered at his continuing to speak Kenan, but she had an odd intuition that he was doing it for comfort's sake, the same as she clung to English. "The borders aren't stable. The locals say a *kshtathit* is coming, and I don't think we want to see it."

The alien word moved her as common sense hadn't. Jerking forwards, Saffron followed a relieved-looking Leoden through the junkheaps, flinching only a little as another burst of spiderweb lightning lit up the storm-green sky.

Their conference had run late, and now it was later still, the two moons in their disparate phases winking through the window like the eyes of some monstrous cat. Trishka had long since returned to her rooms, escorted by the same guard who'd brought her to begin with, while Matu had likewise recognised the signs of Amenet's exhaustion – and had doubtless been near his own limits in any case – and led her out not long after. Luy knew something of the poison Leoden had used on her, and could scarcely reckon what strength it took for Amenet to appear even half as composed as she so often did, regardless of cane and brace.

Their numbers thus decreased, but with Halunet still present, Gwen promptly set about quizzing the priest on what they might do to recover Luy's memories, using the same combination of sevikmet and ahunemet that he and Aydi had used on Sene a Sati. Luy was too grateful to be embarrassed by the intervention; his stomach still churned to think of the violation, and only the pressure of Rikan's hand on his enabled him to meet Halunet's gaze.

"It's hard to say," the priest said at last. "In the case of the late ambassador, the bulk of the damage was due to the sheer carelessness with which her thoughts were rifled. There was no precision, no targeting – just a greedy sort of… *rummaging*." He pronounced the word with profound distaste. "Think of Sene's memories like words written on a slate: what was done to her smeared the chalk around, but didn't wipe it clean, so that when new words were layered on top, neither they nor the originals were truly legible. But with Luy, it's as if they reached out to the same written slate and carefully removed only one or two words with a damp cloth, expunging the chalk completely. Do you see?"

"Not entirely," said his bloodmother, in the guarded way that meant she was trying very hard not to be furious at the wrong person.

"I think I do," said Luy, quietly. He ducked his head, wishing fervently in that moment for the privacy of his Shavaktiin veils. *It's always so much easier to look than to be seen,* he thought, and let his fingers tangle with Rikan's. Glancing at his mother, he said, "He means that Sene a Sati only needed help to unsmudge the chalk, to gather back knowledge that was scattered and smashed, but not truly erased. Whereas the memories taken from me were stolen complete and entire. There's nothing to call back."

"Actually," said Halunet, speaking over the top of Gwen's shocked gasp, "that's not *quite* right. I mean to say that, while I doubt the ahunemet can help Luy recover what was lost, he might yet be able to do that for himself. I wouldn't have confidence in such an outcome in the ordinary course of things, inasmuch as any of this is ordinary, but for a dreamseer... well."

"How?" asked Pix, face lit with curiosity. Beside her, Viya looked equally intrigued, though when she caught Luy's eyes on her, she had the grace to blush. To his own surprise, Luy found himself smiling back, a slight shake of the head to indicate no harm done, and felt relieved when her posture straightened in response. He liked the fledgling Cuivexa, sharp and brave and stubborn and wary; admired the fierce way she *tried*. Pix he might chaff for tactlessness, but Pix was a courtier who ought to have known better: Viya just wanted to understand, the same as Luy himself.

"To stick with the analogy," Halunet said, "though individual words are gone, Luy might yet divine them from context. The root memory is gone, but subsequent judgements and actions are not, and if–" he flicked his gaze back to Luy again, "–if you were to let the ilumet guide you in meditation – if you were to try and view that web of thoughts, its progression and displacement, as a pattern in need of completion–"

"Ah!" said Luy, understanding. Hope sang through him, a pure note rung from a waterglass. He beamed at Halunet, not wanting to get ahead of himself – there was still no guarantee the suggestion would work, after all – and yet he had neither the desire nor the ability to check the relief that flooded him at the prospect.

"What *I* want to know," said Pix, addressing the room in general, "is why Luy's thoughts were taken so cleanly when, so far as we can tell, there was no such care taken with Sene or the worldwalkers. Why did he merit special treatment? Or were the various thought-thefts effected by different kemeta, with Luy's the more talented thief?"

"If you'll permit an opinion, lady," said Halunet, waiting on Pix's nod before continuing, "I would be very surprised if more than one kemeta was involved. There is a lingering sense… It's hard to explain to those without magic, but though the ambassador's thoughts were scrambled, the damage there had a similar imprint to that inflicted on Luy."

"Like calls to like," Gwen murmured, almost to herself.

Halunet shot her a surprised, approving look. "Exactly," he said.

"Then why the difference?" Viya asked. It was the first she'd spoken in some time, and her voice was fainter than usual.

A brief silence followed the question – broken, somewhat unexpectedly, by Rikan.

"Perhaps," he said, then faltered, as though belatedly uncertain of the welcomeness of his opinion. Luy squeezed his hand and shot Pix a warning look – she raised her brows in protest, but said nothing – and after a moment, Rikan gulped and tried again. "That is, perhaps it's because of the ilumet. They had no fear of 'prisoning the ambassador with their worldwalkers, so why not do the same to Luy? It's not as if there's many would've questioned a Shavaktiin's disappearance. Sorry," he added, shooting Luy an apologetic look, "but you've got to admit–"

"I know," he said, and kissed Rikan's cheek, delighting in the subtle flush this produced. "You were saying?"

"Well, I mean." Rikan fidgeted, rubbing the nape of his neck with his free hand. "They didn't kill their prisoners. They could've done, quite easily – easier than chaining 'em, I'd've thought, given it was all a big secret – and that makes me think that, whatever it is they wanted to know, they never found it out; they needed to ask more questions, so they kept them around for seconds. And likely that was true of Luy, too, or else he would've been dead – so why not chain him up?" He looked around the room, as though expecting someone present to answer the question, and when they didn't, he shrugged. "Because he has the ilumet. Because, whatever else they did, they couldn't stop him dreaming – they must've known he was talking to other Shavaktiin, but they didn't want anyone thinking that something was wrong."

"That makes a great deal of sense," said Gwen, looking on Rikan with increased approval. And then, with feeling, "Damn them! What a callous waste! If they'd done what they did to the worldwalkers in haste or ignorance, that would still be terrible, but to know they could've been careful about it – to think they left them all, all metmirai by choice–"

"Metmirai?" Luy asked sharply, startled. "Now, there's an odd word for it."

His mother looked equally surprised. "You know the term?"

"I'm more surprised that you do."

"It came up earlier," Pix said, glancing between them. "When Trishka was talking about the anchored portal."

"It was just before you arrived," said Gwen, a touch apologetically, and at Luy's impatient look she promptly launched into an explanation: jahudemet and maramet; stone mortared with blood; the mysteries of Ke's Kin and the fear of absent portals chewing away the world.

The words sank into him like stones, and when she finally quieted, Luy's head was spinning, an odd, discordant nausea in the seat of his spine and stomach. He reached into his thoughts and felt, the same as he had in Rikan's bed, that conspicuous, socket-like absence of a knowledge which ought to have been there. Yet unlike before, he also felt a remnant thread, some lingering pull in what he couldn't help but think of as the right direction. The ilumet was hard to master when awake, but Luy reached for it – and reached for the thread – with every scrap of focus he could summon. At first it proved intangible, obstinate, drifting further from his recollection the harder he tried to grab at it, until he remembered Halunet's talk of webs and patterns and took a step back, the better to view the whole.

The sensation, when he managed it, was not so much of a key successfully turning a lock, but of a lock's tumblers spin-snapping open in precise and satisfactory order, a chain reaction whose component parts, though hidden from Luy, were nonetheless profoundly felt, the summoning of an outcome both intuitive and, in some bizarre sense, predestined. For a moment, his vision was doubled, the room around him overlaid with the silhouette of his dreamscape crossroads, and then it all greyed out entirely, blackness crashing into him like a tarry wave.

A suspension of seconds passed, though Luy had no real awareness of them, and when he came to he was lying sprawled on the floor, his head in Rikan's lap as his lover worriedly called his name, his bloodmother anxiously crouched nearby and demanding Pix send for a healer.

"I'm all right." The words came out a quiet rasp; he forced

himself to repeat them, louder. "I'm all right. I'm here."
And then, when he was sure enough in himself that it was
really true, "I just remembered something, that's all." He cast
around for Halunet and found the priest standing at Viya's
side, a look of tremulous relief on his face. Trying for a smile,
Luy said, "I used the ilumet, just as you said. It worked."

Halunet didn't speak; just nodded and sank heavily into
the nearest chair, exhaling a shaky breath.

A confusion of movement followed, wherein Luy tried to
rise unassisted, found that he was shakier than anticipated,
and ended up letting Rikan and Gwen help him into a chair.
Once upright, he sat quietly for some minutes, aglow with
triumph at having bested Leoden but nauseous with the
effort of having done so, while Viya busied herself in brewing
a fresh pot of tea. It was a surprisingly simple blend, but all
the more restorative for it, and when the first cup was set
before him Luy inhaled greedily, letting the familiar scent
wash through him as he drank.

"I didn't get it all back," he said at last, hating the flash
of disappointment in his mother's eyes, "but that word you
said, metmirai – it triggered my awareness of a stolen thing,
a memory." He grinned, sharp and victorious. "So I stole it
back."

He took another sip of his tea, as much to steady himself as
because he was parched, and spoke. "The Shavaktiin collect
stories. Most, we share. Some, we trade. And others, we keep
only for ourselves. One such fable touches on what it means
for a thing to be metmirai. And in this context..."

He tailed off, much to Pix's clear aggravation. Gently, Gwen
nudged him. "Louis?"

Luy gulped, the full implications of what he was saying
hitting him like a wall. "Understand, I'm already half a
heretic for what I've done, for acting on an interpretation of
the Great Story disdained by the Shavaktiin enclave, for all
that I can't recall the heart of it. And I know, I understand

that Leoden stole it from me first, but I was unwilling then, and telling you – speaking it aloud, with intent – if I break this vow, too – if I share this story, and the sharing becomes known–"

Gently, Rikan asked, "Do only the Shavaktiin know this story, then?"

Luy considered the point, exhaling in a steady breath. "To the best of our knowledge, yes," he said. "But I am not, at present, speaking as a Shavaktiin – not in the strictest sense." He gestured to his unveiled face. "Participant, not narrator. But still. *Still.*"

He quieted, a mulish silence stretching as he weighed the point. Beside him, he felt his mother's protectiveness like a tangible thing, and smiled to know that, should anyone chivvy or push him, she would bristle in his defence. But then, he realised abruptly, he was in Gwen's world, and had been since the moment he'd first come to Karavos. He'd never resented the fact that the majority of the people in his mother's life were unaware of his existence: she'd always been honest about her motives and her love for him in his childhood, and as an adult it would've been hypocritical, given his own choices. Nonetheless, there was a comfort – and, he realised, a strange sort of power – in being known to the people here as Gwen Vere's son, and not just as an anonymous Shavaktiin.

It was this fact that decided him, and when he spoke again, his conscience was clear.

"I would ask that the story I'm about to tell you not leave this room, but we have allies enough who might yet need to hear it that the request would be moot. Instead, I ask that you refrain from disclosing it without reason, and never to someone you don't trust to be likewise circumspect. Are we agreed?"

"We are," said Pix and Viya, just as Gwen and Rikan said, "Of course."

Only Halunet hesitated. "With respect," he said, "and as much as I would value such a confidence, my inclusion in this conference seems unnecessary. May I have leave to retire?"

"You may," said Viya, inclining her head. "You've served well, Halunet. We thank you for your attendance – and for your discretion."

Bowing deeply over his cupped hands, Halunet murmured thanks and, with a final parting glance at Luy, who felt profoundly grateful for the priest's willing abstention, left the room.

Luy waited a beat, drained the rest of his tea, and began. "All right. This story – I will not tell you our name for it – is one of the oldest the Shavaktiin keep, and the most important. We still debate its origins, as the true provenance is lost. Were it any other story, that would see it accounted a moon-tale, but instead… well. It's the oldest usage we've found of the word metmirai; indeed, it's as if the story exists to explain the term, and if what Trishka says of Ke's Kin is true, then they must know some version of it, too. As she suggested, in order to be metmirai, a place must be over-exposed to the jahudemet – so many portals opened, the world's weft ripped and ripped again, that it sunders forever. Which is why, in this particular case, the lack of any provenance is so meaningful. It's not just that we lack any historical records to correlate the tale, or that the name of the earliest teller is missing, or that we don't have an original written copy. It's that we don't know if the story comes from Kena – or from anywhere else in this world – at all."

"I think," said Viya, after a brief, stunned silence, "that we ought to hear this tale in full, the better to judge for ourselves."

"I can't relate it verbatim –"

Pix raised an eyebrow. "Can't or won't?"

"Both," he said, somewhat tartly. "It was never given to me to carry, but even had it been, I'm only willing to bend my oaths, not break them." He laughed, rubbing his face. "Now, *there's* a thing I never thought I'd say."

"Such is life," said Gwen, smiling wryly.

Luy's mouth quirked in acknowledgement. "Well. What I can say is that the tale concerns a place called–"

He broke off, mouth abruptly dry as the truth slammed into him.

"Called what?" Viya prompted, after a moment.

Luy swallowed. "Vikasa," he said, thoughts full of Sene a Sati's last words. Across the table, Gwen swore under her breath. "Vikasa was a place, not a person – a city, a country, a world; I don't know which – but somewhere where portal-magic was commonplace. Those at the centre of Vikasa's power grew rich on trade and conquest, raiding weaker worlds, bartering with those of greater or equal strength, and all the while amassing wonders for themselves.

"Yet after many years of this prosperity, they began to notice that their borders were disintegrating, fraying at the seams. Debate arose within their... I think the best word is government; the tale has clearly been passed through many languages, with many nuances lost in the process–" Gwen snorted in understanding, "–but though the jahudemet was identified as the source of decay, those in power refused to check its usage, believing that Vikasa would endure. But the fraying – the metmirai – only increased, and though some survivors fled before it swallowed them entirely, Vikasa was lost forever. That phrase, too, is deliberate: not *destroyed*, but *lost*." He spread his hands. "With so much history lost in the Years of Shadow, we can't be sure if Vikasa was once a part of this world, or if it belonged elsewhere. But as we have the tale, it must have had some connection to Kena at some point – and if, as his theft of the story suggests, Leoden has a vested interest in Vikasa's fate, or the jahudemet, or metmirai, or all of them together, then I'm disinclined to view it as unrelated to his capture of worldwalkers."

"But what in the worlds does he *want*?" asked Gwen,

frustration in her voice. "What did Sene know, and why does some lost realm matter at all? It doesn't make any sense!"

Luy spread his hands. "He told me once that he had no need of other worlds – we were speaking of the jahudemet and Trishka's value in wielding it, but he wasn't interested. I didn't think he was lying at the time, but I was clearly mistaken."

A debate ensued then, the five of them tossing theories back and forth, but nothing they came up with hung together. There was simply too great a discrepancy between Leoden's actions and his stated goals, his claims and their consequences. Luy fell silent, letting the discussion pass from his hands, and the next thing he knew Rikan was nudging him awake, his expression a mix of fondness and concern.

"It's late," he said. "You should rest. We all need to rest."

This sensible suggestion was met with belated murmurs of agreement. It had already been agreed that Matu would speak to the worldwalkers the following day, and Luy felt a similar need to contribute. "If nothing else," he said, rising alongside Rikan, "I should try to reach Kikra in the dreamscape, see what our allies are doing. Safi, too, if I can find her."

His mother made a face like she wanted to tell him not to overextend himself, but bit her lip at the last second, flashing him a Look instead.

With that, the gathering disbanded, each of them heading wearily to their respective beds – all except Rikan, who stayed to accompany Luy to his.

As drained as he was, they were halfway to Luy's quarters before he recalled, with a sudden and visceral clarity, the strange young man he'd encountered in the dreamscape after his last conversation with Safi. He stopped dead, heart pounding in belated recollection. *Do you realise you're missing pieces?*

"Gods," he whispered. "He knew. He looked at me, and he *saw*."

"Who looked at you?" asked Rikan, puzzled. "What did he see?"

Luy shook his head, too tired to articulate it. "I don't know," he murmured. "But damned if I'm not going to find out."

10
Shattered Skies

Saffron and Leoden were a good half hour away from the weird junkyard and its impossible Escher-outlook, the heaps of metallic refuse replaced by a barren plain, when a storm that wasn't quite a storm broke over them. The malachite sky grew fractal with lightning, sideways-jagging spiderweb cracks proliferating so quickly that it looked like some invisible god had cast a net over the heavens. Whipping static filled the air, a stinging stillness that prickled Saffron's skin with electric shocks. Beneath her bare feet, the rubble strewn on the silver-black earth began to tremble as if at an earthquake, red rocks dancing like frightened crabs.

"The kshtathit!" Leoden yelled, pulling his goggles up over his eyes, the chunky bronze casing giving him an insectoid look. "We need to find cover, quickly!"

Too frightened to speak, Saffron broke into a run beside him, struggling to keep pace with his longer stride. Ever since they'd left the junkyard, the ground had sloped faintly but consistently upwards, and though the incline was gentle enough to make little difference while walking, running was a different thing entirely. Saffron's calves soon ached, throat burning as the ozone-bleach scent in the air grew stronger, making it increasingly hard to breathe. Drifts of static buzzed through the air like greyscale wasps, the very sight of them making her eyes water. The ground shook harder than before, upsetting her balance; hard red rocks dug into her soles and made her stumble. The silvery earth loosened and sucked at her feet, as though she were running through sand.

A sob caught in her throat at the oppressive, terrifying strangeness of it all. She didn't know if the kshtathit could kill them, but as their featureless plain offered no obvious hiding spots – and as she needed every scrap of air to just keep running – she was glad she couldn't ask.

Nearby, a static drift solidified and exploded, a shocking burst of acidic sensation washing over her. Saffron yelped and tripped again, harder than before, her ankle creaking ominously as she tried and failed to right her balance. But even as she flailed, a strong hand gripped her arm and hauled her upright, sliding down to grab her hand and tug her unfailingly forwards.

"Keep close!" Leoden panted, adjusting his grip on her. "If we can make the dome, we'll be fine, but we need–"

He broke off suddenly, and for an awful moment Saffron thought he'd been injured somehow, until he burst into hard, relieved laughter and surged forwards again, waving his free arm at a distant shape on the horizon.

A shape that was rapidly getting closer.

As dazed as she was, it was several long seconds before Saffron managed to resolve the sight into anything comprehensible; once she did, however, she nearly fell all over again, and not just because of another nearby static explosion. Coming towards them – or *loping* towards them, more accurately, with long-legged, gambolling, ground-eating strides – was an enormous blue creature, taller than an elephant and substantially longer than one, bearing what appeared to be a single human – or humanoid, at any rate – rider. The closer it drew and the faster they ran to meet it, the more alien details stood out: the six legs ending in taloned paws; the long, iridescent hair, limned faintly with peacock green; the four eyes, round and liquid black, set high on a head whose tufted ears and diamond-shaped skull contrived to look both leonine and snakelike.

Her first day in Kena, Saffron had been awed and impressed by the sight of a roa, but as strange as they were, at least they looked and acted enough like big, bipedal alpacas to be vaguely familiar. This was something else entirely, and even with the kshtathit bursting around them – even with the heavy warmth of a murderer's hand holding tight to her own – her heart expanded with joy and fear and wonder at the sight.

"Leoden!" yelled the rider, waving frantically on the final approach. What followed was a string of words in the third, indecipherable language with which the Vex had previously tried to communicate with Saffron. Then, with a complex twist of the reins, their saviour pulled the creature to a halt beside them. Tossing its head – which, up close, proved to be far bigger than a person – the creature made a rumbling, chuffing sound and went to its knees, allowing the rider to jump down. Fearless of those massive, toothed jaws, they stood at the creature's head and spoke urgently to Leoden, shouting to be heard over the roaring of the kshtathit. He answered in the same language, dropping Saffron's hand to gesture at her, at the path they'd walked, at the magic storm around them.

And it was magic, or something so far beyond her understanding of science as to be indistinguishable from it: on that point, Saffron was clear. She didn't have to know what the kshtathit literally was in order to be terrified of what it might do to her.

Like Leoden, the rider wore a thick pair of glass-and-bronze goggles – protection against the elements, or so Saffron assumed – and sturdy leather clothing. Unlike Leoden, they also carried a weapon slung across their back, the shape of it reminiscent of a bayonet or rifle, the tip of it glinting over their right shoulder. Their skin was black, their tight-curled hair cut as close to the scalp as Saffron's own, their gender indeterminate. Turning to Saffron, they gave her a quick, assessing look and then motioned at their giant mount – or, more specifically, to the handholds set in the side of its sizeable saddle.

We have to ride. An obvious conclusion, and it wasn't as if they had time to spare debating the point, even if the three of them had shared a common language. Even so, the circumstances were so oddly reminiscent of her first day in Kena – the alien mount, the androgynous stranger coming to her rescue – that she found herself fighting hysterical laughter. *And what would Luy make of this all, I wonder? A meaningful pattern in the Great Story, or just common coincidence? Do the Shavaktiin even believe in coincidence? Irony? Random chance?* A phantom memory tickled her, a true conversation from the dreamscape sliding belatedly into her waking thoughts. *What was it that he called the worlds – an accident of stars?*

Focus, a calmer voice whispered, *and you might yet live to ask him.*

It was all the push she needed. Before either Leoden or the rider could prompt her to respond, Saffron took a deep breath and stepped up to the blue beast's shoulder – or in between two of its shoulders, assuming the word applied to whatever joint moved its middle legs, their musculature bulking out what should have been smooth flank – and grasped the protruding saddle-grips like a rock-climber seeking leverage. She could feel the big beast breathing, barrel-chest expanding beneath the various girth straps, and yet the rumble this provoked was vastly less disconcerting than the ground-quakes of the kshtathit.

Eyeing the distance from ground to saddle, the placement of what looked to be toeholds in the leather, Saffron inhaled sharply and climbed, heart pounding as she scrambled onto that big, broad back. From the ground, she'd worried that the saddle would function like an uncanopied howdah: that the only way to sit in it would be sidesaddle, because how could she possibly sit astride so massive an animal? And yet she could, with surprising comfort: though flat on top, the saddle was built high and, compared to the creature, narrow. There was no question of steering with her legs in such an arrangement – but then, Saffron wasn't driving.

As Leoden and the rider mounted in turn, there was a quick, scuffling adjustment as they took their seats, Leoden as unsure as Saffron had been, the rider unslinging their weapon and securing it elsewhere. The saddle had seemed massive when Saffron sat in it alone, but with two more adult bodies aboard, the space contracted rapidly. The final arrangement saw Saffron pressed between Leoden and the rider, his arms set around Saffron's waist and hers around the rider's, their proximity less intimate than it was practical, their feet snugged in stirrup-like grooves on the saddle's overhang.

Above and around, the kshtathit intensified, sideways lightning cracking the sky as static burst and red rocks danced and the big blue creature came to its feet, an upright lurch that reminded Saffron vividly of her one and only camel-ride. The rider twitched the reins and shouted – a command, a prayer, an exultation, Saffron didn't know – and the creature responded, turning with a speed and grace that ought to have been impossible, given its size. And then they were off, the real wind roaring in Saffron's ears as they picked up speed. Beneath her, the creature's six-legged stride produced an undulation that felt like the pitch and cresting of a wave that could never break; only build, and build, and build again, the three of them rocking in balance as they clung to it and each other.

Behind her, Leoden began to speak – in Kenan this time, his chest rumbling against Saffron's back. For a horrible, irrational moment, she thought he'd realised her deception and was issuing a threat, until she unfroze enough to actually listen. Once she did, however, she almost wished she hadn't.

Leoden was praying.

Not to Ke or Na, the heads of Kena's heavenly pantheon, as Saffron might have expected, but to Sahu, goddess of wisdom, in whose service Matu had learned to use the zuymet. Indeed, it was thanks to Matu that she recognised the prayer: a plea for guidance for the lost.

Low and fervent, Leoden murmured:

"Find me, bright one.
Find me and keep me, your willing servant;
save me from the dark that comes
with ignorance, from false paths chosen, false words trusted;
save me from myself.
Yours is the song in silent places,
yours the name intelligible
when language fails
and temples fall
and the silver bell that sings the world
is cracked and broken;
yours the truth
and yours the guidance.
Sahu, bright one, aid your child:
for I am lost, and the world is wild."

Saffron shuddered, the words too resonant to ignore. She didn't want to feel sympathy for Leoden, let alone kinship, and yet it was impossible to pretend herself completely unmoved, for wasn't she lost, too? She tried to be practical; to remind herself, sternly and in detail, of his many abuses, betrayals, cruelties. Her subtlety was as nothing to his, and Leoden was a master manipulator besides. As some unknown person had sent her to him, who was to say that he – that *they*, whoever they were – didn't know exactly who Saffron was and what languages she spoke? Ever since the junkyard, she'd been silently congratulating herself on the cleverness of feigning incomprehension, the better to act as a spy, but what if Leoden knew it for a tactic, and was taking advantage of it in turn, presenting himself in a purposely favourable light?

Zech had prayed to Sahu, too.

"Oh, gods," Leoden said, the words so soft, they were almost unintelligible. "What am I doing here?"

Saffron swallowed, an ugly lump in her throat. Above them, the sky cracked and shattered, booming flashes of light and noise like a heavenly systems failure. She thought of the captured worldwalkers, their thoughts and memories violated, and felt her missing fingers throb. For a moment, the Vekshi tattoo around her wrist burned like a shackle, as though she, too, had been chained in a dungeon beneath the palace instead of sitting the Trial of Queens in the heart of Yevekshasa.

Something about the thought pricked at her, though she didn't know what, and it struck her, abruptly and with no small degree of anger, that even in travelling other worlds she'd fallen into the habit of accepting that the adults around her were basically trustworthy, their information free of contradiction or falsehood. Which, on the one hand, was sensible – at the outset, she hadn't known enough about Kena or Veksh for any political criticism to be informed by anything other than bias. Though she cringed to think of it now, her first sight of Kadeja, who'd looked nothing like Gwen's quick description of a Vekshi woman, had prompted her to doubt Gwen's word, and look what had happened next! It was Kadeja who'd cut Saffron's fingers, Kadeja who'd murdered Zech–

Kadeja.

Even pressed between two warm bodies, Saffron went cold all over. All this time, she'd trusted in the firm assertion of Gwen and Yasha, Pix and Matu that Leoden was a danger to Kena; Leoden, who'd met Kadeja long before Vex Ralan's death, and who, despite his apparent desire to hold the throne alone – despite his months-long marriage – still wore his hair in a singleton's cut. Though he'd allowed it to happen, Leoden had not been the one to whip Viya bloody with star-nettle in penance to Ashasa; had not put a temple knife through his daughter's throat or severed Saffron's fingers in a fountain. Certainly, she'd been told of his actions by others – most prominently the attempted murder of Amenet and the actual death of her sister, Tevet, whose body he'd hung from the palace walls – but she had no details; hadn't ever thought to ask any *questions*.

She shook her head, frustrated, breath whumphing out in a sudden gust as the still-nameless creature hurdled some unknown obstacle, big paws thumping the silver earth as the rider clicked an approving noise and patted it on the neck, *thump-thump*. Through some sympathetic sensory alchemy, the tactile sound made Saffron belatedly and acutely aware of her own discomfort. Fine grains of sand whipped into her like insects, their sting underwritten by the constant electric fizz of the kshtathit, and combined with the cold – the temperature must have dropped, and dropped sharply; she hadn't been chilled in the junkyard – the end result was a constant acidic prickle against the bare skin of her arms, face, feet. Something small and sharp lodged painfully in her eye; she yelped and scrubbed it frantically away, which action meant loosening her hold on the rider. Not wanting to fall, she grabbed them again as soon as she could, and though it pained her not to look, she squeezed her eyes shut against further intrusions, the loss of one sense enhancing her awareness of the lolloping creature beneath her.

Start with what you know, she told herself, the wind of their passage and the kshtathit's anger screaming in her ears. *The ahunemet can alter thoughts and memories, though Ke's Kin considers it barbarous, and that's what was done to the worldwalkers. And Luy said –* she strained to remember, chasing after raggedy scraps of their dreamscape conference – *Luy said the Vekshi ambassador was with them, too, and that they thought a kemeta, one of the arakoi, was responsible for it. But why even bother with arakoi when he already had the temples? No, no, I'm getting too far ahead – go back again.*

Gritting her teeth against the omnipresent sting, Saffron pressed her cheek to the smoothworn leather of the rider's coat, hands locked around their waist, and thought. *We always knew Kadeja was dangerous. Nobody ever claimed otherwise. But even with her heresy, the omen she sought in the Square of Gods –* her fingers pulsed again, aching and absent – *it never made sense to think she was the one in charge, because how could she have been? She wasn't leading some Vekshi plot to take over Kena – she was exiled, heretic – and if she'd planned on using Kena to retake Veksh, she ought to have allied with Yasha, not burned her out.*

But we never knew why she was exiled in the first place...

And Leoden didn't go after her. She jerked with the thought, incongruous and alien when contrasted with the decorous press of his chest to her back, the way he gripped his own forearms where their loop encircled Saffron's waist in preference to touching her directly. Perhaps that detail was a small thing, a Kenan thing, a courtesy she might expect from any murderous despot who'd nonetheless been raised without a sense of entitlement to female bodies; and yet it struck a chord, contrasting in her memories with the sharp, compulsive misogyny of Jared Blake and too many others like him. She tried to imagine Mr Gryce or Mr Laughton being so considerate in a comparable situation, and found she could only imagine them being awkward about it, their manner sure to provide whatever discomfort their actual contact missed.

A primitive judgement, instinctive and politically baseless and very possibly dangerous, as it had no correlation to Leoden's goodness otherwise: *I trust him not to assault me.* Surely the lowest possible bar for anyone to jump, and yet she'd long since grown accustomed to how few adult men met even that basic requirement. The summer Saffron had turned fourteen, both she and Lyssi had kept a running tally of catcalls received over the Christmas holidays – not in competition, but because they couldn't quite believe it kept happening.

Lyssi. The thought of her was an ache, and Saffron was already hurting. She shoved it aside and risked a glance at the passing landscape, wincing to see her frigid, sand-whipped limbs visibly streaked with grime and scratches – and then she froze in place, blinking dumbly, as she looked at the land ahead.

Or rather, at the lack of it: instead of stretching on, the plain – no, the *plateau* – abruptly stopped, shearing away into a cliff edge. Rising up in the space beyond was a huge, translucent protuberance, so massive that she didn't initially realise it was symmetrical. Leoden had mentioned a dome, and this must be it – the promised shelter from the kshtathit. Yet how were they to get down there?

As if in rebuke of the unasked question, a brighter than usual burst of sideways lightning cobwebbed overhead, accompanied by a burst of static thunder. Behind her, Leoden swore, while the rider gave a frustrated growl and snapped the reins sharply, so that the creature turned to run parallel to the plateau's edge. Saffron heaved an internal sigh of relief. Introspection forgotten, she focused on picking out a narrow cliff-track through the gloom ahead, a path cutting down from where they were to the base of the silvery dome.

If not for the Trial of Queens, the descent that followed would have been one of the more terrifying experiences of Saffron's life. Instead, it left her manic and exhilarated, laughter bubbling in her throat with every downwards juddering step of their alien mount, its thick muscles bunched and tensing as the rider held it at a speed just shy of breakneck. Considering the nearby dizzying drop to the valley floor – a valley whose soaring dome protected a luminous bustling city, a colourful sprawl of lights and motion that seemed to go on forever – Saffron's memory of falling off her roa back in Karavos ought to have choked her; and, for one awful instant, it nearly did. But though she wobbled in her seat, the rider in front remained firm, and Leoden, as if sensing her sudden precariousness, tightened his grip. She did not fall, and down they thundered, down and down and down and down the switchback trail, until they reached the valley floor and, shortly, the dome's edge.

From the plateau's vantage, Saffron had seen that the dome was translucent; even so, she'd been thinking of it as glass or plastic or some such tangible substance, and was therefore taken aback when it proved completely permeable. The rider clearly knew this, as they urged their mount through without hesitation; Saffron barely had time to open her mouth in shock before an opaline shimmer passed over them, faint as a veil of water, and then–

The kshtathit stopped.

Or, no: that wasn't right. With the great beast finally slowing to a walk, Saffron turned in the saddle, staring back the way they'd come, at the fracturing sky above. It wasn't that the kshtathit had stopped, but that the dome was shielding them from it, the static bursts and whipping wind and stinging electricity all gone.

"Oh, thank god," she mumbled weakly, laughing as she pressed her face between the rider's shoulderblades. Behind her, Leoden exhaled in pained relief, while the rider contented themselves with patting the creature, gloved fingers skritching into its thick blue ruff. The creature gave an answering rumble – was it tired, Saffron wondered? She'd lost all sense of time, had no idea how long it had been since their rescue – fifteen minutes? forty? ninety? – and no notion in any case of whether such a period of activity counted as strenuous for such a massive beast.

With the immediate danger gone, she let herself look about at their new surroundings, which proved to be the outskirts of the nameless city. Unlike Karavos, there were no gates through which to pass: just two massive, carven pillars, each one several stories tall, made of some gleaming greenblack substance that was equally reminiscent of stone and crystal. The idea that they were gemstones seemed absurd, given their sheer size, but was the prospect really so much stranger than the existence of magic?

Just then, Leoden spoke in that other language, voice pitched for the hearing of the still-anonymous rider. Saffron had no idea what he said, but the rider's response was an indignant snort, followed by a longer verbal reply. As they spoke, they took one hand off the reins to rummage in the pocket of their coat, eventually flourishing their closed fist with a noise of triumph. Without quite looking around, they passed whatever they'd located back to Leoden, who took it, grunted approval – and then, to Saffron's complete surprise, tapped his knuckles against her arm, as though it were really meant for her. Confused, she swivelled in her seat – now that they were travelling at a reasonable pace, it was easier to make some space without putting herself at risk of falling off – and tilted her head at Leoden, miming confusion.

His lips quirked. Holding out his hand, he showed her what was on his palm: a fat white pill. He mimed swallowing it, then proffered it again. When Saffron didn't take it, he blinked, paused, then reached into his own coat pocket to pull out a leather flask of what, when opened, appeared to be water.

Saffron stared at Leoden, mouth working soundlessly. She had no idea what the pill would do, if it was meant as preventative or sedative or some other miscellaneous thing, but her fear of what it could potentially lead to was acute. In that moment, the only thing that stopped her from knocking it to the ground in abject refusal was the knowledge that Kenan medicine, being almost entirely dependent on the sevikmet and maramet, had little to no concept of pharmaceuticals, and Gwen had never said that Leoden had any knowledge of Earth. In all probability, he had no idea why taking an unknown pill from a stranger was, in Saffron's world, a thing whose dangers had been thoroughly emphasised since she was old enough to talk. Which was why, after another beat, she found herself accepting the pill, weighing it in contemplation. If either Leoden or the unknown rider wished her harm, they could have easily left her to the mercy of the kshtathit...

But what if it knocked her out? She thought of the worldwalkers, bound and captive beneath the palace; thought of human trafficking and roofied drinks.

She thought of Lita.

Saffron reached a decision. Fingers closing over the pill, she gestured with it and said, in her best approximation of broken Kenan, "What is?"

Surprise lit Leoden's eyes. "So you do speak Kenan!" And then, when Saffron continued to feign blankness, he sighed and said, enunciating slowly, "You understand?"

"Little," said Saffron. She shook the pill again, harder than before, and let her fear bleed into her voice. "*What is?*"

"Words," said Leoden quickly, brows shooting up in surprise. "It gives you language, I don't know how, but I took one, too–" He broke off, recalling her supposed lack of comprehension, and said again, firmly, "Words. Please?"

It wasn't what Saffron had been expecting. She looked at the pill again, wondering if this apparent language delivery system was scientifical or magical or something else altogether. *He could be lying*, she told herself, but it was a dutiful thought, and one at odds with the fact that Leoden, a newcomer lacking the zuymet, appeared to speak the local language fluently after very little time. *If I take this and it does what he says, then I'll be able to talk to him – and he'll be able to ask me why I'm here.* Not an optimal outcome, given the reason she'd kept silent in the first place. *But if it's really the local language, then I won't be reliant on him to figure out how to leave.*

The little voice in Saffron's head that sounded like her anxious mother shrieked in protest as she held out her hand for the water flask. *Nothing ventured, nothing gained.*

With a swig of lukewarm water, she swallowed the white pill.

For all the internal buildup, it was rather anticlimactic. Shrugging, Saffron handed the water flask back to Leoden, who conscientiously recapped it, and wondered what was meant to happen next. Her stomach churned slightly, but no more than it usually did after taking a pill on an empty stomach, and apart from a vague, suffusing warmth, she felt nothing out of the ordinary.

Then the rider said something, the words twisting oddly in Saffron's ears in a way they hadn't before. Leoden replied, and it was like listening from underwater, the meaning distorted but tangibly just out of reach. She shook her head, which was suddenly buzzing, rubbing at the triple scars that ran across her scalp. As Leoden and the rider continued to talk, their words flowed in and out of comprehension like bursts of chatter through white noise, as though some part of Saffron's brain were scanning through the FM band in search of a radio station.

And then, like flicking a switch, it happened.

"...takes effect at different rates," the rider was saying. "Some fast, some slow. It all depends on the person, the mind, their basic capabilities – it helps if they're already multilingual, but even so–"

"Hello," said Saffron, somewhat dazedly. An alien, unfamiliar word – *vevak* – and yet it felt no stranger on her tongue than if she were speaking Kenan or Vekshi, as instantly familiar as the knowledge that this new tongue was called Trade. "I, ah... does this work with science or magic?"

"Ahah! There she is!" the rider crowed, turning just enough

in the saddle to flash them both a brilliant smile. Saffron was startled to realise that they'd pushed their goggles up to their forehead, revealing a pair of bright brown eyes. "A very quick adaptation! To answer your question, the tablet is a little of both, though don't ask me how it all makes sense – I'm a paladin, not a mendicant." They took a hand off the reins and tapped two fingers twice against Saffron's cheek – a greeting of sorts, which some newfound instinct suggested was equivalent to a handshake. "I'm Nim, and this–" they gestured proudly to the big blue creature, "–is Maza, my *roshaqui*."

Languages, as Saffron was beginning to learn, were peculiar things. English was not a grammatically gendered language, like French or German, and nor was Kenan, which hinted at the hierarchial faith of its speakers in other ways. Vekshi was gendered, but as the feminine form was the overwhelming default, with the masculine variant used only in a smattering of instances – or, depending on context, if the speaker wished to be insulting – it scarcely registered. But Trade was very decidedly gendered, offering up a plurality of forms with which Saffron had little experience. The form Nim had used for their introduction was one of these, indicative of the speaker's identity, and Saffron almost laughed out loud to realise that her mental ungendering of the rider hadn't been far off the mark. Saffron knew of no English pronoun that was quite equivalent to Nim's own, and so borrowed a Kenan equivalent for ease of internal translation; thei were not so much androgynous as genderfluid, a distinction thir language reflected more easily than her own.

"It's a pleasure to meet you," Saffron said, as all this flashed through her head – then added, as seemed only polite, "And to meet Maza, too."

Nim grinned, broad and approving. "By what name may I know you?"

"I'm –" Saffron paused, slackjawed as her new knowledge

of Trade instinctively proffered a literal translation of her own name: *sitka*. Apparently, wherever she was – *Noqevai*, the language whispered, meaning *Nexus* – had crocus plants and a saffron crop, or knew of some close enough equivalent to have named it, and while the temptation to name herself that way was briefly strong, what came out instead was, "–Safi. You can call me Safi."

"You know *my* name, I trust?" asked Leoden, somewhat wryly.

Almost, Saffron answered honestly, but realised at the last what a bad idea it was. Admitting to knowing a tiny smatter of Kenan was one thing; confessing to knowing Leoden was another. "I don't," she said, not quite daring to face him as she said it. "I don't even know why I'm here."

Behind her, Leoden heaved an exasperated sigh. "Why am I not surprised?" he muttered in Kenan – then said, switching back to Trade, "I am Leoden. Am I right to assume you're a worldwalker, someone who's been to Kena before?"

"You are," said Saffron – cagily, not knowing where this was going. "I wasn't there long; I passed through on my way to somewhere else. The portal that brought me here..."

She broke off again, not sure what to say. A lump rose in her throat at the thought of her family: their loss and treatment of her was a subject she had no intention of raising, and yet how else to explain why she'd willingly fled to an unknown world? And then she remembered what Gwen had said back in Yevekshasa; that keeping track of the lies you'd told was harder than making them up. *Partial truths, then, where possible.* She took a steadying breath.

"I was... stuck," she said, forcing herself to turn and look at Leoden. "The place I was last, I was stuck there, and when the portal opened–"

"–you took the opportunity," Leoden finished. A strange gleam lit his eyes, though his expression was somehow sad. "Well, then. I suppose that means I have some explaining to do – though I'd prefer to be somewhere more comfortable first." Tilting his head to look past Saffron, he pitched his voice to Nim. "My thanks, by the way, for rescuing us. I'd thought the kshtathit would come later."

"That's because you're a traveller, and therefore foolish," Nim said amicably. "Which is why paladins exist." Turning to Saffron, thei explained, "Among our other duties, we keep a watch on who comes and goes from the dome, so that if a kshtathit blows up unexpectedly, or early – and they often do – we can round up any caught in it."

Now that she had access to Trade, Saffron was startled to realise that kshtathit meant *reality blizzard*, an intriguing concept she filed away for later investigation. Instead, she asked, "Do all paladins ride roshaqui, or is that just you?"

Nim laughed. "It's not just me. Roshaqui are ideal – they're intelligent, loyal, and native to Noqevai, which means the kshtathit doesn't scare them. All those static explosions, the electric currents? Maza doesn't feel them, because her coat protects her." Thei gave the beast another pleased pat on the neck.

"What does she eat?" Saffron asked, fascinated. "It must take an enormous amount to feed her – to feed all of them, if you keep so many tame."

"Oh, they'll eat almost anything, provided it stays still. Every six to eight days, we turn a pack of them loose on the Nakhereh–" the Trade name for the plains beyond the dome "–and let them graze as they will, with maybe a novice paladin along to watch over them. While they're in barracks, though, they eat mostly *joh*."

"Joh," Saffron echoed, dumbstruck by the meaning of the word. "You mean they eat *gemstones*?"

"Not *all* gems, obviously," said Nim, wrinkling thir nose in distaste. "Just joh. It's native, too, and it grows very quickly. Wild roshaqui eat it all the time, and it's not bad powdered down." Thei waved a hand at their surroundings. "You see?"

Saffron looked. They were still on the outskirts of Noqevai, the Trade name for both the city beneath the dome and this whole world in general. The broad avenue down which they rode was unpaved, the hard earth pounded flat by the passage of paws and feet alike, yet missing the parallel cartwheel ruts that Saffron had half expected, given the presumable lack of cars. This far out, the buildings were all permutations of two basic designs, being either tall, square and shuttered or longer, lower and open-faced. Probing her newfound knowledge of Trade for clues, she determined that the former were hostels and warehouses, the latter roshaqui stables and paladin barracks.

And everywhere else, along the road and between the buildings, were well-tended gardens, and vegetable plots, their deliberate symmetry marred by jagged, crystalline juts of joh growing haphazardly amidst the flora. The smallest outcrops were barely bigger than Saffron's arm, while the largest were like boulders, their unpolished facets – none quite the same colour, pinks and browns and golds and blues – reflecting the flashing light of the kshtathit overhead.

"It's beautiful," Saffron said, softly.

"I'm glad you think so," Nim replied, reining Maza to a gentle halt. They'd stopped before an incongruously L-shaped building: a stable with a barracks attached. Saffron's eye was caught by noise and movement, more leather-coated figures emerging to investigate their arrival. Nim murmured a command to Maza, and with a surprisingly canine *whuff*, the roshaqui knelt down, the sudden jolt of it setting the three of them rocking like buoys on a wave.

"You'll have to dismount first, Leoden," Nim said. "It's too crowded for the rest of us to sling a leg over otherwise – you're the only one with room to manoeuvre."

Leoden snorted. "That's easy for you to say – you're used to this lumbering forest." But he moved nonetheless, bracing against the saddle as he felt out the same handholds he'd used to ascend and clambered awkwardly down. Saffron waited until he stepped back from Maza's side and copied him, unable to keep from grinning as she did so. Last of all came Nim, who didn't so much climb as jump, a lithe, practised ascent that nonetheless betrayed a spark of showmanship. Saffron was on the brink of asking thim how long thei'd been a paladin when a nearby shout distracted her.

"Well run, Nim! You found the traveller?"

"Him and a newcomer both," Nim replied, turning to address the speaker. "Well met, Tsai!"

Either Saffron was acclimating to life as a worldwalker, or else there was a hard limit to how much shock she could register in a given day. The person approaching – Tsai – was humanoid, but clearly not human. Though she – and it was she; the grammar of Nim's greeting made that much clear – wore full-body leathers, her hands, throat and face were covered with pale green scales, the faint beginnings of amber striping evident at throat and wrist. Her eyes were wide, sideways-blinking and liquid black, and a webbed crest rose and lowered against her skull, reminding Saffron oddly of a cockatoo. Her voice was full of clicks and whistles even when speaking Trade, and yet was deeper than Saffron, once she'd processed all this, had expected.

"Leoden, Safi, this is Tsai, Guide-Paladin of the Second Approach. Tsai, these are my travellers. Permission to escort them further?"

The configuration of Tsai's eyes made it impossible for her to visibly roll them; instead, she gave a quick up-down flick of her crest, her cheek- and throat-scales pulsing faintly lilac as she made a clicking noise, a triple combination that somehow contrived to give the same impression. "I have little expectation of stopping you," said Tsai. "Be back by the second chime."

"My thanks," said Nim. Moving as one, they exchanged the same brief cheek touch with which Nim had greeted Saffron, and then Tsai turned and began calling instructions for Maza's care to other nearby figures, all of whom scrambled to obey.

"Roshaqui are too big to be groomed and unsaddled by just one person," Nim said, in answer to Saffron's unasked question. "The novice paladins all take turns. Now, come!" Thei began to walk, pulling Saffron and Leoden in thir wake like metal after a magnet. "I'll see you to your lodgings."

"There is no need," said Leoden, but the words were a formality: he made no further protest to Nim's presence, a small smile lurking in the corner of his mouth.

It hit Saffron then, with the suddenness of a freight train, that she was starting to *like* Leoden – to trust him, even. Which was utterly absurd, given everything she knew of his actions, to say nothing of how little time she'd actually spent in his company. She knew he was a liar and a manipulator, someone canny and cruel enough to fool Gwen into thinking he was something he wasn't; and yet that knowledge was secondhand, less immediately real than her own experiences.

His pleasantness, his consideration, even his mumbled prayer – it was all a façade, a trap designed to lull her into a false sense of security. It had to be, as smarter, more knowledgeable persons than Saffron had declared it so, and who was she to go against their reasoning?

Her earlier thoughts came back to her, muddled and foreboding. Kadeja, the ahunemet, the captive worldwalkers: none of it made sense to her, but that didn't mean there was no sense to be made; only that she lacked the necessary information, the right perspective, to see the true shape of it. And if that was true of Saffron, then maybe it was true of Gwen and Pix and the others, too.

I miss Yena. The thought sang through her, blooming into an ache between her ribs. Yena, with her glossy curls and quick, vulpine humour; Yena, who understood politics and people, knew how to parse the difference between pragmatism and self-deception, change and irreverence; Yena, who was so completely and beautifully herself that she glowed like a sun was trapped beneath her skin.

Yena, who was worlds away in Yevekshasa, accessible only through the dreamscape. Just like Luy and Gwen and Viya, and anyone else she desperately wanted to turn to.

Determination welled in Saffron. Whatever it was that Leoden planned to tell her – whatever he thought she was there to do – she would find a way to tell her friends; to uncover the truth and return to Kena.

"I'm over the rainbow," she murmured in English, recalling one of her earliest conversations with Gwen, "but that doesn't mean I'm waiting on tornadoes. I can do this." And then, with a sudden gulp at the truth of it, "I'm a worldwalker."

"I don't think I've heard that language before," Nim said, sounding faintly surprised. "You must have come from far away!"

"I really did," said Saffron, and let the paladin lead her into Noqevai.

Despite the lateness of the hour, the knock on Yena's door wasn't unexpected. After her meeting with Ksa and Mesthani, she'd tried to arrange a conference with Halaya, but the Shavaktiin had been busy, promising instead to speak to her later that evening. Apparently, the time had come, and though she was yet to finish her meal – her ordeal in the sun's mouth and subsequent healing had left her ravenous – she called out an easy *Come in!*, not bothering to look up.

"So this is where you've been."

Yena froze, the words sinking into her like hooks.

Yasha.

"*Namahsi,*" Yena said, setting down her bowl, her voice as calm as her pulse was not. Since their stranding in Yevekshasa, Yasha had insisted Yena refer to her by the Vekshi word for grandmother, even when they were speaking Kenan, as Yasha had just done. Anything else, she said, would be disrespectful, and what if someone overheard? *You need to fit in, child. They won't tell you anything, otherwise.* Yena clenched her jaw. "I was under the impression that you had no access here without my say-so."

Yasha snorted. "Counting on it, were you?"

Yena turned to face her, cheeks burning. "And what if I was?"

"It's my fault," said Halaya, stepping into view. Like the other Shavaktiin, she still wore her veils and robes, though their hems and cuffs were starting to show signs of wear. Following Yasha into Yena's quarters, Halaya shut the door behind them, her tone apologetic. "I would have warned you, but–"

"–but what we have to say," said Yasha, cutting her off, "was too important to risk your refusal to see me."

"Sit, then," Yena said, resigned. "Be welcome."

Yasha made no reply to this, but settled herself on the end of Yena's narrow bunk, clucking like an affronted hen at the uncomfortable surface. Yena's lips twitched; she suppressed the smile, waiting as Halaya claimed the sole spare chair; waiting out a silence as soft and sudden as snowfall.

As Yena looked at her grandmother, she noticed with surprise that, though her head and face were bare, she was dressed otherwise in Shavaktiin robes – a disguise to gain entry, she assumed, or the remains of one. Yasha studied her in turn, taking in her now-bald head, the faint new scars on her arms. Yena braced for praise, for censure – she honestly wasn't sure which gambit would be worse – and was therefore completely wrongfooted when Yasha said, with uncommon softness, "I never thought I'd miss your curls."

Yena swallowed hard. "I never thought you would, either. You always called them a heresy."

"I did," conceded Yasha. "But perhaps... perhaps they were a gentle one, all things considered."

"All things considered," Yena echoed. "And what does that mean?"

"That Veksh is ungentle," Yasha said. "I always knew it to be so, and yet–"

She broke off, visibly frustrated. The whole exchange was so out of keeping with what Yena knew of her grandmother's character that she was rendered speechless; certainly, it was sharply at odds with Yasha's recent behaviour.

"Namahsi?" Yena said, when Yasha remained silent.

Yasha sighed. "You chose to distance yourself from me. I was angry at you for that, until I understood what you meant to do, and why; and then I was angry at myself, for forcing you to act without my aid. I am… conflicted. Veksh had changed, and yet it hasn't; I have changed, and yet I haven't. Nothing aligns as I feel it ought, and in that dislocation I am thwarted. Veksh meant power to me, but in my return I have none. It has passed from my hands." She proffered her open palms to Yena – and then, in a shockingly Kenan gesture, cupped and bowed over them, body tight as she resettled her empty hands in her lap. When she looked up again, her eyes were bright. "But that is as it should be, is it not? A mother's power is a daughter's inheritance. Or a granddaughter's, in this case."

"And what of my mother's power?"

"Power she has aplenty, but it was never mine. She made her own, and that is a different inheritance. One you share with your sister. Shared," said Yasha, the words a sudden rasp, "with both your sisters."

Zech's ghost sat between them then, so real that Yena almost sobbed. "Is that what you came to say to me? That you accept my claim on her?"

"I always did," said Yasha, softly. "Never doubt that."

"We came," said Halaya, when Yena failed to speak again, "to tell you what we've learned about Kadeja."

At that, Yena sat bolt upright. "Are they going to start her trial? Have the queens passed judgement?"

"Nothing so sensible," Yasha growled. "But exile as I am, I still have ears and eyes and the wit to use them – or I did," she amended, "once a certain granddaughter reminded me of the fact. And if I lack my little birds–" the euphemism she'd always used for her spies in Kena, "–I can make do with Shavaktiin."

"We are *so* honoured," Halaya said wryly.

"Yes, yes." Yasha flapped an impatient hand, though the quirk of her mouth conceded the matter. "The salient point is this: though nothing is yet being *done* about Kadeja, a great deal is nonetheless being *said*. And one of the secrets most whispered of – the question many queens have asked, and yet which the priestesshood has declined to answer – is this: for what specific crime was Kadeja exiled in the first place?"

Yena jerked in shock. "You mean the *queens* don't even know?"

"It would seem so." Yasha's tone was grim. "Unlike mine, her exile was handed down by the First Voice of Ashasa, head of the Great Temple, whose word was as law, and only a handful of whose seniormost priestesses were ever rumoured to have known the crime." She raised an inquiring eye at Yena. "What does that suggest to you?"

"That her dismissal was either arbitrary," said Yena, exhaling hard, "or so heinous that the First Voice was ashamed to make it known."

"And based on her subsequent actions," Halaya murmured, "I somehow doubt it was the first of those. Or if it was, her notion of revenge is rather odd."

"I'd always assumed she was pushed out for her views on the gods," said Yena. "That she espoused to the priestesshood the same ideas she brought to Kena, about declaring the Kenan pantheon a facet of Ashasa."

"So had I," said Yasha, after a beat in which Yena felt certain she would be laughed at. "But while her views in that respect are illogical and heretical, neither are they entirely new – oh, don't look so shocked," she added, as Yena felt her brows shoot into her now-theoretical hairline. "Veksh is strong and Ashasa wise, but pantheism is not a new ailment, which is why the Great Temple traditionally takes the time to be public about its erasure. In Kadeja's case, I'd thought their silence might have been kept to spare her motherline undue shame, or out of embarrassment that such a high-ranking priestess had espoused such drivel. I might have probed the matter further, but there were no rumours to chase, while her decision to cleave to Leoden seemed proof enough in itself."

"May I take this speculation to indicate that you have not, in fact, discovered the true reason for her expulsion?" Yena asked, not quite impatiently.

Yasha flashed her a knowing look. "No," she said, after a moment. "We have not. But we have discovered a rather intriguing coincidence." To Yena's surprise, she gestured for Halaya to continue in her stead.

"Just as all queens must sit their Trial, so must all senior priestesses sit theirs. They call it the Trial of Knives, though Ashasa's Knives have no exclusive claim to it. Each ritual is held sacrosanct; few women ever attempt – or, indeed, are permitted to attempt – both, not least because failure tends to prove fatal."

"And Kadeja tried to sit both?"

"No," said Halaya. "But having already passed the Knives, she asked to take it again not long before her expulsion. She was denied, of course, but it's an anomaly. The Shavaktiin know of few queens or priestesses who survived their failure of either Trial, or who, having succeeded in one, attempted to sit the other. But asking to resit a Trial successfully passed? Neither I nor Yasha can recall another instance of it happening."

Yena blinked, considering what little she knew of the Trial of Queens or the Trial of Knives. By the evidence of her eyes, they were physically dangerous: both Safi and Zech had emerged with scars, and among the ranks of queens and senior priestesses alike there was scarcely a woman whose body did not bear some kind of permanent injury. Whatever combat the Trials involved – whatever rules their supplicants adhered to – it was clear survival came at a cost. Why would Kadeja want to repeat the experience?

Then it clicked. She looked at Yasha, seeing the truth of her conclusion writ in the matriarch's face. "It wasn't that she wanted to resit the Trial," she said. "It's that she wanted access to where the Trial is *held*."

The catacombing tunnels beneath Yevekshasa.

"We believe so," said Yasha. "You know I've sat the Trial of Queens. Even as an exile, I protect those secrets; whatever Veksh thinks of me, I understand the value of my oaths. And as I never sat the Knives, I do not know – can only guess – at what similarities might lie between them; the places Kadeja may have wished to access, the knowledge she might have coveted. But you, Yena – Halaya tells me you have plans to visit the Archives?"

"I do," said Yena. "Ksa a Kaje has arranged it."

Yasha nodded, for once making no comment. When she spoke again, her voice was hard. "I cannot in good conscience encourage you to research the Trial of Knives. Those secrets are not for you, Yena, and it would breach my faith in Ashasa – in the will of Her temple, Her servitors and daughters – to even suggest it. But."

"But," said Yena, understanding at once, "if I were to encounter some, some *relevant information* in my search for other details, and report it to you...?"

"Quite," said Yasha, shortly.

Belatedly, Yena realised that her grandmother carried no staff: in order to pass for a Shavaktiin, she'd had to leave it behind. It made sense, of course, yet now that she'd noticed, the absence struck her as a kind of nakedness, like seeing a crab without its claws.

She turned to Halaya. "Out of curiosity, why did you agree to bring my grandmother here? You could've told me all that yourself without taking any risks."

"I agreed," Halaya said quietly, "because she is the Queen Who Walked, and because she asked it as a boon of me, in that name, in return for the fact that I knew her story, but did not truly know *her*. And," she added, "if you'll forgive my meddling, she is your grandmother. She needed to see you – as you, I believe, have needed to see her."

Yena nodded, abruptly unable to speak. She looked at Yasha, at Halaya, and thought what it must have cost her grandmother's considerable pride to beg a Shavaktiin's aid.

Trembling only slightly, Yena stood and crossed the room, bending to drop a quick, cool kiss on Yasha's wrinkled cheek.

"Namahsi," she murmured. "Thank you."

And for the first time in a long time, she found she meant it.

11
Moon-Tales

Noqevai was a patchwork city, luminous and fey. So far as Saffron could see – and that was, she freely admitted, not very far at all, her knowledge and assumptions both still skewed to Earthly norms – it was a chaotic jumble of magic and technology, a magpie's nest assembled from the trappings of an itinerant multiverse. More and stranger creatures than the roshaqui roamed the mazelike streets, though none were quite so large, and as strange as she'd found the paladin Tsai – who belonged, said Nim, to a race called the Qashqa – she was far from being the only non-human around. Yet all of them, unquestionably, were people: people riding unfamiliar bipeds and quadrupeds; people in armoured palanquins; people zipping past her on gleaming, personalised hoverboards; people, people everywhere, and not a one she knew.

Saffron's head spun with it, giddy and half-terrified, elated to the point of nausea. It was like being perpetually caught in the moment where a lucid dream became a nightmare, only without the horror: a visceral, all-over jump that said *it's real and you're here and you need to stay calm or you can't control it,* written right down to her bones. Nim, who was clearly no stranger to overwhelmed newcomers, made no fuss of her gawking, but guided her gently through the crowds with a hand on her elbow, thir patter meant more as background noise than incitement to conversation. For his part, Leoden took in the alien markets, with their tiered fountains and colourful buildings and unpredictable denizens, with a sort of calm equanimity, as though he were not so much acclimatised to the setting as aloof from its implications.

"You are staying at the Baroeht, aren't you?" Nim asked him. The three of them momentarily split up, navigating separate paths through the cheerful outspill of a packed hostelry, the milling patrons all with a drink or food in hand and talking over the distant strains of music. When they came back together again, Nim added, as though there'd been no interruption, "I ought to have asked earlier, but I just assumed–"

"I am, yes," said Leoden, shooting thim a wry glance. "Though I'm not sure I ever said as much."

"You didn't have to," Nim replied. "It's in the paladin records, and even if it weren't, the Baroeht is usually where the touts send human first-timers." Saffron did a slight doubletake at that, the word *human* having a somewhat broader definition in Trade than in English, the better to account for the various differences that distinguished them across different worlds.

Leoden raised a brow. "Even the disreputable touts?"

"Especially them," said Nim. "Or else they'd answer to us."

"Why?" asked Saffron, interjecting for the first time in nearly ten minutes.

Nim waved a bare hand – thei'd long since removed thir gloves – at the surrounding cityscape. "Noqevai looks wild, I know, but it functions as it does precisely because we adhere to rules of order. Travellers coming here must be able to trust that they'll encounter a certain degree of safety, and that any patrons they bring in the future will do so, too. Some merchants thrive on risk, but few prefer it, and stepping between worlds is already danger enough for most. And we in turn can't afford to let a reputation for lawlessness hurt our trade, or else we couldn't function." Thei flicked a meaningful glance at the dome.

Saffron blinked, confused. "Why not?"

Leoden eyed her curiously. "What manner of world do you come from, that it's not obvious?"

There was no obvious sting in the question, or Saffron would have bristled. Instead, she felt very young, head ducked as she struggled to answer. "We have many large cities where I'm from. And they're full of, of *businesses*–" again, the word meant something subtly different here, "–but they don't work like this. Trade doesn't work like this. The companies own the factories where their products are made; almost everything is made in bulk, on a massive scale. The companies sell their products to shops, and the shops sell them to customers, and it's all… I mean, you do get people who sell the things they've made themselves, but it's smaller, rarer, and everything can be sent so far, so quickly, from one side of the world to the other – within a few days, I mean, not weeks or months – that we don't have travelling merchants. Just big businesses with lots of different stores in lots of different places, and smaller businesses whose owners support themselves and their shops, but still buy their stock from the bigger ones, or who need licences to be reputable."

"And what about food?" Nim asked, fascinated. "Is that all made the same way, too?"

"Sometimes," Saffron admitted. "There are farmers, but they mostly sell to companies, not shops or people. At least, I think that's how it works – the cities are so big, with so many surrounding, um–" there was no word for *suburbs* in Trade, forcing her to improvise, "–residential districts, that most people don't grow up with farms unless they live on one."

Leoden made a thoughtful noise. "So this city, this place – you have no reason to wonder how it can feed itself, sustain itself, in the absence of arable land?"

"We passed all those gardens –" Saffron began, then stopped, wincing as the illogic of it hit her. Of course a city of this size would have to get its perishable goods from *somewhere*, and if the kshtathit came regularly enough – and was dangerous enough – to render the surrounding plains useless for farming, of course they'd be reliant on traders. Outside Noqevai's protective dome, only the native fauna was safe. "Oh," she said, embarrassed. "I see now."

She half expected Nim and Leoden to laugh at her, but neither did. Nim just gave her a friendly clap on the arm, steering them through an octagonal plaza full of milling foot traffic.

"Most of our fresh produce comes from the Qashqa," thei said, scattering a small – flock? pack? – of scavenging, furred-and-feathered animals that appeared to occupy the same ecological niche as pigeons. Like the roshaqui, they had four eyes and six limbs, which was evidently a local speciality, though their colouration was more conservative, black and tan bodies with golden accents in their feathers and downy white underbellies. In fact, they reminded Saffron of nothing so much as tiny gryphons, hissing and tussling like kittens as they fought over scraps, their shiny wings flapping angrily; she made an involuntary noise at the sight, resisting the urge to try and scoop one up. Nim, oblivious, carried on: "Their enclave is one of the oldest in the city; they've had representatives here almost since the founding. Their world is easily accessed, full of game animals and edible flora, but prone to earthshakes and flooding, with few more tangible resources. Trading benefits us both." And then, as they turned the corner: "Ah! Here we are."

The Baroeht turned out to be a sturdy, eight-storey inn – two below ground, six above – with bathing facilities in the first lower level, a communal space serving food and drink on the ground floor, and rooms overhead, with each floor costing slightly more (and offering more comforts) than the one below. Leoden, it emerged, was staying on the moderately priced third tier, but at the rumbling of Saffron's stomach, he ushered them all to a vacant table on the ground floor and flagged down a human servitor, ordering a suite of dishes and a pitcher of what Saffron hoped was a non-alcoholic beverage.

It was only then, as she sank into her corner of the padded bench, that she realised how utterly sore and exhausted she was. It felt like a lifetime since she'd fled her childhood home in nothing but her clothes, and since then she'd jumped worlds through an unknown portal, run from the kshtathit, ridden a roshaqui into an alien city of trade, learned a new language and seen more sentient species than she'd ever dreamed existed, all while in the company of an enemy and a stranger.

Slowly doubling over until her forehead hit the tabletop, Saffron started laughing. The soles of her feet were swollen and tender, throbbing now that she finally had the luxury of noticing. Her face and arms were chapped raw from the wind and sand; her muscles ached from riding. She was laughing too hard, too loudly, tears leaking out from the corners of her eyes, but she still couldn't make herself stop.

Beside her, Nim bent down until thir head, too, was resting on the table. Saffron glanced at thim, wheezing in and out.

"Would patting help?" Nim asked kindly. "I don't know your soothing rituals, but patting seems to help a lot of people, especially the ones without feathers."

"It might," gasped Saffron, the noise she was making no longer strictly laughter. "Sure."

Not lifting thir head, Nim stroked her back in long, slow sweeps, up and down. It was grounding, and Saffron felt no shame in leaning against Nim's shoulder, eyes shut as her breathing steadily evened out and the terrible pressure inside her chest abated.

"There," said Nim, withdrawing thir hand as Saffron finally sat up again. "Better?"

"Much," Saffron admitted. "Though my feet still hurt."

"You've no shoes!" Nim clapped a horrified hand to thir mouth, eyes wide in belated shock. "Oh, and we made you walk all that way – we'll have to find you some! And some clothes, too," thei added, taking in the filthy state of Saffron's shirt and pants. "But only after you've eaten."

"And bathed," put in Leoden, somewhat unexpectedly. "The baths downstairs are rather good."

"I don't have any money–"

"You have me," said Leoden. "As you were sent to help me, I can hardly leave you straggling like a... what is that charming phrase you have, Nim?"

"Like a one-winged *sehket*," Nim said, grinning – an expression Saffron shared when her Trade-knowledge informed her that sehket were the pigeon-gryphons she'd seen earlier.

"Thank you," Leoden said, lips quirking. "Like a one-winged sehket, indeed. And besides," he added, voice lowering as the servitor returned with their food, "I believe I owe you an explanation."

Once upon a time four months ago, Saffron's mother had teased her for being a picky eater. It hadn't been a completely fair accusation even then – she was usually willing to try new things; she just didn't like particular foods cooked badly, or in combination – but it certainly didn't apply now. Ravenous, she tore into the local fare without hesitation, a thick noodle dish strewn with ribboned green vegetables and chewy pink morsels that looked like a cross between morels and unshelled scallops. There was a shared platter of some larger, many-legged creature like a prawn or a water bug, served whole in a buttery white sauce; Saffron watched Nim expertly shuck the head and carapace before, much more inexpertly, copying. She ended up dripping sauce to her elbows, but the effort was worth it: the meat inside was tangy and succulent, with a consistency closer to softened pork than fish, and she'd downed five before she could stop herself. The remaining dish was lighter, sweeter, full of different sliced tidbits of varying shapes and flavours – a palate-cleanser, Gwen would've called it. With the exception of a pale blue variety that tasted strongly of aniseed, Saffron enjoyed them all, though her favourites were the thick, pink wedges with a beetroot texture that tasted like salted melon.

Fit to bursting, she washed it all down with a deep draught of the unknown drink, a lilac-tinged liquid that tasted of flowers on the tongue, but burned like whiskey when swallowed. She coughed hard, eliciting an unsympathetic cackle from Nim, who was being far more conservative with thir own cup. Saffron managed a choking laugh, sniffing at the residue.

"Is this an intoxicant?" she asked, unable to find a closer word for *alcohol*.

"For most humans, yes," said Nim. "Though not an especially strong one, despite the taste. For the Qashqa, it might as well be water."

"You might've warned me!"

"You might've asked."

"And besides," said Leoden, interjecting with another small smile, "you seemed so focused, I hated to interrupt."

"There is no shame in hunger," Saffron said, with as much dignity as she could muster, snagging another one of the prawn-things as much for want of something to do with her hands as because they were delicious. Meanwhile, some internal voice was caught between panic and laughter: *God, is he actually* teasing *me?* She couldn't reconcile anything in Leoden's behaviour with what she'd been so explicitly warned against, and no matter how hard she tried to remember that deception was his master-skill – that the lack of outward warning signs was, in him, synonymous with a red flag – it was difficult to try and so completely ignore her own, more immediate instincts.

"*Ahhh,*" said Nim, sitting back with a satisfied sigh. "That was good!"

Leoden favoured thim with an amused look. "Paladin, did you walk us here solely to justify a meal at the Baroeht?"

"Not *solely*," said Nim. "I am also enjoying your company. But I do have a weakness for *krata*–" thei indicated the grim remains of the prawn-bug platter, "–and they're always excellent here."

"Here, and nowhere else?"

"Among other places," Nim conceded, "but none quite so unsuited to the dignity of a paladin, who ought to know of better eateries than those frequented by travellers. And yet."

"And yet," said Leoden, smiling.

Oh, thought Saffron, looking between them with dawning comprehension. *This is flirting. I think. Is this flirting?*

Leoden and Nim continued smiling at each other, forgetting to look away for a good three seconds.

Definitely flirting.

"Well," said Nim, coughing as thei stood. "As pleasant as this has all been, I believe the two of you have business to attend to, while I have a daring rescue to document for posterity."

"Paperwork," said Leoden gravely. "I do not envy you."

"A dangerous foe," said Nim. "Should you wish, in a spirit of charity, to verify my survival, you are welcome to inquire after me at the barracks."

"Should time permit, it would be my pleasure."

Standing, Leoden touched his fingers to Nim's cheek, a gesture thei returned with just a hint of self-consciousness. For the first time, Saffron wondered how old Nim was, and found herself stumped. She'd never considered that interpreting someone's gender played a part in how she guessed their age, but perhaps it did; or maybe it was a combination of factors, like clothing and manner and language, that were here rendered universally strange, and therefore devoid of clues. Either way, when Nim leant down to exchange the same parting touch with her, she found herself staring just a little too long, looking for crows' feet at the corners of those lively eyes. Yet all she saw was laughter lines, and when Nim raised a querying brow, she laughed in turn and said her own farewell, hoping they'd have occasion to meet again, too.

Leoden watched Nim go, his forearms braced on the tabletop, waiting silently as the servitor came to clear away the empty plates and refresh their pitcher of drink.

"How is it you have money here?" Saffron blurted suddenly. At Leoden's surprised expression, she remembered she was meant to have no knowledge of his origins, and hastily added, "You seem to be a traveller, not a merchant, so I just wondered–"

"I'm not a merchant," Leoden said. "Nor am I quite a traveller in the usual sense. But I am resourceful." He tipped his head back against the wall, eyes closed in remembrance. He had a mellow voice, one that was easy to listen to, and Saffron found herself hanging on every word. "When I first arrived, it was under tempestuous circumstances. I was fleeing my home, for reasons which... well... I'll explain that part shortly, as much as it can be explained. The point is that I was alone, confused, my thoughts an utter scramble." He opened his eyes and looked at her, as though something had just occurred to him. "You're a worldwalker. Does travelling ever disorient you, confuse your memories?"

Saffron blinked at him. "No," she said, puzzled. "It doesn't."

Leoden sighed. "I thought not. It seems to be a peculiar weakness of mine. Regardless, I arrived here with nothing, and though I'd conducted a little research into this place–"

That's one way of putting it, Saffron thought.

"–I didn't speak the language. But I did have the good fortune to arrive closer to the outskirts than you, which is where a tout found me."

"A tout? You mentioned those before, but I wasn't sure–"

"A sort of local guide," said Leoden. "Individuals who look out for newcomers to the city and earn their keep by showing them – or us, I suppose – how everything works: how to find lodgings, where to sell our wares, explaining the rules for good conduct, which are mostly good sense and courtesy. The paladins patrol the city and the Nakhereh, the mendicants give healing to all and keep watch on sanitation, the judiciars pass judgement for any wrongdoing – it's an oddly fascinating system, all penance culturally weighted to fit the sensibilities of both the accuser and the accused, which is rather a difficult prospect here – and apart from one or two basic civic functions, everything else is the purview of the various mercantile guilds.

"So: a tout found me, and gave me the language pill, though not before conveying that I'd need to find a way to pay for it. I accepted her terms, and once I could speak we discussed potential revenue options. There are, as it turns out, a great many things to be bought and sold in Noqevai, even should you show up naked and blind – and I'm told some do." He shrugged. "I sold myself."

It took Saffron a good five seconds to process this statement, jaw gaping steadily open.

"Forgive me," she said at last, "but that phrase has a very, ah, a very *particular* meaning in my home language, and I'm not sure you meant – I don't know how to ask..."

Leoden cocked his head, parsing her embarrassment. Then, to Saffron's utter astonishment, he burst out laughing. "Oh! The selling of sex, it's a shameful thing to your people?"

"I suppose it is," said Saffron, somewhat dazedly. "Though it shouldn't be."

"In my world, there are countries that have this attitude, too." He shook his head in bafflement. "I've never understood it. Why devalue that which you wish to purchase? It insults the buyer and demeans the seller, and that is no good way to treat a natural thing. In any case, it seemed the most expedient option. The mendicants run the pleasure-houses here, which is only sensible, the novelty of bedding travellers sets the value high, and the itinerant nature of participation is understood. I worked one night, and earned myself enough to live a month."

Saffron stared at him, unable to find the words to respond. It wasn't that she thought what he'd done was shameful; it was that she had no reference for Leoden being the sort of man who, whatever his Kenan thoughts on sex, would engage in selling it. He was born royalty – surely he had other skills to trade, a strong enough sense of entitlement to preclude the act? And yet she knew, even as she wrestled with the problem, that she was butting one sense of cultural assumptions up against another, to say nothing of knowing next to nothing of Leoden's true personality. Pix and Viya would know better what to make of it, but they weren't here, and in their absence she could only try to glean more information.

"Did you…" Saffron began, then licked her lips. Started over. "If I wanted to earn my own money, what other options are there? I'm not trying to insult you, but I couldn't – for me, it wouldn't–"

"You?" Leoden looked horrified. "Gods, of course not – you're far too young! Who would even…" He broke off, rubbing the bridge of his nose. "No," he murmured. "Don't answer that question. I know enough of people to know the answer, but I wish I didn't." He coughed, recalling himself, and said, "If you truly want coin of your own, a tout could aid you better than I, but there's always something. The mendicants buy blood and seed and marrow, if you're not too squeamish. Some vendors buy hair, though–" he grinned, indicating her shaven head, "–you'd have to wait some time to sell it. I'm told some of the mages here buy memories, and there's always menial work, grinding joh or sweeping stalls–"

"Leoden," said Saffron, cutting him off. "Why am I here?

Why are you?"

He exhaled slowly. "Ah. And so we come to the crux of it."

Saffron felt her pulse speed up, a terrible tripping beat. Leoden was silent for a long moment, and when he finally spoke, his voice was quiet.

"For many years," he said, "I was a scholar. I knew I was in line for the throne, that I might one day be called to rule, and while I was prepared for it, in an abstract way, I never truly considered it as an option." He lifted his head, gauging her reaction, and Saffron tried to look suitably impressed-slash-startled at the revelation of his royal heritage. Presumably, she did a good job, for Leoden flashed a quick smile and continued, with a laconic shrug, "The ruler – the former ruler, I mean – was my uncle. I don't know how things work in your world, but in my homeland, in Kena, our marriages are plural. The true ruler – the *Vex* or *Vexa*–" he used the Kenan terms, visibly frustrated with the restrictive nomenclature of Trade, "–takes a primary consort, a *Cuivexa* or *Cuivex*, and each of them – the Vex and Cuivexa, in my case – is entitled, expected, to take another three partners in turn, *sehet* and *halat* and *mara*, to represent the qualities most wanted in a family – in a *mahu'kedet*, as we say – to honour the attributes and organisation of the heavenly hierarchy of the gods."

"That sounds... complicated," said Saffron, who'd thought as much when Gwen had first explained it to her, and who still thought so now, albeit with less startlement at the particulars.

Leoden gave a wry laugh. "It certainly can be," he admitted. "What is important to understand is that not every partner in a mahu'kedet beds every other, though I understand that many beyond my country expect this to be so. I say this, not because I suspect you of prurience, but so you understand, when I tell you that my mother belonged to my uncle's – her brother's – royal mahu'kedet, that there was no incest involved. She was *Cui'Sehet*, a lesser consort of his Cuivex. My father-by-blood, as we say, was the *Vex'Halat*, a man my uncle married for his beauty and charm, though he loved his Cuivex before all others." He hesitated, then said, in a strangely detached, wistful voice, "They're all dead now, or else gone from court."

Technically, Saffron had known this; even so, she'd never quite heard it spoken of so baldly, nor in such tones as to make it seem a tragedy. Some of this must have shown in her face, for Leoden waved a hand and said, in the same tone, "Not all at once, if that's what you're imagining. There was no great catastrophe, except that my uncle Ralan was enamoured only of men, yet so content with the peace of his realm and the love of his family that he made no rush to secure his inheritance by naming an heir." A look of fond remembrance suffused his face. "The few times we spoke of it, he said he was waiting to see who might yet be born better suited to the task than those of us living. I never took offence at his not naming me, though I suspect my cousins—" he grimaced at the word, though whether at the reminder of Amenet and Tevet, or at the inaccuracy of the Trade-term, Saffron didn't know, "–felt otherwise.

"Regardless," he continued, "my uncle let his mahu'kedet decline without thought of renewal. His *Vex'Mara* and *Vex'Sehet* were both old when he married them, prominent women already admired in Kena, who bore no children. My mother, who was his elder, predeceased him by several years – a canker of the lung, an ailment beyond the remedy of our healers."

"I'm sorry," said Saffron. She'd lost an aunt to cancer, though she'd been so small when it happened, she scarcely remembered.

"Thank you," said Leoden. "And the others... well. My father-by-blood had a rather dramatic falling-out with Cuivex Tahen over my uncle's affections many years ago – I would've been, oh, eight at the time. Things between them all became too tense to bear; in the end, it was easier for him to plead a halat's grace and retire to an estate in the far south, away from us all. We exchanged letters for many years, but none... none recently." He frowned, as though perturbed by this detail, then blinked it away, resuming his narrative. "The only shock death was Tahen's – he passed the year after my mother did, though he was the youngest and healthiest. A sheer reckless accident, breaking his neck in a fall from his horse. My uncle took his loss hard; he was urged to take a new consort, but he loved Tahen deeply and had no wish to dishonour his memory for the sake of, as he put it, rounding out the numbers."

A brief flicker of smile, there and gone. "Which left him, at the time of his own passing, with only two marriage-mates, Tahen's Cui'Mara and Cui'Halat. They'd been married themselves, to each other alone, before their partnership was ever made an aspect of the royal mahu'kedet, and almost the first thing they did at Ralan's death was retire to their old holdings. Which left me, the only child born to the mahu'kedet, and my two elder cousins, Amenet and Tevet, who were the daughters of my uncle's royal-born brother, as his only likely heirs."

Amenet, whom you betrayed and poisoned. Tevet, whom you killed. The words were poised on Saffron's tongue, and yet she didn't speak them, fascinated despite herself by Leoden's account.

"And what were you doing through all of this?" she prompted, when he lapsed into silence.

"Me?" Leoden reached for the pitcher, pouring them each another cup of the lilac liquor. He took a long sip from his own, though Saffron merely cradled hers, uncertain of its potency and unwilling to risk accidental inebriation. "I was, like my mother before me, a scholar, engaged in scholarly pursuits. I had this fascination with moon-tales – that is, with the stories we tell our children – and the idea that some of our lost history might be hidden within them. For so much of our history *is* lost, in Kena. And I thought, if I could only find the right clues and follow them, that I might unearth something spectacular and important. I must have looked quite odd, taking so many trips to old ruins, consulting with magic-users and storytellers and foreigners to see where their versions of things matched up with mine, or where they differed, but I loved it. And that's how I met her."

"Her?" asked Saffron, so caught up in the story that she'd forgotten the proper context, and felt her stomach lurch at the look on Leoden's face.

"Kadeja," he said, smiling. "She's my Vex'Mara now, but back then, before Ralan died, she was the first person I'd ever met who shared my enthusiasm for moon-tales, for the idea that the past could be recovered. She wasn't from Kena – she'd been cast out of Veksh, a nation to our north – and I met her outside Yavinae, during one of my research trips. She had such ideas..."

He trailed off, eyes going vague as he stared into the distance, and Saffron felt something sick and ugly curl through her stomach at the realisation that there was no good way for Leoden's story to end.

Finally, he snapped back into himself, and said, "We began to work together, she and I. We didn't plan to marry – her people don't, and I understood – but once Ralan died, it was different. Important, that she be with me. That we not be interrupted." His gaze took on that strange gloss again, as though he were speaking at a remove. "And in the palace, we discovered an artefact. Old and powerful. Kadeja knew what it was, she knew – her people had different stories, sacred stories – and so we found a helper to unlock its purpose, to show us how to make it into a portal. And with his help, she showed me what we'd lost; what my realm had lost. A missing piece of itself, of Kena's very heart – a stolen scrap of world – that I, as the Vex, had a duty to reclaim. A duty that superceded all other concerns."

Saffron found that her hands were shaking. To still them, she took a sip of liquor, motioning silently for Leoden to continue. Which, to her mingled dread and astonishment, he did.

"And I was Vex, then. There'd been talk of my marrying Amenet and Tevet – sensible talk, in its way – but Kadeja made me see the danger in it. They couldn't be trusted with what we were doing; they wouldn't understand. And so she – I – that is, we acted, we–" a strange and frightening interplay of emotions crossed his face, "–we were forced to remove them both. And then a more suitable Vex'Mara was found, who wouldn't interrupt, and I found new help in a storyteller, who knew more secrets than we'd ever hoped to find, and the ambassador helped us, too, though she'd refused at first. But then the Vex'Mara ran, and after that, nothing went as it should: the palace was attacked, Kadeja was stolen away from me, and I was forced to come alone. Or at least, I thought I was alone, but only because I'd forgotten about Naruet. And then he sent me you."

"Naruet?" asked Saffron, leaping on the name. "Who's Naruet?"

"My ally in Kena," Leoden said. "One with a gift for portal-magic." His expression was friendly, conspiratorial. "He's the one who brought you here."

"Why, though?" The words came out a helpless rasp. "Why me?"

"Because you're a worldwalker," Leoden said, as if it were obvious. "Because he must think you can help me find it."

"Find what?"

"The missing heart of Kena." Leoden's eyes shone, wild and dark. "The moon the wolf swallowed, which wasn't a moon at all, but a piece of our living world, dislocated and set adrift and lost. Our ancient place. Vikasa."

12
Over Star & Under Ocean

Luy sat at the edge of his crossroads, fingers tapping impatiently as he waited for Kikra to appear. Prior to falling asleep, he'd been eager to find help and answers, but furious at himself for missing the clue from Naruet about his stolen memories. *Missing pieces indeed!* Luy felt stung, though more by his own heedlessness than the cryptic nature of the hint, and doubly so when he realised that, in the chaos of Sene's suicide, he'd completely forgotten to ask about the youth. The thought of Leoden rifling his thoughts, his memories – the violation of it, knowing he'd given up Shavaktiin secrets – left him feeling sick; as did the fact that Naruet, a stranger, had been able to sense the absence through the dreamscape, while Luy had felt nothing amiss. But now that he was forced to wait, surrounded in the most literal sense by his own subconscious, part of him wanted nothing more than to run.

It was Yena who really needed to hear it, but Yena was in a temple warded against the ilumet, so Kikra it would have to be.

"You're very still tonight."

Luy whirled, hands clenching. There was Naruet, summoned as if by thought. He ought to have been angry, and for half a heartbeat, he was – and then he laughed, his faith in the Great Story reasserting itself.

"I suppose I am," he said. "Or most of me is, at least. I keep fidgeting my hands."

"Dream-hands," Naruet pointed out. "Your real ones are as quiet as the rest of you."

"That's true." He inhaled, lips quirking as the youth's strange effect on his dreamscape started to make itself known, the coloured drifts and crystalline mushrooms just as compelling as they'd been the first time. "You never told me how you know me in waking."

"I didn't," Naruet agreed.

"Will you?"

A lengthy pause. "Maybe."

Luy didn't know whether to laugh or cry. "Now?"

"Does it matter so much?"

"It does. It does. You said that–" the words caught in his throat, forcing him to stop, start again, "you said I was missing pieces. And you asked about my friend."

"Oh, Safi – yes! And I found her, too." Naruet beamed at him, the broad smile transforming his face. "I opened a door to where she needed to go, and she went quite beautifully." His smile fell away as swiftly as it had come. "I couldn't speak her words, but she was sad where she was. She wanted to leave." And then, more softly, "I know what that feels like."

Luy went cold all over. "You have the jahudemet?"

"I do."

"And you... you opened a portal to Safi? Sent her away from Earth?"

"I did."

"You brought her to Kena?"

"Of course not!" He wrinkled his nose, offended. "She wasn't needed here, not yet. I sent her away to help."

"Help? Help who?"

"Leoden."

Luy sat down heavily, thumping onto the crossroads grass.

"Thorns and godshit," he whispered. He looked up at Naruet, more helpless than he'd felt in years. "Why in the worlds did you do a thing like that?"

"Because it needed to be done." Naruet cocked his head, forehead creasing slightly. "I don't understand. Why aren't you pleased? You helped him, too."

"He took pieces of me!" Luy shouted, surging back to his feet. Naruet cringed away from him, hands flung up as if to ward off a blow. "That's what you told me, isn't it? That I was missing pieces?"

"Yes, but –"

"But nothing! Leoden stole them from me, and you –" He fell back, appalled, an entirely new thought occurring to him. *Jahudemet.* "Blessed Scribe. You're the one who helped him, aren't you? The one who opened the anchored portal, the one the Most Honoured of Ke's Kin is sending us."

All at once, Naruet looked very young indeed. His shoulders hunched, head ducking like a bird's. "I am," he said, softly. "I know you won't believe me, but I never meant for anyone to be hurt."

Luy exhaled hard. He felt adrift, wrung out, unable to reconcile this shy, flinching boy with the beautiful dreamscape to the idea of a person so cold-blooded as to sanction the kidnapping, torture and imprisonment of worldwalkers. "I don't understand. Why did you do it? Why did you help him hurt all those innocent people?"

"He didn't do it!" Naruet cried. His head snapped up, fresh tears on his cheeks. "He's a good man, he was Inside, he was kind to me and he said… he told me they were criminals, and I believed him, but Ktho says they weren't and I think now, I think… I think–"

"What?" snapped Luy, too frightened for tact. *"What is it* that you *think–"*

Naruet gulped. "I think he's missing pieces, too."

•••

Gwen's awareness of the dreamscape came on her slowly, as though she were rising up through a honeyed lake. It was the very strangeness of this thought that brought her the rest of the way to lucidity, laughing under her breath. The landscape around her was striking in its vivid impossibility: to her left, great staticky swathes of unreality hung in the air like eldritch sheets from some invisible washing line, while to her right was a maze of junkheaps, metals and woods and plastics all mingled together. The ground underfoot was red stones strewn on silver sand, the sky a tempestuous bruise-green riven with sideways lightning cracks. Gwen's first thought was that she'd stumbled into a stranger's dreamscape – it had happened once or twice before, always to curious effect – but there was a peculiar feeling of intrusion to those encounters that was absent here, and so she discarded the theory. More likely, this was an echo of somewhere real, and she'd been brought here for a purpose.

Rubbing her eyes, she came slowly to her feet and called for the likeliest culprit, gaze caught by a flicker of movement off between the junkheaps.

"Louis? Is that you?"

A figure emerged, eyes wide.

"Gwen?"

"Oh!" Gwen exclaimed, awash with relief. It wasn't her son: it was Saffron, and as the girl pelted madly towards her, Gwen flung out her arms and caught her, wrapping her into a tight, hard hug.

"Gwen!" Saffron choked again, the name almost a sob, and Gwen held her tighter, swallowing against the sudden threat of tears. Of course she'd worried about the girl, but until that moment she'd been able to hold her fear at a distance, the better to deal with more immediate threats. She tried to push it back again, to be a composed and knowing adult, but then she felt Saffron shake against her, thin ribs moving under her arms, and realised the girl was crying, face mashed hard to Gwen's collarbone.

All the air went out of her, and for a perilous, breathless moment, she felt her waking self flicker, the strength of the moment almost enough to catapult her out of dreams entirely. But Gwen was long practised at resisting such currents, and so she held firm and let herself cry, too.

Tears were odd things in the dreamscape, their presence the product of memory and emotion. The heat of them, the faint taste on her lips – Gwen knew it wasn't real, not in the bodily sense, but the mind has its own realities, and it seldom paid to do them a discourtesy. She rode out the feeling, making an effort only to breathe steadily, and when they finally pulled back from each other, Saffron's cheeks were utterly dry, the phantom salt evaporated like dew.

"Damn me, but I missed you," Gwen murmured, laughing as she clapped a hand to Saffron's shoulder. "I won't say I should've gone back with you, because I don't know that it would've made things easier, but I've wished I did all the same."

"I've wished it, too," said Saffron, softly.

Gwen took in her tremulous smile, the stubborn set of her shoulders. "Tell me," she said, and did not specify *honestly*, knowing in her bones that Saffron wouldn't lie. "How bad was it?"

Saffron's eyes sparked, their green as shattered as the sky above. "They wanted to save me from what I'd already become. They wanted to turn back my heart like a clock, and when I said no, they thought I needed fixing." Her smile faltered, sharp and sad. "And perhaps I do, at times. But not like that, and not from them. Never again."

"Oh, girl." Gwen took her hand and squeezed it, as her heart squeezed in her chest. "Are you sure?"

"I've left them," Saffron said. "I ran away, but they won't find me. I'm safe from that, at least."

Gwen was on the verge of commenting on this when the

significance of their surroundings suddenly hit her all over again. If she was right, and this was a real place, then Saffron had to have brought her here – but this was demonstrably *not* a place on Earth.

"You mean you left the world," Gwen breathed, seeing the truth of it in Saffron's face. "But Trishka never sent a portal."

"I know." Saffron gulped a laugh, a shaky hand running across her stubbled head. "I mean, I know that now for sure, though it didn't really register at the time – the magic looked different to Trishka's, but my parents were chasing me after I left the house, and I–"

"They were *chasing* you?"

Guilt flashed over Saffron's face; Gwen inwardly cursed and bit her tongue, forcing herself to speak more gently. "Start at the beginning. Deep breaths. Go as slow as you like, but tell me what happened." And then, with a flare of maternal wryness she couldn't quite quash, "Louis was hardly forthcoming with the details."

"That's not his fault," said Saffron. "It was hard to contact him at all, but I think, being here–" she broke off, shaking her head. "No. OK. I'll start at the beginning, like you said."

And so she did, hands clenching whenever her telling faltered, voice surprisingly even as she told Gwen everything: about the police, her teachers and school and social worker; about her parents and what they'd done; about Jared Blake, the boy who'd tried to ruin her; about Lyssi and Lita and Ruby. It was a story both familiar and alien to Gwen, so that her heart ached in sympathy. She'd always known that going back would be difficult, but she'd hoped, however foolishly, that it might be somehow easier for Saffron than it had been for her.

"And then I felt the strangest tug," said Saffron, who'd just described her flight to the train station, "like something had hooked in my stomach and *pulled*. And then the portal appeared, and I just – I didn't know where else to go, what

else to do. So I stepped through, and ended up in this place."
She waved a hand to indicate their bizarre surroundings.
Her lips twitched briefly, as if in remembered humour; then
the expression fell. She took a moment to steady herself,
and when she next looked at Gwen, her face was studiously
blank. "Leoden was waiting for me, here. Not that he had
any idea who I was," she added quickly, answering Gwen's
shocked inhalation, "but the portal was made by his ally in
Kena, a jahudemet-user called Naruet, who meant to send
me as help to him, though neither of us is quite sure why
beyond the fact that I'm a worldwalker. But, Gwen–"

"Has he hurt you?" Gwen gripped her hand again, fearful
and urgent. "I can speak to Ke's Kin, get you back to us – I
swear, if he's done anything–"

"He hasn't," said Saffron, voice oddly pained. "Gwen,
listen, I don't... I don't know how to explain it, I know I
shouldn't trust him, but he's said some things... The way he
talks about Kadeja, about what she's like – about how they
met, what they were doing together – god, it's so messed up,
and you know what Luy said about the worldwalkers, about
their memories being stolen? I think Kadeja's the one who
did it, not Leoden; I think she did it to him, too." And before
Gwen could quite process this stunning suggestion, Saffron
launched into a different narrative, speaking more quickly
than before: running ahead of a reality storm, their sudden
rescue, Leoden praying; the rider Nim, their walk to the
boarding house; Leoden's revelation of his sources – Kadeja,
Shavaktiin, ambassador – and, more terribly, his purpose,
hunting a missing piece of a world whose name was stolen
from Louis' memories.

*Vikasa. He's looking for Vikasa, and he's doing it in the Nexus. It's
why he stole the worldwalkers.* It was a vital piece of intelligence,
the very clue they'd been looking for, yet overshadowed in
the telling by Saffron's unexpected defence of Leoden.

"No," said Gwen, when Saffron had finished. Her stomach

was churning, thoughts whirling at hurricane speed. "No, he's complicit, he has to be, no matter Kadeja's role. Everything he's said and done, the way he changes – his *voice*, gods, you've never – you've never truly seen him, girl, never been there when the veil lifts and he shows his true face, the *venom* of it all." She shut her eyes briefly, thinking back to that last frantic dash through the shaking palace, Leoden's sharp tongue cutting Viya, Louis; the way he could switch between cruel and calm without so much as blinking.

"I know I haven't," Saffron said, voice edged with desperation. "But Gwen, the way he is here – he asked me if I'd experienced memory loss after using portals, or if it was something that only happened to him. And I know I don't know much about how the ahunemet works, but mind-magic, rifling thoughts... if it can be used to take memories, why can't it also be used to change them, or create them? I just... I keep thinking – did any of you ever meet Leoden, speak to him, before he knew Kadeja? Because if he was always like this, well, that's one thing, but if it's a change..."

"I don't know," said Gwen, feeling sick to her stomach. "I never knew him before her, and I don't think Pix did, either – she was part of old Vex Ralan's court, but he was never much in attendance..." Her voice tailed away, the incongruity of the statement striking her like a blow.

"Ralan!" said Saffron, seizing on the name. "He told me – Leoden did, I mean – he explained his whole family to me, what happened to Vex Ralan's mahu'kedet. They're mostly dead, but he said that his father – his bloodfather, I mean, the old Vex'Halat – he's meant to be still alive, retired to his estates. They used to write letters to each other, but Leoden said they'd stopped. He sounded confused about it, as though he didn't remember why, and from the way he was talking I think it happened around the time he first met Kadeja – I think he said it happened at Yavinae, but I didn't know the name–"

"*Yavinae?*" Gwen exclaimed, shocked. "Kadeja went to *Yavinae?*"

"Is it important?"

"It could be. Gods!" She ran a hand down her face, an ugly knot of guilt in her chest. "If there's even a chance you're right – and I'm not saying you are, just that it's a possibility – but *if* you're right, then all this time she's been using him, hurting him, right out in the open, and none of us ever noticed." She shuddered. "Do you know, I think that might actually be the worse sin? To have accidentally helped a monster take the throne is one thing, but not to have seen that he wasn't a monster at all – to have blamed him for what was done to him..." She fell silent, momentarily overwhelmed. Then:

"No," Gwen said again, more calmly than she felt. "One thing at a time. You might be right and you might be wrong, but either way, we need more evidence – and either way," she added, in belated recognition of the fact, "you've done extraordinarily well to find out as much as you did." She smiled, the expression coming more easily than she'd expected, and said, "I'm proud of you."

Saffron made a small, involuntary noise at that, and something in Gwen clenched hard as a fist to think that no one else had told her so, when Saffron so clearly deserved and needed to hear it. She tried to think of what else to say, but found herself forestalled when Saffron suddenly tensed up.

"What is it?" Gwen asked.

"I don't know." And yet Saffron was taut as a bowstring, eyes scanning the impossible horizon. "I think... you told me once that Earth was hard to access with the jahudemet; that magic was fainter there. I think that's why I've had so much trouble reaching Luy or staying in the dreamscape before now. But this world, this *place*? It's ragged at the edges. Permeable, somehow, magically and otherwise."

"Metmirai," Gwen breathed. "In Kenan, that's the word for

it – metmirai. It means magic-ragged."

Saffron nodded, digesting the term. "That makes sense. I barely had to try to get here at all. And all this debris–" she gestured again at the junkheaps, more sharply than before, "–it's like flotsam and jetsam, lost things washed up here from different worlds, or blown on the kshtathit. The reality storm," she added, answering Gwen's confusion. Gwen nodded, belatedly recalling the term, and motioned for Saffron to continue. "And just now, I felt something like… I don't know." She set a hand to her abdomen, pushing in slightly. "A jolt. A tug in my stomach, just like I did on the train station, before the portal came." She frowned, eyes downcast. "It sounds silly, when I say it like that. It's probably nothing."

"Or it might not be," Gwen pointed out. "If Noqevai, the Nexus, is really so magically dense, you might well be sensing something. We–"

A booming thunderclap cut her off mid-sentence. The dreamscape shook around them, hard enough that they stumbled. Saffron cried out in shock; Gwen grabbed her arm, determined not to be cast away – or cast awake, which was much the same thing – and looked frantically for the source of the disturbance.

"Is this the ksht… the reality storm, whatever it is?" she asked, voice raised to carry over the sudden roaring wind.

"I don't know!" Saffron shouted back. "But if it is, we should run!"

"Why?" Gwen asked, even as she complied. Her hand found Saffron's, and as the dreamscape shuddered and groaned, she let herself be towed through the junkheaps, wondering at the sudden scent of bleach and ozone.

"Because I brought us outside the dome!"

"You *what?*"

"The dome, there's a dome over the city that protects it from the kshtathit, and Luy told me once – I think it was him,

I don't know how else I'd know if it wasn't..." She swore, dodging sharply as the rising wind flung some alien object into her path, "...he told me that the dreamscape echoes the worlds, that there's a geography to it, a closeness, and I think–" the sky lit up, a jagged spraddle of cracking light through angry jade, "–I think, the jahudemet and ilumet are enough alike that a reality storm can affect both! Or maybe it *is* both, I don't know, but this, what's happening–" another sonorous crack, the ground jumping under their feet, "–it feels like it did in the waking world, and if I'm right we really don't want to get caught in it!"

"Then wake up!" said Gwen, a prickle of sweat at the nape of her neck – a detail she'd seldom felt in dreams. "We both wake up, and nothing happens!"

"I'm trying! Are you?"

"I am now!" Gwen said, but even as she spoke, she chilled to realise the difficulty. It felt as if something was holding her there, a tacky, staticky interference like white noise jamming a radio frequency. Which, she realised abruptly, was probably quite close to the literal truth: if the kshtathit really was a wild blend of jahudemet and ilumet, a natural phenomenon concerned less with the human delineation of magical disciplines than ripping holes in the worlds, then their proximity to it likely meant the sheer scope of its magic was cancelling out their own, much smaller talents.

Gwen felt a kick of real fear, then. She began to run faster, heart rabbiting as she dropped Saffron's hand in favour of keeping pace.

Beside her, Saffron let out a terrified bark of laughter. "I wonder if the paladins patrol here, too? Dream-riders on dream-roshaqui, Nim to the rescue again–"

"Sounds like quite the sight," Gwen panted, and then–

Several things happened at once, distinguishable as separate occurrences only in the aftermath.

The kshtathit rolled over them, burning like bleach and

turning the dreamscape crystal-blue as an old star's heart.

A skinny, frightened youth with wild black hair materialised alongside Gwen, grabbed her hand and shouted, "Sorry!", yanking her fiercely sideways and down, the landscape parting around them like theatre curtains.

Saffron let out a startled yelp as a bright gold light flared out from her stomach, irising into an all-over halo that hurt to look at, until she was like a firework ghost, an afterimage seared on the eyes forever.

The dreamscape shuddered and warped. Gwen clung to the unfamiliar hand as her sole point of contact, coughing as she fell and failed and finally tumbled to her knees on a patch of grass, head swimming with the strangeness of it. Her hands were empty, she realised: she had a feeling the youth was nearby, but beyond that, her senses were disarrayed.

"Mother!"

"Louis?" she croaked, shocked to find her son standing over her, eyes wild and worried as he helped her to her feet. "What happened?"

"He brought you! He was here one minute, and then he started babbling, and then he vanished, and now you're here... you're both here," he amended, casting a furious gaze on Gwen's rescuer, "and there is, presumably, a relevant explanation as to why."

"The kshtathit," the youth said. He was coughing too, bent double at the waist, and when he straightened up Gwen was startled to find that she recognised him: Naruet, the acolyte of Ke's Kin who'd so obligingly opened the portal to Avekou that fetched Amenet, Matu and Jeiden. "It was going to take them both, and Safi was safe, but your bloodmother wasn't."

"Kshtathit?" Louis asked, just as Gwen said, "Safi was safe?"

"Yes," said the boy – said Naruet.

Naruet.

Gwen stared at him, struggling to understand. "You're

working with Leoden," she said. "You sent Saffron to Noqevai."

"I did."

"But you saved me, just now."

"Yes."

"He doesn't seem to know whose side he's on," said Louis, not without rancour. "Though he's also been trying to convince me that Leoden's being controlled by someone–"

"Saffron had the same theory," Gwen said, cutting her son off. "And not, I think, because Naruet suggested it to her."

"We haven't spoken, Safi and I," said Naruet, not unhelpfully. "I knew she could help, but there wasn't time to talk–"

"The kshtathit," Gwen said, suddenly urgent. "You're sure she's safe? The way she lit up–"

"– is why she's safe," said Naruet, calmly. "And why I sent her to Leoden."

"How do you know?" asked Louis, curious. "What makes you so certain of any of this?"

Naruet frowned. "I scry the worlds and the dreamscape," he said at last. "I used the jahudemet to look, the ilumet to map – it's all a web of tangled things, but full of patterns, full of paths."

"Like a crossroads," Louis breathed. His gaze bore intently into Naruet. "That's what you're describing, yes? You made a crossroads in your dreamscape, looking for possibilities?"

"That is accurate," Naruet said, blinking in clear surprise. "Yes. I did that."

"Damn me," Louis said, looking Naruet over with new respect. "You're a Shavaktiin. Not formally," he added, preempting Naruet's startled response, "but what you're doing, looking for patterns, following them out – sending people where you think they need to go, the way you did with Safi? That's Shavaktiin work." Almost, he laughed. "No wonder the Story sent you here."

"Not to disparage your faith," said Gwen, in a tone just shy of snapping, "but I'm more concerned with where the kshtathit sent Saffron."

"It didn't send her anywhere," said Naruet. "I told you, she was safe."

"But how do you *know* that?"

Naruet didn't reply, his gaze fixed on a distant point. Gwen heaved an exasperated sigh and turned to Louis. "Is he always like this?"

"Apparently," Louis said, "but in his case, I think it might be more… what's that English phrase?" He paused, considering, then switched languages, grinning broadly. "More a feature than a bug."

Any reply Gwen might have made was forestalled by a sudden shout from the distance. She turned, surprised, and saw a yellow-robed figure approaching. She tensed, unable to place the man's face, but relaxed again when she realised it was Kikra, the Shavaktiin dreamseer.

"Hoy, Luy!" called Kikra, walking up to them. "I didn't know your mother would be joining us."

"It's something of an accident," Gwen said. "Though hopefully a fortuitous one, if it means we all get to talk." She took a breath, steeling herself as she turned to introduce Naruet to Kikra–

But Naruet was gone.

It was like being caught in a hurricane, a vortex of clawing light. Saffron choked and tumbled, the kshtathit snapping at her heels like an angry dog, and yet the light, whatever it was, continued to whisk her onwards in a rushing roar of gold. Her stomach burned with it, a bellydeep ache that made no sense, as sharp-edged as if she'd swallowed something–

<scale-sister>

The words thumped into her, hard as blows and just as sudden, jarring as the light winked out and dropped her in a single, hurtling instant.

Saffron crashed into consciousness like a carcass into the bed of a truck, her body slick with sweat. She sat up, gasping, fumbling in the dark. For a horrible moment, she thought she was back in the tunnels under Yevekshasa, until her hands clenched and felt bedding, not dirt. *I'm in the Baroeht,* she thought, struggling to calm her racing pulse. *I bathed downstairs, the proprietor took my clothes to wash, and her wife loaned me a nightshirt.*

The mundane details settled her. She drew a shaky breath, and as her eyes adjusted to the dim light she made out the shape of Leoden's room: his bed lay flush to the opposite wall, and Leoden was fast asleep in it, clothed chest rising and falling in a steady rhythm. Saffron watched him a moment to make sure, but his stillness didn't seem feigned, and as there was nobody else in the room but them she forced herself to lie back again, her blank gaze fixed on the ceiling.

Slowly, she pressed a hand to her stomach, fingers probing for a hurt she couldn't find. She tried to tell herself she'd imagined the voice, that sibilant thought-echo whispering *scale-sister*, but couldn't. She knew exactly what it was, the same way she knew what had caused the light, no matter her inability to explain how it had worked.

"Scion," she whispered, the Vekshi word soft in the air of Noqevai. Beneath the weight of Yevekshasa, within the humid, crystal-growing sphere of an impossible egg, Saffron had swallowed a single golden scale as part of the Trial of Queens – had bound herself to a creature she could only name as *dragon*, shared its thoughts and actions as they fought another of its kind, with Zech's heart riding pillion. That was the burn she'd felt when Naruet's portal opened; the burn she'd felt again before the kshtathit rattled the dreamscape, tugging behind her navel like a fiery hook.

Somehow, the dragon had sensed her. Warned her. Saved her, even, pulling her back to her body. And now the connection – the dragon, the scale, whatever it was – had gone again, leaving Saffron alone with her questions, time ticking by like the wheel of stars as she lay awake, and yearned, and wondered.

PART 3
New Song's Measure

13

New Hands, Old Keys

If Veksh could be said to possess a culture of hospitality, it wasn't one that readily extended itself to foreigners, heretics or anyone suspected of colluding with them. Yena, who had experienced precious little since arriving in Yevekshasa to disprove this assumption, was therefore shocked to find herself woken politely by an anxious, eager acolyte with the news that she had a visitor, and would she like some breakfast first, and maybe water for washing?

"Yes," said Yena, blinking in confusion. "That would, ah... that would be lovely."

Ducking her head in obeisance, the young woman hurried off again, leaving Yena to sit up in her cot and wonder if the world had fundamentally rearranged itself while she slept.

The acolyte returned within minutes, accompanied by another, equally awed girl who'd evidently been drafted into carrying the water. Not having expected the courtesy, Yena exclaimed in surprise to find that it was warm from the bathhouse.

"My thanks," she told them, eliciting a pair of high blushes. Fighting a rather inappropriate grin – they were both quite pretty, and Yena had always had a weakness for blushing – she turned her attention to the tray of Vekshi delicacies the first girl had produced. Along with a cup of hot *mege*, there was a bowl of spiced sour soup, a selection of small glazed breads still hot from the oven and a platter of sliced fruit. Yena, who'd spent the past week being fed like a temple novice, derived a certain grim satisfaction from having earned the right to eat like someone important.

Opting for cleanliness ahead of food, she shucked out of her nek and washed in the warm water, forcibly ignoring the presence of the two girls. It was a perfunctory wash, but a satisfying one, and by the time she'd dried and pulled on her clean clothes her breakfast was still warm enough to steam. She devoured it all with relish: it was far more than she usually ate, but after yesterday's healing, it felt just right.

"I'm ready for my guest, now," she said, and as they scuttled off to bring whoever it was, taking the wash-water and empty tray with them, Yena found herself bracing for another encounter with Yasha.

Instead, to her considerable surprise, they returned with Kikra in tow, the Shavaktiin dreamseer robed and veiled in his customary shade of yellow.

"If you need anything further," the first girl said, "just call for us." And with that, the two acolytes vanished, leaving Yena alone with her visitor.

"You have news?" she asked, as Kikra perched on the edge of her cot.

"I do," said Kikra. He kept his voice lowered, as though worried the acolytes might be eavesdropping. "Last night, I met with Gwen Vere and Luy in the dreamscape. Much has happened, and it may yet affect us here."

Heart racing, Yena listened with rapt attention as Kikra detailed what had happened. Hearing that Safi was stuck with Leoden in some alien world was shocking enough to knock the breath right out of her, as was the suggestion, however nebulous, that Leoden's guilt might really be Kadeja's. The as-yet unknown significance of Vikasa piqued her curiosity on multiple counts, and she hardly knew what to think of Naruet, but hearing that Sashi was set to act as interim Vekshi ambassador made her spirits lift, albeit briefly: the implications of Sene a Sati's suicide made her stomach churn.

By the time Kikra had finished, Yena's head was spinning. Kikra, sensing this, didn't press her for conversation beyond a confirmation of her planned visit to the Archives, for which Yena was grateful; she squeezed his hand in parting, and sat quiet for several long minutes after he left. Her heart ached to think of Safi stranded even further away than she had been before, and Yena allowed herself the brief indulgence of yearning, quietly and fiercely, for her return.

And then, with a shake of her head, pragmatism reasserted itself. The Council of Queens didn't need to know about Safi's worldwalking or the problem of Naruet, but they were entitled to learn the fate of Sene a Sati.

Standing, Yena moved to the door and poked her head into the hallway, feeling slightly foolish as she called out for the acolytes. Her lips twitched in amusement when both girls came running in response; evidently, surviving the sun's mouth had earned her something of a reputation.

"I need to speak with Mesthani a Vekte," she said. "Might a meeting be arranged?"

Of course, was the answer; *just wait here, we'll find her.* Amused at their deference, Yena returned to sit on the cot. In their enthusiasm, the two girls failed to shut the door all the way, which rendered audible a fiercely whispered argument in the hall outside Yena's room as to which of them was to have the honour of playing messenger for her. As shutting the door immediately would have alerted them to the error, Yena bit her lip to keep from laughter and waited until they departed, still debating the point in earnest, to do so.

Anticipating a longer wait, she was again surprised when the second acolyte, who'd evidently won her bid for messenger-status, returned inside of fifteen minutes, reporting that Mesthani a Vekte was waiting to see her now.

"She's in the temple gardens," the acolyte explained, her voice a rush. "I think she'd come to see you herself, which is why I found her so quickly."

"My thanks," said Yena, but didn't follow the acolyte out. She took a moment to compose herself, hands smoothing reflexively down the fabric of her new clothes. Both *kettha* and *dou* were dyed a deep burnt orange, a colour that suited her skin especially well, and which was another small sign of respect from the temple, being as close to the whites and reds reserved for queens and priestesses as women holding neither title could legally wear. *Either they feel guilty about the sun's mouth, or there's been a collective change of heart.* Yena's lips quirked at the thought: Ashasa's daughters weren't known for their sudden charity, but they certainly understood politics.

Straightening her shoulders, Yena took a deep breath and went in search of Mesthani.

Rationally, Naruet knew, there weren't all that many people in the audience chamber – not compared to, say, the temple dining hall during midmorning meal, or the cool of the scriptorium on a hot day. Why, there were scarcely more people present than he had fingers! But it *felt* like a crowd; felt as though every eye (and there were twice as many of those as people) was fixed on him. Straining to breathe in a binder that once more felt increasingly tight, he stood silently by Ktho's side, head cocked at a straining angle as he focused on a distant point devoid of eyes or judgement. Words flowed around him, remote and unheard, hanging in the air like the static drifts of Leoden's bazaar world. He'd scryed for the Vex last night, relieved to see that Safi was safe in his company; that the ebb and flow of the dreamscape felt *right* when he contemplated their togetherness.

He pointedly did not think of everything that had happened after: his conversation with Luy, who leaned against the far wall; his rescue of Gwen, who stood beside him. That he had met them both in dreaming ought to have been a source of reassurance in meeting them now: instead, it only made him feel more anxious. Drumming his fingers on his thigh in a calm-down rhythm helped a little, but the context was overwhelming: there were too many people, too many expectations. Naruet was trying his best to do the right thing, but did anyone present truly believe him? Did they think he was monstrous for trusting Leoden, for failing to help the worldwalkers? Was he monstrous?

Beside him, Ktho subtly shifted her weight from one foot to another, so that her hip bumped his. A barely discernible motion to the rest of the room, but to Naruet it was as if she'd shouted. He fought the urge to break into a beaming smile, which would surely be inappropriate, and yet his mouth twitched anyway. This, *this* was why Ktho was Inside, forever and always: the contact was deliberate, bringing him back to himself whenever he threatened to drift too far astray. As focused as she was on Cuivexa Iviyat and her duties as Most Honoured, still she'd noticed Naruet's discomfort.

If Ktho could be so considerate in giving attention, what excuse had Naruet not to try? Not necessarily to succeed, for he knew Ktho would understand in either case, but the attempt itself – that was what mattered.

Inhaling as long and slow and deep as the binder would allow – and that was further than he'd expected; perhaps the tightness he'd felt before had only been an illusion – he forced himself to look at the Cuivexa, who was speaking, and to listen to what she said.

"... understand you have some related news you wish to share with us?"

"I do," said Ktho, standing imperceptibly straighter. Without turning around, she raised a hand and beckoned forward the archivist-priest who'd accompanied them from the temple, his thick arms laden with vellum. "Given the recent verdict of the House of the Mortal Firmament, I thought it only proper to consult the archives of Ke's Kin for any legal precedents which might prove useful in our current circumstances. Happily, that search was not in vain." She nodded, and the priest approached the royal dais, stopping at the base to not so much bow as bob as the courtier, Pixeva, relieved him of his papers.

"If I might summarise for the benefit of those present," said Ktho, after a beat, "the precedent dates to the reign of Vexa Yavin – or rather, to its end. There has always been speculation as to what ultimately became of her, but that she vanished from Yavinae – and from Kena itself, never to return – is a matter of historical fact. As she was still Vexa at the time of her disappearance, replacing her called for extraordinary measures. The precedent I cite can surely give no offence to the House of the Mortal Firmament, as it was their predecessors in that office who signed it into effect, the record entrusted to Ke's Kin rather than their own judiciary, not for secrecy, but safekeeping. Vexa Yavin's rot went far, and they wished to ensure the document survived.

"They ruled as follows: *A Vexa or Vex who abdicates this world abdicates likewise from Kena, their throne and mahu'kedet, who may disband or else reform without them in the choosing of a new monarch. Such is the will of Ke and Na, and the ruling of the House of the Mortal Firmament.*"

Absolute silence fell in the wake of this pronouncement. Naruet fidgeted, one hand coming up to tug at the edge of his binder through his robes. Then Amenet ore Amenet spoke, her voice a little breathless.

"Our sincere thanks, Most Honoured, for your invaluable research. Pixeva shall, of course, convey your findings to the House, who will doubtless wish to view the documents themselves–"

"Of course," said Ktho, with the slightest of bows.

"–but even so," said Cuivexa Iviyat, smoothly picking up the thread, "we do not anticipate any disagreement. We gladly take your acolyte into our custody and under our jurisdiction, and look forward to planning our coronation with the full support of Ke's Kin."

"Naruet idi Ke," said Amenet, "please step forward."

Shaking only slightly, Naruet complied. He risked a brief glance at her, but she was altogether too much, too bright; he fixed his gaze on the floor instead and tried to remember to breathe.

"I understand," said Amenet, "that you are the one responsible for activating the anchored portal in Vexa Yavin's vault."

Naruet swallowed. He hadn't been asked a question, but as the silence stretched and Amenet didn't speak, he realised he was expected to answer as if he had been. "Yes, highness."

"Tell me, please, how you came to serve Vex Leoden in this matter."

"He... Some time ago, he sent to Ke's Kin to request the expertise of someone familiar with the history of the jahudemet. I was the one who received his messenger, and as I have such knowledge, I went to see him myself. We talked. He was..." Naruet licked his lips, fingers clenching and unclenching in the fabric of his robes, acutely conscious of his audience in general and Ktho in particular, "...he was kind to me. Interested in my research, which few people are."

He paused here, hopeful that Amenet might ask about his studies, too; they were the one topic on which he never failed to speak fluently, but Naruet had learned from experience that, even within Ke's Kin, his unprompted monologues on the topic were seldom appreciated. Amenet, however, did not ask, and after several more seconds of silence, Naruet resigned himself to her disinterest and continued.

"Eventually, he asked me to look at the portal. He stressed the secrecy of our work, and as he was both Vex and Inside, I said nothing to anyone else. I learned how to activate the portal, how to control where it opened, but I never went through. Vex Leoden told me it was research only; that he wanted to learn more of Kena's history." He ducked his head, flooded with sudden shame. "I did not see the worldwalkers taken, but I saw them there, in the pit. He told me they were criminals, and I believed him. He told me not to look, so I did not look. I trusted him. I trust him still." With terrible effort, Naruet forced himself to meet Amenet's gaze. "I believe he was deceived by *her* – by Vex'Mara Kadeja." He looked down again, cheeks burning. "She frightened me."

"Do you know who used the ahunemet on the worldwalkers?"

"No, highness."

"Do you have any suspicions?"

Naruet shook his head. "I never saw anyone in the vault except for the Vex and Vex'Mara."

Amenet's voice was cold and clear. "And do you have any proof of Vex Leoden's innocence, Naruet idi Ke? Anything to support his exculpation beyond your trust in him?"

Naruet shut his eyes. He wanted not to answer, but though Amenet was not Inside, she was still an authority, and as Ktho had been the one to give him into her care – as Amenet and Iviyat, not Ktho and Leoden, were now the people to whom he owed his service – he had no recourse but honesty. Fingers shaking, he reached into his robes and drew out the necklace on which the key was strung, pulling the whole thing over his head and holding it at arm's length. The key was ancient, made of some silvery metal that wasn't actually silver, incised on the flat with finely carved Kenan script. Instead of being toothed at one end, it spiralled down in odd waves and ripples that caught light, trapping it.

"Vex Leoden gave me this," said Naruet. "He told me I had to keep it safe and hidden, even from the Vex'Mara. He was upset that day, but the next time I saw him he acted like he didn't remember. But it's something, isn't it?"

Amenet extended a hand. "May I see it, please?"

Until that moment, Naruet hadn't quite noticed that Amenet and Iviyat were sitting side by side on a single throne, which was in turn raised on a dais. He approached them nervously, shoulders hunched, and felt a wash of gratitude when, rather than snatching the key from him, Amenet held out a palm instead. The silver gleamed against her skin, the chain hissing softly as it folded up into her hand. Amenet murmured thanks and held it up to the light, examining it.

"It's beautiful," said Iviyat. "For a key."

Amenet made a noncommittal noise. "Do you know what it opens? Is it part of the portal?"

Naruet shuffled his feet. "Vex Leoden said it opened Vakti's door. I don't know what that means, but it sounded important."

For an awful moment, he thought that Amenet would confiscate the key. His anxiety flared sharply at the prospect, but before it could truly take hold she handed it back to him, dropping it as neatly into Naruet's palm as he'd dropped it into hers.

"Keep it," she said. "We all know that Leoden can be charming when he wishes. All of us here were fooled by him at one time or another; it would be the worst sort of hypocrisy to hold you in contempt for doing the same. Provided you swear to serve us faithfully – provided you keep your faith with us – I will not hold your past transgressions against you."

"I will serve you faithfully," said Naruet, bowing over his cupped hands. "I swear by Ke and Na."

"Excellent!" said Amenet. "As it happens, Naruet, I have a task in mind for you; one that requires the particular use of the jahudemet."

Naruet jerked his head up. "You do?"

Amenet smiled her crooked smile. "My new Vekshi ambassador and her entourage are in urgent need of a portal to Yevekshasa. Not this moment, of course – we still have some arrangements to make – but within, say, the next few hours. Can you do that for us?"

Naruet smiled, a ball of warmth in his chest. "Oh, yes," he breathed. "I can do that."

Yena had expected informing Mesthani of the ambassador's suicide to be a formality: a necessary courtesy, yes, but also an opportune means of assuring the Council of Queens that Zech's body would soon be en route to Veksh. She had not expected Mesthani to turn white as a bone and sit down heavily on a stone bench, her face upturned in bewilderment.

"Suicide? Sene?"

"Yes," said Yena, sitting down beside her. She felt unpleasantly guilty at her failure to anticipate Mesthani's reaction. "You, ah... you knew her, then?"

"I knew her," Mesthani said softly. "She was an Archivist once, did you know? Oh, her work was never popular, of course, but she was an exemplary scholar. She had this glorious habit of wetting her blade in wine–" a peculiarly Vekshi expression, indicating the profanation of the sacred in pursuit of the mundane; she filed that titbit away for future examination and continued listening, "–and while I admired her, she always skirted far too close to heresy with little care for consequence. It's why she was sent south, in the end: ambassador to Kena has never been an overly popular post." She bit her lip, an expression of sad reminiscence crossing her face, and asked again, "Suicide?"

"Suicide," Yena confirmed. "But not unprovoked."

Mesthani's brows rose sharply at that, and Yena explained it as best she could without betraying the existence of the captured worldwalkers, saying only that Leoden and Kadeja had, for unknown reasons, rifled Sene's memories and imprisoned her, the shame of which had prompted her suicide. Yena hadn't thought it was possible for Mesthani to get any whiter, but by the time she finished the queen was as pale as if she'd spent a decade indoors.

"That is... profoundly disturbing," she said at last, as shaken as Yena had ever heard her. "Of course, I understand – and I'm sure the Council will agree – with the need to appoint an interim ambassador to return your sister's body. And Motherless Kadeja, for her part, must also be held responsible. I can't imagine Vex Leoden would've had any use for a lone Vekshi woman had Kadeja not suggested it to him, assuming she didn't perpetrate the crime herself, for own dark amusement."

"We could... That is, I believe the plan is to return Sene's body to Veksh along with Zechalia's, assuming there are no objections."

"I cannot imagine there would be," said Mesthani. "Anymore."

A silence fell then, one weighted with mutual loss. And yet Yena couldn't help wondering: what had Sene a Sati known that had seen her expelled from the Archives? What secrets had she betrayed to Leoden and Kadeja? It would've been a grave coincidence if whatever it was had nothing to do with Leoden's plan to relocate Vikasa, though that still covered a vast range of potential subjects. Perhaps she'd helped them unlock the anchored portal, or betrayed some Vekshi intelligence of worldwalkers, which topic, while not strictly taboo, was nonetheless zealously guarded.

Yena was just on the verge of speaking when Mesthani, who'd been slouching forwards, sat bolt upright. "She tortured Sene a Sati," she said urgently, as though this hadn't already been established. "Thereby causing her death, however indirectly."

"Yes?" asked Yena, not sure what the queen was thinking.

"We reclaimed her in Ashasa's name, as the right course of action, in rebuke of heresy, but it was a political action, not a legal one, and in any case, the Knives never like to expose the faithful to heretics if they can avoid it. But Sene's death, her abuse beforehand – that's a new crime, a separate offence to be weighed and measured." She squeezed Yena's hand, her grip calloused and strong. "Do you see it?"

Almost, Yena shook her head – until she recalled her previous conversation with Mesthani and Ksa; her demand to know why nothing was yet being done with Kadeja. The implications bloomed in her like fire. "*Oh*," she breathed, eyes widening. "The Knives won't grant you access to Kadeja without proof of Zech's death, but they have no grounds to stop you asking questions about Sene."

"Precisely." Mesthani glanced around, confirming their privacy in the temple garden, and lowered her voice. "We have a very narrow window of opportunity here. An accusation of torture, whether through direct action or complicity in the actions of another, is a serious thing. And right now, we're the only ones who know of it." A slight twist of question coloured her words; Yena nodded confirmation.

"I haven't told anyone else."

Mesthani exhaled, nodded. "Keep it that way. I'll have to name you as my source for the charge, and as a queen's sister that ought to be sufficient for the Knives – for now, at least – and once I do so, it won't stay secret, which means that other factions can potentially make use of it. But for now, it should be enough to gain us a way in; enough to get us access. Or get me access, at least," she amended, cutting Yena an apologetic look. "A queen's sister you might be, but as Sene is no kin to you, that status grants you no rights to pursue this case. But in this, I will act for you – for all of us. I swear by Ashasa's fire."

She rose, and Yena rose with her, fear and excitement quickening her pulse. "I'm due to tour the Archives today," she said, her voice surprisingly steady. "If you need to reach me, that's where I'll be."

"Of course," said Mesthani. "Whatever happens, you'll hear from me as soon as I'm able to come."

"My thanks," said Yena.

Mesthani smiled, and just in that instant, she looked as

young as Yena was, the bright morning sunlight glancing off her hair. "For Veksh," she said, and with a parting squeeze to Yena's hand, she turned away and left the garden, vanishing into the temple.

Saffron woke to an unprecedentedly vivid recollection of her night's adventures in the dreamscape, which she'd half expected to melt away after she fell back asleep the second time. She was pleased beyond words that she'd managed to reach Gwen, but worried that the kshtathit might have harmed her. Fear would eat at her if she let it, and so she shoved it to the back of her mind, bracing instead for whatever Leoden might ask of her. She understood his desire to find Vikasa, at least in the abstract, but at a practical level she wasn't sure what the quest entailed. Over breakfast, in response to her awkward querying, he told her he'd sought out Noqevai precisely because of its status as an access-point, somewhere both linked to and known by many different worlds.

"I wanted information," he said – Saffron shuddered, thinking of the captive worldwalkers – "and this seemed the best place to look for it."

"But what is it you want from *me*?"

"Be my guide," he said, waving a genteel hand as if in conjuration of the obvious. "Naruet clearly sent you here for a reason. We'll explore the markets, let you get a sense of the place, and if you feel a pull, an instinct, anything suggestive of a probable course of action, you let me know."

"You want me," said Saffron, somewhat disbelievingly, "to act like a, a…" there was no direct translation for *divining rod* in Trade, and after a moment's internal fumbling, she settled on, "…some sort of magical compass?"

"Ideally," Leoden said, unflustered, "yes."

And that was precisely what they set about doing. With Saffron barefoot in her freshly-laundered Earth clothes and Leoden in a lighter version of his Nakhereh-venturing leathers, they made for something of an odd couple, wandering, with what Saffron was prepared to call purposeful aimlessness, around the endless markets of Noqevai.

Which was, on the one hand, an undeniably fascinating experience. For all that the local population treated the sehket as nuisances, Saffron was captivated by them. Leoden indulged this fascination with poorly-concealed amusement.

"I'm sure they'll lose their charm soon enough," he said, the fifth time Saffron stopped to watch them play. "Once they've shat on you, perhaps? I hear that's the usual source of disillusionment."

"Hasn't happened yet," said Saffron, and kept on throwing them bits of whatever food she had to hand, fingers itching for a camera she didn't have. Given the plethora of goods on offer from worlds both technological and magical, it occurred to her that the markets might have something cameralike for sale, too, and why not suggest to Leoden that they look for one, as he was so determined to take her lead? It was exactly what Ruby would've done in the same situation, and the feeling of grief and fondness the thought produced was strong enough that Saffron couldn't act on it; could only swallow against a loss that wasn't a loss, and focus on the strangeness of their surroundings.

And so she did, at first. But after several long hours of hunting on foot for she didn't know what, the novelty was starting to wear thin.

"This might work better," Saffron said, a note of peevishness in her voice, "if I understood what it is you expect me to do for you beyond–" she made aggressive air-quotes, deriving a certain angry satisfaction from Leoden's lack of comprehension, "–*being a compass.*"

"If I could explain that," said Leoden, maddeningly Zen, "I wouldn't need you to do it."

Saffron didn't quite stifle a groan. "Does that mean we keep walking?"

"It does," said Leoden. "Lead on, please."

Saffron groaned, but complied.

As calloused as they were from her barefoot weeks in Kena, Saffron's soles weren't impervious to aching, especially not after hours spent trekking over hard ground. Though loath to admit it, she was also more than a little disquieted by the sky above the dome, which continued to flash with lightning. There was no sun, no stars, no moon – yesterday, she'd assumed the kshtathit was obscuring them somehow, but this was evidently the Noqevaian norm. The ambient light ought to have been as erratic as the lightning, except that in this, too, the dome provided, smoothing it out via some unknown magic or mechanism into a steady, not-quite-twilit glow.

"So," said Saffron, as much for the sake of conversation as out of curiosity, "how will you know Vikasa when you see it?"

Leoden cocked his head at her. "What do you mean?"

"I mean, how are you going to recognise it? Do you have a way to tell? Is there a test you perform, a spell for the truth, a particular landmark you think will be there – anything like that? Or are you just going to find a world, or a piece of one, that *looks* like it might be Kenan and say *job done*?"

"Oh, that." He blinked, as though momentarily puzzled by his own answer, then patted one of his many pockets. "I have a way to tell."

"Can I ask what it is?"

"You can."

"And will you tell me?"

The slightest twitch of smile. "I might."

I do not like this man, Saffron sternly reminded herself. *I do not trust him, and I'm not convinced he's innocent.* Even so, she found herself grinning back. "You're a tease, you know that?"

"So I've been told," said Leoden dryly.

They continued in silence for just long enough that Saffron had given up hope of an answer. Then Leoden said, offhand,

"I suppose it can't hurt to tell you. We – that is, Kadeja and I – in our research, our explorations, we found a fragment of Vikasa – a piece of the earth itself, tucked away in a forgotten archive."

"That seems... convenient," said Saffron, frowning slightly.

Leoden laughed. "You say that because you don't know how hard it was to find, how many years it took. But when Kadeja showed it to me–"

"Kadeja found it?"

"We both did," Leoden said. "I was there, too – she just picked it up first." But his eyes went vague as he said it, the same way they had the night before. "Either way, as soon as I saw how it had been catalogued and under what name, I knew what it had to be. I'd found my proof, and thanks to that finding, as you say, I have a way to verify the final location. I have a mining tool, one used in Kena to verify the provenance of particular natural substances, like gemstones, which I've had one of the local establishments modify for the purpose. I've fastened it to my Vikasa sample, and it ought to produce some small amount of warmth and a clear light when we reach its world of origin, with both effects becoming more pronounced the nearer we get to a more specific source. Does that satisfy your curiosity?"

"Yes, actually," said Saffron, who hadn't expected anything quite so sensible. "Thank you."

"Of course," said Leoden, "I have no means of testing it if we never leave Noqevai. That's why I was out on the Nakhereh yesterday – I wanted to see if any of those ragged edges might trigger the proximity light, but it didn't work. Instead, I ended up with you."

He said it lightly, but Saffron felt a pang of guilt all the same. She came to a halt at the junction of three streets, standing just to the side of the main foot traffic. They were on the crest of a hill, the farthest expanses of Noqevai's endless commercial realm laid out below like a patchwork blanket, buildings and towers and stalls and storefronts all intermingling: a city built from scraps. Which, Saffron supposed, it was – in a manner of speaking.

Sighing, she cracked her neck and tried to understand what it was that Leoden wanted from her. She'd already told him she had no inherent gift for magic – accessing the dreamscape hardly counted, especially as she had so little control over coming and going – and with that option exhausted, she didn't know what else she could possibly do that might provide him with guidance. It wasn't as if she had any reason *not* to help him find Vikasa: if it actually did exist, and with what she knew of Kena's loss of history since Vexa Yavin's reign, it would likely be an invaluable resource. Assuming, of course, that no one else had colonised it in the meantime, or that any old ruins remained if they hadn't; there were any number of potential obstacles, but all of them stubbornly hypothetical until or unless the world itself was found.

And somehow, Naruet thought that she could do it.

For obvious reasons, it wasn't a duty Saffron had been treating with any seriousness up until now: she'd never left Earth before her first trip to Kena, and the idea that she might possess some secret knowledge regarding the location of a lost world was nothing short of ludicrous. But then, she supposed, she would've once said the same thing about the existence of magic and a populated, interconnected multiverse, and *they'd* turned out to be real enough. *There are more things in heaven and Earth, Horatio, than are dreamt on in your philosophy.* She almost snorted to recall the quote, but even so, she realised she'd made up her mind. For the sake of her own curiosity – and, if she was being honest, Leoden's puppy-dog look – she ought to at least try *something*.

Feeling slightly ridiculous, Saffron closed her eyes. *Vikasa,* she thought, her inner voice tinged with a scepticism she struggled not to project. *How do I get to Vikasa? How do I find the way?*

Warmth in her stomach. A tug behind her navel.

Saffron's eyes flew open in shock. She shut them again almost instantly, pulse racing as she tried to stay calm. Maybe she'd just imagined the sensation.

(She hadn't. She knew she hadn't.)

Show me the way to Vikasa.

Another tug, more insistent than the first. Saffron followed it forwards. Years ago now, she and Lyssi (*don't think about Lyssi*) had dressed in crop tops and fake navel-rings for a birthday party. The rings had pinched, but they hadn't been able to resist fiddling with them, laughing and making dumb jokes about what it would look like if bulls were led around by belly-rings instead of nasal ones. One hard tug and they'd come right off, but there'd still been a reflex to chase the pull, if only to avoid the scratchy, pincering bite of the cheap metal.

Saffron felt similarly now, except that the burn-tug didn't abate when she changed direction. Wide-eyed, she looked at Leoden, a strange lump in her throat.

"I think," she said, and swallowed. Stopped. "I think I've got something."

Leoden's eyes lit up. "Show me."

Vikasa, Saffron thought again, and followed the burning pull.

14
What Once Was Lost

The Archivist looked Yena up and down, then down and up for good measure. She was of middling height, which meant she was half a head shorter than Yena, and yet she exuded such presence that she came across as taller. Her eyes were sharp and grey, and in deference to the complex status of the Archives and their guardians within the hierarchy of Ashasa's priestesshood, her head was half-shaved, a high, continuous undercut contrasting with a longer fall on top. This excess hair was pulled back in a practical tail, bound tightly with a thin strip of leather.

Grey hair, though the Archivist hadn't yet reached her middle thirties.

She was shasuyakesani. Like Zech had been.

"This is Evai," Ksa said, proudly. "My eldest daughter."

Already blindsided by the Archivist's resemblance to Zech, Yena's thoughts came to a stumbling, screeching halt at the revelation that Evai was *Kadeja's sister*, and therefore Zechalia's aunt. Wide-eyed, she stared at the beautiful calico pattern of Evai's skin, so like and unlike Zech's, standing out against the dark ochre of her robes, and felt her throat tighten.

"Why?" she asked – of Ksa, of Evai, of the room in general. Her voice was a shaky rasp. "If Kadeja's sister is one on whom the sun both smiles and frowns, then why would she give up a child born the same way?"

"Do you wish an honest answer?" Evai asked. Yena nodded; the Archivist's lips twisted in a humourless smile. "Two reasons: superstition and jealousy. What I am – what my young niece was–" a weight of bitter grief in the words, "–is the subject of many stories. One such concerns the tendency of our colouring to run in families." Her voice turned scathing. "It is said that our status – which is to say, our goodness; whether we are blessed by Ashasa or damned by her – can be told by the ordering of our births. Mottled sons, of course, are always morally suspect, but every second mottled daughter is one meant for greatness."

"Foolishness," Ksa muttered vehemently. "Utter foolishness."

"Quite," said Evai. "And yet there are many who cling to it, especially among the priesstesshood and certain of its more prominent motherlines. In the record of our family, I was such a second daughter. And Motherless Kadeja–" a flicker of loss crossed Evai's face, "–though she never claimed to believe, cared deeply what people thought of her." More softly, she said, "Growing up, she envied me my apparent destiny, as though I had made myself this way to spite her. It isn't hard to imagine that, when Zechalia was born, she feared that her daughter's very existence would be contrasted with mine, and held lacking. And so she let her go."

"And *murdered* her," spat Yena, furious and hurt. Evai and Ksa both flinched, and she ducked her head, ashamed. Kadeja's actions weren't their fault, but they wore the guilt all the same. "Forgive me. That wasn't – I didn't mean–"

"I know," said Evai. "The fault is Kadeja's, not yours. Or mine." She glanced at Ksa. "Or ours."

Taking this for a cue, Ksa stepped away, her head inclined towards Yena and Evai. "Assist her in her research," she said, eyeing her daughter. "And if Yasha a Yasara sends her little birds–"

"–I'll know what scraps to feed them," Evai finished.

"Just so," said Ksa, and exited the Archives with a final, stiff bow.

Evai waited until she was gone, then turned her full attention to Yena. She didn't quite smile, but her eyes were warmer than before. "So," she said. "Am I to understand you wish to research helpful legal precedents, should your newfound status be challenged?"

Yena thought of Kikra's news and her subsequent conversation with Mesthani a Vekte, who even now might be in conference with Kadeja. What should she tell Evai she'd come to research? Sene a Sati, who'd known something important enough that Kadeja had destroyed her for the sake of stealing it? Vikasa, a lost piece of Kena that might not exist, but which Leoden had jumped worlds to reclaim? The secrets of the Trial of Knives, and thus the truth of Kadeja's expulsion from the temple?

In a flash of defiant humour, Yena imagined telling Evai the truth, laying everything bare like unwashed linen. It certainly made for an entertaining prospect, but not, she was forced to admit, a practical one.

Suppressing a sigh, Yena hedged instead. "Eventually, yes, I would like to research precedents," she said. "But in honesty, I've always wanted to see the Archives. Growing up in Kena, with Yasha – I had such stories as she told us, and her copy of the Ryvke, but the longer I stay in Yevekshasa, the more I realise how little I truly know of Veksh." Which was entirely accurate, and somehow a more personal divulgence than she'd intended. She bit her lip, belatedly wanting to take a different tack, but Evai was looking at her with new interest, a thoughtful expression on her face. She was narrow-jawed, her mouth slightly crooked, and when she smiled it gave her an endearingly lupine appearance.

"Come with me," she said, and held out a dappled hand. Yena took it, a slight thrill running through her at the contact, and let Evai lead her into the Archives proper.

Entering as she had from the Great Temple, whose own scriptorium was linked to the Archives by a covered walkway cutting through a scribe's garden, Yena hadn't managed to get much of a sense of the structure's size. The open, columned hall in which they'd met was, according to Ksa, a kind of neutral ground. Indeed, as Yena glanced around, she saw various women in the blood red robes of senior priestesses – and the lighter reds and whites of their junior sistren – working alongside others in the distinctive Archivist's ochre. As they passed a bench where one such pairing sat, Yena did a double take, brows shooting up as she realised that the Archivist in question was male.

Catching her startlement, Evai huffed out a laugh. "The priesteshood does not admit men to Ashasa's service," she said, "but then, the Archivists are not quite priestesses, are we?"

Yena was hit by a sudden memory: walking across Yevekshasa with Safi, explaining who was eligible to serve Ashasa, and why. She'd felt confident in her knowledge at the time, but that was before Safi's departure and Zech's death had forced her to negotiate the mesa on her own terms, without the status afforded by either novelty or connections. Something twisted in her chest, half pain, half mirth. "Yasha never mentioned that," she said, faintly. But then, why would she? Yasha had precious little use for men at the best of times.

"It's always been a controversial exception," said Evai, leading her through a new maze of columns carved in the shape of trees. The huge hall was so strangely proportioned, the height of the roof and floor and the shapes of the columns so intermittently varied, that the eye was tricked as to size and distance both. Yena craned her neck, trying to track the changes without losing her footing. "There aren't many men who serve with us, compared to the number of women, but the ones we do have stand out. Ah! Here we are."

She'd brought them to an arched doorway hidden from sight until you were almost upon it by the wall's gentle curvature and the placement of nearby columns. The door itself was old, polished rhyawood: it had a central keyhole, but no handle. Reaching into her robes, Evai withdrew the lower loop of a necklace on which dangled a crystal key – or rather, a short spike of crystal that bore no visual resemblance to any key Yena had ever seen, except that it functioned like one. Once inserted in the lock, the crystal flared briefly with some magic light, dying again as the door swung smoothly and silently inwards.

"A shortcut, of sorts," said Evai, stepping through. She paused on the other side, waiting for Yena to join her, then tapped the crystal against the wood. The door swung shut of its own accord, a faint crackle of magic sparking along the jamb. Evai grinned. "Most guests aren't brought this way, but you, dear Yena, are a *special* guest."

"Because I'm a queen's sister?"

"Because you are that, yes, but also because you are *my* guest." The grin sharpened, wolfishly savage. Evai walked briskly as she talked, leading Yena down a narrow switchback stair, voice echoing against the stone. "You'd think it would be easier to find credit for your successes among people who think you're born to them, but no – whatever I do to the good, it's never through my hard work or skill, but always by Ashasa's grace or Her sungiven luck, or some other wretched platitude with no bearing on my competence. But at least I'm the good second daughter; at least the sun smiles on me more than frowns. And then, what should happen but that my disgraced sister's child is made the youngest queen in over a hundred years, and the sun both smiles and frowns on her as well! Why, then, something must be wrong in the arithmetic, the superstitious robewives say. After all, we cannot *both* be good."

As Evai drew an angry breath, Yena mouthed the word

robewives, a piece of Vekshi slang she'd never heard before, but which she assumed from context was a disparaging term for conservative priestesses. She filed it away to ask about later – she had no wish to interrupt – and returned her attention to Evai, face flushed as she aired her grievances.

"And then, adding insult to injury, the young queen dies before her worth can be truly judged! Ashasa forefend that I might grieve her death on my own account, as a niece unknown yet more like me than any living kin – no, no. I must instead be subject to the speculations of those who see her murder either as proof of my goodness or as a betrayal of hers. I am not *quite* an Archivist in social exile, Yena, but I have grown perilous fond of non-judgemental silence." She shook her head, frustrated, and shot Yena an apologetic look. "But now, here you come: a queen's sister! One who represents her nascent clan – and yet Kenan-raised, and yet newly penanced, and yet, and yet – and every other objection under the wide blue sky; you'd think we dealt in tattle alone – but even so, you are here, you can pass judgement, yes? You can deny me and elevate her, or deny her and elevate me, or so the robewives think. But you aren't here for that, are you? You're here for *research*, because *you*, Yena–" they arrived at another locked door; Evai used her crystal-key to unlock it, the motion smooth and practised, "–*you* remember what these Archives *mean*."

The door swung inwards, and Evai waved her hands in a flourish, gesturing Yena to enter ahead of her. The room on the other side glowed with light, and as she crossed the threshold Yena was briefly blinded. She stumbled, panic searing through her with the memory of fire, and for a sickening instant she was back in the sun's mouth, struggling to breathe. And then she steadied, and Evai was there, a featherlight touch on her elbow keeping her upright.

"I'm all right," Yena gasped, though she felt shaky down to her bones. "I'm all right."

"There is no rush," Evai murmured. "Catch your breath."

Yena did so, gulping in air as her heartrate settled, spots swimming through her vision like midges skimming a pond. Slowly, the rush of fear faded, and as her eyes adjusted to the brightness, she lost her breath for a different reason, mouth falling open in unabashed awe.

"We call it the Lightwell," Evai said, softly. There was a smile in her voice, though Yena didn't look to see. Instead, she stepped forward, hypnotised.

They stood at the edge of a stone balcony, curved to enclose a massive, circular shaft that opened onto the sky and dropped down into the bowels of the mesa. The space was easily fifty paces wide, and when Yena peeked over the balustrade she could see other Archivists working on the levels below. But what made it extraordinary was the light: a steady, impossible outpouring of translucent gold down the body of the shaft, like an airy waterfall. As with the bulk of Yevekshasa's open constructions, there must have been a barrier in place to keep out the wind and rain, though whether it was also responsible for the viscous glow, Yena didn't know. Looking closer, she realised that the very top of the shaft was lined with massive crystal mirrors, while smaller glasses curved around the inside – or the outside, Yena supposed – of the various balconies, a spiral pattern designed to trap and funnel the sunlight downwards. It could have been merely a mundane effect, some cunning trick of geometry that only gave the appearance of magic, and yet there was something in the way the light fell, the sheer gleaming solidity of it, that suggested otherwise.

"It's beautiful," said Yena, tearing her gaze away for long enough to look at Evai. The Archivist, who'd stepped up beside her, leaned her elbows on the balcony rail, chin tilting to indicate the lower levels.

"The Archives were built around it," she said. "Or at least, it predates them. There are different accounts as to how and why it came to be, but like so much else in Veksh, it's difficult to know the truth."

Yena gaped at her, shocked. "But I thought the Archives were complete, detailed!"

"Oh, we have plenty of records," said Evai, wryly. "And if you want to know exactly what a revered queen or priestess said at a certain time on a certain day, there's none more accurate. But when it comes to history, trade, architecture, culture... well. There is, shall we say, an overriding tendency for such facts to be filtered through the lens of Ashasa's divine preferences, and while that shows a very admirable devotion to Her will, it's not actually very useful, historically speaking."

"But–"

"Has Yasha a Yasara given you such an unbiased accounting of Veksh and its history as to raise your expectations?" The question itself was cutting, but the delivery oddly gentle. "Or did you merely hope that the rest of us were better than that?"

Yena snapped her mouth shut, cheeks burning with misplaced shame. Mesthani had already told her that Sene's research had seen her sent away; what reason did she have to assume that practice was more exception than rule? Yet even as she moved to apologise, Evai clicked her teeth in negation, dismissing her own harshness.

"It's not your fault," she said. "It took me years of study to realise the problem, and whenever I suggested it might be such, I received only blank stares and accusations." She snorted. "Once I secured my current rank, I formally dedicated my research to correlating objective facts across historical accounts by filtering out the Vekshi bias. I thought, how *provocative* of me! The robewives will have a fit! Instead, they took it to mean that Ashasa was guiding my hand, helping me to root out old heresies for the good of Veksh. One of the greater ironies of my life, that."

"Compared to the lesser kind, you mean?" Yena asked,

unable to resist the gentle tease.

Evai grinned. "Absolutely," she said, and gave Yena a comradely clap on the shoulder. "Come, then. The Lightwell is certainly beautiful, but it's not the heart of the Archives. Let me show you what we *really* do."

Viya stared at Zech's blank face and wondered why, with everything she had to do, she felt so furiously conflicted over a dead girl that she couldn't focus on anything else. It wasn't as though they'd been particularly close: aside from the shared aftermath of the battle of the Envas road, their meaningful interactions were limited to a single dreamscape conference and their tense run through the palace. And yet she'd set aside her correspondence, her notes on the trade of the Bharajin forest and a dozen other things to come alone to the *nineka*, the laying-out room, and stare at Zechalia's body as though it could answer whatever unasked questions compelled her attendance there.

"You betrayed me," Viya said, voice echoing on the nineka's tiles. Just as fiery Yemaya governed life, it was Nihun, god of water, who guarded death, and as such their imagery was everywhere in mosaic, the whole room covered from floor to ceiling. Yet Zech, who'd died a queen of Veksh, was shrouded not in Nihun's blue, but a faded red that came perilously close to Yemaya's carmine. It was unsettling, and not just because there was a moon-tale about a girl whose lover shrouded her body in red and bargained with the gods to bring her back; it made it hard to see her as dead at all.

My bloodmother is dead, too. The knowledge was an ache in her, and yet it felt unreal in a different way. She'd missed Hawy's funerary rites, and in the rush following their reclamation of Karavos, she'd had no time in which to seek the grave in her family's holdings, no will to tie a final blessing to the marker-sapling or burn a lock of hair. Nihun guarded death itself, the watery passage of the soul from one state to another, but it was Lomo of the earth who kept their bodies, transmuting old life into new.

Hawy's body, yes – but not Zech's, which was now finally destined for Veksh and a blasphemous burning rite; as was Sene a Sati, Viya supposed, though it was harder to feel upset about that. Allowing it was the correct thing to do. Viya understood that much, she did, but the red shroud – the fire that ought to signify Yemaya's sovereignty over life used instead to show death – and the lack of other, smaller rites all felt disrespectful. As angry as she'd been at Zech, Viya still wanted her laid to rest with honour. But these rituals were alien rituals, and Zech's funeral, like Hawy's, was a thing Viya wouldn't see. Even as Cuivexa, there was nothing she could do about it; or nothing worth starting a war over, at least.

"You betrayed me," she said again, and this time there was a rasp in her voice, a sting in her throat and nostrils as she struggled not to cry. The hole in Zech's throat where Kadeja's blade had struck was hidden, bound beneath a strip of red cloth; her eyes were closed, her skinny, mottled shoulders visible at the top of the shroud. The maramet, the blood-spark, kept her free from putrefaction, but there was a telltale greyish cast to her skin, and her eyes, now shut, would never open again.

"I ought to hate you for that. You gave away the Bharajin Forest, you *lied* to me, but you were meant to stay!" Her voice cracked on the word. "How can I be angry with the dead? Whatever god will judge you now, I have no say in it, and I ought... I ought to be accepting. I should forgive you, or not, and feel at peace." She swallowed, and said, more softly, "But I am not good at peace. I try to be, but there's a quickness in me I cannot seem to choose away."

A noise behind her, muffled but distinct. Viya whirled, mortified at being discovered, and found herself staring at, of all people, Trishka.

"What are you doing here?" she demanded, swiping the

tears from her cheeks.

"Looking for you," said Trishka. Her amber gaze, so like yet unlike Yasha's, fell on Zech's shrouded body. "And her."

Viya exhaled in a rush, guilt prickling her neck. She'd never paid much attention to the relationship between Zech and Trishka, but of course they'd had one; of course Trishka grieved her loss. "Oh," she said: a wholly inadequate sound. And then, stupidly: "I wanted to see her again. Before they take her."

"I was her mother," Trishka said, softly. "In every way that mattered. And yet I have no right to bury her here."

"Oh." The simple admission made Viya want to weep again. "I'm sorry."

Trishka's expression, which had hardly been sharp to begin with, softened. "Don't be. Grief is a strange and lonely thing, even when shared. Or perhaps especially when shared. The same loss can mean something different to everyone."

Viya stepped wordlessly aside, watching as Trishka came to stand by Zechalia's bier, smoothing a gentle hand across the scruff of grey hair.

"It means something to me, that you've come to see her," Trishka said, her hand falling back to her side.

Viya swallowed, feeling suddenly awkward. Soon enough, Zech's body, like Sene's, would be moved for transport, transferred to the custody of Sashi, Gwen and Luy for their final journey to Veksh. Viya felt like an interloper: she didn't want to intrude on Trishka's farewell, but she didn't want to leave her alone if she wanted company, either. "Do you, ah… Do you want me to stay?"

Trishka smiled sadly. "No, thank you," she said, and turned her eyes back to the nineka's bier and the small, still body of Zech. "I'll be fine."

"Of course," Viya rasped, and fled the room, a terrible lump in her throat.

•••

Yena felt at home in the Archives in a way she had nowhere else in Yevekshasa – or in Veksh, for that matter. Evai was good company in her own right, and even if she hadn't been the Archives themselves were utterly distracting.

After showing her the Lightwell, the upper library and the main scriptoriums, all of which were beautiful, Evai led her down to the stacks, a lengthy series of catacombing rooms carved into the mesa stone. The air down here was cool, but not unduly so, smelling faintly of old paper and minerals. According to Evai, it was where the bulk of documents were kept – "It's only newer records and copies we keep upstairs," she said, "because they're the most commonly borrowed things, and therefore likely not what you're looking for." Evai waited a beat at that, and then, when Yena didn't speak, said, "I'm reasonably sure you didn't come here just for legal precedents, Yena – not after what it took to get your status. What is it you want to see?"

It was a delicate moment: Yena didn't want to lie, but neither was she so certain of Evai's discretion – or of Ksa's – as to blurt out the obvious answer. After a moment's consideration, however, she decided to take a risk.

"There is one thing I'm curious about," she said, injecting as much coyness into the statement as she dared. "I'd heard the current Vekshi ambassador, Sene a Sati, used to be a scholar here, and as – as she's bringing my sister's body–" she didn't have to feign the sudden gulp in her voice, which had the added bonus of concealing her lie, "–I thought it might be good to know more of her. Of her history, her ideas – if it comes up in conversation, I'd rather not be blindsided. Assuming you know where the records are, of course."

Evai looked intrigued. "Huh. Not what I'd expected, but certainly manageable. If memory serves, we haven't had a new ambassador in at least a decade, so anything a former scholar published that long ago that hasn't entered general circulation – and I'm sure it hasn't done, or I'd have recognised the name – ought to be... this way!"

She led off through the stacks, Yena striding happily in her wake. After several minutes of rummaging and a great deal of muttering on Evai's part, Yena found herself set up at a stacks-desk, a stone bench-and-chair carved into and from the living rock, the whole setup a functional alcove consuming no valuable hallspace. A sheaf of documents lay before her, thick as two fingers: it seemed to her a reasonable starting place, but Evai was clearly dissatisfied with her findings.

"That can't possibly be all of it," she said, frowning at the writings of Sene a Sati.

"What makes you say that?"

"Scholars number their works, and some of the numbers are missing. That's not so uncommon – as I said, if a work becomes popular or accepted, it usually gets taken up to one of the higher libraries – but in that case, there ought to be an Archivist's note explaining the absence."

"And there isn't one?"

"There isn't," said Evai, looking sharply at Yena. "Why do I feel that you're not as surprised as you ought to be, hm?"

Straightfaced, Yena said, "I live an exciting life. It takes a lot to surprise me."

Evai chuckled. "Fair," she conceded. And then, with an irritated huff, "Even so, I mislike the idea of a scholar's writings going astray. Maybe someone hid them on purpose, but maybe they've just been misfiled." She turned to leave, then hesitated. "Will you be all right here, if I go to look?"

Yena stared at her, nonplussed. "Why wouldn't I be?"

"No good reason," Evai said. "Some visitors just find the stacks oppressive, is all."

"I survived the sun's mouth," Yena said dryly, priding herself on the perfect stillness of her hands, the lack of shake in her voice. "I think I can survive a library."

"Also fair," said Evai, and gave her a friendly pat on the shoulder. "Well, enjoy your reading! Ashasa willing, I won't be gone too long."

With that, she strode away down the corridor, leaving Yena to her research.

Rolling her shoulders, Yena scanned the titles of Sene's papers, all of which seemed to focus on Vekshi history: motherlines, clan holdings and their changes over time.

"Perilous dry stuff," Yena murmured, "but such are the sacrifices we make."

She turned the first page, and began.

It was slow going, not least because Sene's handwriting was cramped and urgent, impenetrable even if it hadn't been weeks or months since Yena had last had cause to read anything written in Vekshi script beyond half-memorised passages from the Ryvke. Still, she did her best, and after the first page she fell into a rhythm. To her surprise, she found that Sene's work was interesting: her style was good, and though she wrote at times like a woman intent on obscuring her own point, Yena had a talent for reading between the lines. That being so, she soon divined that Sene a Sati had cared about borders, both literal and metaphoric. It was a theme that spanned her essays, even in relation to ostensibly different topics: what caused some things to change, and others to remain steady? If all Vekshi were Ashasa's children, what did it mean to separate their motherlines the way they did, paying little or no heed to paternity? Why were the oldest clan territories divided into such neat parcels of land, as though each great matriarch had endeavoured to hold an equal share with every other?

Niggling questions, related yet not, and all of them hinting at something larger. Yena felt like the proverbial child of Kenan legend, the one who'd swallowed the absent third moon and so taken on the burden of its stories. There was a conclusion to be had here, a point that Sene, in her obfuscating fashion, was driving at, but Yena couldn't interpret it. But then, if Evai was right, and the missing papers were no coincidence, she likely wasn't meant to.

Frustrated, she skipped around and found a new essay, one that came just before the first major gap in her folio. Unlike its predecessors, it was about the Vekshi language: Sene had been tracking changes in word use, pronunciation and meaning across a variety of old documents, which lead her in turn to speculate about their origins. It was exactly the sort of thing that captivated Yena; she dove into it with a will, and had read nearly the whole thing when a particular argument leapt out at her. Yena read it three times, fingers twitching as she traced the lines:

> We have no language but Vekshi, but that language has always been strange, as though we have put it to work at a task for which it was not meant; indeed, as if we have hammered it into a mirror, showing now the opposite of its origins. And yet, it is not glass: the bumps & pits of modification remain, if we care to look for them. Our masculine forms are used only crudely, and yet are among our oldest grammatical structures; we have gained none, but lost many. Our magical lexicon far outstrips our oldest capabilities in both theory & effect; such terms, we are told, were only ever invented for use in stories, and yet it is largely newer tales that use them thus, not our oldest. But to my eyes, the most egregious instance is one hidden in plain sight, at the very core of Veksh. We say we are led by the Council of Queens – of Queens, when Veksh has never come within spitting distance of being a monarchy! And yet the word itself is ancient, not borrowed from the Kenan or Kamnei forms of our neighbours, nor from any more distant tongue, but is rather one of the most unchanged, least dilute terms in Vekshi.
>
> We cannot even plead Ashasa's influence, as our Mother Sun, though She has many names, has never been called Queen. We mean no overt monarchical influence by our use, and yet our oldest stories make clear the meaning that

underlies our own. Truly, our most radical change is the
pluralisation. We are ruled, not by a single monarch, but
many – a tyranny of queens – & though we all know the story
(or some of the story) of how that came about, still it begs the
question: why did we have the word before the concept? Who
were we, truly, in the days before Veksh was Veksh?

"Who were we then?" Yena murmured, reverent. "Indeed, who are we now?"

She stared at the paper, trying to gather her swarming thoughts. *Borders.* Safi had been curious about borders, though they'd had little time to discuss it. Borders and queens and language bent around on itself–

She realised, with an abrupt chill, how very silent it was in the stacks. How long had Evai been gone? Yena had lost track of time with her reading, but it must have been an hour at least by how many essays she'd finished.

"Evai?" she called, voice echoing against the stone. She swung her legs over the bench and stood, back popping as she craned to peer down the hallway. "Evai, are you there?"

Nothing came back at first; and then, very distant, she heard an answering *pat-pat, pat-pat,* the rapid sound growing louder as it approached. Footsteps, she realised: someone was running towards her, though they hadn't called out, and there was no reason, no logical reason at all why such a simple sound should suddenly feel so ominous, except that it *did*, and the hairs on her neck stood up.

"Evai?" Yena whispered, taking a half-step backwards in fear of she knew not what.

But the runner wasn't Evai. It was Jesit, the priestess who'd played messenger during Yena's penitence and healed her burns in the aftermath. She'd always been disapproving before, but did not look so now: she was out of breath, redfaced and flushed – and not, Yena realised with horror, merely by dint of exertion. There was blood on her cheek, a spatter of red still wet enough to drip, thin rivulets tendrilling under her jaw like rootlets in search of water.

"You have to come with me," Jesit gasped. "Yena, you must – you're needed, we need–"

"What's happened?" Yena asked. "Whose blood is that?"

"Mesthani's," Jesit gulped, and only then did Yena see she was crying. "Mesthani a Vekte is dead. Kadeja killed her." She gripped Yena's shoulder, fingers digging into the bone, and when she spoke again, her voice was edged with hysteria. "Do you hear me, Yena a Trishka? Kadeja killed her in cold blood, and now she's escaped, though we don't know how, and *we need you to help us find her.*"

15
The Weight of Scales

It hadn't yet sunk in for Naruet that he no longer belonged to Ke's Kin. His secondment to the palace was official inasmuch as Amenet and Iviyat and Ktho had all declared it so, but it didn't *feel* real, for all he'd sworn his obedience. How could it be, when Ktho was yet to announce it to the temple? How could it be, when he hadn't yet tried – and therefore been prevented from – going back? He thought of Leoden, who had been as deceived in his understanding of things as Naruet himself, despite his good intentions; of hated Kadeja, whose fault it all was. He thought of Safi, the worldwalker girl he'd sent to Noqevai, and of every resonant thread that surrounded her in the dreamscape, futures and truths and shapes half-glimpsed that sang in confirmation of the choice. He thought of Luy, who'd suggested approvingly that Naruet was acting like a Shavaktiin, and what it might mean to become so in truth, if such a course was ever laid open to him.

He thought of the captive worldwalkers, and the debt he owed for his role, however unthinking, in their imprisonment. Leoden's key, worn once again beneath his robes, seemed heavier than before.

With his service pledged, Naruet found himself abruptly superfluous: as Amenet had said, there was other business to be dealt with first. Permitted to sit in one of several vacant courtier's chairs at the edge of the audience chamber, the enthusiasm Naruet had felt on being asked to employ his magic steadily ebbed, transmuting into anxiety. He hadn't quite expected Ktho to say farewell, but when he looked up after a long period of introspection and found her gone, he very nearly panicked. It wasn't her absence that distressed him so much as its implications: he was alone with strangers, and though he'd met both Gwen and Luy in the dreamscape he didn't know how to approach them in waking, let alone who any of the others present were. He started rocking, trying to soothe the sudden burst of agitation this produced, when suddenly two strangers came and sat down on either side of him.

Like Naruet, they were much younger than everyone else in the room: a pretty, feather-haired boy who looked to be little more than twelve, and a girl his own age whose hair was cropped short in a sculpted singleton's cut, emphasising her wide, dark eyes and elegant jaw.

"I'm Sashi," said the girl, and tipped her chin to indicate the boy. "That's Jeiden."

Naruet nodded, not sure what sort of response to give; clearly, they already knew who *he* was.

"I'm the new Vekshi ambassador," Sashi said, "which is rather unexpected. And Jeiden will be my equerry, if only so he doesn't end up stuck here with no one to talk to."

Beyond them, the to and fro continued; Iviyat was no longer present, but several honoured swords had appeared who hadn't been there before.

"Is it always like this?" asked Naruet.

"Worse, usually." Jeiden sighed. "Seems like the only time they agree is when they're telling me what to do – if not, I'm sure they'd argue until the stars fell down."

"Or longer," Sashi added. "We're just lucky Pix isn't here–" Pix meant Pixeva, who'd taken Ktho's legal documents to the House of the Mortal Firmament, "–or you'd really be in for a show."

"Pix is Matu's sister," said Jeiden. "And both of them are my blood-cousins, because their bloodmother is *my* bloodmother's full sister. But my old mahu'kedet... I was the youngest child, which wasn't so bad, until everything got, ah. Complicated."

His expression turned inwards; Naruet, who sympathised, was moved to speak in turn.

"My mahu'kedet was *loud*," he said, lips curling on the offensive word. "So much *noise*, and I only wanted quiet. Not that the temple is always quiet, either," he added, in strictest honesty, "but there, if I take myself off to work in peace, no one follows me."

Jeiden nodded, not quite looking up. "I do miss them all sometimes," he said, "but living with Pix and Matu and the others is still better. Even... even without Zech."

At that, Sashi reached across Naruet's lap and squeezed Jeiden's hand, but pulled back before he could start to feel uncomfortable. "She wouldn't mind you saying it, you know. She'd want you to be happy."

Naruet said nothing at this. He knew that Zechalia was one of the dead women whose transport was being argued about nearby, but beyond that he didn't feel qualified to comment. Zechalia's loss belonged to other people, and as they were not Inside with him, he didn't know what to say. Happily, neither Jeiden nor Sashi appeared to expect him to comment: instead, they kept him company, talking in an easy way that invited Naruet to contribute without pressuring him to do so. By the time they were finally called away again he felt inexplicably better, and when, not long after, Gwen approached him and said, "It's time," he found that he was ready.

Eager to help, Naruet let Gwen shepherd him outside, her hand hovering over his shoulder without quite making contact, a Ktho-ish courtesy that helped to set him at ease. Because of the wards, they had to depart from outside the palace; Naruet knew this, and found he was relieved when

Gwen assumed that knowledge, steering him down towards the gates without explaining why.

"Here," said Gwen, and gestured ahead to where a small crowd of people now waited, just on the citywards side of one of the lesser – and therefore less populated – gates. A sensible place, just far enough beyond the wards to risk no entanglement with them, yet still out of sight of the city proper. Naruet tested the ebb of it in the jahudemet, like strumming the strings of an instrument to check its tuning, and found it to be neither closed-off nor overly worn: a good choice all around, then. He wondered if Ktho had suggested it; although, he supposed, the jahudemet was not so regularly used for portal-making as to have made a rarity of suitable locations.

The hearse was small, the tray enclosed by a low roof, the whole just wide enough to fit the two coffins abreast, pulled by two matched grey horses and driven by Luy. The whole array was saturated with the preservative magic of the maramet, yet missing the traditional, interwoven tang of the *kedebmet*, the magic of soil and stone, that ought to see new plantlife take root when the bodies were buried in Lomo's sight. But of course, these bodies would not be buried in Kena, but taken to Veksh. That thought troubled Naruet enough that he momentarily stopped walking, and so suddenly that Gwen almost crashed into him. He had to think it out in silence before he could continue: they were Vekshi, their rites were Vekshi – that was proper, wasn't it? *Yes*, he decided, and walked again, Gwen rising further in his esteem when she neither rebuked nor commented on his pause.

The honoured swords stood in formation around the hearse, three on each side. Jeiden waited off to their right, holding the reins of two baggage-laden roa and chatting quietly with Matu who, along with Iviyat, had come to see them off. And there, beckoning almost impatiently to Naruet and Gwen, was Sashi – or at least, he thought it was Sashi.

Naruet blinked, confused for a moment by her Vekshi clothes and newly shaved head, until he recalled that Vekshi women cut their hair, and of course a Vekshi ambassador, even an interim one, would need to show the same deference. Lengthwise, it wasn't really that far off from the close crop she'd had before, but the starker lines didn't frame her face the same way: it made her look harder, somehow.

"Now there's a look I never thought I'd see on you," Gwen said, not unkindly.

"Don't say it suits me," Sashi said. "I already know that Yasha will, and that's about all the praise of it I can take."

"You can grow it out again soon enough."

"I know."

"I know you do." She ruffled the hair Sashi didn't have – Sashi swatted her away, but playfully – and went to confer a final time with Matu and the Cuivexa.

Sashi ran a palm over her head, making a face at the texture. Then, quite abruptly, she burst out laughing.

"Is something funny?" Naruet asked, concerned that he'd somehow missed a joke.

"A little," said Sashi. "I just realised, I've been standing here thinking what Yena, my sister, will say when she sees my hair like this – we never wanted to have Vekshi hair, but our grandmother, Yasha, wouldn't ever unbend so far as to let us have fully Kenan cuts – and then I realised, she'll already have had to shave hers too, as part of her penitence in Yevekshasa."

"Penitence?" Naruet asked, intrigued.

Sashi blushed slightly. "She's... well. She needed to be accepted as a full Vekshi there, but it wasn't enough that she cut her hair, because she took Kara's choice and changed her body, and all at a Kenan temple, you see? They thought it was blasphemous that she hadn't done it in Ashasa's sight, and so she had to sit a penitence."

Naruet digested this. Carefully, he said, "I'm one of the

trickster's children, but I never took Kara's choice. Will that count for me in Veksh, do you think, as a lack of blasphemy, or against me, for being male?"

Sashi looked momentarily dumbstruck. "I don't know," she said, thoughtfully. "I don't think it will really matter. I mean, it might do, if you were to stay there, but you're not Vekshi, so the same rules don't apply. They'll likely look down on all of us for one thing or another – me for not being Vekshi enough, Gwen for being a foreigner, you and Luy and Jeiden for being men, the honoured swords for being too Kenan to fight properly, by their standards – but unless diplomacy fails us, they're unlikely to make much mockery to our faces. Yasha might, though, when she comes with us," she added, face falling slightly. "My grandmother is... difficult." And then, with sudden fierceness, "But I won't let her say anything rude to you."

Naruet felt oddly touched. "That's kind of you," he said. "We call it Kara's choice, but some people don't seem to understand that it *is* a choice. I am myself, and my body is mine, and though there are days when I want to change it, I worry what else that choice might change that I didn't want altered." He hesitated, but Sashi was already on the threshold: he might as well bring her fully Inside, now that he knew he liked her. "I don't think like most people; not the ones I've ever met, anyway. I take too long sometimes, or I go too fast, or I miss some things and pick up others that nobody else is bothered with, but *I* like who I am, even if not everybody does. And nobody's ever said to me that changing my body would change that, too, but they can't prove it wouldn't either. And..." he faltered slightly, embarrassed, but took strength from the fact that Sashi wasn't laughing at him, "... and I like to sing, sometimes. To myself, or to the temple cats. But if I changed, I'd get a new voice, and what if it wasn't any good at singing?"

Sashi smiled shyly. "Would you sing for me, some time?"

Naruet felt his ears go hot. "I might," he said, "but only if you listen with your eyes closed. It's too much, being looked at. Cats are all right, though. Cats judge everything and everyone, so even when they're judging you, you know it isn't personal."

"I can't argue with that," said Sashi, and grinned again.

"All right!" said Gwen, striding over to them. "Let's try and make a clean getaway, shall we? I think I've just about managed to cut us free of Matu's vicarious wanderlust, but I wouldn't put it past him to chase after us if we don't hurry." She turned to Naruet, tucking a lock of hair behind her ear. "Now. Do you know where you're taking us?"

"Oh, yes," said Naruet, brightening at the prospect of using his magic. "I've scryed the mesa before. I know just where to take us."

"Do it, then," said Gwen, and Naruet obeyed.

He didn't have to close his eyes to picture their destination, but it helped. He felt the warp and weft of the world, the thinness of air and distance. He saw the mesa of Yevekshasa, a stone fist punched through the skin of the earth, and charted a web from *here* to *there*, precise and clean and perfect. The jahudemet flared in him, an oilslick of power. As though he was parting a curtain, Naruet raised his hands and opened a portal – one large enough for all of them to walk through abreast, though the effort was draining; he found that he wanted to show off, just a little. Just this once. He stretched it down through the cobbles and across the street: a perfect oval limned with sparking rainbows.

"It's beautiful," Sashi murmured. Naruet dropped his hands, not needing them raised to keep it open, and found that Sashi had cocked an elbow, offering him the chance to link arms with her. "Together?" she asked.

"Together," Naruet said, and slipped his arm through the loop of Sashi's, stepping across the portal's threshold.

In that split second of transition, everything pitched

sideways. Naruet felt it as a suckerpunch, his magic roiling against his control like a rudder caught by raging seas. He'd never felt the like before, a drawn-out moment where everything pitched and yawed and colours tasted like music. Electricity sang through him and into Sashi, as though they'd been jointly struck by lightning; his head throbbed, bright lights hammering into his eyes until he had screwed them shut. And then he was stumbling, lurching forward, Sashi panting in his wake, though Naruet dared not look at her. Something had gone wrong, badly wrong, but it was taking all his strength just to keep the portal open.

Then the pain hit, an aching burn against his sternum and a piercing ache in his head, the former hot as an iron and the latter cold as ice. Naruet yelped, clawing at his chest as he yanked away from Sashi.

"What's wrong?" asked Sashi, panicked. "Are you hurt?"

"I don't know! I don't know!"

"Make way!"

That was Luy's voice, accompanied by the clatter of horses and honoured swords as the hearse and guard came through. And then, Gwen's voice, cutting above the sudden din, "Naruet! We're all through!"

"Oh, good," Naruet whispered, and let the portal go. The burning pain in his chest winked out, as sudden as snuffing a fire, and only then did he realise that the source of it was Leoden's key. He went to his knees without meaning to, trembling in every muscle, too shocked and exhausted even to flinch when Sashi put an unexpected hand on his shoulder.

"Naruet." Gwen's voice, hard and urgent. "Naruet, look at me. Open your eyes."

"It wasn't his fault!" cried Sashi. "Auntie, something went wrong and I think–"

"Wait your turn, Sashi." He felt movement in front of him, calm and controlled and therefore, in all probability, furious. "Naruet. Can you open your eyes?"

"It hurts."

"I know it hurts. But can you?"

Naruet considered this. Nodded. Tried, through the wrenching ache and suddenly gummed-up stiffness of his eyelids, to do as he was asked. Succeeded.

Gwen crouched before him, a look on her face that Naruet was not equipped to read. "What just happened, Naruet?"

"The key," he gasped, struggling to pull it free of his robes. He yanked the chain over his head, thrusting it sharply at Gwen. "The key, something happened, I don't know what. It interfered with the jahudemet when I stepped through the portal, it was burning, it hurt – my magic's never gone wrong before, I don't understand…"

Gwen took the key from him, hissing between her teeth: it was still faintly hot to the touch, which at least helped prove that something had happened. She looked from the key to Naruet.

"Did you mean to bring us astray, then? Or were you forced?"

The question made no sense. "Astray?"

"We're nowhere near Yevekshasa. We might not even be in Veksh!"

"Where are we, then?" asked Naruet, his voice small.

Gwen clicked her teeth. "I don't know," she admitted, rising to her feet. She hesitated, then held out a hand for Naruet. He considered refusing, but his legs were too unsteady for pride. Gwen's palm was warm against his own, her grip firm without being painful as she helped him stand.

They stood at the top of a rocky rise, the ground in three directions broken and bare. There were few trees, and all of them strange in some respect, with odd-coloured leaves and twisted limbs. The sun was clearly Kena's sun, as low in the sky as it had been in Karavos, albeit seen from a different angle; if not for that, Naruet might have wondered if he'd accidentally taken them through the worlds, the landscape was so strange. Even the soil was odd, shot through with reds and whites he'd never seen before.

"Hime's breath," exclaimed one of the soldiers. "What is *that*?"

Naruet turned and looked up the hill, heart rabbiting in his chest. Above their vantage point, the land was crowned with ruins, massive and fey and crumbling. The remains of a city, sprawling upwards across the rise and over its crest, so that their long shadows darkened the slope like the wings of some mythical bird. Instinctively, Naruet reached out with the jahudemet, and though his magic was drained and raw, still he felt the vulnerability of the place, the world's weft thin as gossamer.

"Oh, no." Luy leapt down from the hearse, his tone one of dawning horror. He looked at Gwen, at Naruet and Sashi and the honoured swords, and gulped, his throat a bobbing knot. "I know where we are. And I rather wish I didn't."

"Where?" asked Sashi.

"Yavinae," Luy said, heavily. The name produced a general shudder; one of the guardswomen swore. "Vexa Yavin's capital, where Leoden met Kadeja."

Saffron stumbled through the markets, nearly running now. The closer she came to whatever it was, the greater the intensity of that burning tug, so that she had no choice but to follow it. Leoden strode beside her like an overprotective bodyguard, glaring fiercely at anyone who obstructed her chosen path. Which was, she felt certain, far from being the most convenient course they might have taken: whatever strange magic was involved, it was leading her as the crow flies, a sharp pang accompanying her every necessary detour around various stalls and buildings. She was trying very hard not to think about the source of this improbable guidance, partly because it was taking all her concentration to keep a straight course without crashing into anyone, but mostly because, deep down, a part of her already knew the answer. What she didn't know was why or how or what the implications were, and so she shoved it all away and kept on going, gritting her teeth against the discomfort.

As little as she knew of Noqevai and despite her decidedly split attention, it hadn't escaped her notice that their current surroundings were rather more run down than they had been earlier. It had been at least a half hour since she'd first felt the pull, and in that time they'd crossed multiple districts, the pattern of wares and storefronts shifting in accordance with some unknown mercantile prerogative. Fabrics and craftwork had given way to trinkets and crystals, raw materials and raw produce and now, finally, to livestock – or at least, to live animals. Saffron didn't recognise anything here except the ubiquitous sehket and, far off, a glimpse of something that might have been a roa. The smell was pungent, worse whenever they passed pens or corrals or, on one occasion, a building that stank like a slaughterhouse, which it likely was; Saffron gagged more than once, and even Leoden unbent enough from his eagerness to put a hand over his mouth.

The pull intensified, protesting at the necessity of going around the corner of a building.

"Just hang on," Saffron muttered in English, "hang on, I'm doing my best..."

The building had an open front, a colourful awning hung out to shade the trio of resident vendors. One dealt in creatures Saffron assumed were birds, or bird-relatives, being either feathered or winged in various combinations; another stood before a large glass tank whose interior swam with ribbon-finned creatures, beautiful and strange. And yet, as she came to a stumbling halt, her gaze was drawn to none of these, but to the single creature offered by the third vendor: his only piece of merchandise, unless the rest was very well-hidden indeed.

Resting on top of a broad stone plinth was something the

size of a cattledog, web-winged and red-scaled. A fine gold chain – gold in colour, yet likely made of some sterner metal – ran from the collar around its neck to the pillar's base, while matching gold weights like heavy piercings were attached to the sensitive tips of its wings, the better to keep it grounded. Its large eyes, owl-round and lava-hued, stared beseechingly at Saffron, a mournful fluting sound in its throat as it half-raised the webbed, spiny crests set on either side of its skull.

<scale-sister>
<stolen>
<help>
<home>

A distant voice, silent to all save her, yet irrefutable. Saffron stared at the baby dragon – a creature the queens of Veksh called a scion – and felt her understanding pivot, facts and inconsistencies shifting into alignment like a miscellany of disobedient moons. Saffron thought about borders; about the impossible world-egg trapped beneath Yevekshasa and the crystal-strewn landscape it contained, complete with living dragons.

Comprehension dawned like light along some alien horizon.

"Oh, god," she whispered. "Vikasa isn't Kenan at all. It's *Vekshi*."

Yena stared at Mesthani's body, willing her hands not to shake. The queen – or former queen, now – was laid out in the Vekshi equivalent of a nineka, a room in the temple where bodies were kept, viewed and, if necessary, examined prior to burning. Her robes, once white, were now so drenched with blood as to make her seem a daughter of Ashasa's Knives, at least when viewed from the front; Yena had no desire to roll her over and check the full extent of the change.

Her throat had been slashed open. The wound gaped like a mouth.

"How?" she asked, the word a rasp. She looked from Jesit, who'd fetched her here, to Ksa, whose command she'd obeyed. "How did Kadeja get a knife? Why didn't Mesthani fight back?"

Which was, in Yena's mind, a greater anomaly than the former Vex'Mara somehow securing a weapon. Mesthani was – had been – a great queen, skilled with a bladed staff and certainly proficient in unarmed combat. And yet there were no defensive marks on her, no signs that she'd fought back. Most damning of all was the neatness of the cut: the line across her throat was straight and deep and utterly unjagged, as though she'd simply held still for it.

"I don't know," said Jesit, just as Ksa said, "I have my suspicions."

"And they are?"

"Unpleasant," Ksa said, darkly.

Yena felt a surge of temper. "If you're not going to tell me, then why–"

"Peace." Ksa held up a hand. "I don't mean to antagonise, but a great deal of harm may come from my speculating without evidence."

"Harm," said Yena flatly. She tipped her chin at Mesthani's body. "More harm than this?"

Ksa had the grace to flush. "Perhaps," she said, softly. "And perhaps not."

"Kadeja has a head start on us," Yena pointed out. "If you want me to help you find her, we need to act *now*, not wait about for permission!"

"You say that," said a new voice, gravel-rasping and flinty, "only because you do not know what ills may come from premature action. And in any case, the Knives are hunting her."

Yena turned, heart pounding. There stood Kiri a Tavi, the broken blade who'd vouched for Zech at the Council of Queens; who'd spoken in favour of Yena's own bid to be recognised as Zech's sister. Her hair was white and her eyes were sharp, and in her wake came Yasha, grimly pale as she bobbed her head to acknowledge Ksa a Kaje.

"What is *she* doing here?" Jesit hissed in shock.

"Witnessing," snapped Kiri a Tavi, "as is both her right and my request." Her voice dripped sarcasm. "Or should I defer to your wisdom in such matters, Jesit a Gathi?"

Jesit went pale and ducked her head. "My apologies."

Yasha didn't respond; just looked to Yena, a quick once-over as if to confirm that her granddaughter was unharmed. Ksa, however, was clearly disapproving.

"Yasha," she said, as cool as mountain air. "How good of you to join us."

Yasha bared her teeth. "How good of you to have me. We are made family, after all."

"No thanks to you."

"Zechalia was more to my credit than yours."

"A low bar indeed, as I had none of her raising. She credited herself, not you."

Yasha made to reply, but Kiri cut her off with a harsh click, glaring at them both. "Sharpen your wits when better blades don't want the whetstone. We have a purpose: stick to it!"

Ksa inclined her head. "I cede you the floor, and gladly. Speak your piece."

Kiri exhaled hard. She stared at each of them in turn, including Mesthani's corpse; and yet it was Jesit her gaze lit on the longest, as though she were assaying whether to send the junior priestess away. Jesit clearly realised this and stayed stock-still, like prey in fear of a predator; Kiri huffed and waved a hand, but did not, in the end, object.

"What I say to you now," she said, voice low and hard, "I say only in need. When Motherless Kadeja was expelled from Veksh, it was at the will of the then First Voice, Nehvati a Sathon – a woman now dead, but one I was proud to call a friend. Few in the temple knew the true cause of Kadeja's dismissal, though many speculated that it had to do with the heresy for which she was later known in Kena." She paused, shooting Ksa a look that might almost have been an apology, and in that moment, it hit Yena powerfully that Kadeja was not only Ksa's child, but a killer of queens twice over.

"That is a partial truth, yes, but not the whole one," Kiri went on. "Kadeja was expelled, not because she questioned Ashasa, but because she threatened the heart of Veksh. Having once sat the Trial of Knives, she requested leave to sit it again. This was denied her; she asked again. Nehvati asked why Kadeja wished to repeat the process; Kadeja gave no satisfactory answer, but demurred sufficiently that Nehvati, though perturbed, considered the matter closed.

"Three nights later, Kadeja broke temple faith and entered the sacred catacombs where the Trial is held, though not under Trial conditions. She was seen going in and seen coming out, though what passed in the interim is known to Ashasa alone. But in the hours of her absence, her quarters were searched for clues as to her motives – searched by Nehvati herself, who spoke of it to me. There were, in Kadeja's possession, certain heretical writings which suggested a blasphemous attempt to remove – to steal – an... an artefact, I shall call it, from the very heart of the Trial.

"When Kadeja emerged, she was not caught immediately. No artefact was found on her person, but she'd had time to hide it somewhere. When questioned, she denied both the intent to steal and that anything had been taken, as well as asserting further heresies which, though Nehvati did not disclose them to me, were considered grievous indeed – a cancer coiled at the heart of Veksh, unspeakable and false. And yet, Nehvati said, she managed to reach an accord with Kadeja. She must leave in disgrace – must suffer the indignity of cut fingers and expulsion – but only if she recanted her worst heresies before Ashasa. This she did, and it must have been to Nehvati's satisfaction, else she would never have set her free from Yevekshasa. Thus was she released, and thus do we count our sins." Kiri fell silent, gripping the head of her staff.

A heresy at the heart of Veksh. The words rolled through Yena like thunder, sparking off a chain reaction as thoughts connected, clacking together like beads on a string. She looked at Mesthani's body, forced herself to gauge again the perfect neatness of her slit throat. She thought of the worldwalkers taken in Kena, their thoughts and memories muddled with the ahunemet, which the Vekshi called *tahka'zin vakh*, heart-into-mind; thought of Sene a Sati's writing, borders and words that made no sense; thought of the Archives, and documents gone from a folio.

"The Trial of Knives and the Trial of Queens," said Yena, slowly. "They are different, yes? Different tests held under different auspices in different parts of the catacombs?"

"Yes," said Yasha, frowning only slightly. "Why do you ask?"

Yena gathered her courage, voice taut with the effort of keeping it steady. "Honoured Kiri. Honoured Ksa. Namahsi." She glanced at Yasha. "Though I would never ask you to betray the secrets of either Trial to one uninitiated, there are two questions to which I request an answer."

"Ask," said Kiri, nodding at Ksa, "and if we are permitted to answer, we shall."

"Thank you." Yena took a breath. "The artefact that Kadeja stole from the Trial of Knives. Might it have granted her the power of heart-into-mind?"

Kiri inhaled sharply. "Ashasa," she whispered. "Yes. It might have done, though I never considered..." She broke off, horror in her eyes. "Oh, Mother Sun. No wonder Nehvati let her go!"

"Arsegullet!" Yasha swore, equally appalled. "Never mind Nehvati – no wonder Mesthani didn't fight. She couldn't!"

Yena swallowed, ugly prescience twisting her guts like

a swallowed fish. "Yasha. Ksa. If Kadeja stole Mesthani's memories of the Trial of Queens, what might she know of the catacombs – of a way to leave this world, or of somewhere within them that might not be of this world?"

Yasha and Ksa both stared at her, but it was Yasha who spoke. "Yena," she said, voice deadly calm, "if Safi has betrayed her oath to Veksh by breaking her sacred trust, even to you–"

"She told me *nothing*!" Yena shouted, too riled for politeness. "It wasn't her at all, it was Sene a Sati! She killed herself in shame because Kadeja stole her knowledge of something secret, and in the Archives I had Evai show me her writings. There was a piece about language, about why we call our leaders queens when Veksh has never been a monarchy, about all these Vekshi words that don't fit our culture, and all the time, namahsi, she was asking about borders, too, the same as Safi was. And Kadeja, if what we've been told is true, Kadeja has been using the heart-into-mind on Leoden, controlling him all this time, which means that *she's* the one who was interrogating worldwalkers; the one who has Leoden searching the worlds for a lost place called Vikasa. But why would Kadeja care about a chunk of Kena stranded elsewhere? Why would she risk expulsion from Veksh for something she didn't care about?

"She wouldn't! Because Vikasa doesn't come from Kena at all, and nor does it come from Veksh. It's where *Veksh* comes from, don't you see?" She clenched her fists, staring down their horror, staring down the lies of centuries. "There's something that proves it hidden deep in the mesa, something that made Kadeja question the first time she sat the Trial of Knives. It's why she wanted to go back down there, why she was researching heresies – maybe it's even why she wanted to twine Ashasa with Kena's gods, to prove that our people have a rightful claim to be here. We're colonists, namahsi. The very first Vekshi were worldwalkers; they came to this world from somewhere else, fleeing a realm that they destroyed through overuse of portal-magic. That's what Kadeja's looking for; that's where she's trying to go."

"Merciful goddess," Kiri breathed. "It can't... I won't believe it, I won't–"

"It doesn't matter what you believe," said Yena fiercely. "Not if we can't find Kadeja in time. Because the way I see it, there's only one reason why someone like her would go looking for a scrap of dead world, and that's because there's something there she thinks she can use – an artefact, or a source of power. Something worse than whatever it is she has already that lets her use the heart-into-mind. Something bigger."

Ksa made a choking noise. "Ashasa help us."

"Ashasa might not," said Yena, grimly. "Better to help ourselves." She turned on Ksa, on Yasha, on Kiri. "Now tell me, secrets be damned: *what is it that she wants?*"

"Two things," said a satin voice from the doorway. "The heart of Veksh, and you."

Yena whirled, terror in her throat.

It was Kadeja.

16
Unlocked, Unlooking

"How much for the dragon?" Saffron asked.

The vendor smiled thinly, looking her over with evident distaste. He was tall and green-skinned, his thin fingers blessed with an extra joint, dressed in a single swathe of opalescent cloth reminiscent of a Roman toga. "More than you can afford, I think," he said, in crisp, accented Trade.

"Perhaps," said Leoden, coming to stand at Saffron's side. "But perhaps not. Name your price."

The vendor named an amount in the local currency. Leoden looked taken aback, and Saffron felt her heart sink. The dragonling looked miserable.

The vendor smiled a thin smile, showing two rows of small blue teeth. "As I suspected."

"It seems a hefty sum," said Leoden, offhand, "for such a meagre beast. Especially one thus bound. Is it truly so fearsome?"

"Oh-ho! And I suppose you think you'd fare better at capturing your own?" The vendor made a chuffing sound which Saffron took for laughter. "I doubt you know the first thing about dragon-hunting!"

"I don't know." Leoden affected a maddening drawl. "If you can do it, I can't see that it's all that difficult. Why don't you tell us where you found that runty thing, and we'll try our hand at it?" He paused, grinning. "Or are you afraid we'd serve as competition?"

Another chuff, louder than before. "From the likes of you? Hardly. And yet, if you cannot buy my dragon, perhaps you would care to trade for directions to his world of origin, hm?"

"By all means," said Leoden.

This stumped the vendor, who'd clearly expected the tactic to be a bluff. But as they continued to stare at him – Leoden with one brow raised, Saffron with barely contained anger at the dragon's unhappy state – an opportunistic look crossed his face. He sized the pair of them up again, more slowly than before.

"All right," he said, "but understand, this trade is my livelihood. I could not part with the information for any less than, say..." He named another amount in the local currency, much lower than the cost of the dragon, but still more expensive than anything else that Saffron had seen for sale.

And Leoden, who ought at least to have haggled – Saffron fought back inappropriate laughter at the thought of the gourd-buying scene in *Monty Python's Life of Brian* – shrugged and said, calmly, "That sounds very reasonable."

Anger crossed the vendor's face, and for a moment Saffron felt certain he would rescind the offer, despite the fact that the two neighbouring merchants were both unsubtly eavesdropping on the conversation. Then Leoden pulled out his purse, and anger was replaced by greed. *Oh*, thought Saffron, irritated. *He wasn't angry we said yes; just angry he didn't think to charge us more, if we could afford to pay without haggling.*

Leoden extended the purse, then jerked it back again. "Is the dragon's world of origin accessible from Noqevai?"

"Of course!" said the vendor, his eyes on the money. "All you need is the right designation to pass on – and money to pay the fee, of course – and the Doormakers in the main bazaar will see you through."

Saffron hadn't heard of the Doormakers before, but she

could take an educated guess as to their function in a place like Noqevai. "And what about how to get back?"

The vendor glared at her. "That," he said, "would be your own responsibility. I'm selling you a way in, not a way out – how you get back is your own affair."

Saffron wanted to argue the point on principle, but Leoden shook his head. "Naruet," he reminded her, before turning back to the vendor, counting out the full amount into his waiting hands. "Here, then."

"Excellent!" cried the vendor, and after a swift double-count he deposited Leoden's money into a lockbox, though judging by the buzzing when it opened and shut Saffron suspected its protections were more magical than mechanical. Reaching into a drawer of his desk, he pulled out a clean piece of parchment, grabbed a penlike implement – then hesitated, cocking his head at Leoden.

"You understand, of course, that having just spent no small amount of money to obtain this location, you'd be foolish indeed to share it?"

"Believe me," Leoden said, "I have no intention of doing so."

The vendor appeared to assess this reply, then gave a quick, sharp nod and jotted a string of details onto the paper. Saffron opened her mouth to point out that they wouldn't be able to read whatever it was themselves, and therefore couldn't verify it, when she caught a glimpse of the scrawl and realised, to her shock, that it was comprehensible. Evidently, the pill that had taught her Trade didn't share the same limitations on script as the sevikmet did, a detail she filed away to bring up with Matu later. Assuming, of course, she ever saw him again.

It was a wholly unuseful thought. *Don't think like that,* she told herself, and fixed her attention firmly back on Leoden.

Or at least, that's what she tried to do. But Leoden was already leaving the vendor's stall, directions in hand, while she was still fixed on the lost, chained dragon, that echoing plea of *scale-sister, help* still ringing in her heart.

"I'm sorry," she told the dragon, feeling both brave and foolish. "I'll... I'll try to come back for you, later." And then she turned and hurried after Leoden, the vendor's chuffing laugh burning in her ears.

It was then, and only then, that she understood the consequences of her epiphany.

"Leoden!" she called. He was walking briskly, but stopped when he heard her. "Wait!"

"What is it?" he said. "I hope you're not about to tell me I've just paid a fortune for directions to somewhere that *isn't* Vikasa, because if so–"

"No, it's not that – I mean, assuming the vendor didn't lie – I recognised the dragon..." She stopped, took a breath, and shakily held up her three-fingered hand, the one Kadeja had cut. Leoden's eyes widened slightly at the sight, as though he'd never really noticed it before, but it wasn't until she started to speak in Kenan that she saw he understood. "You see this? Kadeja did this to me. I was her omen, the girl she cut in the Square of Gods. I lied to you back at the Nakhereh when I said I didn't speak Kenan, and I'm sorry for that, but I didn't know – you have to understand, we didn't realise what she'd done to you, what she made you do–"

"What she did to me?" Leoden asked. He didn't yet sound angry, but his voice was flat, and edged with something too scared to be pure confusion. "I don't know what you mean."

"That's just it!" Saffron said, then bit her lip, trying to get her thoughts in a coherent order. She'd panicked, she saw that now, leapt into a revelation that required more tact than she possessed, but having started the conversation there was no way to simply let it drop. She tried to think what Zech would say – Zech, who'd had such a knack for putting the pieces together and getting the right conclusion. All at once, a memory struck her: the night she and Zech had accidentally spied on Leoden and Kadeja through the dreamscape with Luy, an encounter Saffron hadn't remembered at the time, but which had ultimately made Zech think that she might be Kadeja's daughter. The memory of Zech's murder crowded in close, as it always did, but though her throat tightened in grief, Saffron shoved it aside, focusing on that tantalising fragment from the dreamscape. What had Leoden said back then? Something about Viya?

One second, two; then it clicked, and she felt her face light up in understanding. "You're the one who persuaded Kadeja to call off the search for Iviyat," she said, willing him to see it. "Remember? You told her that letting Viya run to Veksh was a perfect excuse to move your soldiers north, but Viya never went to Veksh – she went to her other allies, to Rixevet and Kisavet and Amenet. And I think you knew she'd do that, didn't you? Or at the very least, you wanted her to get away."

Leoden stared at her. A muscle twitched in his jaw. "How do you know about that?"

"Does it matter? It's true, isn't it?" She reached for another dreamscape memory – like the dreamscape itself, they seemed to be more accessible here – and latched onto something Luy had told her of Leoden's flight from the palace, the truth of it clicking into place like a dislocated joint. "When Gwen and the others took the palace, you didn't need to let yourself be taken prisoner, because you already knew the anchored portal wasn't a weapon. But you *did* know the captive worldwalkers were chained down there, and that we wouldn't find them without help. That's why you made Gwen take you to the vault – so that they wouldn't die in the dark! So we'd know what was happening! I think Kadeja made it so you couldn't tell the truth to us directly, but you found a way around it, just like you found a way to keep Luy with you, a way to let Viya escape."

"No," said Leoden. He was breathing hard, a high flush on his cheeks. "No, that's not... Kadeja is mine, my sworn

Vex'Mara – she loves me and I love her, she could never...
she *would* never–"

"Leoden, please. Think." Saffron gripped his forearm,
almost begging now. He was poised on a precipice of fight or
flight, and she didn't know how deep Kadeja's manipulations
went, what failsafes she might have imprinted on him to
counteract the truth. All she could do was try her best and
hope. "You told me that you've been losing memories since
you came here – since you ran away from *her*. That's not a
normal consequence of the jahudemet, Leoden; that's more
like what would happen if whatever she did to you with the
ahunemet is starting to wear off. I don't know how or why,
exactly, but it's a sign that something's wrong."

He tried to pull away from her. "I don't need to listen to
this."

"Yes, you do! Leoden, Vikasa isn't part of Kena at all –
it's part of *Veksh*. The magic that let me find the dragon, it's
because of something I did in Yevekshasa; that's how I know–
"

"And what does that distinction matter?" Leoden jerked
out of her grasp. "We lost so much in the Years of Shadow, it
could well be that certain territories now belonging to Veksh
were originally Kenan. Kadeja even suggested such a theory
herself, when we discussed the relationship between the
celestial hierarchy and Ashasa. Whatever Vikasa is, I mean to
find it. Why are you trying to stop me?"

"I'm not!" cried Saffron. "Or not entirely – it's just that
Kadeja's hurt a lot of people, and if she's the ultimate reason
you're here, then we need to stop and think what it is she's
looking for, and whether it might be dangerous – to you, or
to Kena, or even to Veksh."

"Vikasa is a ruined world," said Leoden, with icy patience.
"It's dangerous to nothing and nobody."

"You don't know that!"

"Perhaps not, but I believe it." He drew a deep breath and

stepped away from her. "If you don't want to help me further, then it doesn't matter: I have what I need."

He turned and started walking away, his long legs eating up the distance.

"Leoden!" Saffron ran after him, made a final grab at his sleeve. He shook her off, annoyed, but she dogged his heels like a terrier. "Who really found that piece of Vikasa, the one you're using for your detection spell? You didn't find it somewhere together; Kadeja gave it to you. Didn't she? Leoden, answer me!"

"If she did," said Leoden, through gritted teeth, "it's no concern of yours." He stopped dead, so suddenly that Saffron nearly fell trying not to bump into him, and gripped her by the shoulder. "I'm grateful to Naruet for sending you to me. I'm grateful for your help in finding Vikasa's coordinates. But I cannot listen to this, and I have no more need of you. Go home, Saffron. Leave me to my research."

And with that, he gave her a hard shove – hard enough that Saffron, who was still off-balance and on the lower part of a slope, fell backwards onto the ground. She yelped in shock, arms flailing, and managed to catch some of her weight on her hands. Her palms smarted painfully, the impact jarring through her hips. Leoden's eyes went wide, as if he hadn't intended such a dramatic consequence – and then, before Saffron could recover, he turned and fled through the markets, vanishing into the crowd.

Cursing, Saffron struggled upright. One hip twinged, but she ignored it, hurrying in the direction that Leoden had gone. But the markets of Noqevai were vast and strange, and whereas Leoden had some navigational sense of their layout, Saffron had none. On her own, she was soon hopelessly lost, and by the time she found someone to point her in the direction of the Doormakers, Leoden was long gone.

"Well," said Saffron faintly. "Shit."

She strode along her chosen path, mulling her limited

options. She didn't think it likely that Leoden would bother going back to the Baroeht before jumping worlds, if only because there was no point: he'd already paid for his room in advance, and Saffron knew it was his – and therefore, as of last night, hers – for at least another week. Which meant, if she didn't catch him up, that she wasn't immediately in dire straits, at least as far as getting back to Kena was concerned: all she had to do was contact her friends through the dreamscape and have either Trishka or Naruet open a portal.

She'd crossed another district before she remembered what the vendor had said about the Doormakers charging a fee, and swore again. The money had all been Leoden's; even if she could somehow catch up to him before he left for Vikasa, he could simply decline to pay for her. If Saffron wanted to chase him, she was going to have to find another way to do it.

But was there a pressing need to follow? Saffron bit her lip, considering the point. If she went back to the Baroeht, rested and slept and made contact with Luy, she could tell her friends what she'd discovered – or what she'd theorised, at least – and let them suggest a course of action. It was sensible, but at the same time she had no idea what was going on in Kena or Veksh, what other problems might have arisen since she last spoke to Gwen. What if she couldn't access the dreamscape this time? She shook her head, frustrated.

"That's not the problem," she muttered in English, forcing herself to walk faster despite the burn in her calves. "The problem is that he doesn't know why he's going to Vikasa in the first place, and I don't trust that Kadeja hasn't brainwashed him into doing something dangerous. The *problem* is that I can't conjure a portal out of thin fucking air–"

Several recent memories flashed through her all at once: the tug of the swallowed dragon-scale; her escape from the dreamscape's kshtathit; Nim riding out to her rescue on the Nakhereh.

Saffron sucked in breath. It was dangerous, but it was a

plan, and hers, and something she could at least attempt to do *right now*. Which didn't mean it wasn't also terrifying to contemplate, but Saffron was sick of always being on the back foot, scrambling to react to the chaos of other people's scheming. At least this way she'd be dealing with her *own* damn chaos, and anyway, what good was it to have chosen to be a worldwalker if she wasn't ever brave enough to try it alone?

Filled with new determination, Saffron approached a nearby stall and asked for directions to the nearest paladin barracks. And then, with a burst of energy, she started running.

"We can't stay here," Gwen said. She'd managed to refrain from yelling only by dint of the fact that Naruet had been demonstrably shocked by what had happened, and whatever else could be said of the boy, she doubted he was a good actor. "Naruet, can you get us to Yevekshasa from here?"

Several seconds of silence followed; she bit her cheek, reminding herself that he wasn't being purposefully rude.

"Yes," he said eventually, "but not... not right now. And not this close to the ruins. I fought what the key was doing, and it's drained me." He hugged himself, thin arms around a lanky body. "I don't like being drained."

"That's all right," said Gwen, who was used to working with Trishka's limitations. "How long will it take you to recover?"

Naruet squinted into the sunlight. "An hour? Two hours? I don't think it's ever taken longer than that, but I've never fought a magical key before, so it might be different."

"Two hours." Gwen considered the prospect. "We can afford to lose two hours. And in the meantime–" she glanced at the ruins of Yavinae, a shiver of trepidation running down her spine, "–I might as well see what's here."

"Do you really think that's a good idea?" asked Louis, voice lowered so as not to spook the honoured swords – a rather redundant courtesy, as he was speaking in English. "Mother, this is *Yavinae*. I know you have a soft spot for archaeology, but this isn't the safest location."

"You think I don't know that?" Gwen shot him a withering look, then softened it with a sigh. "Believe me, I'm well aware of the dangers. But I also can't help noticing how often Vexa Yavin's name has come up in conversation lately; how everything that's happened seems beholden to things we've lost. Things that *she* lost, or that she made."

Louis blinked. "Damn me, you're right. The anchored portal. The precedent Ktho found for Viya and Amenet's rule. Naruet's secondment from temple justice. Even Vikasa, if we count the history lost in the Years of Shadow."

"And now, perhaps, this key." She curled her fingers around it, wondering where Leoden had found it, what impulse had moved him to entrust it to Naruet. "I want to see what's here. I don't trust these ruins, and I certainly don't trust this key, but I need to know why it brought us here." She looked sternly at Sashi. "You're in charge, ambassador. If anything happens to me–"

"–or to me," added Louis. "I'm coming with you."

"–or to Louis," Gwen affirmed, resisting a fond roll of her eyes, "to either of us, I suggest you wait as long as it takes for Naruet to recover, walk as far from here as necessary to portal to Yevekshasa, and you do what we came here to do. All right?"

"Yes, auntie," Sashi said, ducking her head.

"This isn't any shame on you," said Gwen, sharply. "Understand? I'm not making you stay here while I do something fun because I'm an adult and you're my niece who made a mistake; I'm *asking* you to stay here while I do something dangerous because we're both adults and you're more important than me. You're needed in Yevekshasa: I'm not."

Sashi looked momentarily stunned; then she laughed,

swatting affectionately at Gwen's leg. "Go on, then. Try not to play with any dangerous magic, won't you?"

"I'll do my best," Gwen said, and gave her son, who was staring rather wistfully at Rikan, a shove in the guard's direction. "Go on, you great lump. Go and talk to him. I can stand to wait three minutes while you reassure your man."

"Your tact is as gentle as newfallen snow," Louis muttered, but did as she suggested all the same. Gwen snorted and started up the hill: the footing was rough enough for the slope to play merry hob with her knees, which meant there was little danger of her outpacing anyone, even with a headstart.

Louis joined her soon enough, a slight warmth to his cheeks in response to whatever brief farewell he'd shared with Rikan, and when Gwen swore and slipped on a rock he courteously lent her his arm.

"Glad to know I raised you right," she said, accepting it gratefully. "Thank you."

He grinned at her, impish. "In fairness, it was mostly bloodfather Naku who taught me manners. You and firstmother Jhesa always tended more towards swearing and a gratuitous use of raised eyebrows."

"Oh, fuck off," Gwen said in English.

Louis burst out laughing.

The laughter stopped, however, when he noticed Gwen turning the key in her hand.

"Can I see that?"

"Be my guest."

She watched as Louis examined it. The key was long and heavy, incised with writing that Gwen, though sure the script was Kenan, couldn't quite make out. She'd removed the chain when Naruet gave it to her, preferring the subtle heft of it in her palm. The spiralled tooth gleamed like a narwhal's horn, and the more Gwen looked at it, the more she felt like she wasn't ever seeing quite the same object as before, as though it were a liminal thing in more ways than one. It was a disquieting thought.

"Can you read what that writing says, along the side?" Gwen asked.

"Not at all. Can you?"

"No. But I feel like I ought to be able to."

"Me, too."

Gwen sighed. "Do you know," she said, "there are days when I feel quite utterly sick of magic? Just when I think I understand it, the damn stuff goes and twists itself out from under me."

"Twists, turns and unlocks, sometimes," said Louis, and passed the key back to her keeping.

As they crested the slope, the later afternoon light contrived to seem both brighter and murkier, the temperature fluctuating from a creeping chill to sudden bursts of warm air. The tarnished ruins gleamed like the sharpest edge of a broken promise, gold stone married with blackish streaks like the legacy of fire. Gwen was no expert on Kenan architecture, but even destroyed it was clear that Yavinae had been unique. The surviving half of a ruined arch hung overhead, the stone worked so finely and with such crisp precision that it might have been carved yesterday – a thing incomplete, not broken. Yet barely three paces on, the tumbled remains of a statue bore every sign of its four centuries of exposure: green plants grew through the cracking base, the detailing so eroded by wind and rain that the subject, a crouching animal of some sort, was difficult to identify.

Gwen thought it looked a little like a dragon.

"History is written by the victors," she murmured, "and time always wins in the end."

Louis laughed softly, the sound fragmented into echoes by the passing of some mischievous breeze. "I can't tell if that's morbid or beautiful."

"It's neither," Gwen said. "Just true."

"I do miss our talks," said Louis. And then, with a sudden

rawness, "I miss our family. I haven't been home in far too long, and I want... There are people I want them to meet. Want you to meet, too. All together."

"Halaya and Rikan?"

"Yes." Louis laughed again, but though the sound was stronger this time, it didn't carry as it had before. "I know they haven't met yet, but I feel... I think it could work. I think they, we, could work."

"I'm glad," Gwen said, too moved to say more. She put an arm around his shoulders, giving him a brief squeeze. "I'm glad for you."

"You approve of them?"

"Louis." She caught his gaze, a smile tugging her lips. "Do you really think I'd be silent if I didn't?"

"Stranger things have happened."

"Like you becoming a Shavaktiin?"

It was an old tease between them, if occasionally fraught; Louis opened his mouth to respond, but before he could speak Gwen yelped to feel a sudden heat in her palm. She opened her hand and stared, angling it so Louis could see, too.

The key was glowing.

"We should turn back," said Louis, shakily. "Whatever that signifies, I doubt it means anything good for us."

"Agreed," said Gwen; and yet she hesitated, a strange thrum running through her. "And yet, I do wonder..."

"What?"

"It's just." She took a step forwards, moving further into the ruins. Her blood was pleasantly warm, as if she'd been drinking whiskey. "You know I've never believed in the Great Story, but this feels... There's something about this place..."

"Mother?" Louis sounded truly alarmed, which Gwen knew ought to have bothered her more, and yet she kept walking, guided by the key's silent compulsion. "Mother, please. Put the key away, it's doing something to you–"

"I know," said Gwen, more calm than she ought to have

been. "I know it's the key. But it doesn't feel *wrong*, Louis. I've felt wrong magic before, and it wasn't like this."

"That doesn't mean you should trust it!"

"I know that, too. And I could put it down, I think. If I truly wanted to." She navigated around the remains of a forecourt fountain, stepping under the lintel of what had once been a door. The open sky beamed down on her where the roof was gone, the sunlight full of dancing motes. Gwen almost fancied they formed a pattern, some secret alphabet of light and air in which all Kena's hidden things were written.

Louis grabbed her arm, tugging at her; Gwen shook him off, not unkindly, but didn't falter. "You don't have to come with me, you know."

"Of course I do!" Sharp terror edged his voice. "You're my *mother*!"

"I am that," said Gwen. She stepped between two melted pillars of glassy slag, their slate-blue facets streaked with lighter grey. Some flash of instinct said they'd once been part of something magnificent, the entryway to a grand space: it wasn't time that had broken them so, but an act of deliberate violence. "I'm also a worldwalker, Louis, and have been since before you were born. Do you really think this is the most dangerous risk I've ever taken?"

"I don't know." He was frustrated now; she risked a glance at him, stray coils of hair springing out from where he'd tied it back. "I want to trust *you*, but I don't trust *this*."

"I'm your mother, Louis. Trust me."

Louis had no answer to that, but he didn't leave her side. Reassured, Gwen passed through the broken remains of another tall door and into a room – again, the roof was gone – whose metal floor gleamed beneath her feet, as mirror-bright and perfect as if it were newly laid.

"Here," she said, in response to another surge of whatever-it-was from the key. "It's somewhere here."

"What is?"

"The door," said Gwen. Her voice was distant, the words not entirely her own, drawn up from a deeper well of knowledge. "Vakti's door."

Gwen stopped, scanning the metal hall. She tilted her head, frowning at the naked air, then took a few paces on the diagonal, squinting. A bare shimmer rippled in her peripheral vision: she fixed on it as it wavered, sidestepping to keep it in view, half bumping into Louis when he didn't move quickly enough.

"Mother?"

In her hand, the key hummed with approval. Gwen took a final step, exhaling relief when a sheet of rippling static appeared before her, a door that both was and wasn't. It was metmirai, she realised: a weakness in the world just like the ones she'd seen in Saffron's dreamscape, albeit more predictably located.

"Gwen?" Louis asked, voice small. "Who's Vakti?"

Gwen jounced the key in her palm and gripped the haft, looking for the best point of entry. Distantly, she was aware that her son was frightened, that she ought to stop and reassure him, but at the same time she knew it could wait; that what she was doing now was more important. Even so, he'd asked her a question, one she also knew she needed to answer. Speaking was hard, but she made herself do it, her tongue feeling thick in her mouth.

"You are, I think," she said. She lifted the key, gaze narrowing on a single bright knot in the static door, an inward spiral like the core of a tiny vortex. "Or her heir, at least."

"No, wait–"

Gwen shoved the spiral-edged key in the lock. A flash like lightning strobed through the room as the doorway opened, and in the split second before she crossed over, Gwen could've sworn she heard two women laughing.

And then she was falling, tumbling through a well of light; she clung to the key, to the tremulous hope that her instincts hadn't failed her, and shut her eyes against the searing onrush of a billion tiny stars.

Reality returned with a roar.

Gwen hit the ground, hard, and collapsed into darkness.

Kadeja stood barefoot in the temple doorway, dressed in a blood-spattered nek, her stolen knives gleaming in her hands. She was the most frightening thing that Yena had ever seen, projecting a greater air of danger even than the sun's mouth. A feral grin warped her features out of beauty, faltering only when she recognised Ksa, and then but briefly. "Unmother," she said, and sketched a mocking bow. "It's nice to see you again."

"Kadeja," Ksa said, winded. "Please, you have to stop this. Whatever it is you're seeking–"

"*Don't.*" She bit the word out fiercely. "Do not presume to tell me to *stop*, as though I'm some miscreant child to be brought to your beck. Our history is a lie; our *temple* is a lie, and anyone who questions it is thrown out to starve! I know that I have done terrible things, but you – all of you – necessitated my actions a thousand times over. Veksh is a body with rot where our heart should be, and though I love Ashasa, She is more than this. She was *always* more; Her flame contains multitudes, spat out in sparks. But we, who ought to honour Her, have shrunk ourselves, and so shrunk Ashasa with us." Kadeja's eyes glittered dangerously; she stalked the room like a hunter. Her wicked knives dripped fresh blood on the stone, a terrible soft noise. "But I can change all that. I can give Her back the world she deserves. Her world and ours, as it always should have been."

"This is blasphemy," Kiri hissed. "You are a traitor, a liar, corrupt–"

"*I am not a liar!*" Kadeja lifted her chin at Yena, defiant, an ugly smile on her face. "That one had the right of it. This world wasn't always ours. We claimed it for Ashasa, but we left Her heart behind." She lifted her hands, blades angled in an aggressive stance. "I intend to bring it back."

Kiri was fast, but Kadeja was faster. As the old priestess raised her staff, Kadeja snuck in under her guard and slashed across the inside of her wrist: a violent disabling move, deep enough to strike bone. Yena's stomach roiled as blood gushed outwards, slick and dark. Kiri shrieked and dropped the staff, trying desperately to grip the wound shut with her good hand, and all the while Kadeja was still on the attack, as graceful and deadly as a razor-edged whip. Time seemed to slow, giving Yena no choice but to watch it unfold in hideous detail. Flowing effortlessly from high stance to low, Kadeja pivoted away from Yasha's retaliatory staff-strike and took her out at the hamstring. Yasha staggered, dropping to one knee, but still retained enough control to convert her staff's downswing into a backwards jab, the butt of the weapon catching Kadeja square in the ribs.

Kadeja went sprawling just as Yasha collapsed, panting in ragged pain. Seeing an opening, Ksa lunged forward, aiming to bring her own staff down on Kadeja's head, but the former Vex'Mara rolled away, the staff connecting with stone. Kadeja leapt to her feet, circling Ksa with her blades raised.

"Would you really kill me, unmother?" she asked, her voice gone viper-soft. "I thought you abhorred filicide."

"So I do," said Ksa, her features twisted with grief and rage, "but as you say, you are not my daughter. Not any more."

At Yena's side, Jesit was frozen with fear; had been so since Kadeja's sudden entry. But now, as the two women circled each other, Yena saw her eyeing the door, and realised what she was planning.

Fear seized in her chest. "No," she whispered. "Jesit, don't—"

"I can make it," Jesit hissed back, "I can get help—"

"You're a healer! Help *them*, help Kiri and Yasha—"

"No," said Jesit, shaking with fear, "no, I'm going—"

"Jesit, wait–"

The healer broke and ran, the sudden movement startling both combatants. Ksa's eye widened, horrified; Kadeja whirled and threw her right-hand blade. It wasn't a proper throwing knife, the balance of it all wrong for such a shot, but she'd reacted fast enough that Jesit was barely halfway to the door. The blade took her solidly in the back, driving in with a wet, awful *thunk*: Jesit staggered, flailed for balance, made an awful gurgling noise and fell, blood spreading out around her.

Blood, thought Yena, numb with shock. There was so much blood on the floor that, for an awful moment, she had the continuity of it backwards, wondering if Jesit had only slipped in Yasha's blood, or Kiri's, the knife in her back an afterthought.

"Stand down, Ksa a Kaje." Kadeja switched her remaining blade from left hand to right. "Your allies still live; let me leave with the girl, and you might yet save them."

The girl.

Yena.

On the floor, Yasha groaned in protest. Yena was rooted to the spot.

"What do you want with her?" Ksa rasped, gaze flickering to Jesit, Kiri, Yasha. To Mesthani's body, cold and still on the slab.

"What do you think?" Kadeja snapped. "You, all of you robewives here, you stole my daughter from me. But this one–" she cocked her head at Yena, "–was her sister. And though she is rightfully one of us, her mother is not. Is the pattern not clear to you? Ashasa means for her to come with me."

"Will you kill me?" Yena asked. Her voice was flat, a mimicry of calm. "If I come with you, will you kill me?"

Kadeja looked at her, wildness in her eyes. She was smiling, terribly so, and the worst of it was that Yena knew the expression was sincere. "No, Yena," she murmured. "I won't kill you. Mothers don't kill their daughters."

"But you killed Zech."

Kadeja stiffened. "*They* killed her," she snarled, gesturing sharply at the other Vekshi, cutting her blade through the air. "Their rules, their pride, their fear – if I'm a weapon, I'm one they shaped. I did *not* kill her!"

Her voice broke on the denial, piercing and ragged.

"Yena," Yasha whispered, reaching forwards to clutch her ankle. "Don't. *Please.*"

Yena looked at Kadeja; at the trio of injured, dying women sprawled on the temple floor. Perhaps help would come if they held out a little longer, but given the likelihood that Kadeja had used her stolen magic on even one of Ashasa's Knives – and Yena would bet it was more than one, to judge by her equally stolen blades – it wasn't a chance that Yena could sensibly take.

"If I come with you," she said, exhaling the words to hide her fear, "if I do that, and Ksa stands down, you'll leave the others alive?"

"I will," said Kadeja, straightening. "I swear by Ashasa's name."

"And you won't…" Yena gulped. "You won't use the heart-into-mind on me?"

"I won't," said Kadeja, her voice as soft as her smile was not, "provided you obey me."

"I'll obey," said Yena. She was shaking, fine tremors that ran through her muscles like shocks. She looked at Ksa, quietly pleading with her not to fight. Ksa tensed, jaw working soundlessly, but under Kadeja's scrutiny, she lowered her staff and stepped aside.

"I yield," she whispered. "Ashasa forgive me, but I yield."

"Good," said Kadeja. "Yena, come."

I'm sorry. The words sat on her tongue as she looked at Yasha, but Yena couldn't speak. As Kiri groaned, still clutching her wrist, Yena stepped over the spreading blood – there was so much, she couldn't avoid getting some on her shoes – and stood, trembling, at Kadeja's side.

"Good girl," Kadeja said, and gripped Yena's wrist with her three-fingered hand. "Now stay silent, and do as I say."

Not waiting for a reply, Kadeja dragged her from the room, stepping disdainfully over Jesit's still-spasming body in the process, leaving Yena to nearly trip on her outflung arm.

The last thing she saw before Kadeja yanked her out of sight was Ksa reaching for Jesit, kneeling in Yasha's blood.

What followed was a nightmare run, Yena's fear of what Kadeja might do – to her; to anyone who got in her way – warring constantly with fear of being deemed her willing conspirator should she be caught. It was terrifying: Kadeja clearly knew her way around the temple, and whatever she'd done to throw the bulk of Ashasa's Knives off her scent, the place was still full of priestesses and acolytes, any one of whom might sound the alarm. Every time they caught sight of someone – whenever Kadeja dragged her back behind a corner, into an alcove, bloodied knife glinting as she waited for a chance to move – Yena considered screaming, making a break for it; doing anything to get away. But then she thought of Jesit, who might already be dead, and shuddered at the thought of more violence being wreaked on innocents. Revealing Kadeja's presence to those who couldn't possibly stop her would only ensure that others would die or be injured in the attempt: if she was going to act, it was better to wait for a real opportunity.

And then, of course, there was the other thing: under her terror and anger, under her worry and desperation, Yena was curious. Where was Kadeja going, and why did she want Yena with her? Claiming that Veksh was ultimately responsible for Zechalia's death while insisting Ashasa wanted Yena to be her substitute daughter was abhorrent, wrong; and yet it still made a twisted kind of sense. What didn't fit was the fact that she'd risked her own recapture to lay claim to Yena *now*, when her real goal clearly lay in the catacombs – as unfamiliar as Yena was with the Great Temple's layout, even she could see that they were heading steadily downwards. Down, where there were fewer people and more secrets and, if Yena's earlier suspicions were correct, maybe even a portal-point.

What was it Kadeja had said of Vikasa? *I intend to bring it back.* Worlds united, new and old – it ought to have sounded positive, and yet the very notion raised goosebumps on Yena's arms, not least because Kadeja's initial search for such unity had involved her cutting off Safi's fingers in the Square of Gods. *What is it you're trying to do, Kadeja?*

They came to an abrupt halt before a locked door, Kadeja muttering under her breath as she jiggled the mechanism. She must have been doing something clever to open it, though Yena didn't know what – and then, at no discernible signal, the door swung silently open. Kadeja made a satisfied noise and dragged Yena through, taking care to shut and relock the door behind them. Up ahead was a flight of stairs, steeper and narrower than any they'd yet used, and as they began their descent, Kadeja grinned viciously.

Down, down, down. Carved stone stairs and twisting turns and motifs of fire and sunlight, symbols that ought to have invested Yena with reverence, but which now were meaningless. On and on they went – there was no sign of anyone else down here – with only the occasional lightstone to keep the path from total darkness. Yena thought of Safi and Zech making this same descent – or had they taken a different route? There seemed to be more than one, with different paths branching off in other directions – and drew strength from the thought. *They both survived whatever's down here. So will I.*

She didn't let herself dwell on the fact that Zech, who'd survived the Trial of Queens, had not survived Kadeja.

All at once the latest stairwell, broader and more ornate than the others, opened out into a long, stone hallway lined with soaring columns. Two impressive double-doors stood at the end, flanked by pedestals topped with what Yena guessed was magical fire; she couldn't imagine how it would stay lit otherwise. The doors were closed, but not – as it turned out – locked; one side swung open at Kadeja's push, admitting them into a massive stone cavern studded with crystals.

Again, Kadeja shut the door behind them. She still carried her stolen blade, but though it was still bloody it no longer dripped, a tacky streak of carmine marring the metal. She hefted it, making sure Yena took notice. Yena's eyes widened, wondering if Kadeja had only brought her here to kill her after all. Kadeja eyed her consideringly, then snorted, lowering the blade and, finally, letting go of Yena's wrist.

"Ahead is a maze of sorts," said Kadeja, after a moment. Her lip curled disdainfully. "The robewives use it for the Trial of Queens, the truth of Veksh hidden in lies and ritual." She grabbed the hem of her nek and used the knife to cut off two long, ragged strips, holding them up for Yena to see. "There is some natural poison in the tunnels ahead, a spore that feeds you your own terror. Tie this over your nose and mouth and try to breathe only shallowly. It will pass soon enough."

Yena took the cloth strip, not knowing what to think. "I don't understand," she said. "Why am I here? What do you want with me, really?"

Kadeja paused. It was a hunter's stillness, laden with intent. She looked at Yena, really *looked* at her, and when she spoke, her voice was soft.

"In Kena, I prayed for a rightful child, and Ashasa chose you for me. I didn't lie about that – why else would you be what you are, who you are?" She gestured with the bloody blade, a single flick to encompass everything Yena was. "My daughter's sister, motherless in law, a Vekshi raised beyond Veksh, but half-Kenan by blood–"

My sire was Kamnei, Yena thought, but didn't dare voice the correction.

"–and valued by all who disdain me?" Kadeja laughed, dark and ugly. "I know you don't understand me, Yena, just as you don't truly know Ashasa. You think of us both as cruel and strange, but that's why you need to come with me. You need to see the truth."

"I know the truth," said Yena, trembling. "The Vekshi come from another world – that's what you mean, isn't it? I already figured it out."

Kadeja visibly startled. Then she smiled, a slow, creeping horror; she stepped up to Yena and gripped her shoulder, hard.

"So you *do* understand," she whispered, eyes bright with fervour. "Ashasa showed you the truth, the same as She showed me. *That's* why she gave you to me; that's why we have to act. She needs us to be Her hands and bear Her witness."

Yena didn't know what to say to that, and so said nothing. Evidently, this was the right decision: Kadeja gave a sharp, pleased nod and gestured to Yena's scrap of cloth.

"Tie it on. We've work to do."

Hands shaking, Yena obeyed. Kadeja crouched, depositing her blade on the ground, and used both hands to do likewise, snatching up the knife again before Yena could so much as think of taking it from her. This time Kadeja didn't grab her wrist, but held out a hand for Yena to hold, as easy as if they were sisters at a crowded market.

"Come."

Again, Yena complied, and soon found herself being lad through a crystal-studded cavern. The cloth rasped against her cheek, fluttering against her nose and mouth with every breath. It was a small mercy that her makeshift mask had no blood on it; the same was not true of Kadeja's, but if the ex-priestess minded at all it didn't show. They only stopped once, when Kadeja decided to prise a longish crystal fragment from the wall – "We'll need it later," she said, pressing it into Yena's free hand – and then they were off again, the distant sound of water echoing strangely around them.

Eventually, they came to a place where the path split into three. Yena felt a flash of fear at the thought of walking into darkness, for all that Kadeja unerringly chose the lefthand path, and when the crystal in her hand, which had been glowing softly, suddenly went dark, her breathing began to quicken.

Kadeja squeezed her hand sharply.

"This is the poisoned walk," she murmured, quickening her pace. "Remember? Slow breaths. The darkness is real, but the fear is not."

"All right," Yena whispered, and stumbled after her.

Knowing the source of her terror only went so far towards alleviating it. Trying to control her breathing made her more conscious of each inhalation, which ratcheted up her anxiety; far easier to pretend there was nothing wrong at all. Perversely, it was Kadeja's presence that made it somewhat bearable. The physical contact meant she wasn't alone, while having someone lead the way removed the lurking fear that she was about to crash into a wall or fall down a hidden chasm.

Epiphany struck like a slap to the face. Not only had Zech and Safi walked this path – or Safi had, at least – but Yena's presence here now was a blasphemy. She was not sanctioned to sit the Trial; she had no right to its mysteries. But if what Kadeja said was true – if Yena's own conclusions about Vekshi history were correct – then she'd already sinned against Ashasa; or against the Great Temple, at least.

And isn't that Kadeja's point? That we have a right to know? That Ashasa, if she exists, is not defined by what the temple says of her? It was a thought made all the more terrible by its appeal to her intellect; she didn't want to agree with Kadeja in anything, but Yena had harboured too many secret doubts about Veksh to dismiss it on those grounds alone.

Poison in her lungs and heart, she plunged on through the darkness.

When the tunnel finally ended – when the crystal glowed again – Yena felt as if she'd undergone her own, private Trial: not one the Council of Queens had ever intended, but one perhaps more precious because of it. Panting, she ripped the mask from her face the second Kadeja did, head swimming as she took in the narrow stone bridge on which they stood, the soaring dark around, above, below.

And opposite, pressing out from within the rock, an absurd, smooth curve of powder-blue *something*, speckled with silver and gold.

"The world-egg," Kadeja murmured. Dropping Yena's hand, she reached across and reclaimed the newly gleaming crystal, hefting it like a second blade.

Yena gawked. "That's an *egg*?"

"Of sorts." Kadeja walked towards it, her smile both sharp and pleased; Yena had no choice but to follow. "It's more like an anchored portal." She didn't touch the surface, but motioned for Yena to do so. "What does it feel like?"

Yena laid a palm to the egg. It was thick and membranous, pulsing slightly under her hand. She pulled back sharply, disquieted. "It feels alive."

"I'd read as much. A clever trick, that." Kadeja tapped the egg with the tip of her stolen crystal. "On the other side of this barrier is another world. I don't know what plurality of magics the ancients of Vikasa used to render this, but render it they did. Self-maintaining, self-replenishing – a closed magical system. Once I open a path for us, it'll close back up again. Whole and perfect."

Without waiting for a response, she took the crystal, punched it into the side of the egg, and yanked it jaggedly downwards, ripping an entryway. Pushing at the resultant flap, she held it open and gestured Yena inwards.

"You first," she said.

Yena hesitated. Whatever lay on the other side, she hadn't forgotten the scars accrued by all who survived the Trial of Queens. But in Kadeja's other hand was the bloodied knife, and Yena knew that, daughter-heir or not, she wouldn't hesitate to use it at the first sign of disobedience.

Gulping, she squared herself and pushed through the shuddering membrane, eyes shut against the strangeness of it all. She was half prepared for Kadeja to abandon her, but still the Vex'Mara followed, stepping through the gap.

"There, now," said Kadeja, pulling on Yena's shoulder. She opened her eyes as Kadeja spun her around, just in time to see the egg-wall close seamlessly behind them. "You see? A very clever magic."

Yena opened her mouth to reply, then froze.

There was something large moving behind her.

"Ah!" said Kadeja, softly. "So the scions are real, after all."

Yena turned and stared, heart hammering in her throat.

Scions.

It was the only name that fit the two massive creatures, winged and scaled, who stood and stared at them. One was massive and white, wings mantled to show extensive scarring across its flanks; the other was smaller and bronze, with a clever-looking head cocked sideways at the pair of them.

"My apologies," Kadeja said, still in that same soft voice. Yena felt a sudden lurch of fear – had Kadeja only brought her as bait for the scions? Was she about to be mauled and eaten? – that only abated when the ex-priestess stepped past her, bowing reverently to the creatures; her words were meant for the scions, not Yena. "We do not mean to come unannounced, without the proper rituals, but need and the will of Ashasa Herself compel us."

Kadeja straightened, the bloody knife still in hand. The white scion blinked its orange eyes at her, so slowly that it almost looked like nodding: if either creature saw Kadeja as a threat, they gave no obvious sign of it. The bronze scion snorted, the webbed crests on its head flicking up and down. It snaked its neck, peering at her from a new angle: its eyes were purple, and when it opened its jaws a crack, the slender tongue that flicked between its many teeth was almost the same shade.

Not conscious of having held her breath, Yena exhaled steadily. "Are they safe?" she asked.

"They serve Ashasa," Kadeja said, which answer was neither helpful nor, from Yena's perspective, encouraging. Still, it wasn't a warning, which counted for something. Yena knew very little of Ashasa's scions beyond their near-mythical status and their purported guardianship of Yevekshasa's secrets. If they objected to their sacrilege, it didn't show, and if they were nothing but dumb, hungry beasts, they'd surely have displayed some hostility by now. Which left a third option: that they were intelligent, and therefore acting in accordance with a different set of priorities unknown to Yena – or to Kadeja.

Taking comfort from this assessment, Yena looked past the scions in favour of their surroundings – *Vikasa,* she reminded herself, *this is another world* – with belated, breath-stealing awe. The air was humid, the sound of water loud in her ears, and everywhere were strange, curled ferns and crystal clumps and long, lilac grasses, the combination unlike anything she'd ever seen.

"Scions," said Kadeja. "We seek pilgrimage to the anchors. Will you take us there?"

For a moment, nothing happened. And then, to Yena's utter astonishment, both scions began to move, the white fore and the bronze aft: a joint guard leading them onwards into a strange new world.

17

Into Vikasa

It took Saffron nearly two hours to track down Nim, and a further twenty minutes to persuade thim that she knew what she was asking for.

"You're insane," Nim said, not for the first time, extending a hand to help Saffron climb aboard a newly harnessed Maza. The roshaqui, at least, was eager to participate, and Saffron felt a surge of gratitude towards the big alien creature. "All travellers are the same; I don't know why I bother to listen to any of you, let alone *help*."

"Don't lie," Saffron panted, clambering into the saddle. She was exhausted, settling herself flush to Nim's back with a groan of relief at taking the weight off her feet. "Your life would be boring without us."

"True," Nim said, resettling Saffron's arms around thir waist. "But let me say, I've heard a lot of terrible traveller ideas as a paladin, and this is just about the riskiest. Well." Thei paused, considering. "Maybe second riskiest. Third at most."

"Your faith in me is truly inspiring."

"It should be," Nim said, more serious now. "I'm still helping you, aren't I?"

"Yes," said Saffron. "You are. Thank you."

"Don't thank me yet," said Nim. "Thank me when you've

survived, and I can claim the honour of having failed to kill you." Thei clicked thir tongue to get Maza moving; the big roshaqui rumbled assent and started up a fast walk, heading out of the paladin barracks and up the broad, bare avenue that led past the border of Noqevai's dome, out into the wilds of the Nakhereh.

Back to where Leoden had found her.

"You're lucky there's not a kshtathit due," said Nim, when they passed the joh-gardens. "Or else I really couldn't take you anywhere."

Saffron was silent a moment, digesting that. "I'm not sure I really believe in luck any more, not the way I used to. It's like... there's coincidence, and then there's patterns, you know?" She rested her cheek against Nim's leathers, watching the scenery. "Or maybe there's not. Maybe I'm just making it all up to make myself feel better. Total, uh–" she hunted around for the right word in Trade, but couldn't find it, and was forced to resort to English. "Total *solipsism*."

"What does that mean?"

"It means, ah... not selfishness or egotism, exactly, but thinking you're more important than you are. Thinking you're the centre of things, because it's easier than acknowledging how much bigger and more complicated the world really is. Worlds, I mean." She chuckled, still somewhat amazed by the plural. "I didn't know there was more than one until recently. My world, where I'm from – we have a lot of technology, but all our magic is hidden. Until I saw a portal, I didn't know it was real at all. Just thought it was something in stories, you know?"

"Not really," said Nim. Thei waved a hand at Noqevai's dome, at the sideways lightning spiderwebbing above it. "Look at where I live. I was born here, raised here. My parents are merchants – they're settled in the city, but they still travel. I went with them from almost before I was old enough to walk. I can't imagine what it's like to grow up thinking any of that is impossible."

"Lucky for you."

"I thought you said you didn't believe in luck?"

"Maybe." Saffron laughed, a strange weight easing from her chest. Up ahead, she spied the carved pillars that marked the exit from Noqevai and sat a little straighter. "Maybe luck believes in me."

"Now, there's an encouraging thought," said Nim. With the way ahead clear, thei kicked Maza into her loping run. The roshaqui picked up speed, Saffron whooping delightedly as they made for the winding switchback up to the plateau. Ascent soon proved to be even more fraught than descent: Saffron clung to Nim, terrified she was going to fall backwards off the too-big saddle. Nim only chuckled and urged Maza onwards.

"Don't worry, traveller. I've never lost a passenger, and I don't intend to start now."

Saffron tried to be reassured, and failed spectacularly. It felt like a small eternity before they reached the summit. Fear-sweat plastered her shirt to her back, toes cramping where she'd gripped the stirrup-dents in the saddle.

"Still with me?" Nim asked. "I felt like I could breathe for a few seconds there. I wondered if you'd fallen."

"Sorry," Saffron mumbled, flushing as she eased up her death-grip on Nim's ribs.

"Oh, you're fine. I'm only teasing. Here, now – are you happy if we go fast on the flat? The sooner I drop you off, the sooner I can head back again, and it's dice-night at the barracks."

"Fine by me," said Saffron, and clung on again – although less tightly than before – as Maza surged forwards, long legs eating up the distance. Without the fear of the kshtathit distracting her, she was able to see more of the Nakhereh than she had on the way in, and found it not so featureless as she'd remembered. Natural clumps of joh sprouted here and there, some staggeringly tall. A flock of sehket wheeled through the sky in pursuit of some larger winged thing, scolding it with angry shouts like lorikeets after an eagle. It was alien and dangerous and beautiful, and Saffron found she was unable to imagine now what her adult life would be like – what *she* would be like – if she'd never followed Gwen through Trishka's portal.

I chose this, she thought, smiling into the privacy afforded by Nim's broad back. *I chose this, and I'd choose it again. I'm sorry for a lot of things, but not for wanting this.*

She shut her eyes, focusing on the triple-thump rhythm of Maza's gait, the steady in and out of Nim's breathing. Was she taking too big a risk? Inwardly, she snorted. *A risk compared to what? Just being here is a risk in itself. At least this way, you'll know you tried to do something meaningful.*

And if I die? a different part of her asked. *Will trying still have been worth it then?*

You already know the answer to that, the first voice said. *You've just been raised to think that it ought to be* no.

Saffron went quiet at that – so quiet, in fact, that she actually fell asleep. Not deeply enough to touch the dreamscape, but enough that, when Maza finally halted, she was startled awake by Nim saying, "Safi? Hey, we're here. Are you here?" And then, incredulous, "Were you *napping*?"

"I've had a very long day," said Saffron, with as much dignity as she could muster. "And it's about to get longer." She yawned, stretching, and looked around the junkyard. Maza stood at the edge of the junkheaps, staring out at the static drifts and mind-hurting landscape beyond. At Nim's signal, the roshaqui folded down on her knees for Saffron to dismount.

"You're quite delightfully peculiar, has anyone ever told you that?" said Nim, as Saffron's feet hit the red and silver earth. "Do try not to get yourself killed. I'd hate for a perfectly good source of chaos to go to waste."

"I'll do my best," said Saffron. She peered up at Nim,

grinning with a sudden rush of adrenaline. *I'm really doing this.* "I'm grateful for all your help, paladin."

Nim waved an airy hand. "It's what we're for, apparently. But do feel free to look me up whenever you're next in Noqevai, if only to let me know you're still alive. We can get a drink and talk about what a reckless idiot you are."

"It's a date," said Saffron – and realised, in a belated burst of comprehension, that this was exactly what Nim, who was smirking at her, intended. Saffron flushed at the prospect, wondering how she'd explain her obliviousness to Yena; then realised, with an equally affecting jolt, that Yena would likely *approve*. *Oh*, she thought, and found herself grinning even wider, new inner worlds unlocking in a happy microcosm of their larger and no less magical counterparts. "I do plan on living, you know."

"I know," said Nim. "It's something I like about you."

Smiling, Saffron turned and strode out to the static veils. *Vikasa*, she thought, reaching for the dragon-voice that had guided her in the markets. *Scale-sister, if you're there, I need to get to Vikasa. Can you help me?*

A burning tug behind her navel; an inner flash of fire-blue eyes, owl-round and knowing.

<yes>

Inhaling deeply, Saffron walked forward. The static drifts rippled around her, buzzing against her skin like swarms of static shock. Beneath her bare feet, the ground alternately froze and burned; a discordant humming sounded in her ears. Distantly, she was aware of Nim's scrutiny, or possibly of her speech – the world was blurring, buzzing turned to stinging as she pressed into that Escher-space, the metmirai place where the world was thin. *Vikasa*, she thought, the name both prayer and anchor. *Vikasa. Vikasa. Vikasa.*

<fours are sacred> the dragon-voice murmured. *<come, scale-sister>*

Around her, the air lit up like fireworks. Between one

second and the next, Saffron felt her body jerk as if she'd been electrocuted; everything tumbled forwards and sideways, back and around and under.

<hang on!>

But it was hard to hang on, least of all because she had no idea of what to cling to. It *hurt*, her senses burning in confusion, tasting sight and scenting pain and screaming in colours, round and round and round and round, like being stuck in the mouth of some kaleidoscopic Gravitron–

Saffron hit the ground and stayed there, lying in a boneless, shivering heap. She felt as though she'd nearly drowned, or possibly as if she *had* drowned, and was feeling the afterburn of resuscitation. She felt like she was going to be sick, but stubbornly refused her own nausea, pressing her head to the unmoving stone to cancel out its spinning. It was a near thing, but though her mouth watered fiercely, she swallowed and swallowed, breathing deeply through her nose until the dizziness stopped; until she could push herself to her knees and blink her surroundings into focus.

Wind whipped past her, hot and dry. The stone beneath her hands was dark red and gritty, veined with slashes of pink quartz, but she wasn't underground: she stood on top of a natural mesa, high and bare and exposed. Though wary of the precipice, she was close enough to the edge to confirm that she was further off the ground than she'd ever been in her life, and as the last starbursts cleared from her vision, Saffron found herself staring.

The view was like nothing she'd ever seen or ever would see on Earth.

It was one thing to know in the abstract that Vikasa was a ruined, metmirai world, and to imagine what that might mean; it was quite another to see the mindbending unreality of it. Heart pounding, she came to her feet, taking a few shaky steps forwards.

•••

The sky was pale purple and dawn-streaked, except where it was ink-black and starshot, the livid, shifting interplay a tiger-striped jostle for dominance. The sun was reduced to boiling gold facets, invisible in the night-swathes, but refracted like mirror fragments across all the lilac air. A pale shattered moon, mammoth and triple-ringed, slunk through the darker patches like a sullen eye, visible in all of them, yet never all at once, the inverse of an optical illusion Saffron recalled with black dots on a white grid. Far below, the land stretched out from the mesa's base in a patchwork of ruins, grandiose structures still identifiable as such despite their centuries of decay. In some places, the ground was gone altogether, terrifying sinkholes yawning into emptiness between vast stretches of rucked earth and jagged geological protrusions, great chunks of stone and crystal, soil and metal breaching the surface like terrible whales. And there, at the edge of it all, a sawtoothed horizon, the raggedy edge of a broken world where curtains of debris fell upwards, spiralling into the sunmoon sky: a massive, inverted waterfall of perpetual terra infirma.

And through it all in the middle distance, untroubled by their shifting surrounds, a flight of dragons soared in an arrowhead formation, their solidity only serving to heighten the intemperate strangeness of everything else. Their bodies gleamed beneath the sun and shone beneath the stars, their shadows flickering between each powerful wingbeat, here and gone, here and gone.

Saffron had no words for the beauty of it in any language; none could do it justice. She made an inarticulate noise, the thin sound stolen away by the wind, and shut her eyes against the threat of tears.

<scale-sister?>

The voice was louder here than in Noqevai, a sonorous burr in her head, heart, thoughts. Unlike before, it was also accompanied by a very tangible *whuff* of hot air against her nape and the rattle of claws on stone.

Not quite laughing, Saffron opened her eyes and turned.

The dragon was every bit as beautiful as she remembered, as tall as the tallest Shire horse and covered in liquid gold scales. Bright wings shifted, settling against its – no, *her* – scarred flanks. One of her ear-fans was badly damaged, torn down to nothing but a stump. In its place were more scars, long clawmarks raking back from around one eye and along her skull, their distribution a perfect echo of Saffron's own. She swallowed, heart full to bursting at the sight. Slowly, reverently, she raised a hand and laid her palm to the dragon's scaled cheek, marvelling all over again at the way her scales, so soft when stroked in one direction, instantly turned razor-edged in the other.

"Thank you," she whispered. "Thank you for bringing me here."

The dragon dipped her massive head. It spoke into her mind with a voice that wasn't a voice, in words that weren't quite language but the telepathic translation of intention, meaning, thoughts, each burst of communication redolent as much with images and feelings as what Saffron perceived as speech. <*the hatchling?*>

Saffron flinched, remembering the tiny dragon chained on Noqevai. "I'm so sorry. I tried to buy her freedom, but the one who stole her wouldn't let me. I'll try again when I go back, but…" Instinctively, she reached again for that strange scale-magic, transmitting the impression of frustration, money, an exchange bound by rules and customs whose parameters could be neither met nor cheated. The dragon flicked her remaining headfan.

<*I understand*>

"I'm so sorry."

<*I understand that, too*>

Saffron swallowed, struggling to regain her focus – no mean feat, under the circumstances. *You came here for a reason, remember? See the sights some other time.*

"Can we get down from here?" she asked, a terrible swoop in her stomach at the thought of having to fly.

<that depends on where you wish to go>

"I don't know." She ran a hand over her head, frustrated. "I was with a man, Leoden, who came to Vikasa by a different door. He wants to find out the truth of this world, and I'd like to trust that it's for a good reason, or at least a harmless one, but he's being manipulated by someone else, and I think something bad is going to happen. That's why I came here; I need to find him, talk to him." For emphasis, she projected the image of Leoden as she'd seen him last, dressed in leathers and fleeing through the bazaar.

The dragon hummed in her throat, a sound that was almost like purring. *<I have not seen him within the mesa, nor have any of my sisters, but that doesn't mean he can't be found>*

Saffron's heart sank. As ruined as Vikasa was, Leoden might have appeared in any number of places. What if he'd landed somewhere on the other side of the ruined world, and she was already too late to stop whatever Kadeja had planned for him?

Projecting amusement, the dragon bumped Saffron gently with the tip of her scaled nose. *<if he seeks knowledge, he will come here, to the place where all doors open>* The thought was accompanied by a jumble of confusing impressions, all seemingly derived from some draconic sixth sense that Saffron didn't possess, but which helped the dragons navigate the metmirai of their home. As best she could tell, it meant that the mesa had a sort of fragile gravity, an attraction that made it harder for external portals to open further out. *<I will help you look for him, and if he is not yet here, we will search until he is>*

"Yes, please." Saffron gulped. "But, uh – you didn't answer before, about the flying?"

The dragon chuffed and swung her head, walking across

the top of the mesa. Saffron paced alongside, and was relieved to find an open stairwell carved in the rock, a winding path that led down out of the elements and into the caverns below.

<walk carefully, little one. this high up, the stone is worn thin in places>

"I'll do my best," said Saffron, and followed the dragon down into the dark.

Gwen groaned, swimming into consciousness with a pounding head and a cramping back. She struggled to make sense of time, blinking dimly as a clump of pale lilac grass resolved itself in her vision. Testing her limbs, she found to her considerable relief that all of them were in working order. The key was still clutched in her outflung hand, and as she maneuvered herself to her knees, she realised she'd been lying on a bed of milky, crystalline stone, its points and faceted edges digging into her flesh. For a moment she was disoriented, uncertain how she'd come to be where she was.

Then she remembered Naruet, Louis and Yavinae, and the key's insistent whisper. Remembered stepping through air and light at the heart of a ruined city.

"Fuck," she muttered, wincing as she pushed herself to her feet. She staggered slightly, reaching out to brace herself on a nearby wall: not only was she dizzy, but the lumpy, slippery floor didn't exactly make for the surest footing. There was no sign of the static door through which she'd entered, but then, she hadn't expected there to be. Instead there was only that uneven crystal floor, milky and strange and studded with clumps of purple grass. The walls were white, too, but smoother, long flat planes of crystal arcing up to a ceiling where toothy crystal stalactites hung down like gleaming fangs. The room – or cave, she supposed; if this was a manmade place, she could see no sign of it – was several stories tall, but only about as wide as the living room in her parents' house.

A single gap in the stone, just wide enough for a single person to shoulder through, stood opposite her: not a natural door, and likely a tight fit, assuming it even led anywhere, but absent her magical point of entry, it was the only option she had.

Or would be, once she started moving. First, she needed to clear her head.

Shoving aside her anger at having left her son behind in so distracted and careless a fashion – thorns and godshit, but Louis was going to have words for her! – she tried to focus instead on what she'd felt directly before crossing over. Opening her palm, she stared at the now-quiescent key. Its colouration had changed, appearing more opaline than previously, the spiralled end looking now more unicorn than narwhal.

"Vakti," Gwen murmured, recalling the feel of the name on her lips. She knew it had been important when she said it, but trying to fathom why was like grasping at the last threads of a dawn-broken dream. "Vakti's heir? What the Many does *that* mean?"

Light sparked from the key, a tiny ripple of stars. Gwen cried out in shock and dropped it, her spoken echoes mixing with the clatter of its fall.

The stone lit up around it, glyphs and sigils showing in the facets like alien algebra. For a moment, the whole cave glowed with light, bright enough that Gwen raised a hand to shield her eyes. When she opened them again, it had subsided: all except for a line of light that ran from the key's tip and out through that single crack in the wall, a ribbon of blue-white.

Gwen stared at this newfound magical effect as if it had personally offended her. Slowly, she stooped and brushed the key with her fingertips, prepared to snatch back her hand at the first sign of any negative effects.

Nothing happened.

Scowling, Gwen snatched up the key, half expecting the light to disappear again. It didn't: instead, a key-shaped imprint in blue-white remained behind on the flat crystal facet, blinking gently on and off like a cursor.

Gwen gripped the key, stepped away from the safety of the wall, and tapped a sturdy boot-tip against the glowing line. When nothing further happened, she heaved an exasperated sigh and stepped forward normally, gripping the key with slightly excessive force.

"Follow the glowing brick road it is," she said, and snorted out loud at the thought of singing munchkins.

Yena found out the hard way not to touch the scions. As the white creature led them through the humid, fern-strewn cavern and into a broad stone tunnel, the footing changed, small stones and a slight, uneven upslope replacing the comparatively smooth crystal. Yena, distracted by her simmering fear of both Kadeja and the scions themselves, misstepped, pinwheeled and fell backwards, crashing into a solid, scaled body. Insinctively, she grabbed at its neck for purchase, then yelped in pain as the sharp-edged scales cut into her exposed skin. Even that brief contact left her forearms thinly ribboned with blood. *No wonder Safi and Zech came back so scarred,* she thought, and shuddered at what other trials they'd had to endure to earn the rest of their injuries.

For its part, the bronze scion was demonstrably unfazed by her clumsiness. When she finally regained her footing, it nudged her gently in the back, a sort of *keep-going* gesture, but otherwise didn't falter. In contrast, Kadeja narrowed her eyes, beckoning Yena onwards with a threatening flick of the knife.

"Keep up," she said.

Yena swallowed hard, endeavouring to comply. Wincing a little at the sting, she wiped her bloody forearms on her clothes: there wasn't much blood, but it smeared her skin in a tacky layer, red on brown. She thought again of Jesit, Yasha, Kiri, Mesthani, all the awful blood they'd shed, and found herself breathing harder, faster at the sight of it still drying on Kadeja's blade. Panic clawed at her, fear and guilt and rage and terror, everything commingled like a paralyzing toxin shot straight to her heart. She wanted to stop, felt her legs go faint at the very thought of sitting down, and for a few steps her vision swam with the effort of keeping upright. Now of all times and here of all places she couldn't afford the luxury of reacting like a person, because Kadeja didn't see her as one. In her eyes, Yena was a tool at best and an ornament at worst, and if she broke down – if she lashed out or screamed or did anything other than obey – it wouldn't be met with kindness.

She wants an audience. The thought came from somewhere deep inside, and Yena clung to it. *She wants me to witness whatever it is she's doing here.*

"What are the anchors?" Yena asked, her voice betrayingly thin. She coughed, balled her hands into fists and tucked them in the small of her back, forcing herself to step closer to Kadeja. "What is it we're doing here?"

Kadeja's answering smile was terrifying. "I mean to restore the heart of Veksh."

Naruet was just starting to relax when the commotion started. He came instantly to his feet, Sashi a half second behind him, in time to see Luy come bolting out of Yavinae's ruins.

Gwen was nowhere to be seen.

"What happened?" Sashi cried, rushing over to him. Naruet followed her, anxious and gawky, as did the honoured sword, Rikan. "Where's auntie?"

"Gone," said Luy. He was covered in sweat, his face ashen. "We were talking, and then the key – I don't know. It lit up, did something to her. She used it to open a portal, and I think… I think she's gone to Vikasa, though I have no proof, but she said something before she left – she called me Vakti's heir–" He broke off, clearly agitated. "Gods of the Many, I don't know what to *do*."

Silently, Rikan moved beside him, putting an arm around Luy's waist. Luy made a pained noise and leaned against him, eyes shut as he tried to master himself.

Sashi looked as if she'd been slapped. "We could... if you wanted, we could look for–"

"No." Luy's eyes snapped open again. His voice shook, but his gaze was steady, so much so that Naruet couldn't bear to look at him; had to stare at the ground and breathe slow and evenly, in-in-hold, out-out-hold, his fingers tapping a calmdown rhythm until his own pulse settled. "She gave us an order. We need to get to Yevekshasa, just like she told us to."

"Do you feel stronger now?" Sashi said.

It took Naruet several seconds to realise that she was speaking to him. He didn't look up, but considered the question, probing his ragged magic.

"I do," he said, finally. "We just need to get a bit further away from the ruins." He bit his lip, frowning, then said in an awkward burst, "And I can get us closer to the city. I know we didn't want to just materialise in the middle of Yevekshasa, but I can find a clear spot on the mesa trail that's near the gates and land us there, so we don't have as far to go. Then I can scry the worlds for Gwen until you need me again."

"You're sure?" asked Luy. "You'll really do that?"

Naruet didn't know if he was questioning his ability to open a portal so close to Yevekshasa's gates or the sincerity of his desire to find Gwen, but either way, the answer was the same. "Yes. I really will."

"Then let's get going," Sashi said, and started to lead the group away from the ruins.

Squeezing through the crack in the wall, Gwen found herself at the apex of a branching series of tunnels, all around the same height and width, distinct only by virtue of their placement and, in the case of the rightmost path, the presence of a glowing line leading steadily down its gullet. The only other illumination came from intermittent clusters of luminescent fungi sprouting from the walls, pale green mushrooms shaped like gnome-hats speckled with violet dots.

Gwen followed the light, and gripped the key, and tried very hard to remember why this felt like a good idea.

The floor of the tunnel was pale pink quartz streaked here and there with milky white. The walls, however, were made of something else entirely, darker stone that was cracking in places and pitted in others, the fungi clumps growing wherever the smoothness gave way to hard-packed dirt. Though the tunnel twisted and turned, the blue light led her on an unerring upwards path, a single clean line always visible even when the pathway branched and branched again. Dutifully, Gwen tried to keep track of the various turnings, but even if she was forced to turn back, she had no means of reopening the static door.

Suddenly, the tunnel jagged sharply, opening into a hemispherical room whose curving walls, level floor and domed roof were all made of a single piece of flawless, unbroken quartz. It couldn't possibly have been natural, and yet Gwen couldn't think how it might have been manufactured, either. Magic was the obvious answer, of course, but even after all these years, she savoured the prospect of a little mystery. Who had made the room, and to what purpose? She had no idea what kind of structure she was in, whether she was above or below ground, but compared to the unpolished roughness of the first crystal room – *a geode*, she realised belatedly; the whole thing had been a damn *geode* – the presence of this space suggested something rather more complex than a cave network.

Beneath her feet, the glowing line led into the room and up the curve of the wall, terminating in what was, as far as Gwen could see, the only break in all that seamless crystal: a single keyhole, pulsing blue on pink.

"A hole in the wall at the end of the world," she murmured, and stepped into the room. Her footsteps echoed against the quartz as they hadn't in the tunnels, making her wonder what the difference was. She glanced at the key, half expecting it to change or glow or start misbehaving again, and squinted in suspicion when it remained inactive. Her lips quirked as she weighed it up, glancing at the keyhole and back again.

"What, no backchat?"

Nothing.

Curling her fingers over the key, Gwen wondered what had triggered its magic the previous times. She was tempted to think it was geographical, but in each instance she'd been nowhere near the location the key seemed to want her to find, except in the most general sense. But she *had* been talking – first to Louis, and then to herself. She frowned, trying to recall her exact words, and felt her mouth fall open as they came to her.

Shavaktiin, she'd said in Yavinae, and then on arrival, recalling that strange, key-imparted knowledge, *Vakti*.

"Oh," Gwen whispered, stunned.

She raised her hand and snugged the key into the keyhole. The quartz chimed, the guiding line of light receding from the floor and hall, but otherwise nothing happened.

Winging a brief prayer of apology to Louis, Gwen cleared her throat and said, in tentative Kenan, "I speak for the Shavaktiin, Vakti's heirs."

The quartz wall lit up like Christmas.

Gwen stepped backwards, eyes wide as the sudden flash of light and colour coalesced, projecting itself from the key into – she blinked, choking on inappropriate laughter – a sort of magical hologram. Occupying the space where Gwen had stood only moments earlier was the translucent form of a life-size, middle-aged woman, blinking as she stared ahead. She was olive-skinned and dark-eyed, dressed in wide loose trousers blousing where they tucked into tall black boots, a loose white shirt beneath a stiff, ornately embroidered vest and a broad black belt, the leather tooled with curlicue designs. Her hair was light brown, bound in four braids that coiled up into a knot.

Marriage-braids, Gwen thought. Or at least, they looked that way to her: the key came from Kena, after all, though the woman herself might have been from anywhere.

"Who are you?" Gwen wondered aloud – in Kenan, not English. "*What* are you? Can you understand me?"

The hologram turned towards her voice, which was unsettling on several counts, and began to speak, in antiquated but intelligible Kenan. Passion carried in her voice, the ghost of a woman-who-was, and Gwen felt a shiver of premonition run down her spine to hear it.

"If you have found me, perhaps you know me," the woman began. Laughter lines crinkled at mouth and eye, but swiftly gave way to grief. "More likely, however, you do not, and so an introduction is in order. I am Vakti ore Yavin ki Sha, Kenan ambassador to the daughter-realms of the firmament, speaking now in the Year of White Stars, 1279, on the eighteenth day of the seventh month. Yavinae has fallen, and my beloved has, of necessity, fled both Kena and our world, though not before entrusting me with this, my final duty as Vexa'Sehet. I do not make this record in an attempt to salvage either of our reputations; that damage has been done beyond repair, and in any case, the sabotage at least protects our people from knowing how very close we came to utter destruction. Fear makes for unsteady hands, and if there's one thing Kena needs in the wake of this crisis, it's steady guidance. I can only pray our sacrifice is sufficient to ensure it.

"I speak now as a provision against any future resurgence of the schemes of Nasheth arat Nasi, a Vekshi nationalist who, though unbeknownst to most, very nearly succeeded in killing both his nation and ours."

Vakti paused to gather the breath she no longer had, and in that moment Gwen felt as if some fundamental internal axis had suddenly spun backwards. With no other means of recording the speech, she hung on every word, striving to commit it to memory: if Halunet could use the ahunemet to recall the final testimony of Sene a Sati, what was to stop him performing a similar service for Vakti ore Yavin?

"Know this," said Vakti, ghost-shoulders firming as she spoke. "The Vekshi are our neighbours, but they were not always thus. They first appeared hundreds of years ago, in the wake of a series of terrestrial calamities throughout Kena – earthquakes and other such cataclysms which, our histories tell us, broke open the chasm we call Yemaya's Cut and caused the formation of the great lake Nihun's Heart, diverting the flow of the Dekan River. The northern plains were home to nomads before then, with whom we had some complicated commerce and many border skirmishes, until, quite suddenly, they vanished. The exact manner of their vanishing is unknown to me, though some records suggest the survivors fled to Kamne, integrating with one of the local clans; what matters is that the Vekshi came to our world from another one – from the world in which, if you are listening to this, you must now stand; a place we now know only as Vikasa.

"I do not know why the Vekshi, in the centuries since their flight, either forgot or consciously discarded any knowledge of their origins; nor is it clear that their desperate ancestors understood the cataclysms their arrival would wreak on Kena. In finding Vikasa, I have learned what it is they ran from, and as you stand now where I once stood, you may yet learn it too, and from a source more knowledgeable than I could ever be. What matters to this story is the fact that the Vekshi, a culture now ruled by warrior-matriarchs, fled a world where men held power and abused it grossly. Now their men hold different roles, unaware – until the researches of Nasheth arat Nasi proved it so – that things had ever been otherwise.

"In Vekshi history, there are other records of male rebellions against the established order, but none has ever been successful. Nasheth wanted to change all this. He came to Kena as a scholar, as one gifted with the jahudemet, but whose gender barred him from receipt of the proper training in his native land. We welcomed him; Ke's Kin trained him; I studied with him; Vexa Yavin supported him; and in return, Nasheth used his knowledge to further our research into new forms of magic."

Vakti paused again, hands forming into fists, and when she next spoke her voice was raw with a rage Gwen knew too well.

"We never suspected the depths of Nasheth's disdain for us; of his hatred, not just for the women of Veksh, but for *all* women, even those who called him friend. Kena gave him a home, but once he learned of Vikasa, he considered that his heritage had been denied him; that the only right course of action was to wipe clean the slates of Kena and Veksh by smothering them with the ruins of Vikasa. For Nasheth learned that the heart of Yevekshasa is an anchored portal – one both like and unlike the one he helped us build, at such an exhaustive cost – perpetually bound to Vikasa, a shard of the old world buried in the bleeding heart of the new. The ties that bind Vikasa to Veksh are old and strong, but Nasheth endeavoured to sever them. And having used Kena and her libraries, he fled with his plans, and left us no choice but to chase him.

"And chase we did, though the cost was terrible. In his wake, he stirred up violence against Vexa Yavin, poisoning the innovations of her reign with lies and half-truths. I will not pretend that Nasheth was the only opposition she encountered in her reforms – indeed, if he had been, he would not have been so effective. We stopped him, yes, and so saved Kena from annihilation, but at the cost of everything else we sought to change, everything we worked so hard to achieve."

The recording bowed her head, an awful catch in her voice. "As much as Nasheth hated women, he hated the Vekshi more. His final taunt to me promised that his plan to bring Vikasa's ruins to Kena would live on; that he had laid clues, left hints and instructions sufficient that some future Vekshi malcontent would take up his cause, even if he – or she, he said, and *laughed* as he spoke – had no notion as to his motive, or even his existence. And though I have worked hard to ensure no trace of that poisonous legacy remains, still I leave this key, this record, to ensure that the worst never comes to pass.

"So, if you are hearing me now, take heed. The magic that binds Veksh to Vikasa can be undone in one of two ways: the first will sever their connection, destroying forever that piece of Vikasa lingering within Veksh, while the second will cause this ruined world to collide with ours, preserving it from further decay, but at horrific cost. The latter plan is what Nasheth intended to do, and what I stopped him from doing; the former, if you are threatened by his heirs, is the only true way to ensure they can never succeed."

Vakti gestured at the room; behind her, on the flat curve of quartz that formed the wall, the image of two artefacts appeared. Both were large, heavy spheres of crystalline stone attached to complex metal settings, incised with glyphs, encircled by various hovering components and aglow with magic: almost, they looked like orreries. One was primarily lilac and white; the other was red and gold.

"Together, these devices keep Veksh and Vikasa in balance," Vakti said. "Destroy them both at once, or smash only Vikasa's sphere, and the two worlds part forever. But if only the Vekshi anchor is broken, what little remains of Vikasa's world will collide with ours. Just forging that connection broke our land, rerouted rivers, killed thousands of innocent people; to bring the whole of Vikasa through would be unconscionable."

Vakti lifted her head, a fey glint in her eyes. "The anchors reside in this mesa; they are not hard to find. Listener, whoever you are, you must now wonder – why make this record, when I might just as easily destroy them both myself? Would it not be easier, safer, better for Kena?" Her jaw clenched. "Perhaps. Perhaps it would be. And I have wrestled with my conscience, with the ghost of gods in whom I no longer fully believe; have argued with the woman I love at a time when such debate was the last thing either of us needed. Yes, I could break the anchors. But I do not know what the consequences would be for Veksh, and for all who dwell in the city of Yevekshasa.

"The first Vekshi were refugees, women in flight from a dying, brutal world. I will not forgive them the deaths they caused in crossing over, but I understand their actions, and though there are many other crimes I might yet lay at their daughters' feet, I cannot and will not claim that any Vekshi now living is so culpable for the sins of their ancestors as to merit death. The heart of Yevekshasa's mesa is bound to Vikasa: removing that connection would have consequences. Any physical damage caused – and I assume there would be some, however minor compared to the alternative – would be as nothing to the cultural, the spiritual damage of such a separation. Though the Vekshi themselves have forgotten it, Vikasa is the centre and soul of the rites by which they choose their queens and priestesses – what bloodshed would result, should an outsider choose its destruction? What sectarian violence, what instability would follow, were I to act as arbiter of justice? To risk the murder of innocents in terror of strangers – to condemn the heart of a culture for the sake of a single zealot – is to become the very thing you fear. And it would be fear that drove me, were I to take that final step;

and I am *sick* of fear.

"So, key-bearer, you who stand where once I stood and choose where once I chose: I beg of you, choose wisely."

Vakti smiled, and Gwen, who felt as though her heart was being squeezed in a vice, smiled back at her, not caring that the other woman was centuries dead and gone beyond recall. Had Vakti known what her legacy would become? What would she think of the Shavaktiin now? Had the key responded to her name alone, or to the implications of her heritage?

The hologram winked out, leaving Gwen alone in a pink quartz room. Heart pounding, she sucked in an overdue, laden breath and moved to reclaim the key, still glowing faintly, from its slot in the wall. It was warm to the touch, but chilled even as she held it, and for several long seconds all she did was stare at it, overwhelmed by its consequences.

"I was not expecting that."

The voice came from the doorway, soft and masculine.

Gwen jerked her head up, eyes going wide as she found herself staring, once again, at Leoden.

18

Scion's Heart

Yena shoved her terror aside as they kept on through the tunnels, hands clenched, eyes down. As the white scion led them on through twists and turnings, she let herself lose time. Her body had to keep going, yes, but her mind didn't have to be present, and so she did her level best to distance the one from the other, tethered to the moment only by the beat of her heart, the steady rhythm of breathing.

And then – quite suddenly, from this distant vantage – Yena realised they'd left the tunnels and entered a different place altogether: a soaring cavern toothy with crystalline stalactites and stalagmites. Beyond the many pools of shadow it was lit by the glow of luminescent fungi clumps and, far off, two glowing orbs that looked at first glance like mismatched eyes: one red and gold, one white and lilac, side by side on a distant rise.

"The anchors," Kadeja breathed, and started towards them, giving Yena no choice but to follow. This time, both scions walked beside and slightly behind them, veering only when the great jags of living stone prevented them from taking a straight line. Mind and body resynchronising, Yena belatedly noticed there was a straight path from the entryway to the anchors, a flat avenue of pinkish stone that lolled out like a tongue. In fact, the whole cavern looked increasingly

like some monstrous, inverted mouth, which did nothing
to alleviate the sudden fear of being swallowed whole, both
metaphorically and – given the presence of the scions –
literally.

As they came closer, Yena realised the anchors were ringed
by floating objects, miscellaneous bits of ephemera circling
them like vultures around carrion, presumably held in orbit
by whatever magic fuelled them. And they were magical, of
that she had no doubt – why else would Kadeja be here?

As though sensing the question, Kadeja gestured to the
anchors, her blue eyes eerily brightened by their glow. "I told
you that the world-egg is an anchored portal, yes?"

"You did," said Yena cautiously.

"Well, *these* are the repositories of power that sustain its
presence in Yevekshasa. That one–" she gestured to the white
and lilac orb, "–stands for Vikasa. The other–" she flicked the
knife disdainfully at the red and gold, "–represents Veksh. Or
more accurately Kena, as our nation is the historical interloper."
She was still moving as she spoke, bringing them all – herself,
Yena and both scions – inexorably closer to the anchors, until
they were almost within touching distance. Up close, they
were massive things, each one bigger in circumference than
Yena's arms could reach, swirling energy roiling in their cores
like captured storm clouds. More startling, however, was the
realisation that the orbiting objects weren't really solid at
all, but ever-changing projections from within the anchors
themselves. Yena had no idea as to their significance, but felt
a prickle of deep unease at what they might signify.

"Together, they keep Vikasa and Veksh in balance. Break
both or Vikasa's anchor alone, and the two worlds snap apart.
But break just Veksh, and the two worlds come together."
Kadeja halted, reverence in her expression. "For Ashasa's sake,
the scions have guarded them for centuries, keeping them safe
for such pilgrims as She deemed worthy." She turned to face
the scions, bowing again towards them. "And for that, you

have Her thanks, and mine. But Ashasa has spoken to me, and your guardianship has reached its end." She smiled then, broad and unfeigned and utterly terrifying. "For in Her name and at Her will, I've come to realign your world with mine – to bring the land of Her making to the refuge She provided us." She turned to Yena, who was struggling to encompass the enormity of this declaration. "Don't you see? Out there, beyond these caverns, lies the city of our foremothers. All our lost history – everything the robewives have denied us, every secret the queens of old saw fit to hide – we can reclaim it!"

"What?" said Yena – stupidly, and yet not stupid at all. It was surely impossible that Kadeja meant what she said she did, but what other explanation was there for any of this? "You want *what*?"

The bronze scion hissed in warning; the white gave an agitated growl, wings mantling as it approached. Yena gulped, but though Kadeja spared a glance for the upset creatures, her only response was angry laughter, startling both scions.

"Veksh is a lie, Yena. Everything it is, everything it stands for. Out there, beyond these caverns – *that's* our true heritage, and we can't build a future without it! Why do you think I sought my omens, prayed for unity, if not to ensure that this is what Ashasa wants? This world lies in ruins, yes, but if I bring it to Kena – to Kena and Veksh, to bridge our realms, the old and the new conjoined by earth of Ashasa's own making – it will live again, and so will we! Everything decayed and broken will be restored: the land we've claimed will truly be Ashasa's land, the Mother Sun brought to Her new sky, and the rule of those who've kept us chained in ignorance will be broken!"

"You–" said Yena, suddenly lightheaded, "–you want to crash this world into ours? To *relocate* it? Permanently?"

"Yes!"

"But that will kill thousands! Hundreds of thousands!"

Kadeja smiled softly. "Yes, it will. But Ashasa will spare

those who matter."

Behind them, the scions growled in warning, and Yena realised abruptly that the creatures not only understood what Kadeja was saying, but disagreed with her. Kadeja had clearly reached the same conclusion, albeit belatedly: a flash of real fear lit her eyes as the massive white scion closed on her – and, by dint of proximity, on Yena, who took a quick step back, hands raised. Ignoring her, the white scion snorted and circled Kadeja, positioning itself firmly between her and the anchors, wings half-raised, neck arched. As messages went, it was unambiguous, and for a moment Kadeja was shocked into stillness. Slowly, she lowered her knife-hand, lips quirking as she considered the bristling scion.

"A test," she murmured, almost sounding pleased about it. "Ashasa's will be done."

Kadeja stepped forward, pressing her bare palm to the scion's jaw.

The white scion froze, a sudden barbed stillness that set Yena's skin to crawling. Beside her, the bronze scion flicked its ear-fans, letting out a terrible, confused whine as its purple eyes fixed imploringly on the white. But the white remained utterly unresponsive, a glassiness to its gaze that hadn't been there before.

Kadeja lifted her hand away, smiling, and only then did Yena understand what she'd done.

"Heart-into-mind," Yena whispered, appalled. She stared at Kadeja, pulse beating loud in her throat. "Mother Sun, you used the heart-into-mind on a blessed *scion*–"

The bronze scion let out a furious scream and lunged at Kadeja, who didn't move because she didn't have to. Controlled by her stolen magic, the white scion was moving for her, shrieking like a kettle as it launched itself at the bronze.

The thunder of their impact rocked the cavern, swaying Yena on her feet. She grabbed at a nearby stalactite for balance, watching in horror as the two creatures began to fight in earnest, the bigger white going viciously after the smaller bronze. She was so busy staring, she didn't notice Kadeja's approach until she felt the prick of the bloodied blade at her throat, accompanied by the press of a three-fingered hand on her shoulder.

"You are my heir," Kadeja murmured, "but that doesn't mean I trust you not to intervene. Stay still and silent; let Ashasa's will be done, or I will be forced to use her gifts on you."

Yena felt tears prick her eyes. "This is monstrous. *You* are monstrous."

Kadeja laughed softly. "I am what Veksh has made me, and will become what Ashasa requires. Now watch, Yena – after all, you're here to bear witness."

And to that horror, Yena had no answer.

Gwen stared at Leoden, reflexive shock and outrage warring with the now-rational admission of Kadeja's manipulation. She took in his un-Kenan clothes, his empty hands, the look of confusion in his eyes and said, as calmly as she could, "I wasn't expecting you, either."

Leoden flinched, which was sufficiently out of character that Gwen took a step forward. He didn't retreat from her, but it was a near thing: his stance wavered, throat working as he swallowed, and it was this more than anything else that made Gwen hesitate. In all her prior dealings with Leoden, she'd never once seen him be anything other than perfectly composed: on those rare occasions when his mask – or what she'd thought of his mask – had slipped, it was always anger she'd seen underneath, not fear or hesitation. That he displayed both now, in a moment when he might just as easily have resorted to artifice – he'd clearly been aware of her before she'd noticed him – undid something near to the heart of how she saw him.

"All this time," she said, and stopped, the words coming

out in an awful scratch. "All this time, was it ever you?"

"I don't know." At his side, his hand clenched, open and shut. His expression was utterly raw. "So many times, I remember the things I've said and done, and the voice I hear is always mine, but the words, the *venom* of them... the girl, Safi, she told me it was Kadeja, and I didn't want to believe her, but that recording, that *woman*–" he nodded sharply at Gwen's hand, the one that held the key, "–if what she said was true, then everything I thought I was doing, the work I meant to accomplish... oh, gods." His face took on a greenish cast, his dark eyes pleading. "I would've killed Kena. I would've broken the wrong anchor."

Gwen felt her blood chill. "What?"

"The anchors, the ones that keep Vikasa and Veksh bound together – I was looking for them here, and I thought... She told me that destroying the right one would bring a lost piece of Kena back to us, not that it would do *that*!"

"And the worldwalkers?" Gwen took another step towards him, needing to know. "Naruet, the anchored portal – all of it. What truly happened?"

Leoden looked half-wild. "Naruet was – is still, I think – my ally. He showed us how the portal worked, and I thought it was part of my research. When I found the key, I knew I had to keep it safe, though I barely understood why. I gave it to him, and after... I think I forgot it, after. For a time. But the worldwalkers..." He met her gaze, stricken to the point of nausea. "Gods forgive me, but I thought they were criminals. She told me they were, and I knew, a part of me *knew* when I looked on them that it wasn't right – it's why I showed you the portal when I fled the palace, why I surrendered myself to be caught, I couldn't just leave them there but I didn't, I couldn't form the words, I knew I had to tell you but I didn't know *why*–"

Gwen felt her throat close over. She shut her eyes, the old guilt at having vouched for Leoden realign itself into guilt at having failed to protect him.

She opened her eyes and, for the first time, knew him.

"I should've seen it," she said, voice shaking. "I should've seen that something was wrong."

"How?" he asked. "How could you have known, when I scarcely knew myself?"

"I blamed you. For so many evils, I blamed you."

Leoden laughed, the sound sharp-edged with hysteria. "Of course you did! It was my mouth that spoke, my hand that acted. What reason had any of us to suspect otherwise?"

"Even so–" Gwen started, but was cut off by a resonant animal scream, a roar from elsewhere in the tunnels amplified and echoed by the quartz. "Thorns and godshit, what was that?"

"I don't know." Leoden opened his mouth. Closed it again. Paled. "I don't know, but I feel... oh, gods." He ran an agitated hand through his hair, fingers snarling in black curls as he tugged it free. "I think she's here."

It took Gwen a moment to parse his meaning. "Her? You mean *Kadeja*?"

He nodded, his expression so shuttered that it took Gwen precious seconds to realise he was terrified. "The... the magic she used on me, the ahunemet – every time I've crossed a portal, I've felt it weaken, felt the threads of it burn away, but just now, with that scream, I felt – I can't describe it. Like a whip-hand raised. She's here. And if she's found the anchors–"

"Run," said Gwen, and Leoden obeyed, the pair of them bolting towards that terrible cry.

At Saffron's best guess they'd been walking for almost half an hour when the stair-spiral finally evened out into something approaching level ground. Evidently, Vikasa's mesa was as riven through with catacombs as Yevekshasa's was, which raised the disquieting possibility that the latter was somehow a mirror of the former. Saffron shook her head, bemused by the thought, and concentrated on keeping pace with her dragon-guide, whose strides were understandably longer than her own.

Before, the descent had been steep enough that she hadn't felt inclined to conversation; now, her curiosity finally got the better of her.

"Do you have a name?"

The dragon huffed, which Saffron took for amusement. *<not as you understand the concept>*

Saffron absorbed this. A childish part of her was tempted to name the dragon anyway, but it somehow felt disrespectful to suggest it. Instead, she asked, "Am I your only scale-sister, or have you had one before?"

<you don't know?> The question was shocked enough that Saffron flinched.

"I, ah… didn't come by the world-egg in the usual way. There's a lot I don't understand."

The dragon's wings half-raised and settled again. *<you are my only-scale-sister; such magic only works once, between one dragon and one daughter of your people>*

"Oh. And that's why I can understand you?"

<yes>

"Can I talk to any other dragons like this?"

<no>

Saffron hesitated, not sure she wanted to know the answer to her next question. "During the Trial, when I… when you… when we fought the red dragon: what would've happened if we'd lost?"

<your essence and knowledge would have passed to me, just as the red's scale-sister once passed to her> A series of thoughts and images accompanied this extraordinary statement, and Saffron, who'd thought the only risk was dying, came to an abrupt halt as she parsed their implications. The dragon stopped, too, her big head tilted curiously.

"You… you would've *eaten* me, and because I'd already swallowed your scale, you would've gotten my *memories*?"

<this disquiets you?>

"Yes!"

<it shouldn't>

"Why?"

<it was the bargain struck between your ancestors and mine – a sharing of knowledge and a show of strength in exchange for passage through our territory>

Saffron started walking again; the stillness made her itch. "Why did they need to pass through your territory?"

<because their magic broke the world. everywhere they made their doors, the air unravelled. but this place was ours, and our ancestors defended it from all human incursions, just as we held our other territories. where we nested, no doors opened, so when the world shattered, our home was the only place left that could sustain the world-egg without further damage. that is why the one you seek will come here eventually, even if only to leave>

"Will he be safe, though? The other dragons won't attack him for being here without permission?"

<we do not attack unless attacked. the bargain was for safe passage for all who wished it, not just those who sought to become scale-sisters>

Saffron considered this. "You don't serve Ashasa, then?"

<that name has meaning to your people, not mine>

Saffron didn't laugh, but it was a near thing. Her mouth twisted, questions bursting on her tongue like champagne bubbles.

"Wait, wait. So if I died and you ate me, you'd get my memories?"

<that is correct>

"But I swallowed your scale. Does that mean something happens to me if *you* die?"

<of course. it is the other half of the bargain> She chuffed again, clearly amused. *<should you outlive me, my memories pass to you – but understand, my species lives much longer than yours. the bargain was made in our favour, you see? your deaths*

enrich us, but ours cost us very little>

"When was the last time it happened, then, that a scale-sister outlived her dragon?"

<several of your centuries ago, as the-ones-who-have-lore mark time> An image of several ancient dragons accompanied the statement, the notion of them weighted with deep awe and reverence. *<she was like you; one of the very few who returned to us after she sat our Trial. her scale-sister was ancient and wise, full of deep wisdom; the-ones-who-have-lore still mourn her loss>*

"What was her name?" Saffron asked, as much because she thought Yena might be interested as from native curiosity. "The human scale-sister, I mean."

The dragon hummed in thought. *<Vakti>* she said. *<her name was Vakti>*

"And what–"

The dragon hissed sharply, cutting her off. Saffron froze, obliquely terrified at the prospect of having caused offence, then jumped as a harrowing reptilian scream sounded through the tunnels.

"What was that?" she yelped.

<something is very wrong> The dragon's inner voice was agitated, layered with stress and anger. *<a scale-sister is being attacked. we must go to her, now!>*

Not waiting for agreement or argument, she surged ahead through the tunnels, forcing Saffron to run almost flat out to keep pace.

"Leoden," Saffron panted. "It has to be Leoden, right? What else could it be?"

<many things> the dragon said, and kept running.

Saffron considered the recent twists and turns her life had taken, and decided that arguing with dragons would be a degree of foolishness too far. She swallowed and kept moving, every nerve alive with fright and worry as they pelted towards the noise.

•••

"Call it off!" Yena yelled, twisting against Kadeja's hold. The bronze scion was bloodied all over, one wing snapped clean through at the bone. It was hobbling now, its right foreleg clutched tight to its chest, a warbling whimper in its throat as the white continued to advance. "You're killing it, please!"

"Scions live and die in Ashasa's service," Kadeja said, pressing the blade that little bit closer to her throat. "Bear witness, and be still."

Yena was crying openly, silent tears wetting her cheeks as the white scion screamed and bit savagely at the bronze's neck, tackling it back into a sharp clutch of stalagmites. The bronze keened, collapsed and went still, blood gouting out where the white's reddened muzzle was clamped around its throat. Giving the corpse a final, vicious shake, the white stepped back and bugled in triumph, beating its wings without ever leaving the ground.

"Well done!" said Kadeja, calling out to it. "Ashasa's will is served." She stepped to the side, pulling Yena with her, and gestured at the red-gold anchor, the one that represented Veksh. "Now, destroy it!"

Breath rasping in its throat, the white scion trekked towards them. The bronze, though dead, had fought valiantly, and the survivor was now as much pink as white, blood colouring its scales. As it passed them, Yena shuddered to see the extent of its injuries, the gaping cuts to flank and throat, and swallowed bile as she realised their resemblance to Safi's scars, and Zech's. *Is this the Trial of Queens, then?* she thought, appalled. *To make these creatures fight and kill each other in the service of our ambition?*

Oblivious to this, Kadeja leaned down and spoke by Yena's ear. "You ought to be grateful I brought you with me; that Ashasa chose you, of all women, to be my heir. There is no guarantee that Yevekshasa, let alone anyone living there, will survive this."

Something in Yena snapped.

Unable to press forward, she whipped her head back instead, feeling the satisfying crack as her skull slammed into Kadeja's nose. Kadeja yelped and staggered, losing her hold just enough for Yena to jerk free, wincing as the blade burned a faint line against her throat. She stumbled forwards, turning just in time to dodge Kadeja's retributive swipe, darting around a clump of stalagmites before Kadeja could close the gap between them.

"You–" Kadeja hissed, but whatever she might've said next was lost in the sudden tumult as an enraged gold scion burst into the cavern – half-flying, half-running, bellowing all the while – and launched itself straight at the white, already raising a massive clawed paw to swipe at the Vekshi anchor.

"Defend yourself!" Kadeja screamed, and just in time: the white, which towered over the gold as surely as it had the bronze, turned and caught the attack on its flank, roaring as it bulled the smaller scion back. Gaze darting between this new battle and Kadeja, who still held the knife, Yena didn't even register the second figure running in at the scion's heels until a familiar voice rang out through the cavern.

"*Yena?*"

Yena whirled, and saw, and let out a wrenching noise.

"*Safi! Safi!*"

Heedless of the fighting scions – heedless of Kadeja, wide-eyed and furious, swearing as she backed up towards the anchors – Yena sobbed and ran to Safi, stumbling over the uneven ground. Safi, who was somehow impossibly *here*, dressed in alien clothes with her arms spread wide and a look on her face that was twin to Yena's, fear and shock and furious hope all blended together.

They crashed into each other, clinging on like the world had already ended, pulling back just far enough to manage what was less a kiss and more a shared sob of desperate breath, lips grazing as their foreheads pressed together. Yena was still crying, shaking as Safi's arms tightened around her.

"How are you here?" she gasped, fingers clutching at Safi's shirt. "How did you find me?"

"Luck," breathed Safi, one hand coming up to cup the back of Yena's head. "Luck or the universe, I don't know any more – godshit, Yena, what's *happening*?"

And with that, the reality of the moment reasserted itself. As the brawling scions came closer, the gold scrabbling for a hold on the white's throat, Yena gasped out Kadeja's plans, the two of them jumping backwards as a nearby stalactite came crashing down.

"Gods," Safi whispered, gaze darting to the scions. "Oh, gods, we have to stop her! Where is she now?"

They scanned the cavern as they moved, Yena tugging Safi steadily towards the anchors.

"There!" she cried, speeding up as she caught sight of Kadeja, crouching beside the Vekshi orb. "There, she's there!"

Kadeja ignored them, her focus all on the anchor. Safi held tight to Yena's hand, swearing in her native language as the cavern shook again.

"We can't let her break it!" Yena panted, pulling Safi around the same clump of stalagmites she'd used to dodge Kadeja's blade. "Or if she does, we have to smash the other one, too."

"How soon?" Safi asked, faltering as the gold scion screamed.

"What?"

"If she breaks the Vekshi anchor, how long do we have to smash the other one before it's too late?"

The question struck Yena dumb. "I don't know," she whispered, heart in her throat as she saw Kadeja glance between her knife and the orb, coolly contemplating the impact of the one on the other. "Sun's breath, I don't know, she never said–"

"Quickly, then," said Safi, squeezing Yena's hand. "Let's just go with doing it *quickly*. And as to how–"

A terrible, piercing scream from the scions, loud enough

that even Kadeja turned to look.

The white was down, wings spread awkwardly against the stone, belly-up as the gold gripped it by the throat. Without letting go, it looked up, bright eyes raking the cavern before fixing on Safi. It was only then, as Safi began to tremble, that Yena realised there must be some significance to the fact that she'd entered with the scion, though the details of it escaped her.

And then Safi looked at Kadeja, and spoke.

"I speak for the scale-sisters, those you call scions!" Saffron called, her voice ringing through the cavern. "Kadeja, you have to stop this!"

"You," said Kadeja. Her voice was flat and her eyes were cold, her grip white-knuckled on the knife as she stood. "You *again*."

"I was your omen, once," Saffron said, an ugly twist in the words. "Is that enough to make you heed me?"

"Why should I?" Kadeja shot back. "What can you possibly have to say that matters?"

<hurry! I can't hold her much longer>

The dragon's voice burned through her, laden with pain and fear. Saffron swallowed, trying to keep her voice steady.

"The scions have their own form of the ahunemet, Kadeja – what you did to one, the others all felt, and they're *furious*. You violated their home; you broke the accords that have held since the first Vekshi came here. If you don't undo what you did to the white – if you force my scale-sister to kill her – your own life will be forfeit."

"The scions obey Ashasa!" Kadeja said, but a thread of uncertainty showed in her voice, and Saffron seized on it.

"If that were true, you wouldn't have needed to use the ahunemet to protect yourself! This isn't Ashasa's will, Kadeja, and even if it was, would it be worth dying for? What will your new world matter, if you aren't alive to shape it?" She stepped forward as she spoke, the clasp of Yena's hand a tangible source of strength. "Let the white scion go. Let her live, and her sisters might spare you, too."

Behind them, the white dragon made a feeble choking sound, thrashing against the gold's persistent hold. From the outside, their pose looked static, but within the privacy of their bond Saffron knew the gold was tiring, struggling to keep the larger dragon pinned.

Kadeja wavered, her bloodied blade glinting in the light of the Vekshi anchor.

A clatter of running came from the cavern entrance, shattering the moment. All eyes, human and dragon, turned to look.

Saffron felt her heart turn over.

"Gwen?" she whispered, just as Yena said, equally disbelieving, "Auntie?"

But though she longed to run to Gwen, it was the other figure that stopped her: Leoden, eyes wild with fury, fists clenched as he stared at his former Vex'Mara.

"*Kadeja!*" he shouted, voice breaking on her name. "I know what you did to me – what you're planning to do to Kena! Stand down!"

An ugly twist of emotion crossed Kadeja's face. "Claiming you was *easy*," she hissed, "and as for Kena–"

<STOP HER!>

In a sudden explosion of violent effort, the white dragon threw off Saffron's gold and bulled her way forwards, dark blood gouting from her throat. Kadeja lurched away from the anchor, visibly startled–

Saffron grabbed Yena, darting hopelessly forwards–

Gwen and Leoden moved, but too late–

With a final, terrible scream, the white dragon threw her battered body against the Vekshi anchor, dying as she fell.

The crystal bulged and boiled and *shattered*, shards exploding outwards in a radial shockwave of pulsing magic, strong enough to shred the dragon's body. Yena tackled Saffron down as the shards whipped overhead, the two of them hitting the ground together, the force of the magic blast crashing them hard into the stalagmite cluster. Somewhere nearby, Kadeja screamed, and through her bond with the golden dragon Saffron felt a question asked, and answered it instinctively, as the cavern began to shake and crumble, *scale-sister, please,* please *help us, she'll kill our world–*

For a terrible moment, the words made no sense. And then Saffron rolled to her side, clawing her way upright in time to see the golden dragon, bloodied and beautiful, launch desperately into the narrow air between roof and floor, dodging as the stalactites fell, to drive herself head-first into the remaining anchor.

The second explosion shook the cavern hard enough that Saffron heard the ground crack. With nowhere to duck, she lifted her head, staring in stunned grief as her scale-sister was torn apart–

And then she felt it, power and magic thrumming through her, a tide of secondhand pain and fear and raw determination that hit like the hammer of dawn. She felt herself spasming, shaking under an onslaught greater than her body could bear; was dimly aware of Yena shouting, of different voices raised in chorus, but all she felt was a blizzard of scales, sharp-edged and deathly, razoring into her deepest self, a storm of sensate memories that went on and on and on–

Foam on her lips and eyes rolled back, Saffron blacked out.

The cavern was falling, huge chunks of stone and crystal shaking free of the ceiling as the world fell down around them. Choking on dust, Gwen staggered to her feet as the floor shook beneath her, a steady vibrato. Leoden groaned on the ground nearby, slowly manoeuvring himself upright; Gwen moved towards him, but was forestalled by a sudden, terrified cry from the opposite side of the cavern.

"Auntie! Help!"

Stumbling towards it, she found Yena crouched over Saffron's motionless body, her face tear-streaked and terrified. In her chest, her heart went numb. *Oh gods, no, please no–*

"She's still alive." Yena choked out the words, one hand still clutching Saffron's. "I don't know what happened, she wasn't hit, but when the second anchor went out, she just–"

"It's all right," Gwen said, more calmly than she felt. "It's all right, we'll get her out of here, we just need–"

"I can carry her." It was Leoden, staggering over to help; covered in stone dust he looked as if he'd aged a decade in minutes. "She helped me when she had no need, I can do that much for her."

By way of answer, Gwen stepped back and let him scoop Saffron into his arms, exhaling relief as Saffron, though unconscious, twitched.

"We have to get out of here, now," Gwen said, one hand on Yena's shoulder and the other on Leoden's, shepherding them both towards the exit.

"You know a way out?"

Gwen thought of the key and the geode room. "I hope so," she said grimly. "Because if this whole place comes down, I don't like our chances."

They started to move, bypassing the bronze dragon carcass – Leoden swore as a fissure opened almost beneath his feet, forcing them to speed up – and were nearly at the tunnel entrance when a bloodied, furious Kadeja lurched into their path, her knife raised shakily as her free hand clutched an ugly-looking wound in her side.

"*No!*" she screamed, swaying in place, her face flecked with dust and dragon blood. "This isn't how it goes, this isn't – this isn't *right*, I was *promised*, Ashasa *promised me–*"

A catastrophic boom from behind as a cluster of stalactites crashed down hard, bringing with them a rain of debris. Gwen couldn't help it: she turned to look, and in that moment Kadeja lunged for her, hand outstretched.

Time seemed to slow. Gwen knew the exact moment the Vex'Mara's bare hand closed around her wrist; felt the terrible warping surge of the ahunemet as Kadeja tried to bind her will. It felt like being drunk, her senses fogging and slurring as the compulsion rose through her, blurring out everything other than Kadeja's instruction: *take my knife, kill them, show me the way out–*

And then, with all the sudden stark clarity of a spotlight switching on, the world flooded back to her. There was Leoden, still clutching Saffron; there was Kadeja, her expression frozen in shock–

And there was Yena, both hands gripping Kadeja's blade where she'd driven it up between the Vex'Mara's ribs.

"No," rasped Kadeja, eyes going wide. Yena released her hold on the knife, and Kadeja swayed backwards, bright blood bubbling on her lips. "No. No. No."

"You killed my sister," Yena said, softly. "Zechalia a Trishka. She was never yours."

Mouth working soundlessly, Kadeja fell to her knees, hands scrabbling at the blade's handle. She gripped it, looking up at them; and Gwen, with an intensity born of revulsion, kicked Kadeja hard in the chest, so that she toppled and fell.

Another crash from the ceiling. The walls began to shake.

"Run," said Yena, faintly. She clutched at Gwen's sleeve and started tugging, pulling her away. "Auntie, come on, we have to go –"

"All right," croaked Gwen, and ran.

I killed Kadeja.
  I killed Kadeja.
  I killed her in cold blood.
  I'm not sorry.
  Should I be sorry?

I think I'm going to be sick.

The words rebounded through Yena's head, a tumble of thoughts as cacophonous as the tumble of falling stone. She ran through the tunnels, acid in her throat and fear in her lungs, and wondered how they could possibly escape the collapse. Though Gwen and Leoden never hesitated over which turning to take, it was nonetheless clear that they'd managed to lose their way, and though the loudest crashing was behind them, the floor and walls still shook, sand falling down where the stone gave way in chunks.

"What are we looking for?" Yena asked. "How did you get here?"

"My way is closed," said Leoden, just as Gwen said, "A key, I've got a key – there was a geode, a crystal room where it brought me through."

"And that'll get us out again?"

"Do you have a better alternative?" Gwen asked, somewhat wildly. "How did you get here?"

"The world-egg!" she said. "Kadeja brought us through from Yevekshasa, an anchored portal under the mesa, but it won't still be there – it's what the anchors were sustaining, what they ought to have destroyed."

Leoden swore, jogging Safi in his arms. She stirred again, groaning. Yena swallowed a sob.

"There!" Gwen shouted, pointing to a branch in the tunnel up ahead. "There, there, I remember that path – we're getting close!"

"You're sure?" Leoden panted.

"As sure as I can be!"

Another rumble shook the tunnels, harder than before, and Yena nearly stopped breathing as she saw the roof of their chosen path start to collapse, the passage closing off ahead in a shower of stone and dust. They came to a halt, staring terrified down the two remaining alternatives; one was cracking along the ground, while heavy gouts of earth fell from the other's roof.

"Thorns and godshit," Gwen whispered. "Which one?"

"Which what?" choked Safi, struggling to sit up. "Gwen? What's happening?"

"Can you stand?" asked Leoden, when Gwen didn't answer.

Safi nodded, and Leoden set her gently down. Her legs wobbled; Yena surged forwards to catch her, throat too tight for tears.

"That bad, huh?" Safi managed, clutching her tight.

Yena fought hysterical laughter. "Something like that."

The ground beneath them shuddered; a slab of stone crashed down from the roof and blocked the way they'd come. Over Safi's shoulder, Yena watched as the fissure in one tunnel gaped into a chasm, then had to close her eyes.

"Shh, hey," said Safi, which was how Yena knew she'd been making noise, little hiccupping sobs under her breath. Safi ran a gentle hand across her bare head, trying to smile as she met Yena's gaze. "Hey. They made you cut your hair?"

Yena made a noise that was not quite laughter. "They did. They did, but it'll grow back." She choked on a sob. "It would've grown back, I mean, I–"

Safi kissed her, hot and desperate, and Yena kissed back, refusing everything other than this; refusing to be trapped and dying and terrified in favour of tasting what life remained to be lived, however little. She opened her eyes again, breathing shallowly, face pressed into the hollow of Saffron's shoulder.

"I'm sorry," Leoden said. His voice was quiet, a hairsbreadth away from broken. "I trusted her first. I let her in."

"She trapped you," Gwen said fiercely. "Trapped and abused and forced you, and you aren't at fault for th... ow!"

"What is it?" Safi asked.

"The key," Gwen said, a tremor of hope in her voice. Yena jerked her head up, staring as her auntie withdrew a slender, spiral key from her pocket. "The godsdamned key is *burning*..."

And then, at the mouth of the fractured tunnel, the single most beautiful portal Yena had ever seen irised open, rainbow-edged and perfect.

"*Naruet,*" Safi sobbed, and as the rest of the roof came down, the four of them lunged for the portal, Yena's hand tight on Safi's arm as they tumbled through to safety.

PART 4
On & On

19

All the Pretty Pieces

Later, Luy would sit down with a pen and paper and try to order the day's events into a linear narrative, a fragment of the Great Story preserved for posterity. He would recall the moment when, having brought them within the shadow of Yevekshasa's gates, Naruet went utterly rigid, grabbing Sashi's arm and talking at near-incoherent speed about the city's faltering wards; about the sudden torque he felt in the scrying-web he'd woven from the jahudemet and his subsequent bone-deep certainty that Gwen was in danger. Luy would write, with a calmness he hadn't remotely felt, about the sudden onrush of Ashasa's Knives, furious armed women who knew, as Naruet did, that something had gone wrong beneath the city, but had drawn the conclusion that he and his portal were somehow responsible for it.

He would remember, but not write, the terror he'd felt as Sashi stood firm before the yshra and demanded they let Naruet act, his heart in his mouth as Rikan and the other honoured swords had formed up around her, Jeiden standing bravely by her side. That fear was personal, and though he was a participant in the story, some things he yet wished to keep to himself.

What he *would* record was Naruet, calm amidst the tumult as he shut his eyes and opened a portal directly behind the yshra, who panicked and scrambled away from its oilslick radius. And then there was Gwen – and Yena, and Safi, and even, gods help them, Leoden – stumbling through to Yevekshasa, all of them rimed with dirt and blood and looking as though they'd escaped some exciting new hell, but all of them – still, blessedly, mercifully – alive.

Whether they were whole was a different matter.

Luy ran to his mother, helping her upright as she coughed and staggered. Until that moment, he hadn't realised how worried he'd been, and seeing that she'd clearly come close to danger left him hugging her harder than intended, until she let out a wheezing laugh and said, "Ease up on my ribs, won't you? Breathing's hard enough as it is!" But even that show of levity vanished when she realised where they were, the threat of the regrouped yshra strong enough that Rikan was yet to lower his sword. Luy froze, torn as to whether he should step forward or stay put, but was spared the decision when Safi shoved her way to the fore, eyes blazing.

"I am Safi a Ellen, a queen's equal," she said in Vekshi, pitching her voice to carry. Before the yshra could challenge her, she held up her tattooed wrist, letting them see the twining proof of her status. "These travellers are under my protection. Bring us to Ksa a Kaje at the Great Temple, and you will have my thanks."

Luy had expected the yshra to be resentful, their hostility increased by the challenge to their authority; instead, they gave ground with what almost looked like gratitude, which said more about Yevekshasa's current unrest than Luy suspected they meant to reveal.

Ashasa's Knives formed up around them, an impromptu honour-guard to escort them through the city. Gwen moved to reassure Sashi and Jeiden, leaving Luy to walk alongside Leoden and Naruet. They were an odd pair, the boy looking anxiously at the monarch – ex-monarch? – in near-worshipful silence, while Leoden looked too exhausted for words. The result was a steady build in tension, and by the time they were into Yevekshasa proper, Luy could bear it no longer.

"You're back, then?" he said, not quite looking up.

Leoden looked at him. Opened his mouth, then closed it again, and in that moment it struck Luy powerfully that this was only the second time that Leoden had ever seen him unveiled. The last time they'd spoken had been the day he'd fled through the anchored portal, sneering and angry and utterly dissimilar to the man beside him now, dressed in decidedly un-Kenan clothes and walking as though weighed down with stones.

"I don't know," said Leoden, eventually. Gods, even his *voice* was different, the carefully sharp inflections Luy recalled so well worn down into something vulnerable and rough. He looked at Luy, mouth twisted into a complex line. "She changed you too, didn't she."

It wasn't a question. Luy felt the breath knocked out of him. "Yes. Yes, she did."

Leoden nodded to himself. "I'm starting to remember. Not... not everything, but things that stand out, that don't make sense; things I would never have done, if she hadn't..." His voice trailed off for a moment, and when he spoke again it was flatter, more distant. "She's dead, now. Yena killed her."

"*Yena* did?"

"That is her name, isn't it?" He tipped his head towards her. "The Kenan-Vekshi girl?"

"That's her."

"She's Sashi's sister," Naruet added suddenly.

"Sashi? Who's that?"

"The interim Vekshi ambassador." Naruet held out a skinny hand and pointed. "There, with the hearse."

"The interim... oh. *Oh.*" Leoden paled, hands clenching by his sides. "Sene?"

"Suicide," Luy said, softly.

Leoden made a pained noise low in his throat, but it wasn't until he scrubbed a wrist across his eyes that Luy realised he was crying. The sight stunned him, though it shouldn't have: he of all people should understand the wrenching violation of Kadeja's actions, what she'd done to them both, what she'd made them do–

But Leoden had married her. Had thought himself in love with her. How much of that had been Kadeja's doing?

"Gods," Luy whispered, horrified all over again as the full implications hit him. As in any civilized nation, rape was a crime in Kena, but one committed less often there than in other places for any number of reasons, none of which mattered a damn in a case like this. He reached to Leoden, hovering a hand above his shoulder before letting it drop. Leoden shuddered, leaning into the contact.

"I think," he said, after a moment. "I think I cannot go home."

Startled, Luy said, "To Karavos, you mean?"

"Kena, Karavos – it hardly matters." He offered Luy a fey, sharp smile. "I assume, of course, that the throne is not quite vacant?"

"You could say that," said Luy, thinking of Viya and Amenet. "Yes."

"Ah." Leoden shut his eyes, putting Luy in the strange position of guiding him until they opened again. "She was with me so long, it's hard to tell, but I think... I do not think I ever wished to be Vex. I was a scholar. *Am* a scholar. And now I have woken to find my life's work is either solved or sullied. What I did to Kena–"

"*You* didn't do anything," Luy said, as gently as he could. "Kadeja–"

"Does it matter? To the people, to the worldwalkers, to everyone her puppetry either betrayed or injured, does it truly matter that my hands were unwilling? Could it ever be explained?"

"It could, perhaps. If you so wanted."

"I don't know," said Leoden. "I don't know what I want,

except the peace and space in which to want it for myself alone; to know the choice is mine. But if I am announced alive, here–"

"I could send you away," said Naruet, speaking with that same blithe helpfulness as before. "A portal, back to the bazaar." He paused, blinking into the distance, then added, "I can't always tell, but you looked happy there."

"I was," said Leoden, softly. "I thought I had a purpose. But that particular chore is more than done, now. No, Naruet–" and here he ruffled the youth's hair, an easy show of gratitude that Naruet, grinning, only pretended to dodge, "–I thank you for the offer, but I would rather... I would like to remain in this world, I think. Just not in any capacity where my presence can further damage Kena's peace."

Up ahead, a new commotion briefly arrested their forward progress. Luy felt a lurch of anxiety that swiftly resolved itself into a mix of relief and joy as he recognised Shavaktiin robes draped around two familiar silhouettes.

Halaya! His pulse leapt at the thought of seeing her again, accompanied by a frisson of possibility at being able to introduce her to Rikan – and then, as he glanced at Leoden, a solution presented itself.

"You know," he said, "scholars of any kind are always welcome among the Shavaktiin, especially those with an interest in Kena's stories."

Leoden looked poleaxed. He licked his lips, considering. A slow smile broke across his face, the first and truest such expression Luy had ever seen on him.

"That sounds... very amenable," he said at last. His eyes crinkled at the edges.

Luy wouldn't write that down, either.

"I killed Kadeja," Yena said. She sat at Yasha's bedside, flanked by Sashi and Safi, while Ksa a Kaje watched them all from a corner chair, silent as stone. Her grandmother's injuries had been healed, but the process had left her badly drained, necessitating further recuperation. Though she was physically whole, the resultant loss of energy left her looking as small and old as Yena had ever seen. Kiri, too, had lived, and was resting one room over.

Jesit had not.

Fierce pride flashed in Yasha's eyes. "Of course you did," she said, squeezing Yena's hand. "Ashasa's will be done."

Yena yanked her hand back as if she'd been burned. She stood there, trembling, then turned on her heel and fled the room, a terrible ache in her throat as she choked down tears.

She made it all the way outside before Safi caught up with her. They were both newly washed and dressed – the first thing Ksa had done once they'd arrived at the temple was to see them cleaned up – but Yena still felt as if she was choking, dust in her throat and blood on her arms from the scion's scales and blood on her hands from Kadeja. She turned to Safi and realised, with a relief that permeated her entire being, that she didn't have to explain herself, because Safi had been there. Safi *knew*.

Wordless, Yena fell into Safi's embrace, her cheek pressed to her collarbone. They held each other as lightly as the moment would allow, which was not very; light enough only to breathe without obstruction and to feel the wind slip by.

When Yena finally found her voice, it felt as if an age had passed. "I do want to grow my hair out," she said. "I like having curls."

"I like your curls, too," said Safi, pressing a kiss to her temple. "Think I'll keep mine short, though."

"It suits you that way."

"Mm."

A moment of silence, clear as bells. The sky overhead was velvet-dark and strewn with stars, the moons a bright flirtation in the dark.

"Yena?"

"Yes?"

"You do know I don't want to stay in Veksh, don't you?"

Yena let out a breath she hadn't been conscious of holding. "I do now."

Safi pulled back far enough to give her a quizzical look. "You really thought I would?"

"Safi. You're a queen's equal here. Thanks to Kadeja, Veksh just lost its link to Vikasa, and who knows what that means for the Trial of Queens and the Trial of Knives? Everything is going to change, and you... you could have real power here, if you wanted. You could help shape a whole country."

"So could you," Safi pointed out. "You're a queen's sister, after all, and far more Vekshi than me."

"Maybe I was," said Yena, softly. "Once. Or maybe I never really was at all." She shut her eyes, shivering slightly in the evening cool. "The Vekshi talk about the braided path, but what does that really mean when we're only ever expected to serve Ashasa, serve our mothers, no matter what else we want? Not that *my* mother is quite like that, but Yasha... Yasha made up for it. And I have family in Kena, I could – we could – travel there, or stay at the palace, but knowing what I know now it's clear the worlds are so much bigger than us, aren't they? But you were brave; you left yours. And I think... I think maybe I want to leave mine, too. With you. If you wanted."

Safi held her tight and laughed. "I do want that," she said, and brushed their noses together. "With you."

Yena kissed her, deep and slow, and didn't stop until the moons had moved.

Gwen stared out at Yevekshasa from a temple balcony, watching the lights of the mesa city flicker against the dark. Mesthani's death was an ache in her chest, though she hadn't much known the woman: one more casualty of Kadeja's obsession. Right now, Veksh was calm only because neither

queens nor temple quite knew how to react to having lost a
heritage they'd never admitted to having. The mesa shook
when the anchors broke, but in all the chaos following
Mesthani's death and Kadeja's escape, the world-egg's loss
was yet to be explored.

"That's the part I don't understand," Gwen had said to
Kiri a Tavi earlier, her tongue still stumbling over the harsh
Vekshi syllables. She'd gone to see the injured priestess as
much to avoid being cooped up with Yasha as from a mix of
respect and curiosity, and Kiri had deigned to humour her in
the visit. "How did Kadeja come to have the heart-into-mind
in the first place? What aspect of the Trial of Knives could
possibly grant that power?"

Kiri had laughed, a rattlesnake sound. "As our mysteries
are gone, I see no harm in telling you, worldwalker. There
was a relic there, a magical repository constructed so long
ago we could no longer duplicate its like. As part of the Trial,
initiates who touched it were offered their heart's desire,
which ought to have been a life in Ashasa's service. Any
who chose whatever else the relic offered were refused the
priestesshood, and while there were limits to what might be
granted it wasn't unknown for one thought a daughter to
emerge a son, or for a child without magic to have suddenly
gained the talent."

"And Kadeja wanted the heart-into-mind," Gwen said,
heavily.

"Yes," said Kiri. "Enough so, evidently, that even having
passed the Trial – she must have originally refused it – that
she snuck back into the catacombs to access the relic a second
time, to a different purpose. Oh, she was suspected of theft,
but the gift of magic was not all that she might have taken,
and how could her accusers ever declare her guilty when she
had only to change their minds?" She made a disgusted noise,
tired and sad, and turned her face to the wall. "I would rest
now, Gwen Vere. Give my regards to Yena a Trishka, should

you see her." And then, more softly, "Veksh does not deserve her."

Later, Gwen had dutifully passed on both messages when she'd stopped to talk to Yena and Saffron. Both girls had been on their way to bed, but had made time for conversation, tired yet animated right up until the moment Gwen mentioned Kiri. Yena went very still as she listened, but her answering smile was vulpine.

"She's right," she said, with more conviction than Gwen had heard from her since they'd reached the temple. "Veksh doesn't deserve either one of us. But we deserve ourselves." And with that, she'd put an arm around Saffron's waist and led her off to their chamber.

Gwen smiled at the memory. *All isn't lost,* she told herself. *Kadeja is dead, Leoden restored, Kena saved. We are left tattered, but whole. We endure.* She thought of Louis, Halaya and Rikan, a trio last glimpsed in close conversation, veils and armour set aside as two of them began to know one another. Her smile broadened, hope and pride and fondness mixed together. *We build, and rebuild, and make new stories. And so the worlds keep turning.*

"You're Gwen Vere?"

The voice was female, unfamiliar and expected. Gwen turned, schooling her expression into polite neutrality as she assessed the shasuyakesani woman standing opposite, an uncertain set to her shoulders as she fidgeted with her sleeves.

"I am," said Gwen. "You're Evai a Ksa, I take it?"

"Yes."

"You're an Archivist?"

"For my sins," said Evai, with a wryness that made Gwen take an instant liking to her. "With everything that's happened, I imagine my life is about to get vastly more complicated."

"I believe it is," said Gwen, and pulled out the key to Vikasa. "Quite possibly in more ways than one."

Evai's gaze flickered from Gwen to the key and back again. In all the furore surrounding their arrival, it was difficult to keep track of whose stories had already been told to which people, even those that were ostensibly hers to tell. Gwen had heard about Evai from Yena during their footmarch in from the gates, but as to whether Evai had heard of Gwen herself – or of her trip to Yavinae – she didn't know.

"Do you know what this is?" Gwen asked.

"No," said Evai, "but I assume it's more than what it appears to be."

Gwen weighed the key in her palm, considering her words, the implications of what she meant to do. The key didn't belong to her except inasmuch as Naruet had ceded her its guardianship; if anything, it belonged to Kena. Depending on how much of Vikasa's mesa had collapsed when the anchors broke, both the geode it led to and the quartz screen it activated could already be destroyed, rendering it useless.

And yet.

"This key opened a door from Yavinae to Vikasa," said Gwen, looking Evai firmly in the eye. "I don't know if it will open again; only that it activates at the name Vakti." The key sparked briefly in her hand; Evai's eyebrows rose towards her hairline. Though privately amused, Gwen coughed and continued. "As I understand portal-magic, other worlds are easier to locate if you have a focal point, a person or object to lead the way. And Veksh, it seems to me, has already lost too much of her history. It won't be the same as what you had, but your scholars at least should have some way to explore your past." At Evai's look of incomprehension, Gwen sighed and proffered the key. "Here, girl. Take it. Whatever use I might have for it is not as great as yours."

Evai's eyes widened. "What do you want in return?"

Gwen snorted. "What does anyone want from the future? Peace and knowledge and common sense, and the hope that we learn from past mistakes instead of compounding them."

More gently, she said, "There's been enough violence, Evai. I might not be Vekshi, but that doesn't mean I want to see this country rip itself apart. Take the key or don't – just do what you think is right."

Slowly, reverently, Evai held out her hand, watching as Gwen tipped the key into her open palm. It landed soundlessly, winking in the darkness like a tiny fallen star.

"There you go," Gwen said softly. "Hope."

At dawn, the Council of Queens burned the bodies of Zechalia a Kadeja and Sene a Sati.

Naruet understood little of the ceremony, feeling like an interloper as he shuffled his feet on the periphery of the great amphitheatre. The seats were filled with unknown Vekshi, while he and the other foreigners stood nearby, not quite a part of the ritual but somehow more than spectators, watching as the bodies were laid on a great stone dais, shrouded and veiled in all the wrong colours for Kena, which were somehow the right ones here. After several impassioned speeches in Vekshi, which Naruet didn't understand, the bodies were set alight by a pair of blonde priestesses gifted with the *yaramet*, or whatever it was the Vekshi called their fire-magic. The Vekshi sang as it happened, a mournful song that echoed against the stone. Naruet felt momentarily panicked at the thought that he was meant to join in, but relaxed when he saw that the other Kenans were quiet, too.

He wished he could stand with Sashi, but as the interim ambassador – and, it emerged, a queen's sister, though the newfound status evidently had more to do with Yena than anything Sashi had done – she'd been one of the speakers in the ceremony, and was therefore standing apart with the queens. Instead, he stood with Jeiden, who was similarly adrift. When the younger boy started, silently, to weep, Naruet placed a tentative hand on his shoulder. He'd worried it was the wrong thing to do, but rather than shrug him off,

Jeiden reached up and gripped Naruet's hand with his own, anchoring the contact. It felt like being brought Inside, and though it was surely disrespectful to be happy at a funeral for any reason, Naruet found himself smiling after that.

Smoke from the burning drifted into the sky, a smear of grey-blue against the pinks and golds. He watched it drifting up and up – so clear at first, but steadily dissipating, until you could no longer tell it apart from the firmament beyond. It wasn't the Kenan way of things, but Naruet found himself moved by the sight. He'd never liked cramped, dark spaces, of which earthly graves reminded him, even when they were planted with seeds or saplings. Vanishing into the sky felt more like freedom, more like letting go.

He hadn't known the dead, as the others had. But whichever god had claimed them now he hoped they were happier for it.

It wasn't quite a relief when the ceremony ended, because Naruet couldn't yet relax. Both Gwen and Luy had taken him aside to explain the need for a swift and unobtrusive departure from Yevekshasa, explaining where in the temple grounds he'd been given leave to open a portal and when, exactly, he should do it. He'd listened very carefully and assured them he'd do his best, but the incident with the key diverting them to Yavinae had rattled him more than he cared to admit. Quietly, he was panicked it might happen again, even though Gwen had told him that she'd given the key away, and consequently found himself unable to focus on anything else.

Naruet opened the portal, holding his breath in anticipation of a distortion that never came. He sighed with relief, waited until Gwen and the others had passed through, then followed in turn, snapping the whole thing neatly shut behind them. They were back in Karavos, in the same unobtrusive avenue from which they'd originally departed, and it was only then, as he looked at his companions, that he realised who was absent.

Panic swelled again, a hot lump in his throat. Hurrying to Gwen's side, he tugged on her sleeve and asked, somewhat desperately, "Did we mean to leave so many behind?"

"Yes," said Gwen, "but only because they'd decided to stay." She raised an eyebrow. "We did explain it, Naruet. Don't you remember?"

Naruet dropped his gaze, abashed. It was hard to remember that Gwen, unlike Ktho, didn't always notice those times when he was only hearing words, not listening to them.

"I don't," he said, humbly. "I'm sorry."

Gwen sighed, but not in an angry way. "It's all right. The honoured swords, Yasha and the Shavaktiin are staying to support Sashi, who wants to arrange for a new Vekshi ambassador to come back with her, and Luy and Leoden stayed with the Shavaktiin. On which note, I'd be grateful if you'd keep the fact of Leoden returning at all to yourself, at least for a little while."

"Of course," said Naruet solemnly. "He asked me to do that, too, last night. I just didn't think it meant he wasn't coming."

Gwen's lips twitched. "Just so. Is there anything else you wanted to know?"

Naruet was about to shake his head in the negative when, from the corner of his eye, he caught sight of a bright, unfamiliar banner waving over the palace. He pointed at it. "What does that mean?"

Gwen followed the line of his arm, blinked, and broke into a broad smile.

"It means that Amenet's levies are here, along with Viya's family." She laughed. "It means we can hold the city. Karavos is safe."

Viya stared at the parchment in the vain hope that doing so would help her make sense of the contents. When this didn't work, she looked incredulously from Halunet to Gwen and back again.

"You're sure this is accurate?"

"As true as I can render it," said Halunet.

"It's accurate," said Gwen. "I was there, Viya. They're my memories. Halunet has it word for word."

"Could the recording have been faked somehow?" asked Matu, the barely-suppressed excitement in his tone betraying his desire to be told otherwise. "There's so little surviving documentation from the Years of Shadow that we hardly have anything to compare it to."

"If any of it is true," said Amenet, "then Vexa Yavin is not quite what we thought."

"Is that so hard to believe, under the circumstances?" Pix asked. "After all, neither is Leoden."

Amenet flinched and looked away.

"Pix," Viya chided – softly, as the courtier was correct.

Pixeva flushed. "Forgive me."

"Personally," said Ktho, after a delicate pause, "I see no reason to think it false."

Viya smoothed the document, resisting the urge to read it through for a third time. The revelation that Vexa Yavin's Vexa'Sehet had been the first Shavaktiin – the idea that Vakti had acted as an ambassador to the many worlds of the firmament – had struck a chord in her.

"In any case," Viya said thoughtfully, "the notion of a worldwalker ambassador is arguably a good one. As accessible to the jahudemet as our world is, we ought to have at least some idea of what goes on beyond our borders."

A smart rap on the chamber door disrupted the conversation; all eyes turned as the honoured sword on duty, Sathika, stepped into the room and bowed.

"Cuivexa, your foreign allies are here. Should I send them in?"

"Of course," said Viya, surprised and pleased, and sat up all the straighter as Safi, Yena, Naruet and Jeiden entered the room. She found herself grinning broadly at the lot of them, and when Safi smiled back, her fingers twined with Yena's, Viya felt something click into place. Especially now that Kadeja's captives were readying themselves to return to Noqevai, it was surely prudent to gather intelligence about where they'd come from; to keep a record of which new places and peoples their stories would carry back to. *Worldwalker ambassadors*, she thought, and sent a prayer of silent thanks to Ke and Na, who guarded one world among many.

Perhaps there was use in moon-tales, after all.

20
Gleams That Untravell'd World

Do you want this? Gwen had asked, a day ago and a world away. *It's not too late. You can still go home again, if you truly want to.*

Saffron had tried to be serious, but all that came out was laughter with a quarter-twist of pain. "I think it's a little late for that, don't you?"

"Is it?"

Saffron's mouth quirked. "We might inhabit a multiverse, but time is still fairly linear." And then, at Gwen's look of worried exasperation, "Even if I didn't have a dragon's memories – and yes, I do plan to write them down when they start to make sense, there's no need to look at me like that – even if that hadn't happened, and Viya didn't want us to be her eyes and ears in the Many; even if Yena wanted to stay in Yevekshasa or Karavos, I would still want to go. What I saw in Vikasa, in Noqevai... I love Kena, I do, but there's so much out there, Gwen, and I want to see it. Wouldn't you? Didn't you?"

"Yes," said Gwen, with a happy sigh. "I just wanted to make sure. Go, with my blessing, the both of you." And with that, she'd dropped a kiss on Saffron's forehead: a gentle benediction.

Now, Saffron clung to Yena, shaking with nerves as Naruet,

aided by Trishka, opened a portal for them both, the two jahudemet-users pitting their combined skills against Earth's stubborn rejection of magic in order to choose precisely the right entry point.

"Breathe," Yena whispered, running a thumb across the back of Saffron's hand. "It'll be all right."

"I hope so," Saffron said. "I really, really do."

Hand in hand, they stepped through the portal.

And into Saffron's bedroom.

It was night on Earth, the single moon high and gleaming through her window. As the portal snapped shut behind them Saffron's throat went tight. Even in the silvery light, everything was familiar enough to ache. She wanted to show it all to Yena: to go to her wardrobe and pull down the photo albums kept at the top, full of the proof of her family and childhood, then open her phone and her laptop both, where the selfies and pictures she'd taken were stored. She wanted to pull out her books and clothes, her school things and games and everything else and lay claim to them, but there wasn't time, and never had been, and never would be again.

Swallowing hard, she looked down at her childhood bed. Her parents had left it freshly made, the stuffed toy penguin she'd had since infancy propped up on the pillow. Saffron picked it up, hands shaking only slightly as she pressed a threadbare wing to her cheek. She clutched it tight, breathing in the scent of home, remembering a sense of safety lost before she ever set foot in Kena.

Saffron kissed the faded beak and set the toy back on her pillow.

"Goodbye," she whispered.

Yena squeezed her hand. "Come on, Safi. We have to be quick."

Saffron nodded. "I know. This way."

Quietly, they eased open the bedroom door and stepped into the hall. According to Trishka, who'd scryed the worlds only minutes earlier, both her parents were fast asleep, but that didn't mean they were in no danger of waking. Treading lightly, heart pounding, Saffron lead Yena to Ruby's door and eased it open, the pair of them slipping quietly into her sister's room.

Like their parents, Ruby was asleep. Her hair fanned messily across the pillow, chest rising and falling slowly beneath her hand-me-down Pokémon nightie. Saffron froze at the sight, her own memories of Ruby whirling in competition with a sudden surge of draconic echoes, feelings and impressions all centred firmly on *scale-sister, clutch-sister, family, love*. The force of it rocked her on her feet: she still wasn't used to the strange double-layering of her inherited memories with her actual ones, and had to gulp in air to calm her racing pulse.

Only then did she kneel by the bedside, dropping Yena's hand to touch her sister lightly on the cheek.

"Ruby? Ru? It's me. Wake up."

Ruby's eyelids fluttered. She blinked twice before snapping awake, her eyes going wide with shock. She opened her mouth to speak or shout or possibly scream, but Saffron had been expecting it and clapped a hand over her lips.

"Please," she whispered. "Ru, can you be quiet? I don't have much time."

Ruby's eyes widened even further as she caught sight of Yena. Her room was on the wrong side of the house to benefit from moonlight, but a dim starry night-light glowed in pride of place on her bedside table, bright enough for the purpose. Ruby looked like she wanted to cry, but nodded regardless, and Saffron slowly peeled her hand away, desperately scanning her sister's face for any sign that she was about to yell.

But Ruby didn't call for help. Instead, she scrambled upright and threw her arms around Saffron, face pressed into her shoulder.

"*Saff?*"

"Hey, Ru." Saffron hugged her tight, struggling not to cry and failing dismally. Her voice was a rasp, too loud and too quiet both. "I'm sorry, Ru, I'm so sorry."

"It's my fault." Ruby lifted her head, tears streaming down her cheeks. "I promised I wouldn't tell and I *did*, it's my fault you had to leave–"

"It's not your fault. It's nobody's fault, OK?"

Ruby's face crumpled. "But you're still not staying. You're not, right? That's what this is. You're saying goodbye."

Saffron's heart was an ugly knot. "I am," she croaked. "I am, but not forever. I promised you., didn't I? That I'd tell you when I was going – that I'd make sure you knew where I was?"

With shaking hands, Saffron dug into her pocket and pulled out a scrap of parchment. She shoved it at Ruby, who squinted at it, struggling to make out what it said in the low light.

"What's this?" she asked. And then, with a sudden sharp glare at Yena, "And who's *she*?"

Yena, who didn't speak English but who nonetheless understood that she was being discussed, raised one hand in a tentative wave. It made her look stupidly sweet, and Saffron found herself smiling through her tears.

"That's Yena," she said, voice wobbling only slightly. "She's... We're together, OK? And this, this–" she squeezed the hand in which Ruby held the parchment, "–it's an address where you can write to me. I mean, not write to me like I'll be living there, but if you send letters there I'll find them. Not quickly, but I will, I promise I will, and when I can I'll write back to you. I won't sign my name, but you'll always know it's me. OK?"

"Not OK," said Ruby, one breath shy of sobbing. "*Not OK*, Saff, you have to *stay–*"

"Ruby. Listen to me. Just listen, all right?" She squeezed her hand again, harder than before. "The world is so much bigger than you realise. So much stranger. And where I'm going, what I'm doing... I can't explain it all, and I won't pretend it's always safe, because it's not. But I'm happy. I'm doing something important, something good, and if you ever... when you're older, if you can ever forgive me for this, if you ask me to show you the truth of it all, I will. You write to me, and I'll show you everything. I promise, OK? I love you, and I promise." And just as Gwen had done with her, she leaned in and pressed a kiss to Ruby's forehead.

Behind her, Yena shifted. In Kenan, she said, "Time's up, Safi. We have to go."

"I know," said Saffron, replying in the same language, hating the startled whiplash look on Ruby's face as she stared between them; hating how much she wanted to stay, and how much more she didn't. She stood up, Ruby grabbing at her sleeve, heart breaking and mending over and over.

"Goodbye, Ru."

"Wait," said Ruby desperately. "Saff, no, *please–*"

Yena opened the door and fled to the hall, Saffron close on her heels. Behind them, Ruby struggled to follow, swearing as her legs got caught in the blankets. Much less soundless than before, they opened the door to Saffron's room and stumbled inside a half second before the return portal opened, the rainbow gleam of Naruet's magic shot through with the burning pink of Trishka's. Grasping Saffron's hand, Yena stepped first across the threshold, tugging her urgently along, and for a moment Saffron stood balanced between two worlds, her hand in one and her heart in another.

Ruby burst through the door, hair wild, wet-eyed, and froze at the tableau.

Saffron smiled at her, pained and loving. "Remember what I said, Ru. I love you, OK?"

"I love you too," Ruby choked out, "but Saff, please, *wait–*"

But Saffron didn't, and couldn't, and wouldn't. She stepped through the portal after Yena, eyes on Ruby until the last, until the doorway irised shut forever.

She was back in Kena, surrounded by friends. She'd chosen her new life three times over, once by chance and once in fear and now, again, in knowledge.

"Are you all right?" asked Trishka. She pressed in close, one hand on her daughter's shoulder and the other on Saffron's cheek. "It's all right if you're not, if you're having second thoughts–"

"I'm not," said Saffron, a single answer to both questions. She was crying in earnest, a wreck of loss and joy. "I'm not, I'm not–"

She threw her arms around Trishka's neck, and sobbed and sobbed, and never once stopped smiling.

The sky above was malachite green shot through with sideways lightning. Yena felt her heart expand at the sight of it: a bigger, more beautiful prospect than she'd ever thought existed. Safi stood beside her, ushering the rescued worldwalkers through from Kena to Noqevai. Some of them came from other worlds, but this one at least was a step up from captivity and a doorway closer to home. The great domed city loomed before them, massive and immaculate: the worldwalkers ran to it joyfully, a red-speckled woman side by side with a scale-skinned Qashqa, strangers streaming across the plain like doves let loose from a coop.

Behind them, the portal winked shut, leaving them once more alone. They'd talked about Naruet coming, too, but he'd found the prospect too overwhelming, preferring to stay in Karavos with Jeiden and Sashi and, eventually, the Shavaktiin.

"But I'll be here when you need me," he'd promised. "The ilumet and the jahudemet know where you are, and if you ever want or need a portal, you just come to the dreamscape and say so."

"We will," Safi and Yena had said, and Naruet's smile had

lit up like a festival.

"So," said Yena, snaking an arm around Safi's waist. "Any thoughts on where we should head to first?"

Safi smirked. "Well, there *is* a handsome paladin who wants to buy me dinner – perhaps thei'd like to meet you, too. But only once we've found you a language pill, of course. It won't be much fun if you can't share the conversation."

"Naturally," said Yena, grinning. "I'm an excellent conversationalist. And didn't you say something about a baby *dragon* in need of rescue?" She found she preferred the English term to scion, all things considered: perhaps there would come a time when she would no longer associate Ashasa and Veksh with blood and death, but it wasn't now, and she felt no need to hide it.

"I did," said Safi. Her expression softened, bright and brave and beautiful. "Come with me, then?"

"Always," said Yena, and kissed her soundly.

And then they straightened, arm in arm, and walked out into the worlds.

GLOSSARY

Kᴇɴᴀɴ

Ahunemet – Mind-magic, telepathy. This gift is associated with
  Nihun, god of water.
Arakoi – Soldiers whose service is sworn directly to the
  reigning Vex or Vexa.
Cahlu – A green-blue smoking leaf.
Cui'Halat – One of the three chosen marriage-mates of a
  Cuivex or Cuivexa. The Cui'Halat is traditionally chosen
  for their embodiment of the quality of liveliness or
  vitality (halat), which is usually taken to mean physical
  beauty.
Cui'Mara – One of the three chosen marriage-mates of a
  Cuivex or Cuivexa. The Cui'Mara is traditionally chosen
  for their embodiment of the quality of kinship or blood
  (mara), which is usually taken to mean that they represent
  a favourable political alliance. For this reason, 'mara
  partners within the royal mahu'kedet are generally held
  to be more powerful than their other marriage-mates, and
  can sometimes hold more political sway than a Cuivex or
  Cuivexa.
Cui'Sehet – One of the three chosen marriage-mates of a
  Cuivex or Cuivexa. The Cui'Sehet is traditionally chosen
  for their embodiment of the quality of soul or wisdom
  (sehet), which is usually taken to mean intelligence,

whether scholastic, magical or strategic.

Cuivex – The primary male consort of a Vex or Vexa.

Cuivexa – The primary female consort of a Vex or Vexa.

Enha – An open, sleeveless surcoat, usually ankle length, worn by nobles.

Halat – Vitality, especially in the context of physical wellbeing and liveliness. Halat is one of the three primary attributes by which partners in the royal mahu'kedet are chosen.

Hime – Goddess of the sky, and one of the six gods of the Second Tier of the Celestial Hierarchy. Her counterpart is Lomo, her sacred colour is lilac, and her marital attribute is vitality (halat).

Ilumet – Dream-magic; oneiromancy. This gift is associated with Hime, the sky goddess.

Jahudemet – Portal-magic, worldwalking. This gift is associated with Ke, the star goddess.

Jixa – A clear, potent spirit made from rice and wild honey.

Kara – The Heavenly Child of Ke and Na, and one of the three gods of the First Tier of the Celestial Hierarchy. Kara is a trickster who governs the moons, considered to be both sexless and all sexes. They have no consort, and their sacred colour is silver.

Karavos – The capital city of Kena.

Kashakumet – Telekinesis. This gift is associated with Na, the god of heaven.

Kavish – A type of spice-nut, cooked whole to flavour the rest of a dish.

Ke – Goddess of the stars, and one of the three gods of the First Tier of the Celestial Hierarchy. Her primary consort is Na, her secondary consorts are Yemaya, Sahu and Lomo, and her sacred colour is white.

Kedebmet – Plant-magic, terramancy. This gift is associated with Lomo, god of earth.

Kemeta – Magic-users who aren't bound in service of a temple.

Mahu'kedet – Literally the "many-bond", which is the Kenan equivalent of marriage. Though the royal mahu'kedet has a specific number of partners, all representing ideal virtues and with specific relationships to one another, for most Kenans, the mahu'kedet is a polyamorous union of two or more individuals whose relationships are not always romantic or sexual, but which is constructed around a culturally specific idea of family.

Mara – Blood, particularly as relates to kinship and family. Mara is one of the three primary attributes by which partners in the royal mahu'kedet are chosen.

Maramet – Blood-magic, commonly used to determine paternity. This gift is associated with Kara, the Heavenly Child.

Metmirai – An archaic word meaning "magic-ragged", referring to a place destroyed or distorted by magic.

Na – God of heaven, and one of the three gods of the First Tier of the Celestial Hierarchy. His primary consort is Ke, his secondary consorts are Nihun, Teket and Hime, and his sacred colour is black.

Nashi – A type of tight- and low-waisted pants whose legs are loose enough to resemble a skirt. Commonly worn as provocative or bedroom attire by noblemen.

Nihun – God of water, and one of the six gods of the Second Tier of the Celestial Hierarchy. His counterpoint is Yemaya, his sacred colour is blue, and his marital attribute is mara (blood).

Nineka – Literally "last bed", a room where the recently dead are preserved and laid out prior to their funerals.

Roa – A long-haired, bipedal beast of burden. Friendly, herbivorous and native to Kena.

Rhyawood – A hard, warm-coloured wood from the rhya tree, prized for its polished glow and rarity.

Sahu – Goddess of wisdom, and one of the six gods of the Second Tier of the Celestial Hierarchy. Her counterpart is

Teket, her sacred colour is yellow, and her marital attribute is sehet (soul).

Sehet – Soul, intelligence, strength of character. Sehet is one of the three primary attributes by which the partners in the royal mahu'kedet are chosen.

Sevikmet – Healing magic. This gift is associated with Teket, god of passion.

Shavaktiin – An order of mystics and storytellers who believe that history is shaped by human stories. They go robed and veiled when acting as agents of the Great Story, to signify their participation as interchangeable servants rather than as distinct individuals, but are known to unveil when taking up discreet roles. (Though how they distinguish between these instances is seldom clear to outsiders; and, indeed, is a continuing subject of debate among the Shavaktiin themselves.)

Taal – A traditional Kenan garment made of a single piece of cloth wrapped and knotted around the body in specific ways.

Teket – God of passion, and one of the six gods of the Second Tier of the Celestial Hierarchy. His counterpoint is Sahu, his sacred colour is purple, and his marital attribute is sehet (soul).

Vekenai-asahuda – Worldwalker: literally "all-worlds pilgrim". The word *asahuda* derives from Sahu, the goddess of wisdom, indicating one who travels divine paths in search of knowledge.

Vex – A male monarch.

Vex'Halat – One of the three chosen marriage-mates of a reigning Vex. The Vex'Halat is traditionally chosen for their embodiment of the quality of liveliness or vitality (halat), which is usually taken to mean physical beauty.

Vex'Mara – One of the three chosen marriage-mates of a reigning Vex. The Vex'Mara is traditionally chosen for their embodiment of the quality of kinship or blood (mara), which is usually taken to mean that they represent a favourable political alliance. For this reason, 'mara partners within the royal mahu'kedet are generally held to be more powerful than their other marriage-mates, and can sometimes hold more political sway than a Cuivex or Cuivexa.

Vex'Sehet – One of the three chosen marriage-mates of a reigning Vex. The Vex'Sehet is traditionally chosen for their embodiment of the quality of soul or wisdom (sehet), which is usually taken to mean intelligence, whether scholastic, magical or strategic.

Vexa – A female monarch.

Vexa'Halat – One of the three chosen marriage-mates of a reigning Vexa. The Vexa'Halat is traditionally chosen for their embodiment of the quality of liveliness or vitality (halat), which is usually taken to mean physical beauty.

Vexa'Mara – One of the three chosen marriage-mates of a reigning Vexa. The Vexa'Mara is traditionally chosen for their embodiment of the quality of kinship or blood (mara), which is usually taken to mean that they represent a favourable political alliance. For this reason, 'mara partners within the royal mahu'kedet are generally held to be more powerful than their other marriage-mates, and can sometimes hold more political sway than a Cuivex or Cuivexa.

Vexa'Sehet – One of the three chosen marriage-mates of a reigning Vexa. The Vexa'Sehet is traditionally chosen for their embodiment of the quality of soul or wisdom (sehet), which is usually taken to mean intelligence, whether scholastic, magical or strategic.

Yaramet – Fire-magic. This gift is associated with Yemaya, the goddess of fire.

Yaravadi – literally "fireflask", a cookpot spelled to keep a constant temperature used to slow-cook food while travelling.

Yemaya – Goddess of fire, and one of the six gods of the Second Tier of the Celestial Hierarchy. Her counterpart is Nihun, her sacred colour is red, and her marital attribute is mara (blood).

Zuymet – Word-magic, language transference. This gift is associated with Sahu, goddess of wisdom.

Vekshi

Alikrevaya – Literally, "gift of the soul-skin", a term used to refer both to the magic by which one born in a body that doesn't match their gender is given new flesh, and to such a person generally, regardless of whether they have transitioned. There is no stigma attached to being alikrevaya in Veksh, but as that matriarchal culture prizes girls more highly than boys, there is a greater social cost to coming out as male.

Ashasa – The Mother Sun, the fire goddess of Veksh.

Dou – A square-necked tunic.

Kettha – Loose trousers that wrap at the waist.

Mege – A hot, sweet tea brewed from caffeinated leaves and soup stock, popular with traders.

Namahsi – Grandmother.

Nek – A plain, undyed shift worn by Vekshi women when they shave their heads.

Nekveksanayun – Literally, "neither the right thing nor its opposite". The state of being in between, uncertain or undecided.

Ryvke, the – A series of writings recording the words of Ashasa's most revered queens and priestesses; new wisdom is only added after their deaths, with the choice of who to add and omit the subject of fierce debate by the Archivists.

Shariktai – Literally "sun-tongue", the Vekshi word for language-magic, equivalent to the zuymet in Kenan.

Shasuyakesani – Literally, "one on whom the sun both smiles and frowns", indicating a person born with mottled skin. Shasuyakesani individuals are varyingly considered to be either very good or very bad luck, and as such are treated with a mixture of caution, contempt and respect.

Tahka'zin vakh – Literally "heart-into-mind", the Vekshi term for telepathy, which the Kenans call the ahunemet.

Yevekshasa – The ancient capital of Veksh. The city is built on a mesa.

Yshra – Literally "blade" or "blades" (the singular and plural take the same form). The word refers both to an actual knife, and to warrior-priestesses in Ashasa's service.

Zejhasa – Literally, "the braided path". An important Vekshi concept describing the complicated relationship between mothers and their children, especially as those children age and begin their own lives as adults.

Trade

Joh – A fast-growing crystal common to Noqevai; edible by certain local animals and human species as a dietary staple, though also used for other purposes.

Kshtathit – Literally "reality blizzard", a magical storm that opens portals and wrecks the detritus of worlds on the outskirts of Noqevai.

Nakhereh – Literally "naked earth", the name given to the open plains and plateaux above Noqevai.

Noqevai – Literally "Nexus", a name applied both to the domed city of trade and to the scrap of world on which it resides.

Qashqa – A scaled, bipedal, sentient race of worldwalkers whose homeworld is close to Noqevai, but who also live in an enclave within the city, trading for much of its fresh meat and game. They have head crests and transmit emotions in patterns and colours flashed through their scales.

Roshaqui – A large mammal native to Noqevai, roughly elephant-sized, with six legs, four eyes and a shaggy, iridescent coat in any number of colours. Used by the paladins of Noqevai as mounts, roshaqui are immune to the kshtathit and intelligent enough to form loyal bonds with their riders. They are often fed on joh, but as omnivores, their diet tends to be varied.

Sehket – A small feathered monotreme native to Noqevai, roughly kitten-sized, with six legs, four eyes, a furred coat in shades of tan, black and white, and feathered wings with lighter accents. The locals consider them pests.

Vevek – Hello; a basic greeting.

ACKNOWLEDGMENTS

First and foremost, thanks and praise and all good things to my loving, patient spouse, who gave up many hours of his hard-earned leisure time (to say nothing of the use of his office space) to ensure I finished this book within a vague approximation of deadline. Thanks likewise to my wonderful son, who saw less of me in 2016 than he might've liked, but who nonetheless remains an ongoing source of cheerfulness, enthusiasm and mischief in my life. Thanks to my agent, Jennie, and to the patient folk at Angry Robot, all of whom put up with my many belated and capslocked emails to the tune of OH GOD DEADLINES AND EVERYTHING HURTS – I can only hope the finished product is worthy of your faith in me. Special thanks to the excellent Liz Bourke, for encouragement when I needed it most, and to Sophie Heawood, who kindly granted permission to quote from her essay "Princess Diana Was As Mad As Any Other Woman" at the start of this book. A million thanks to my amazing readers – it hopefully goes without saying, but I wouldn't be here without you, and I'm enduringly grateful to you all.

And last (but by no means least!) a special shoutout to Nora Jemisin, my Deadline Hell writing buddy, whose emails and encouragement helped me get through the last, gruelling chapters of this book, and who never once passed judgement on my critical overconsumption of Red Bull, mixed lollies and chocolate. You are The Actual Best, and I'm pretty sure the rest of the world agrees with me. HORNS UP!

ABOUT THE AUTHOR

Foz Meadows is a genderqueer author, blogger, essayist, reviewer and poet. In 2014, she was nominated for a Hugo Award for Best Fan Writer for her blog, *Shattersnipe*; she is also a contributing writer for *The Huffington Post* and *Black Gate*, and a contributing reviewer for *A Dribble of Ink, Strange Horizons* and *Tor.com*.

fozmeadows.wordpress.com • *twitter.com/fozmeadows*

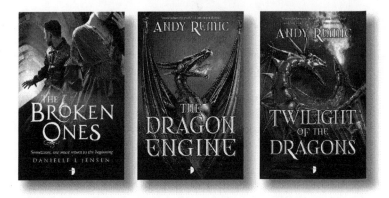

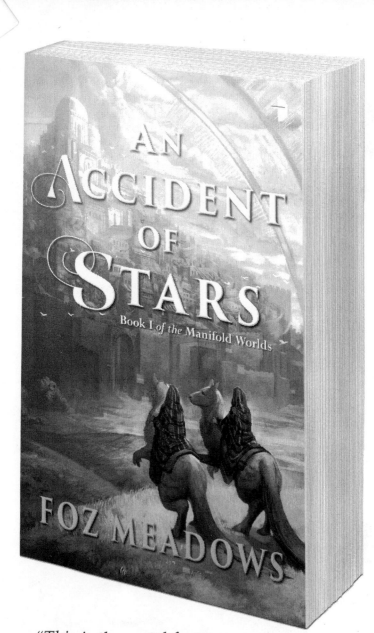

AN ACCIDENT OF STARS

OF

STARS

Book I of the Manifold Worlds

FOZ MEADOWS

"This is the portal fantasy
I've spent my whole life
waiting for." — Tor.com